ROBERT MUCHAMORE
KILLER T

HOT
KEY
BOOKS

First published in Great Britain in 2018 by
HOT KEY BOOKS
80–81 Wimpole St, London W1G 9RE
www.hotkeybooks.com

This edition published 2019 by Hot Key Books

A CIP catalogue record for this book is available
from the British Library.

ISBN: 978-1-4714-0719-2
also available as an ebook

1

Designed by Perfect Bound Ltd
Printed and bound in Great Britain by Clays Ltd, Elcograf S.p.A.

Hot Key Books is an imprint of Bonnier Books UK
www.bonnierbooks.co.uk

Killer T *noun* A type of white blood cell that kills damaged cells, particularly those that are cancerous, or infected with a virus.

PART ONE
THE BEGINNING

1 SLASHED RUBBER

Deion Powell was the king of high school. Stubbled and swaggering. *Powell 03* on the back of his practice jersey and a splayed walk imposed by monstrous thighs. An amber late slip flapped in his hand as the starting quarterback bowled the empty hallway, crunching in desert grit trailed from the parking lot.

'Whatcha staring at?' Deion snapped instinctively as a skinny ninth grader came out of an empty classroom. He had to hook the door with his sneaker because there was a set of textbooks stacked to his chin.

The kid jolted. Catching the door frame with his shoulder, almost spilling *Algebra 2s*, before Deion's bunched fist set him off in a rodent scuttle.

But there was too much in Powell's head to enjoy the humiliation. There'd been a tussle in the locker room after Monday night practice. A minor miracle that the coaches hadn't found out. And that morning, Deion's kid sister bounced for the school bus, but doubled back before clearing the driveway. Uptight and wide-eyed, the nine-year-old blurted that the front tires on his truck had been knifed.

So, the quarterback took a city bus and fifteen-minute jog, missing first period and catching a lecture from a tattooed school clerk, who'd heard too many excuses to care if they were true or not. *Third late arrival since summer recess. Can't come and go as you please, making like you're above the rules.*

Stress bulged Deion's veins. Sweat glazed his oak-brown skin. *Should have taken a picture of my tires to show I'm no liar. Five hundred bucks for new ones. Must have been JJ. Will everything kick off again? What if we bump JJ's crew in the hallway? And no way to avoid it in the locker room ...*

Deion's locker had been decorated by the rally team. *Powell 03*, sprayed through a stencil. *Rock Spring Rockets* stickers and nylon rosettes fixed on with sticky pads. An invite to *Aisha's 18th – Foam Partaaay* poked out of the door. He tried fitting a face to Aisha's name as he turned the locker dial.

Eighteen, six, twenty-two.

There was a grunt of realisation as Deion let his backpack drop off his shoulder. He usually left football gear in his truck on the school lot. The locker was crammed. Books, baseball cleats, protein shake pouches and a Bluetooth boom box he'd tried selling to a teammate who'd never come through with the money.

Maybe it was easiest to keep hold of the stuff. *Dump it in Terence's VW at recess.* But this made the walk to the locker another waste of time, on a day when everything was going bad.

Calm down. Think straight. Don't let stuff get to you.

'This sucks,' Deion raged, smashing his palm on his locker, and kicking the one below with his size thirteen.

His thoughts had been balled too tight to hear the girl who'd turned into the hallway behind. Pink cotton pumps, a *Rock Spring High* gym shirt and milky, vein-pencilled legs. He'd startled her and was about to apologise when . . .

Noise ripped. So loud it hurt inside both ears. Blazing light. Heat. The girl screaming. The yellow locker door, unhinged and smashing Deion in the face. Stumbling. Blood. Tripping on something. A mouthful of dust, and ceiling tiles falling like oversized confetti.

2 NOT HARRY POTTER

The klaxon yowled as twenty-four hundred high-schoolers bustled out into sun-blasted gravel and hundred-degree heat. Out of fire doors and down clanking metal stair treads. A few straddled first-floor windows. Smoke plumed from the Zone C annexe as emergency sirens wailed.

The clueless school security guard kept a wary hand on his taser. Teens from the dance studio felt scorching sidewalk on bare soles and a math teacher rolled a kid in a wheelchair past the cholla cacti at Rock Spring High's main entrance.

'This is *not* a fire drill,' a deputy principal yelled, pit stains showing as he waved students away. 'Do not gather at the assembly points. Just get as far from the building as possible.'

'Is there a shooter?' someone asked, almost colliding with a kid who walked backwards, videoing the smoke.

'Heard shots for sure,' another body close to Harry Smirnov said. 'Five or six.'

Harry followed the crowd away from school on a paved path, his jog slowing as bodies funnelled through mesh gates. He was a ninth grader. Fourteen, slender limbs, floppy black bangs, still more boy than man. He'd only been in Las Vegas eight months since moving from the UK with his aunt.

In the run-up to leaving London, Harry's two best mates joked darkly about American high-school shootings. One even wrote *mind the bullets* in his leaving card and drew a stick man letting rip with an Uzi. Now the joke seemed thin.

'Smoke's from over by the wood shop,' someone behind Harry noted as a guidance counsellor urged teens not to shove at the gate. 'My dad's a carpenter. One place he worked, there was a spark in the dust extraction and the whole joint went boom.'

'Where you going, Harry Potter?' Lupita from Harry's homeroom spat, as he cut off the path. 'Ain't no other gate up there.'

First name Harry, a black mop and an English accent made the nickname inevitable. Even his home-room teacher used it.

Vegas didn't get a lot of rain, but baked-hard ground meant flash floods when a storm hit. The mesh fence around Rock Spring's perimeter ran parallel to a concrete drainage channel, eight feet wide and half as deep. Harry stepped down into the basin, brushing weeds growing through cracks as he started a crouched jog towards the smoke.

He glanced back, but fellow evacuees saw nothing past backs of heads and shuffling limbs. The drain's sides were graffitied, the base littered with occasional pyres made from melted nylon backpacks and black-edged textbooks. These had been squirted with lighter fuel and burnt up by college-bound seniors before summer break.

Harry ducked instinctively as an ambulance skimmed the access road across the fence, lights flashing but siren off. It turned through a set of vehicle gates eighty yards ahead. The storm drain went under this access road, but the thought of snakes in the dark sent a chill down Harry's spine, so instead of charging through he lay against the gently angled wall, checking the scene as the sun cooked the back of his neck.

Smoke had been tamped by a fire crew, and puddled hose water was evaporating into a rainbow haze. This part of the school was single-storey classrooms, with a taller main assembly hall and lunch room behind. Shatterproof panes had twisted out from their frames, and aluminium roof sheets jutted into the air.

But Harry sensed calm. Two relaxed cops guarded the school's service entrance as a lunch lady in kitchen whites led a fire officer round the edge of the building, seeking a shut-off valve. Harry cupped one ear and listened to a police lieutenant briefing the freshly arrived ambulance crew.

'Some kind of explosive. Got the area cleared out and locked down, but don't hang around inside. We can't be certain it's the only device until there's been a full search.'

Harry's mum had been a photographer and journalist. She'd taken a bullet in the Ukraine and won awards for her vlogs from Brazzaville during the Third Congo War. After living in war zones, her death was ironic: wiped out by an undiagnosed heart defect as she jogged in London's Hyde Park.

Harry had been seven. His mother's death had left him with a mortal fear that his heart could explode, a fascination with news websites and an urge to follow her path.

He read biographies of famous correspondents and photo-journalists. He liked war documentaries and obsessed over films like *Spotlight* and *All the President's Men* where journalists kicked butt. A swanky Nikon camera topped Harry's Christmas wish list, back when his mates were still into *Star Wars* Lego and console games.

Until now, the fourteen-year-old's journalistic experience comprised an Under 12s Photography Prize, rugby and cricket reports for his old school in London and a Rock Spring Neighbourhood News blog that he set up at Digital Arts summer camp. But here was proper news, and Harry had the first camera on the scene.

His fancy Nikon was at home, so his phone would have to do. Harry unlocked with an iris scan and flipped to *advanced camera* mode. Sunlight bleached the screen, so he had to click and hope for the best as he shot the little rainbow and buckled roof.

There was a chance the cops at the door would see Harry dash between the storm drain and the side of the building. He was no rule breaker, but he'd waited half his life for a story. Every crunch of gravel felt like a sonic boom, but Harry timed it well and cracked an exhilarated smile as his back hit the wall by an open window.

What if there are more bombs? What if some nut jumps out of a storeroom with a machine gun? This is such a buzz … This is why Mum loved it so much.

Harry wiped a dripping brow on the sleeve of his T-shirt, jumped on to the ledge of the sliding window, then down on to a chair, which kids had used as a step when scrambling out fifteen minutes earlier.

The strip lights were dead. The school's crisply conditioned air had warmed and caught enough smoke to sting Harry's eyes. Most kids had grabbed their backpacks, but there were pens and books on desks, clothes over the backs of chairs and a tatty phone left charging.

The classroom door was closed, with water trickling beneath. Harry took four pictures, then kept his ear to the door, before easing the handle and peeking out. A single hallway ran down this part of the school, lined with yellow senior lockers.

A shut-off sprinkler dripped and mini icebergs of fire-suppressant foam drifted on slow running water. Harry had never seen the hallway with the lights off and he stepped into the gloom, placing his Nikes as quietly as the wet allowed.

To the right, things normalised. A few downed ceiling tiles and the flow of water narrowing as it ran into classrooms. At the far end, light dazzled through skylights where this annexe met the main school building.

Hell lay in the other direction. Water dripped from the ceiling; slow-moving fire foam clumped around a collapsed sub-ceiling that had once held up lamps and ceiling tiles. Some locker doors were dented, others torn open by the force of a blast.

Harry crouched low for a gory snap of a dead rat, its black fur singed to bloody flesh.

Dressed in nylon shorts, he was briefly fascinated as his leg sank ankle-deep into foam. A groan sounded over the sprinkler drips and running water. Then a tortured shout.

'Leave me, leave me, leave me.'

The voice was young, deep, and came from beyond the downed ceiling. Harry edged to the lockers, where the puddle was shallowest, and crept up to the tangle of metal and light fittings blocking the hallway. Beyond the gloom, sun pierced the torn roof.

'Let's have a shot of morphine,' a neon-jacketed medic told a colleague. Then soothingly, 'Just need to move you on to the stretcher, baby.'

Harry pushed a dangling wad of pipe insulation out of the way, making a gap big enough to see through. The gloomy walls and sunlight through the holed ceiling was a photographer's nightmare. Harry played with the exposure controls until the image was usable, then tapped the screen, taking shot after shot.

The explosion had taken place twenty feet beyond the collapsed ceiling. On one side, a dozen lockers had been pancaked. Across the hall, the blast had knocked lockers through drywall, exposing an outer layer of concrete breeze blocks. The floor between was littered with books and athletic gear, all smeared in the creamy fire foam.

The victims had been moved further down the hall. Harry caught drips on his head as he pushed deeper beneath the collapsed ceiling frame and switched to video. After a slight zoom, he filmed a cop helping ambulance crew roll a girl on to a stretcher. She was limp and bloody, but a breathing mask meant she had to be alive.

The other victim lay a few yards beyond, head raised on an air pillow as one of the ambulance staff prepped a morphine jab. His clothes were burnt and face bloody, but Harry knew Deion Powell from his cringeworthy *school spirit; go, team; come to the game and get behind the Rockets* speeches during whole-school assembly.

'Don't move me!' Deion begged.

Harry had visions of some teacher or cop creeping up behind, but kept his nerve, focusing on holding the phone steady, because he wanted his footage to look professional.

'Gotta get you to hospital,' the ambulance guy soothed as he stuck in the morphine. 'Lift you up, nice and slow.'

'It hurts so bad!'

Harry kept filming, his breathing tense and drips hitting his back as a second ambulance team arrived.

'Gimme another shot for the pain,' Deion groaned as four medics circled.

'Lift on three, two . . .'

Deion's scream burst like a grenade as two medics lifted his arms and another raised his feet for a short lift on to a stretcher.

'You did real good, QB,' one medic said. 'That was the bad part. Now we gonna put your stretcher on to the trolley.'

'Your mama's already on her way to hospital, buddy,' a cop standing behind soothed. 'She'll be there waiting.'

'I can beat this!' Deion shouted, grasping the side of the stretcher with a slippery, bloodied hand.

'Again on three.'

As two medics raised Deion's stretcher up to the wheeled trolley, the one at the back felt his heel slip on the foamy floor.

It wouldn't have mattered with a normal-sized patient, but Deion's bulk hung off all sides. As the guy holding the foot end swung the stretcher towards the trolley, the medic who'd slipped didn't follow. The lift was supposed to be smooth and pain free, but the jolt left strips of Deion's burnt skin stuck to the stretcher and his spasm of pain tilted it sideways.

Cops cursed and charged in, as Deion rolled off, crashing the side of the trolley and slapping the wet floor. Harry knew he'd filmed something big as Deion howled in agony, lashing furiously and sprawling the guy who was trying to pick him up off the floor.

'Can't you be careful?' Deion boomed as he stopped flailing and let the medic close in with a respirator mask. 'I'll be suing all your asses!'

'We're doing our best, son,' someone said.

'Deep breaths,' the medic soothed as she held the mask over Deion's face. 'Slow, deep, breaths.'

3 A THOUSAND BUCKS

The dining hall smelled of lunch that would never get eaten as Harry cut between tables, wet Nikes squeaking the glossy floor and phone clutched like a bar of precious metal.

'Why you ain't evacuated?' a chef shouted from deep in the kitchen.

'On my way, sir,' Harry said obediently.

But instead of going out he pushed through double doors into the main part of the school and bounded stairs two at a time. The upper floor hallway was dim and empty and the second door he tried came open. It was a science room, with no sign that anyone had bailed in a hurry.

'OK,' Harry muttered as he took a deep breath. 'Think.'

He knew what he wanted to achieve, but there were a lot of steps and he needed to get them straight in his head. After kicking the door shut, he strode to the back of the room. If he sat at a desk he might be seen through the classroom door, or from outside. So Harry crouched in a space between a desk and storage unit. If anyone came in, he'd act scared and say he'd been hiding.

Harry rested his back against the wall below a window,

tilted his phone to cut reflections and started flicking through photos. The first shots with the rainbow looked cool, but lacked drama. The abandoned classroom pics were poignant, but again not the wow factor that would excite the webmaster of a news website, or a local TV channel.

His best shots were a pair taken after they'd carried Deion out: a grim pic of the bloody floor where Deion had been lying, and another of the locker with what looked like . . .

Harry zoomed in. Fearing that the cops would return and bust him, he'd snapped rapidly. Luckily the shot on his screen was perfect: Deion's football helmet, dented and bloody, in front of a buckled locker door sprayed with his name.

He cropped the image, used a filter to up the contrast and give the shot more kick, then saved the result. Next he watched the video. The audio was poor and the picture full of long shadows cast by harsh light through the torn roof, but you could tell what was going on, including a clear view of Deion tilting off the trolley.

When the clip ended, Harry opened a video-editing app. He'd played around with making videos for years so his fingers dabbed and swiped artfully. Harry brought up the brightness, and applied an anti-shake algorithm to his footage.

Sound was more of a battle, but he managed to damp the hallway echo and tinker with the frequency balance, so that voices were clearer and you could hear the eerie drips of water close to the microphone. To avoid getting ripped off, he added a semi-opaque graphic in the top right corner of the footage that read © Harry Smirnov.

Harry popped his head above the desks when he heard footsteps out in the hall, but nobody stepped in. Back at the screen, he watched his three minutes of enhanced, shake-free, footage. It was good, but few folks had the patience to watch three minutes of anything, so he cut two edited versions.

The first was a thirty-second highlight reel, showing Deion screaming as he got lifted off the ground, him being dropped and then ending on his threat to sue. The second was a zoomed eight-second clip of Deion being tipped off the stretcher, then kicking the medic with his giant leg. Zooming meant the footage was blurry, but the light glistening off Deion's burnt body gave it serious impact.

Harry rendered the videos before pushing the two shorter clips to YouTube. The local phone masts were swamped and the upload bar crept, even though he had a solid 5G signal. Once they were online, he made a short entry on his Rock Spring Neighbourhood News website: *Amazing footage of the aftermath. More later!* Then he posted the video clips to Reddit, Facebook and a few other spots where he thought they'd get attention.

The clips instantly clocked a dozen views and Harry trembled less and smiled more as he surfed websites, grabbing email addresses for the news desks of Las Vegas's three local TV stations, plus a couple of prominent Vegas news and tourist websites. He opened *voice* and quietly dictated an email.

I have posted video footage of the aftermath of the Rock Spring High explosion online. You are welcome to use these clips if you credit me and do not blur my name in the clip. I also have high-resolution photographs of the aftermath and a full three-minute clip. These are available exclusively to the first organisation to contact me and agree to pay $1,000 . . .

Harry stared at the $1,000 figure. He'd never done stuff like this before and wondered if he was asking for too much, or too little. He edited it to $1,500, stared at the number and then put it back to $1,000 before pressing send.

Refreshing the YouTube page showed that his thirty-second clip already had a hundred and fifty hits and seven comments.

Obvs FAKE!!!!

You can see it's Deion by his legs! How could someone fake this when it just happened?

Harry Smirnov made this? Isn't that the Brit kid who looks like Harry Potter?

Yes.

Medics getting ass sued! LOLs

Where's your QB now Rock Spring homos?

JJ Janssen is better anyways! Still gonna kick Mountain Creek on Friday.

The video neared two hundred views as Harry pocketed his phone. Rendering videos had worked the CPU hard and the phone felt toasty as he pushed it down the mesh pocket of his shorts, then grabbed his pack and headed for the classroom door.

'Tits,' Harry moaned as he peered through the door. The hallway was gloomy, but he could make out a cop by the stairs and a woman in bright orange *Fire Department* overalls.

Harry went back to the main windows. There wasn't a soul amidst the wooden picnic tables on the paved courtyard below. It was only one storey up and there was a solid box gutter he could use to dangle and drop. But this idea crashed when Harry dragged at the sliding window and realised it didn't open fully like the ones at ground level.

He thought about waiting it out, but now the video was online and backed up to his Google account, Harry was less worried about some teacher or cop forcing him to surrender the footage as evidence.

'Why in the name are you up here?' Harry heard, the instant he opened the classroom door.

It was a teacher in overstretched brown leggings. She'd just reached the top of the stairs, behind the cop and fire officer.

'I needed my bag,' Harry explained as he reached behind and tapped it.

'And you waltzed back into a crime scene to fetch it?' the teacher wailed, placing hands on hips. 'What if there was another explosive? Where's your common sense?'

The cop seemed more suspicious. It was the lieutenant Harry had overheard by the gate and he noticed the cop now had blood smeared on his shirt sleeve. Most likely Deion's.

'What's your name, son?'

'Harry Smirnov.'

'S M I R N O F F?' the officer spelled, as he jotted the name in a notebook. 'Like the vodka?'

Harry shook his head. 'The proper Russian spelling, with a V, not two Fs.'

'Uh,' the officer said, as he crossed out. 'You know Deion Powell?'

'Not personally,' Harry said.

'And you don't know anything about this explosion?'

'I'd have thought anyone that did would have kept their distance,' Harry pointed out.

'Don't get smart,' the officer rebuked, but his moustache curved into a slight smile as he turned towards the teacher. 'Can you escort Mr Smirnov off the premises?'

Harry followed the teacher's short-of-breath waddle down a paved path and all the way to the school's main entrance. The ambulances had departed, but the service road beyond the school fence was lined with squad cars and a major-incident command truck.

'They're waiting for explosive-sniffing dogs,' Harry's guide told another teacher walking in the opposite direction. 'After that they'll do a manual search.'

'JJ wasn't in school today,' the teacher replied, shielding her mouth like it was some big secret, even though Harry stood right there.

Three TV news vans were parked on the big turning circle by the school's main entrance. The student parking lot had mostly emptied out, while the yellow zone where school buses usually parked was busy, with anxious parents waving out of cars, collecting kids who were too young to drive.

'Got my eye on you,' Brown Leggings told Harry. 'Now scoot!'

Once the teacher was out of sight, Harry checked his phone. He had a message from his running buddy, Matt, three minutes old.

Amazing vid! You crazy! Need a ride home?

Harry didn't reply right away, instead refreshing the YouTube page. After eleven minutes online, the clip was closing on 500 views, with comments off the bottom of the screen. Out of the virtual world, Harry found himself by a lively crowd watching three girls being interviewed for Vegas Thirteen local news.

The producer had selected pretty girls and the trio acted super dramatic, holding hands and tearing up. One girl told the presenter that she was scared they were going to die, while tenth-grade dicks pulled faces in the background.

'Harry, my boy!' Matt Silver said.

Harry looked left and saw his best – and so far only – American friend closing in.

Matt had stupidly tangled blond hair and a solid build. He teetered on the verge of Gothdom, in wrecked All Stars, frayed black cargo shorts and a slate grey shirt with embroidered zombies on the back.

Matt and Harry only shared a couple of classes, but they enjoyed running, lived three blocks apart and trained together at least twice a week. Both were fast enough to make the Rockets Athletic Team, but Harry ran to clear his mind rather than compete, while Matt got booted off the squad after he'd ditched class and got busted smoking a joint with some girl.

'You're insane, bro!' Matt said admiringly. 'Going back in like that! School gonna throw a fit, though . . .'

'You think?' Harry said warily.

'Not evacuating, using your cell on school premises, violating student confidentiality.'

Harry realised he'd not considered all possible consequences as he ran a hand through sweaty hair. 'I got caught up in the moment. My Auntie Kirsten won't be impressed either . . .'

Matt aimed a thumb towards student parking. 'My sis is offering a ride home, but she ain't gonna wait all day.'

'There's a video on YouTube,' Matt and Harry overheard as they went through the gates into the student parking lot. 'It's Deion Powell. Looks like he's burnt real bad.'

'Who's Harry Smirnov?' a titchy girl asked as she watched his vid on her phone.

Harry buried his smirk as Matt thumped him fondly on the back and whispered, 'Superstar.'

4 SOFIA SILVER

A few groups hung around their cars, but the student lot was mostly clear once you got beyond kids hovering round the TV crews. Harry wondered how much trouble he was in, how Aunt Kirsten would react, and desperately hoped some news editor would cough up a thousand bucks to make the risk he'd taken worthwhile.

But his attention flipped the instant he saw Matt's hot sister. Sofia Silver was seventeen, propped on the open tailgate of her Audi SUV. She had brown eyes, cleavage and smooth, freckled skin. A grubby white Havaiana dangled off one foot and her chipped nail varnish and thrift-store vibe jarred with the sixty-thousand-dollar car.

'Found my boy,' Matt said happily.

'You've got some balls, Harry,' Sofia said, smiling.

Matt grabbed shotgun as Harry got confronted by another girl in the back. She was Japanese-American, sat cross-legged, messaging on her phone with black hair streaming down her back.

'Have you met Rie?' Sofia asked.

'Nah,' Harry said.

Rie gave the tiniest glance away from her phone, while Sofia used the dash cam to back out of the parking space.

'Everyone's online saying JJ's behind the explosion,' Rie announced, slipping her phone into a canvas bag as the Audi joined a short line of student cars waiting to turn on to the highway. 'JJ's not a genius, but he's no dummy either. It's just *too* obvious.'

'The teacher who marched me out mentioned JJ,' Harry said. 'Who is he?'

'The Rockets' backup quarterback,' Matt said from up front as his big sister merged into traffic. 'You know what a quarterback is now, don't you, Harry?'

'Shut up,' Harry moaned, before Matt explained for Rie's benefit.

'When Harry first came from London, he didn't *even* know what a quarterback did.'

'But if you came to Britain, *you* wouldn't know what the wicket keeper does in cricket,' Harry said defensively.

Sofia tutted at her brother, then started explaining. 'Deion Powell is a senior and the Rockets' starting QB. JJ Janssen is a year younger. He's backup quarterback, but a lot of fans say he's more talented.'

'Way better,' Rie said.

'Just because you slept with him in tenth grade . . .' Sofia teased.

Rie tipped her head back and smiled. 'And it's not just his muscles that are big!'

'Jesus!' Matt said, thumping the armrest and laughing as Harry flushed with embarrassment.

'Deion Powell has a chance of a college football scholarship,' Sofia explained. 'Coach Henning is a decent guy, so he's kept

Deion as starting QB, because this is his senior year. The college scouts will be out looking for prospects and Coach wants to give the kid a shot. Next year, JJ will be a senior. He'll be starting quarterback and get *his* shot at college.'

'Seems fair,' Harry said.

'But Deion hasn't been playing great,' Sofia continued. 'He's thrown eleven interceptions and just one touchdown in his last three games. Lots of folks say JJ should be made starting quarterback now if Rock Spring is gonna have any realistic shot at state championships.'

'Like JJ even needs a football scholarship,' Matt hissed bitterly. 'The Janssen family are rich.'

'You're not exactly on food stamps,' Harry noted, as he flicked the back of Matt's head rest.

'Our parents are doctors,' Matt said. 'But Jay Janssen Senior owns casinos, hotels, and . . .'

'He owns that strip mall on Flamingo,' Rie added. 'JJ hooked me up with an employee discount card . . .'

'But that's not how Janssen Senior started off,' Matt said. 'JJ's old man spent time in jail for cocaine dealing, and his casinos are the kind of places where you wipe your feet on the way out.'

'I'd bet my last ten bucks on JJ's girlfriend, Fawn Croker, being involved,' Rie said as Sofia stopped at a red light.

'I *hate* Fawn Croker,' Sofia said, shuddering. 'It's *so* creepy. JJ's in eleventh grade and she's, like, twenty-five.'

'So JJ, or JJ's dad, or his crazy girlfriend could be behind the bomb,' Harry said thoughtfully as the light turned green.

'What if it's nothing to do with football?' Rie suggested. 'Deion's a bully, but nobody would dare snitch on a football player.'

'Why not?' Harry asked.

Matt loved it when he knew something Harry didn't. 'If you

snitch and a player gets kicked off the team, you'll have every football fan in Rock Spring lining up to beat your ass.'

'I guess the cops will focus on the explosives,' Harry said thoughtfully. 'It crumpled lockers and blew a hole in the roof, so it was proper gear, not just fireworks.'

'That's it!' Matt blurted, jerking round so excitedly that his seatbelt locked. 'Charlie Croker!'

'Who dat?' Sofia asked.

'I did a project with Charlie at middle school,' Matt told everyone excitedly. 'She's one grade below, but she was in all the accelerated classes. Super smart and a tomboy. When we had science fair, Charlie did this presentation on demolition and explosives. She had this waxy blob the size of an M&M and we all had to go out into the parking lot to watch her demonstration. She'd made it herself and, I swear, the building shook when she set it off.'

'Charlie Croker,' Harry said, indulging his journalistic lust by opening a note-taking app on his phone. 'Tell me more.'

'Charlie is Fawn's kid sister,' Matt explained. 'Low-rent trailer trash.'

'I heard JJ and Fawn got engaged,' Sofia added.

'For real?' Matt blurted. 'JJ's *seventeen*.'

'It's a redneck freak show,' Rie confirmed, as Harry's phone started vibrating in his hand.

Harry didn't recognise the number. 'Hello?' he said warily.

It was a guy named Ellie Gold. Ellie said he was from Vegas Local, a trashy-but-popular news and listings website. He said he'd pay $800 for the full video clip and high-resolution photos, plus half of any royalties earned if they got sold on to other news outlets.

'Sounds good to me,' Harry told him.

5 DEL TACO

Harry spread some of his newfound wealth, tapping his phone at the Del Taco drive-by window to pay for Sofia, Rie and Matt's lunch.

'Nobody drops food in my new car,' Sofia ordered as she rolled into an empty parking bay.

Matt passed back Harry's Sprite and street tacos, plus a cream-topped strawberry shake for Rie. Then he baited his sister by daubing sour cream over an air vent.

'Wipe or walk home,' Sofia ordered, then turned back to look at Harry, who noticed shredded lettuce stuck in her front teeth. 'Thanks for the tacos, Harry. It's *so* cool what you did. Sneaking around cops and stuff.'

Rie lowered her milkshake before nodding in agreement. 'I admire that you want to be a photographer and you're going for it. I have *literally* no clue what I want to do with my life.'

Their praise sent Harry's ego through the panoramic glass roof. Matt saw Harry's involuntary grin and felt a duty not to let his friend's head get too big.

'You sent Vegas Local the files already,' Matt noted. 'How do you know this Ellie guy is gonna pay you?'

'I don't,' Harry said. 'But it's breaking news. Am I supposed to ask for a contract? Wait for my aunt to get home and read it? This time tomorrow, nobody will give a damn.'

'Vegas Local is a well-known site,' Sofia said. 'Don't sweat – baby brother's jealous is all.'

As Sofia drove, Harry checked the thirty-second edit of his video on YouTube. It had clocked 3,000 hits in less than an hour and Vegas Local had put the full version up, together with an article on its home page.

ROCK SPRINGS HIGH EXPLOSION

EXCLUSIVE *FULL VIDEO*: HORRIBLY BURNT QUARTERBACK DROPPED OFF STRETCHER BY BUNGLING MEDICS!

Harry pressed play. A compulsory fifteen-second ad for whitening toothpaste made the site seem tacky and the comparison with his dead mum's award-winning journalism less favourable. And Aunt Kirsten wouldn't be impressed when she found out that he'd risked arrest, expulsion and the prospect of a shooter, or secondary explosion, just to make a gory clickbait video for a third-rate news site.

'Have a good one, Harry Potter,' Rie said cheerfully as he got out of the Audi.

'Cheers for the ride, Sofia,' Harry said, then to Matt, 'Wanna go for a run this evening, when it cools down?'

Matt shook his head. 'Sorry, pal. Seeing a film with Ciara tonight.'

The Sinatra Executive Apartments was a five-storey complex, made of two horseshoe-shaped blocks with a sun deck and pool in the space between. The woman on reception realised Harry was out of school early, but didn't care enough to ask why as he walked past and tapped a plastic fob to access the elevator.

Aunt Kirsten jested about the moody teenager Harry had turned into, but the reality of that hit as he opened the apartment door. Fifteen minutes earlier, Harry had been happy about making eight hundred bucks, with a hot chicken taco and the girls heaping praise. Now he felt like dirt.

He worried that Vegas Local was a sleazy website that would never pay the eight hundred bucks. He had mounds of homework and imagined himself spending the night at his desk, while Matt got frisky with Ciara at the Summerlin Regal.

Harry shouted, 'Anyone home?'

He expected no response and didn't get one.

Harry's aunt, Kirsten Channing, had moved to Vegas to open a swanky restaurant inside the newly built Algarve Casino. The food critics had been kind and tables were booked weeks in advance. This meant Kirsten was crushing sales targets and earning big bonuses, but had little time for her nephew and even less for house hunting.

Eight months after emigrating, they were still in a short-stay corporate apartment. It was twice the size of their old place in London. It had floor-to-ceiling windows with electrochromic dimming glass, a jet tub with sixteen modes and a fridge you could fit a car inside.

But it was a place to live, not a home. Harry loathed the bland abstract art and the smell of the cleaning spray used by the housekeeping service. He couldn't paint his bedroom or put up posters, and the building manager buzzed the intercom when he played music too loud.

Kirsten worked six nights a week and Harry didn't know anyone outside of school, so unless he was hanging with Matt the hours between school and bed were lonely.

It was approaching two in the afternoon, leaving eight and a half hours to bedtime. Harry grabbed sparkling water and a plate of random tapas-type things out of the fridge. He sat on a stool and flipped the lid of a battered MacBook that lived on the kitchen counter. Kirsten had been using it while working on a recipe and the screen had icing-sugar fingerprints and a whiff of orange essence.

Harry's first thought was to transfer the photos he'd taken earlier and see them on a decent-sized screen. But when the iris scan unlocked his phone, the screen showed the notes he'd made while everyone gossiped in Sofia's car.

JJ Janssen Backup quarterback, 11th grader
Obvious suspect (too obvious!)
Threatened to kill Deion in locker room on Monday
Dad is Jay Janssen Sr, \$\$\$ minted businessman
& former drug dealer

Fawn Croker JJ's fiancée.
25yo!!! Money grabber?

Charlie Croker Fawn's brainy kid sister
8th grader
Made explosives for show and tell!
Did science project with Matt

Making eight hundred bucks had knocked Harry's focus away from the locker mystery, but when he read the notes, the thing that stuck out was Matt's personal connection with Charlie Croker. JJ and Fawn would be suspects, but the cops didn't have Matt's personal knowledge, and Harry wondered if they might take a while to learn about Charlie's explosive-making.

Harry dialled Matt's number.

'That Charlie Croker,' Harry began, 'the one who makes her

own explosives. Did you ever go to her place when you did that science project? Did she have a lab, or a shed, or something where you worked?'

Matt sounded patronising. 'Still playing Joey-the-journalist?'

Harry grunted. 'Can you help me or not?'

'She always came to my house because it's nicer,' Matt said warily. 'But I rode in the car one time when my dad dropped her home. I don't know the road name, but it's the corner with the big CVS pharmacy, off North Rainbow.'

'The CVS we pass on the way to school?'

'Exactly,' Matt agreed. 'North Pine Road or Lonely Pine. Something like that. Just after you turn off Rainbow, there's a tire place, then you come to a double-wide trailer home. Blue grey colour, sorta like someone mixed all the leftover paint together. But this was back in seventh grade, so they might have moved since.'

Harry tucked his phone between shoulder and chin so that he could use Google Maps on the MacBook.

'Found it,' Harry said jubilantly as he switched to street view and saw the trailer home, like Matt had described. '1680, Leaning Pines.'

'How you gonna play it?' Matt asked. 'Knock on the front door and ask Charlie if she's blown anyone up?'

'Check the area out, I guess,' Harry said uncertainly. 'I'll grab my good camera. Have a little snoop. Maybe there's a shed with burnt shit, or something. It's a ten-minute taxi and I've got nothing else to do.'

'You need a girlfriend, Harry,' Matt said affectionately. 'Try not to get shot or blown up.'

6 RAINBOW ROAD

Harry googled *Charlie Croker* as he rode in the back of a Prius taxi, with stained seats and a screen blaring ads for Kanye West at Caesar's Palace. Seven hundred and seventy-four search results were topped by a Mr Charlie Croker who sold farm machinery in Iowa and a sweatband-clad Pilates coach. Narrowing the search to *Charlie Croker Rock Springs* proved more productive.

Local Girl Wins National Tech prize

Eleven-year-old Charlie Croker beat out more than 600 rivals, including many high schoolers, to win a $750 prize and a tour of the world-famous materials lab at the California Institute of Technology.

The accompanying photo showed Charlie with athletic build, coarsely chopped blonde hair and a green sponsors-logo T-shirt that reached her knees. Her most striking features were giant blue eyes and no-brand sneakers, with a big toe poking out the front.

There was a link to another article, but the phone started vibrating and Harry recognised the Vegas Local number.

'It's Ellie Gold,' the voice said, packed with cheesy cheer. 'Just wanted to let you know your video is clocking ninety views per minute. USA Network and Cox News want a national TV exclusive. I'm playing them off against each other, but the bidding is already up to seven thousand buckaroos!'

Harry's jaw made a clichéd dive towards the floor of his taxi. 'I get half of that, right?'

'Exactly,' Ellie said. 'And I've put your photos on a news syndication site. Nobody has bought that beautiful bloody-helmet shot yet, but the watermarked preview has had sixty downloads, so it's gonna sell for sure.'

Harry was excited about the money, but sounded wary. 'When am I gonna get paid?'

'Don't you trust me?' Ellie said, roaring with laughter. 'Vegas Local wouldn't last a week if I didn't pay my sources. Bounce me some bank details. My minion Sue-Ann will email your paperwork, and as soon as it's signed you'll get the eight hundred.

'The rest will take time. Big news outlets take months to pay their bills, but people are *loving* the mystery of the blown-up quarterback and your gore-fest stretcher footage has the visual punch to make it a national story. When the dust clears, your cut on this could be well into five figures.'

'Seriously?' Harry gawped, imagining how jealous Matt and his mates back in London would be if he made ten big ones . . .

'You must have a talent for this stuff. Anything else like this happens, you'll call Ellie first, won't you?'

'Sure,' Harry said.

'Stay in touch.'

Wow-bloody-wow! National story! I can handle some flak from school and Kirsten for ten grand. I can afford a light field camera. Drop a grand at the mall. All new running gear, maybe a better laptop. Bet Kirsten will go sensible and make me save at least half for college . . .

The cab had just turned off South Rainbow and they were passing the lot of the big CVS. Harry had used Kirsten's Lucky Cab account and given the 1680 Leaning Pines address, but he could hardly get out right in front of the Crokers' double-wide trailer and start poking around.

'CVS,' Harry spluttered. 'Drop me here.'

Harry wasn't trying to be rude, but it came out that way and the dome-headed driver flicked bitterly at his sat nav. 'It says sixteen eighty.'

'My ma asked me to get some shopping,' Harry lied. 'I forgot. I didn't mean to snap at you.'

The driver stopped sharp, and Harry stepped on to the kerb and pulled on a backpack bulked with his pro-spec Nikon camera.

The CVS had a couple of hundred parking bays, but it was mid-Thursday afternoon and the big pharmacy's only customers were parked in a single row, keeping car interiors cool on the shady side of the building.

Harry pushed on sunglasses as he strode across marked parking bays. The CVS lot ended at a knee-height fence. Matt had mentioned the tire-repair place beyond, but it looked like the Tire Maxx franchise had been closed for years. The corporate logos had blown out of the tall roadside sign, the main glass door wore heavy chains and the sand-blown lot was strewn with beer cans and perished rubber.

Sweat trickled down Harry's back as he upped to a jog. The dirty-blue trailer home came into view as he rounded a self-service car wash with a caved roof. The upbeat feels from

Ellie's call hadn't lasted and Matt's question resurfaced: *How will I play it when I get there?*

What am I hoping to find? Why not turn round, buy a Mars ice cream in CVS and go home? But it sucks being home alone . . . If Mum was alive, would she approve of this? Why do I want to do stuff to impress a mum who was never around much even when she was alive? Do I want to be a photojournalist, or have I been telling myself that for so long I've not considered anything else?

Harry's train of thought got diverted at the far side of Tire Maxx. There was a blackened wall and a saucer-like crater, part filled with litter. The asphalt in the base of the crater had weird ripples, and screws and bolts stuck out, clearly having sunk in when the surface was molten. Harry took out his Nikon, taking time to snap the metal shards and cracks in the wall.

He got a fright when a gust set a Coke can clanking down near the road, and remained spooked as he got close to the 1680 lot.

You're not a real journalist. You'll look a total fool if this turns bad . . .

But Harry didn't give in to his doubts.

There was no boundary between Tire Maxx and the trailer home. The land alongside the house had evolved into a junkyard: faded sections of a kids' plastic garden fort, an enclosed towing trailer with two flat wheels, the rusted hulk of a washing machine and enough other junk to give decent cover.

Harry snapped a couple of wide shots, thinking someone might want pictures of the house if it turned into an important part of the story. The spinning fans of roof-mounted air-conditioners ran full blast, but their grumbling wasn't enough to mask the kid bawling inside.

He edged further round the junk, trying to glimpse the far

side of the house. Harry's idea – that he'd get here before the cops – blew up as he saw two parked police cruisers. One had a plain-clothes officer sitting with the passenger door open, finishing off a cigarette.

The trailer's aluminium door crashed as Harry raised his camera. A cruel-looking cop came out, hands over her mouth as she jumped two wooden steps to the ground. Harry aimed his camera round the side of the trailer, flipped to continuous shooting and took a dozen shots as she bent forward, dry heaving.

'You want some water?' the smoking cop said, grabbing a bottle out of the cruiser's door and striding to her aid.

'Stank in that dump to start with – now the crazy kid has shat himself.'

'Are you kidding me?' the smoking cop moaned, shaking his head as he stubbed his cigarette out under his shoe. 'Where's child welfare? They should be here already.'

A third cop came out, gasping for air as a huge scream erupted and something heavy thudded against the wall inside.

'Kid just screams *no attention* and that he wants Charlie, over and over and over,' the new arrival said. 'Gimme that bottle of water.'

The cop drained the water, then flung the plastic bottle away, which landed in the junk a few feet from Harry.

'What a day! What a day!'

The cop paced angrily towards Harry's hiding spot, hands on hips as he hacked phlegm in the dirt. Harry buried his face, gulping as the cop turned back towards the cruisers, two steps from where he'd have noticed Harry's trailing leg.

This isn't worth the risk. That lieutenant at the school seemed suspicious, and if they catch me here ... At the very least they'll arrest me. Kirsten's face would be a picture at the police station.

As the cop strolled back to his colleagues, Harry retreated at a rapid crawl. When he reached the disused car wash, he got to his feet, his expensive camera in one hand and one knee smeared in black, oily, God-knows-what.

Stupid idea coming here.

Harry moved round the back of Tire Maxx, but only got halfway when a shadow loomed from above. The bright sun silhouetted the figure leaping off the roof. Harry's legs buckled as the body hit him, one arm scraping the metal siding as his palms tore through grit.

A cloud of dirt filled Harry's mouth as he inhaled, setting off a coughing fit as the figure landed on his back. It was a girl, a full head shorter than Harry. She locked a strong arm round his waist. Harry fancied his chances of throwing her off, but before he could move a pistol tip jammed into his cheek.

'Why are you sniffing around?' Charlie Croker demanded. 'Who are you?'

7 BEAUTIFUL FREAK

'Quit your whining,' Charlie said, looking over her back, hoping the cops hadn't heard Harry's coughing fit.

'I . . .' Harry gasped, but the dirt trapped in the back of his throat made him hack noisily again, and grit was scraping around in his left eye.

'Inside,' Charlie ordered, standing up but keeping the gun aimed right at him.

Her voice wasn't confident. Harry wondered if nerves made her more or less likely to shoot him.

'Inside,' she repeated, dragging a piece of metal sheet to expose a tire-propped fire door behind it.

Harry realised his palm was bleeding as he crawled in. Charlie took a final glance towards the house, crouching behind him and pulling the siding back over the doorway

The space was gloomy. A metal roof and no air-con made the heat unbearable. It had once been Tire Maxx's employee break room. There was a wall of lockers, a long-dead drinks dispenser and a shift rota on the wall, over which some joker had inked, *We broke! Ya asses all FIRED!*

Charlie stripped a bottle of water from a pack of a dozen CVS branded bottles and passed it to Harry with a gruff, 'Here.'

Harry gulped desperately, swallowing some and spitting the rest on chequered floor tiles as Charlie threw him a grubby cloth.

'To wipe your hands.'

It took a minute to blink grit, wipe bleeding palms and get the violent coughing down to an occasional hack.

Charlie had run a wire down from a portable solar panel on the roof. It powered an abused laptop, a desk lamp and a fan that pushed heat from one spot to another. She put the gun down, and started inspecting Harry's camera, just as his vision cleared enough to get a proper look at her.

The picture Harry had seen online was two years old, and puberty had kicked in since. Charlie had let her hair grow, framing a face still dominated by huge blue eyes. She was around average height for thirteen, built on a broad frame, and she'd sweated in the heat so that her black bra showed through her pale blue T-shirt. Her chunky legs had a line of scabs from a fall and she had the tough, blackened soles of someone who liked going barefoot.

'So, you're a photographer,' Charlie said as she found the replay button on the camera and flipped through his pictures.

Harry eyed the gun. He was a good runner, but it still wasn't far enough from Charlie's reach to try to escape.

'Is this where you're from?' Charlie asked, turning the camera round so that Harry could see a view of a sunset over a cityscape.

'You've gone past the end to the first pics on that memory card,' Harry explained, trying to tame the fear in his voice. 'I got the camera for Christmas, and took it on a Boxing Day walk with my dad. It's the view over London from the top of Hampstead Heath.'

'Nikon,' Charlie said, inspecting the lens. 'Must have cost plenty.'

Harry nodded. 'It was my main Christmas present two years ago, and I saved money to buy extra lenses and stuff.'

'What's your name?'

'Harry.'

'Smirnov?' Charlie replied sharply. 'You made the video of Deion.'

'Yeah,' Harry admitted, stifling a cough with more of the tepid water. 'That footage is on my phone.'

'Did you follow the cops here?'

Harry shook his head. 'I asked around. People said you made some explosives . . .'

'It's not hard,' Charlie said, nodding. 'Swiped most ingredients from CVS next door, and found the rest online.'

'Mixing explosives sounds dangerous,' Harry said, intrigued that Charlie seemed keen to talk.

'The trick is to practise with tiny batches. The guys who get their hands blown off are the ones that throw sacks of chemicals in bathtubs before doing proper tests.'

Harry laughed, at least as much as you can laugh when your throat is scratchy and the person you're talking to is two feet from a gun.

'But it's been more than two years since I mixed a batch.'

'Why'd you stop?'

'All kids have their phases,' Charlie said dismissively. 'Some get obsessed with guns or knives. Boys light trash on fire, or torture frogs. I was the science geek who blew stuff up.'

Charlie seemed embarrassed, making a little snort and looking down at her grubby feet. The way she was opening up made Harry think he might be on to another story, and gave him hope that the cops wouldn't be finding his bullet-riddled corpse.

'I got into playing baseball, and the advanced programmes at my school opened up a bunch of stuff way more interesting than basic chemical reactions,' Charlie explained, then buried her face in her hands. 'I must sound like such nerd!'

'No way,' Harry said, liking her despite the weird circumstance. 'It's good to have a passion for something. Kids knock anything that stands out, but have no idea what they want themselves.'

'True,' Charlie admitted. 'Not that it matters any more. JJ says he's gonna admit to the bombing, but I still made the explosives. I should have ditched them, but that's hard when you've put a lot of work into a project.'

Harry was amazed by the admission. 'JJ used your explosives?'

'JJ started being nice to me. So much so that my crazy-jealous sister, Fawn, accused me of wanting to screw him. But I guess he just needed to find where I kept the explosives.'

'You and Fawn don't get along?'

'She's so manipulative,' Charlie said. 'Grinds everyone down till she gets exactly what she wants.'

'You've spoken to JJ since the bomb went off.'

'Twice,' Charlie confirmed. 'I was suspicious right away. I wasn't in school because my little brother has been sick. Rock Spring High is only two blocks from here, so I heard the explosion and started seeing posts online. As soon as I heard it was Deion Powell's locker, I came down here to check. I'd hidden two watertight packs of explosive. One pack was gone, along with a tin of detonators.'

'But why would JJ act so dumb?' Harry asked. 'He must have known he'd get caught.'

'He was doing steroids to bulk up for the season,' Charlie said uncertainly. 'They can make you super aggressive. But I don't care *why* he's ruined his own life. It's the fact he might have ruined mine too.'

'That sucks,' Harry said, too wary to offer physical comfort as Charlie propped herself on a little dining table.

'Did you see my brother up at the house?' Charlie asked, her voice wobbling. 'I'm sorry, I never usually cry.'

As Harry got to his feet, he realised he was now closer to the gun than Charlie. He could grab it and run, but he was hooked on the revelations.

'I heard a boy shouting and throwing stuff around your trailer,' Harry said, deciding not to mention that the cops had bailed out of the trailer, complaining that the kid had shat himself. 'Is he OK? You said you were off school looking after him?'

'Ed's ten,' Charlie explained as she rubbed one eye. 'His skull got crushed by the delivery forceps when he was born and he suffered brain damage. Fawn's supposed to be his full-time carer. She gets eighteen hundred a month from Ed's compensation fund, but she's never home. She's practically moved into JJ's place.'

Harry wondered where Charlie's parents had got to, but didn't want to probe and upset her more.

'I heard a cop say social services were coming to collect him.'

Charlie shook her head. 'Ed's a good kid once you know his quirks, but he gets emotional if there's any change to his routine. He picked up a horrible stomach bug, but he doesn't grasp that he'll get better and can go back to school in a few days the way that a normal kid does. And Fawn loses her temper. Calls him *dirty boy*, locks him in the bathroom then drives off. And I am left – literally – cleaning up the shit.'

Harry took another half a step towards her.

'I got pissed seeing you snoop around taking photos,' Charlie told him, 'but I'm not holding you hostage. Go if you want to. Snitch me to the cops and get your pretty bangs on the six-o'clock news.'

'I'll stay and talk if you want,' Harry said gently.

Charlie gave a huge sob and pushed up from the table. She was muscly and Harry stumbled as she locked her hands behind his back and rested her cheek against his chest.

'I don't have a single real friend, Harry.'

'You'll be OK,' Harry said, feeling awkward as he put his arms round her.

Charlie's T-shirt had ridden up and Harry's hand slipped in the small of her bare, sweaty back. Sobs shook Charlie's body as Harry breathed her smell and felt a little turned on.

'I'm such a freak,' Charlie said, staring up with desperate eyes.

'Beautiful freak,' Harry said, and wondered where the hell that came from. He half expected her to recoil, but Charlie cracked a soft, flattered smile.

I want to kiss her, but that's the last thing she wants right now.

Charlie sensed Harry's awkwardness, peeling sweaty hair off her face as she backed up.

'Sorry I put a gun to your head,' Charlie said, wearing a doomed smile as she scratched one ankle with a dirty big toe.

'Maybe it's not that bad,' Harry suggested. 'You made the explosives a long time ago and you didn't know JJ was going to steal them. Maybe, instead of hiding from the cops, go over to the house, surrender and tell them what happened. You're a smart kid, you've never been in trouble before . . .'

'Two flaws in your plan,' Charlie said as she slumped in a plastic chair. 'First, if I was covering my ass, the story I would tell is that JJ stole the explosives and that I knew nothing about it. It happens to be the truth, but will the cops believe me?

'Second, I have been in trouble before. Some kids started teasing Ed at the mall one time. I grabbed a fire extinguisher and foamed the little pricks. One guy slipped and when the foam ran out I belted him over the head with it.'

Harry's eyebrows shot up. 'For real?'

'You can smirk, but I fractured the little turd's cheekbone and Canyon Mall said there was over two thousand dollars in damages. I got a fine, three anger management sessions and the judge said if I put another foot wrong I'd be booking my ticket for juvenile detention.'

'But they started on your little brother,' Harry said indignantly, then jolted as a phone rang loudly behind him.

'What's happening, JJ?' Charlie said anxiously as she answered her cell. 'I'm dangling here.'

Charlie was on the phone for six minutes. Harry listened, but struggled to follow, beyond the fact that it was someone called Mr Elkmann, using JJ's cell.

'JJ's lawyer,' Charlie explained, after the call. 'He's just left the precinct after handing JJ over to the cops. Elkmann says the best thing is for me to surrender too – and don't say *I told you so*. JJ's dad is rich so he's going to fix me up with a good lawyer, and I'm supposed to stay calm and polite, but keep my trap shut until the lawyer arrives.'

'Why would Jay Janssen Senior pay *your* lawyer?' Harry asked suspiciously.

'I guess he has more control over his son's case if my lawyer is in his pocket. Nothing can be worse than the public defender

I had for the fire extinguisher deal. She saw me for ten minutes and basically said *plead guilty, or else.*'

'So, you might get off?' Harry asked.

Charlie shook her head. 'JJ said he'll take the rap for the bomb, but Elkmann says I'll face charges for illegal possession of explosives.'

'Could you get locked up for that?'

'He said it hinges on how badly Deion Powell and the girl are hurt.'

'Last I saw online, the hospital was saying *seriously injured, but not life threatening,*' Harry told her.

'Because of my age, Elkmann says I'd be unlucky to get more than nine months for an explosives charge. I can handle that. It's Ed I'm worried about. He always asks for me when he gets upset and he'll lose it if I'm not around.'

'I'll give you my number, so you can call if you need *anything,*' Harry said. 'Pass your phone – I'll put it in your contacts.'

'Doubt I'll be allowed my cell where I'm going,' Charlie said, but she still passed him her cheapo cracked-screen smartphone. 'If you want to do me a real favour, take that and make it vanish.'

Harry looked up from the phone and saw Charlie pointing at the gun.

'It's covered in my fingerprints,' Charlie said as she reached under the locker units and pulled out a double-length thirty-two-round clip, filled with tarnished bullets. 'I can do without extra hassle over an unlicensed firearm.'

Harry was startled as the clip landed heavy next to the gun. But Charlie wasn't done, reaching deeper under the lockers and coming out with a black, plastic-wrapped package about the size of a house brick.

'Is that what I think it is?' Harry asked.

'If you're thinking five pounds of homebrew C4 explosive,' Charlie said, enjoying Harry's shock. 'It's stable,' she added. 'Drop it off a rooftop or throw it in an incinerator. Nothing will go bang without a blasting cap. If someone sees it sliced up in the garbage, they'll assume it's dried out plasticine. Or break it up and flush it.'

Harry gawped. Before today, the worst trouble he'd ever faced was one-day suspension from his London school for calling a teacher a *petty-minded cow* when he got told it was against the rules to tie his sweater round his waist.

'This stuff will get me in more trouble,' Charlie pleaded, her eyes more desperate than ever. 'Do you want to help or not?'

'I guess,' Harry sighed, knowing he was crossing a line from wannabe journalist to an accessory to a serious crime.

He was already half in love with this messed-up girl and her giant blue eyes, but simultaneously imagined a scene where he got busted carrying explosives and a gun.

'Use this,' Charlie said, grabbing a Rock Spring Middle School tracksuit top off the back of a chair. 'Wrap the stuff in that to keep your DNA off. Cut the explosive in small bits and put it in the trash, then wear plastic gloves and wipe the gun before you dump it.'

'I'll google the best way to clean it,' Harry said.

Charlie nodded as she hunted around the gloomy floor, pushing her feet into trashed sneakers. 'Now get your fancy-pants camera out. You can film me surrendering to the cops.'

8 CHEESY BALLS

Charlie claimed her explosive was stable, but Harry had seen the bloody mess made of Deion, and didn't like having five pounds of the stuff strapped on his back. Nor did he like the massive risk he'd taken to help Charlie out. But those blue eyes, and the smell of her when they'd hugged . . .

Stupid idiot. This situation is a million kinds of crazy. You could get locked up for this and you'll probably never see Charlie again.

Harry walked fast, getting honked at by an old bird driving an RV as he stepped off a kerb without looking. His brain was scrambled egg. The sun was impossibly hot and the pack crammed full, with the gun digging his back.

Once Charlie had surrendered, he'd sprinted back to the CVS, then jogged a mile and a bit down South Rainbow, until he came to a little outdoor mall. It had the usual suspects: Starbucks, Burger King, Kurt's Sporting Goods and Dollar Dominator. He'd been here twice with his aunt and knew he'd find men's toilets by the kids' play area.

Stupid American toilets, Harry thought, seeing a row of aluminium partitions that started ten inches from the floor and stopped below head height. *But nobody's in here and it's pretty clean . . .*

He bolted a stall at the far end, went down on one dirty knee and opened his backpack. The Nikon was Harry's most prized possession, but he'd shoved it in the bag without the lens cap, and it felt horrible seeing it covered in dust, fingerprints and blood from his grazed hands.

But camera cleaning came way down the list. He unrolled Charlie's jogging top, brushing his hand on the gun as he pulled out the plastic-wrapped brick. It had an oily, metallic smell, even though Charlie had sealed it in a heavy-gauge rubble sack wound with several yards of duct tape. Harry tried getting inside with his nail, but he only got a couple of tiny strips off before realising it would take forever.

He needed something sharp. His first thought was a key. He'd carried several back in London, but out here the Sinatra's apartments opened with a plastic fob, he had no bicycle to lock and Rock Spring High lockers had combination dials.

Luckily, Harry had left home in a rush. He'd pulled all the schoolbooks out of his pack, but a bunch of pens and his geometry set still rattled at the bottom. The compass point speared the plastic, releasing a burst of the heavy oil smell. He stabbed and gouged until the explosive brick was fully exposed.

The outer layer had dried to a bluish-green crust, with dozens of dead bugs stuck to it. But when Harry dug in – using his protractor as a scoop – the inside was gooey, like the little French cheeses his aunt liked.

He let a chunk plop into the toilet and flushed, not relishing the idea of having to fish it out if it didn't go down. But it went down fine and he flushed two more lumps, before realising that the swirling water had drowned out the sound of his phone ringing.

'You're having a great day, young fella!' Ellie Gold said cheerfully as soon as he picked up.

'Am I?' Harry said, unconvinced, as he kneeled in front of the toilet, looking at a slab of explosive that could level a house.

'Do you want the good news or the great news?'

'Whichever,' Harry said, straining not to be rude, but desperate to flush the explosive and get out of the restroom.

'BBC Online came in and offered fifteen grand for the exclusive on the video. Those licence-fee-funded English pricks have more money than sense!' Ellie paused before adding, 'No offence.'

'None taken.'

'The even better news is people are loving the helmet shot. Seven newspapers have picked it up in the last hour, plus a dozen TV stations and some online outlets. Each syndication only earns three to six hundred dollars, depending on image resolution and exact usage. But those numbers add up fast.'

'Cool,' Harry said. 'But I'm in the middle of something . . .'

'Have you got anything else for me?' Ellie asked.

'Not right now,' Harry said warily. 'Cheers for telling us, but I *really* have to go.'

Harry had yet to look at the shots of Charlie's arrest, but he'd already decided to ditch them. He didn't want anything publicly linking him to Charlie and the explosives. He planned to upload all the other pictures on the memory card, then smash it into fifty pieces.

'I'll stay in touch,' Ellie said warmly. 'And check your email when you get a chance. Sue-Ann should have sent through a contributor form.'

Harry's hand was trembling and he almost dropped his phone as he pushed it down his shorts. Someone locked a bolt three stalls down, ripping an epic fart as Harry used the protractor, scooping, dropping and flushing until all that remained was a bundle of torn plastic with slimy residue and dead bugs in the bottom.

Plastic would never flush, so Harry balled it with the explosive-smeared protractor and compass inside, reeled off a massive wodge of toilet paper then wound it around until it was a white clump, roughly the size of a volleyball. Harry waited for the guy taking a dump to wash his hands and exit, then put his backpack on.

Why didn't I stay home? Is this the dumbest decision of my life? It's definitely the weirdest day of my life . . .

After a cautious glance, Harry stepped from the cubicle and swiped his hand under an automatic faucet. He made the ball of tissue wet so that it stuck around the plastic and hopefully hid the strong smell. Then Harry pushed the soggy blob through the flap of a wall-mounted trash can. Finally, he disguised it further by dumping heaps more paper towels on top.

A kid of about seven started peeing at the urinal as Harry blasted his hands with four squirts of soap. The bright pink gel stung the cuts on his palms, but he ignored the pain, scrubbing hard and trying to free anything incriminating from under his nails.

It was a relief to get back into the sun, without the fear of exploding. He spent a few seconds thinking about Ellie's call. Eight hundred up front, seven-and-a-half-grand share from the video, more from the helmet photo.

If Ellie pays. He seems decent, but don't count chickens till the payment clears.

The little kid raced past, flapping his wet hands before retrieving a frozen-yoghurt tub from a hot mom with a stroller. Harry thought about the gun. How to destroy fingerprints and DNA?

He sat on a concrete bench outside a Sunglass Hut, vaguely recognising some girls from his school strolling by. Harry made sure full privacy was switched on before searching. Google led him to a hobby site called The Forensic Enthusiast. The article claimed that regular chlorine bleach broke down all DNA in under an hour.

He read carefully, then checked the public comments below the article, to make sure there weren't a bunch of people claiming the advice was bad. A few comments suggested alternatives, such as oven-cleaning foam, but the majority agreed that most criminals would use bleach, because it cost less than a dollar a bottle and was available everywhere.

Harry made a shopping list in his head as he strode towards Dollar Dominator at the far end of the mall: *cleaning cloths, strong bleach, Ziploc bags, rubber gloves, strong plastic sacks.*

Be meticulous. Clean the gun and dump it where it won't be found for a long time. Throw out your backpack and everything inside it. You've got heaps of clothes, these are comfy running shoes but there's probably tiny bits of explosive trodden in the sole and stuff so ditch them too ... What else?

You can't make one single mistake ...

9 DAZED AND CONFUSED

Charlie had surrendered, but the cops still slammed her to the ground, causing a nosebleed. Her clothes had to go for forensic examination, so she wound up on a green vinyl bench in a police cell, naked beneath a disposable paper suit, with drips of blood down the front.

It was hard to keep time in the windowless cell, but Charlie guessed it was early evening when the door swung open. Her nose had finally stopped bleeding, but the clot felt like a thumb wedged up her nostril, and red-splattered napkins were balled all over the floor.

'We need to have a conversation,' a cop with an orange-dyed buzzcut said brightly.

She was at the tail end of her twenties. Chubby tattooed arms, black jeans and the sleeves of a plaid shirt rolled up, like she was about to chop wood.

'I'm Officer O'Banyon,' the cop said, gum in her mouth. 'Don't need to cuff you, do I?'

She took Charlie one floor up, then offered *anything you like* from the vending machine, as if that was the deal of the century. The interview room had been prepped. Files waiting on the table, a stack of disposable cups and a tatty plastic water jug with cling wrap stretched over the top.

'Take a chair,' O'Banyon said.

The officer's movements were all floaty, her voice easy. Trying to play the chilled big sister.

O'Banyon stripped cellophane off a vending-machine sandwich and bit bread stained with mustard. 'You'll have to excuse me. Crazy shift, I'm *famished*.'

'Shouldn't I have a lawyer?'

'You don't *have* to say anything,' O'Banyon explained. 'Obviously, anything you choose to say in this room is being recorded and may be used as evidence.'

She licked mustard off fingertips, then pointed to a camera, up on the ceiling inside a heavy Plexiglas dome.

'What's your full name?' O'Banyon began.

'Charlie Luanne Croker.'

O'Banyon scratched something on a pad. 'And you're thirteen years old?'

Charlie reckoned O'Banyon was trying to ease her into talking by asking questions she had no reason not to answer. Charlie sat upright and tried to sound strong.

'First off, I've already spoken to a lawyer and he told me to say nothing unless he's present. Second, I'd like to report that the officer who arrested me kneed me in the face when I was already pinned with my arms behind my back.'

The cop chewed slow as she considered her response.

'That's a serious accusation,' O'Banyon said finally. 'It's not my department, but I'll pass that along and someone from internal affairs will speak to you as soon as they can. But let's focus on the *big* picture here.'

O'Banyon dragged her chair forward, and locked fingers on

the desktop. The cop's orange nail varnish was the same shade as her stubbly hair, and Charlie thought it seemed fake: putting so much effort into a look that was supposed to show that you didn't care.

'Think of your situation like a ticking clock,' O'Banyon said. 'You're in deep. You're facing serious charges. But if you're honest and you co-operate with us now, the sentence you end up with could be minimal.

'And I'm not talking about a few months' difference, Charlie. Play ball and the state attorney might let you plead down to a charge like *assault with a deadly weapon* and you'll get two to five in juvenile detention.

'But you try to be clever, the state attorney will get the bit between her teeth. Thirteen-year-olds can be tried as adults for murder or attempted murder in this state. That's fifteen years in an adult prison, before you get a sniff at early release.'

Charlie folded her arms. *I'm Buddha. Don't react. Don't make eye contact with this phoney punk.*

'Look,' O'Banyon said, making a theatrical sigh as she leaned in, then lowering her voice for added drama. 'You did something bad, but people will have a *lot* of sympathy. We *all* had crazy teenage crushes. When I was twelve, I fell in love with Todd Pendragon. Are you old enough to remember him?'

Charlie tutted and shook her head.

'Todd was a super-cute Olympic diver. I watched all his fitness tips on YouTube. Spent hours online trying to buy gold sneakers like the ones he wore on *Good Morning America*. I'd stare at his picture and lie on my bed imagining that I could reach across and touch him. When I thought about how Todd didn't even know my name, my body ached *so* bad I wanted to die.'

Charlie shuddered with contempt and broke silence. 'Why are you telling me this?'

O'Banyon cracked a motherly smile, at odds with the black eye make-up. 'We know about the messages you sent to Deion Powell,' she purred. 'We found his practice shirts under your bed. We found hundreds of photos and newspaper clippings on your laptop and a steak knife with pieces of rubber on close to Deion's home.'

'I don't have his shirts,' Charlie said incredulously. 'I've *never* messaged Deion. I've never even been to a stupid Rockets football game.'

O'Banyon let Charlie's words float as she kept talking. 'We haven't run the DNA test yet, but the steak knife has a white plastic handle with a feather design. It's an exact match for the cutlery in your trailer. Your den at the back of Tire Maxx sent the explosive-sniffing dogs into a frenzy. The forensic report will take a couple of days, but I'd bet a year's salary that the explosive residues at Rock Spring High will match the ones we detected on your clothes when you were arrested.'

Charlie had been expecting questions about JJ, the explosives and how JJ got hold of them.

'This Deion stuff is all lies,' Charlie said, as tense fingers dug into her knee. 'Is this some cop trick? Trying to knock me off balance?'

'Who are you trying to fool, Charlie?' O'Banyon said. 'You had a mad crush on Deion and when you realised you couldn't have him, you made sure nobody else could either.'

'I don't . . . Just . . .' Charlie shouted, then shook her head and tried to compose herself. 'JJ already handed himself in to confess. Maybe it was at another precinct. How can you not know what's going on?'

'You can't pin this on JJ,' O'Banyon said, confidently shaking her head. 'JJ was an obvious suspect. Very sensibly, he came here shortly after the attack with a lawyer who works for his father. He was open and honest about *everything*.'

'Was it him that pointed the finger at me?'

'JJ was able to comprehensively explain his movements from the last time Deion accessed his locker on Wednesday night until the explosion this morning. He was at a party all night, and he stayed at his father's house, sharing a bed with your sister, Fawn. The Janssen property has extensive CCTV, and all recorded footage has been handed across.'

'The Janssens are super rich,' Charlie pointed out. 'I'm sure JJ could pay someone to do his dirty work.'

'So where were *you* between the end of school on Wednesday and the locker explosion this morning?' O'Banyon asked, her purr now more of a roar.

'I want a lawyer,' Charlie insisted.

O'Banyon pointed up at the camera. 'What would a jury say if they saw this recording?' she asked. 'If you're as innocent as you claim, why can't you answer a simple question about what you were doing last night?'

O'Banyon looked unbearably smug. Charlie would have loved to grab the water jug and smash it over her head.

'My sister, Fawn, was there when I got home from school,' Charlie said angrily. 'But Ed was getting sick. He made a mess in the bathroom and was crying. Fawn suddenly walked in wearing this stupid party dress and tells me she's going to a club with JJ. We had a blazing row. But she stormed off and there was no *possible* way I could leave Ed.'

'So Fawn left,' O'Banyon said, back to purring. 'Who else saw you between the time Fawn left and the time of your arrest?'

'I was looking after Ed the whole night,' Charlie said, her chest shuddering as she wondered if there was more to this than O'Banyon trying to trick her into an admission.

'Would Ed make a reliable witness?' O'Banyon asked.

Charlie narrowed her eyes. 'You know he wouldn't.'

'And did Ed go to sleep?'

'You're making this stuff up,' Charlie insisted. 'The shirts and the steak knife. Accusing me of planting the bomb, so the other stuff seems less serious.'

'Who are you trying to kid, Charlie?' O'Banyon groaned, standing aggressively, then leaning in with her knuckles flat on the desktop. 'If I told lies in this room, your lawyer would watch the tape and claim I'd tried to entrap you. I'd get yelled at by my boss, investigated by internal affairs and this entire interview would be ruled inadmissible by a judge.'

Can she really not lie? Charlie wondered. *Or is that a lie too . . .*

'All I'm doing is laying out the *real* evidence, Charlie. All you're doing is burying your head in the sand and making your situation worse.'

'I didn't do this,' Charlie shouted, then gasped with delight as she had a brainwave. 'They have CCTV in the hallways at my school. They *must* have it in the High School too. Since you're *so* sure I did this, I'll bet you *two* years of your salary, that you will not see me anywhere near Deion Powell's locker.'

'The video was looked at,' O'Banyon explained, unruffled. 'The closest camera is sixty feet from Deion's locker and only gives a blurry view. But you knew *that* already, didn't you?'

'You're turning everything I say against me,' Charlie spat. 'Aren't you supposed to listen to what I say and investigate? Not decide I did something before I open my mouth?'

O'Banyon kept hammering. 'The memory card recording CCTV footage for the entire ground-floor annexe suffered damage the last time it was reinserted. We can get a data-recovery technician to look into that. But that takes days and costs the police department money, which we can spend on something more worthwhile if you do the decent thing and admit to what you did.'

'I've been framed,' Charlie yelled.

'Who'd frame a thirteen-year-old girl?' O'Banyon said, tutting incredulously as she took a step back from the desk. 'I've given you a chance to make things easier for yourself, but I'm clearly wasting my time.

'So, Charlie, you cool your heels overnight in your cell. I'm gonna drive home, make food, walk my dog and snuggle up in bed with my boyfriend. I'll drop by your cell in the morning. And hopefully you'll be ready for a more constructive conversation by then.'

10 NEW-BABY SMELL

'The person you are calling is not currently able to take your call. If you wish to leave a message, please speak after the tone.'

'Harry, this is me . . . Charlie, from earlier? These calls are recorded so I must be careful. Fawn's not answering, but the custody officer let me get numbers off my cell and yours was still open in the contacts screen.

'I can't think of anyone else and I know you're interested in this story, even if you don't care about me. I'm scared . . . *Really* damned scared. JJ *didn't* hand himself in at all. They're trying to blame me for the bombing, not just making explosive.

'I got grilled by this awful cop. She's talking about stuff they found. A steak knife from my house got used to slash Deion's tires. Deion's football shirts under my bed. Pictures of him on my laptop. They're saying all this crazy stuff and none of— You'll probably hear stuff about me, but, Harry, I swear on my mom's grave it's not true.

'I don't have an alibi, because Ed was sick and I had to stay home. I can't see why the cops would make up a bunch of evidence. It had to be planned before the attack anyway, so someone must have it in for me. My sister Fawn's not answering her phone, but we've been fighting a lot. I got angry and threatened to report her to the trustees who control Ed's compensation money, because she gets eighteen hundred a month but hardly looks after him. I guess it suits Fawn if I'm not around, and if Deion's out of the picture her boyfriend, JJ, gets to be starting quarterback . . .'

Charlie took a deep breath before the words started tumbling again.

'My own sister . . . I know, right? Can't be certain, I guess. You must think I'm some nut-job . . . But you were there when that lawyer guy called, saying he was an attorney and that JJ was going to surrender? You heard that, right?

'If I get a public defender it will be exactly like the fire-extinguisher thing. They'll see the evidence stacked up and tell me to plead guilty. And my eighty-six dollars in Wells Fargo won't get me a real lawyer. So I'm up to my neck, Harry. And, as pathetic as this seems, you're probably the only person in this world who might give a damn . . .'

There was a stifled sob, then Charlie hung up.

● ● ●

The red Nikes weren't as comfy as the ones Harry had binned, but a scraped heel was just pain and pain was part of what he liked about running: the feeling of pushing your heart and lungs, nothing in your head but the next gulp of breath as sweat floods your eyes.

Harry ran a slight hill, on a street between two gated developments. It was no-man's-land. Rooftops and palm trees, glimpsed over twenty-foot block walls. He'd often amused himself with the thought of suburban kids tunnelling out, but today all thoughts were fixed on the gun.

As the street came to a dead end, a smell of trash wafted

through a service gate in one of the walls. Beyond was a parking lot, busy with the type of cars you cram full of kids and a public space centred on four softball diamonds and a play area.

Harry ran past a dad holding a sleepy toddler, then slowed as he cut between two tall SUVs, parked under a row of palms. The kerb here had a big slot-drain to catch runoff from the parkland.

He put one Nike up on the kerb, like he was stopping to tie a lace, glanced around to make sure nobody was in sight, then slipped a drawstring pouch off his back. Breathless and dripping sweat, Harry opened the collar of the pouch, careful not to touch the package inside as it slid out on to the kerb.

He'd used white spirit to scrub the clip and gun for fingerprints and now they were in a Ziploc bag, disassembled and swimming in neon-blue bleach gel to kill DNA. He'd only touched the bag while wearing rubber gloves. Now he flicked it down the hole with his heel and hooked the drawstrings back over his arms as he resumed his run.

There was often a bunch of Venezuelan refugee kids around when Harry ran through the park. They'd always ignored him, but two hands-down-pants tenth graders swaggered over as he stopped at a water fountain.

'You Smirnov?' the bigger of the two stated accusingly.

He straightened up, sweeping away dribbles down his chin. 'Yeah.'

Harry felt wary. But he never took a phone or money when he ran and there were heaps of people around.

'That video's sick, man,' the smaller one said, getting closer than Harry found comfortable.

'Sick,' his pal agreed. 'The photo too, with Deion's cracked helmet and all the blood.'

Harry had spent two hours cleaning the gun, cleaning himself, and timing it so that everything he'd been wearing or carrying earlier went down the Sinatra's trash chutes, minutes before the cart arrived to take it all to the dump. He'd been so focused he hadn't even known the photo had been published.

'Where'd you see it?' Harry asked excitedly.

'Insta, Facebook. It's everywhere,' the little guy said. 'The bloody helmet gave me chills, bro.'

'You get paid for that shit, Smirnov?' the big guy asked.

'Nah,' Harry lied.

Football players liked any excuse to use their muscle, so the last thing Harry wanted were rumours he'd cashed in on Deion's misfortune.

'I wanted it online so people could see.'

'School website says Rock Spring is closed at least until Tuesday!' the big guy said happily.

Harry tapped the face of his running watch. 'Good to talk, but I've gotta bolt.'

He felt better now he'd got rid of everything, but angst still gnawed at him.

What if someone saw me leaving Charlie's den? Or cameras in the CVS parking lot? Or I clogged the mall plumbing with all that explosive? Cops catch pros who spend months planning crimes and I did this on the fly. On the other hand, if JJ has confessed, and Charlie gets a smack on the wrist for making the explosives, why would the cops be looking for me? In which case I just threw out a $160 pair of running shoes for no reason . . .

Running blotted thought, and Harry pushed his body, even though the early evening temperature was up in the nineties. He sprinted the last stretch beneath an amber sunset and caught an open gate as a lady in a casino uniform dashed out of the Sinatra to a waiting taxi.

The TV in the kitchen was on as Harry walked in, trailing drips of sweat. He was sure it had been off when he left, but with so much in his head he figured he must have forgotten. He'd guzzled water from the sink and started peeling his shirt when he saw the message icon on his phone. He guessed it might be Ellie, or Matt bragging that he'd done something with his girlfriend that her father wouldn't approve of.

Harry decided a shower was more important than the message, but only got three steps before a door opened at the top of the stairs.

'There you are,' his aunt, Kirsten, said, with enough acid in her tone for Harry to know there was trouble.

She looked a lot like her nephew. Harry had caught the running bug from Kirsten and they shared the same slender build. She'd been getting undressed, so the belt of her white pants dangled and her double-breasted chef's coat was unbuttoned, showing a grey undershirt beneath.

'You're early,' Harry said, which was an understatement. It wasn't eight and his aunt never got home before midnight.

'I had a couple of diners compliment me on your photography skills,' she said tartly, coming downstairs as Harry unconsciously backed into the kitchen island. 'And an hour ago I had a call from the principal of your school saying that you're suspended until I come in to discuss your actions after the evacuation.'

'School's closed until Tuesday anyway,' Harry noted.

'Don't get cute!' Kirsten snapped, hands on hips as Harry felt queasy. His aunt wasn't around much and they rarely argued.

'I'm not going through this again,' Kirsten said, wagging a finger. 'I grew up with a big sister I loved to bits. I watched her charging all over the world, with everyone telling me how brave and talented she was. But I spent too many nights lying awake worrying about her, and your nan was a wreck every time your mum left on another adventure.

'Your mum almost died when she got shot, and again when she got blood poisoning in Zimbabwe. And then the ultimate nightmare happened. By which time your dad had pissed off back to Russia, and I wind up with a poor heartbroken seven-year-old to look after.'

'Mum died of a heart defect,' Harry pointed out. 'She'd be just as dead if she'd become a librarian.'

Kirsten jabbed the finger into Harry's chest. 'When you turn eighteen, you're free to take that *stupid* bloody Nikon your dad bought you and do what you like. But while I'm your sole guardian you *don't* take stupid risks.'

'It wasn't risky,' Harry said, imagining how crazy she'd be if she knew about Charlie and the explosives.

'You climbed back into your school when it was locked down. Some psycho cop might have shot you, or another bomb could have gone off. There could have been a gas leak, or a live electricity cable . . .'

Harry felt the tear that streaked down his aunt's face. All he could do was stare dopily at his feet.

'It happened at my school,' he said gently. 'It's not like I ditched uni and jumped on a plane to Malawi like Mum did.'

'You edited the videos, and put them online. Found an agency to syndicate the photograph and sell the exclusive on the video. Maybe the explosion just happened, but you knew exactly what to do after. You *must* have put thought into this.'

'It's what I want to do,' Harry said. 'Probably . . .'

'You're fourteen,' Kirsten said. She seemed about to add something like, *you don't know what you want*, but instead she took the last step forward and wrapped her arms tightly round his back. 'I just . . . Don't get hurt.'

Harry was slightly taller than his aunt, and felt loved as he craned his head and caught the crisply laundered smell of her chef's coat. But he kept thinking about the gun and the explosives. And saw a horrible mental image where they were still hugging, but he was dressed in an orange prison jumpsuit . . .

'I love you, Auntie,' Harry said.

'I've got the family heart defect,' Kirsten reminded him. 'Too many shocks might kill me off.'

'I'll try not to,' Harry said softly.

'Love you too,' Kirsten said, looking at the sweat-dripped tiles around Harry as she backed away. 'I remember when you were little. You had that warm milky smell and when nobody was looking I'd pick you up and sniff because I loved it so much.'

'Not now, eh?' Harry said, raising one soggy armpit close to his aunt's face.

'Gross!' Kirsten said, laughing as she backed off and grabbed sheets of kitchen towel out of a dispenser. Harry took his phone off the counter as Kirsten dabbed her eyes, then used the tissue as a foot rag to mop his trail of sweat. 'Now go shower, and you're grounded. *Obviously.*'

Harry wasn't shocked. 'How long?'

'At least until Monday. Then we'll see what your school says.'

Harry's room was upstairs. He'd used his bathroom to clean the gun and he whacked the air-con up to clear a lingering bleach smell. After peeling off his sweaty shirt, he sat on the lid of his toilet and unlocked his phone.

'*You have one new message, received at nineteen thirty-six hours.*' Then after a beep, 'Harry, this is me . . . Charlie, from earlier . . . ?'

61

11 GOON SQUAD

Charlie chased sleep. She lay on the shiny green mat, hearing fragments of the things that went wrong on a Thursday night in Vegas: A cocky pickpocket chatting to the custody officer like some long-lost sister, a weeping college kid and drunks banging their doors and claiming they knew their rights. Charlie suspected they were all in less trouble than she was.

'Croker, ya goin' upstairs,' someone yelled through the door.

Charlie got handcuffed this time. The clock over the custody sergeant's desk said three-fifteen and the third floor was a dead zone. Empty desks, and the only light coming off exit signs.

She was marched down a hall, past a basketball-tall guy working a mop and into a big office. A Nevada state flag and a big stuffed fish hung on the back wall. The unbarred windows had a vista over a lot filled with cop cars.

'Sit there.'

'What's happening?' Charlie asked.

The custody officer left wordlessly as Charlie settled on a spongy office chair, cuffs scraping the desktop. The only light was a triangle from a side door, where she could hear piss spraying into a toilet bowl. Charlie heard the faucet run, hands getting dried, then a gong crash from the lid of a pedal bin.

'Charlie Croker,' a stooped figure said as he came out, silhouetted by the washroom light.

He was bulky, with a man bun, biker jacket and stubble. Blue cop car light flashed the dark office walls as he settled across the desk.

'How's your day been?'

'Had better,' Charlie said as she tried to place the voice. 'Are you JJ's lawyer, Edelmann?'

'Well recognised,' he said, casually drumming a fountain pen he'd taken off the desk. 'Not my actual name.'

'Man of mystery,' Charlie said, stifling a yawn as one of her disposable slippers dropped off. 'I'm guessing you're not a lawyer either.'

'That would be a smart guess,' he said, jamming the pen in his ear then studying the blob of wax stuck to the end. 'I describe myself as a person that can fix things in this town. For instance, I can arrive at a police station at three in the morning and get a suspect taken from her cell for a private chat. And when you look at the custody log in the morning it won't be written down. And if you ask around nobody's gonna remember a damned thing.'

'Is that the same guy who hacked my laptop and put Deion's shirts under my bed?' Charlie asked.

'And slipped your brother the laxative, so you couldn't leave the trailer,' he said, clicking his fingers. 'Don't get your hopes up about data recovery on the Rock Spring High CCTV, either.'

Feeling vulnerable in the paper suit with nothing underneath, Charlie pulled one knee up to her chest and wrapped her cuffed hands round it.

'Are you working for my sister?' she asked warily.

'If I were in your shoes, I wouldn't be gifting Fawn this Christmas,' he smiled. 'But my services come above her price bracket.'

'Jay Janssen Senior?'

'Do you think?' the mystery man said, but nodded as well.

'So two people half burnt to death and my life gets wrecked, all so some rich guy gets to see his son play starting quarterback?'

He stroked his man bun and smiled. 'Crazy messed-up world we live in.'

'But you're here at three a.m.,' Charlie said thoughtfully. 'Haven't you got me already?'

'Got you for sure, Charlie girl,' he said. 'But I sleep better when all the loose ends are tidied away. And Fawn said she wanted your wings clipped, rather than lock you up and toss the key.'

'Isn't that nice . . .' Charlie said.

'Here's the deal-a-roo,' mystery man said as his drumming pen slipped and hit the carpet. 'O'Banyon will come into your cell tomorrow morning and you'll cave.'

'You think?' Charlie spat.

'We'll get you a lawyer. You don't need a superstar if you're not going to trial, but I know a lady who'll fight your corner and cut a deal with the justice department. She'll big up that you could have used a lot more explosive if you wanted to, that you're a good little orphan kiddie who looks after her retarded brother, and lives under a lot of emotional stress, yada, yada.

'The Clark County attorney's office will want a high-profile case like this tied up fast and neat. If you play ball, they'll settle for an assault beef. Your plea will be three to five years, and if you behave, you'll be out in two.'

Charlie looked suspicious. 'Is what you're saying now any more reliable than when you told me JJ was about to confess?'

'It's a plea bargain,' he explained. 'It's how ninety-five per cent of criminal cases get settled in this country. Say nothing to O'Banyon until I get that lawyer in the room with you. There will be a tussle over your sentence and exact wording of your confession. Then it will get rubber stamped by a judge.'

'Just a few years of my life, eh?' Charlie said airily. 'How do you sleep at night?'

Mystery man laughed. 'I sleep soundly, on a mattress stuffed with hundred-dollar bills.'

'Money . . .' Charlie said, shaking her head. 'What if I don't cave? What if I *happen* to have some principles?'

'You seem fond of that brother. I'm sure me and a pal could pay him a visit.'

Charlie put her leg down and shot forward in the chair. 'Leave Ed the hell alone.'

'Or what?' he teased as he stood and moved round the desk. 'You'll come get me, Charlie? Do you think that drooling gimp brother of yours will squeal like a piggy when I tenderise his face with this diamond ring on my big ol' fist?'

Charlie shuddered as he loomed behind, planting a hairy hand on each shoulder.

'You're sweating through that overall,' mystery man noticed as his stale breath hit her face. 'It's not leaving much to my imagination.'

Charlie felt sick as the hands slid to the base of her neck, two fingers putting a slight squeeze on her windpipe.

'Are you going to make this harder than it has to be, Charlie girl?'

She wanted to bite or fight. She wanted to be the mighty

hero, like the white-grin tweens in the Disney shows she watched with Ed. But the mystery man's wrists were as broad as her neck and Charlie had a head for numbers.

One of me against Janssen's whole organisation.

My eighty-three bucks versus his hundred million.

Out of lock-up when I'm barely sixteen, or adult prison till I'm thirty.

You can only play the hand of cards you've been dealt and these people own me . . .

A chill went from head to curled toes as the pressure on Charlie's throat made her croak, 'I'll speak to your lawyer.'

'Nice,' he growled, taking one hand off and edging a slight grin. Then he pushed out his tongue and licked from the base of Charlie's chin to her earlobe. His breath was like rot and she could hear the spit slosh around his mouth as he spoke his final words.

'It's been a pleasure breaking you.'

12 ONE-LEGGED GRANNIES

How much bad stuff can you ignore? Harry kept asking himself. *The world's full of hungry babies and one-legged grannies who stepped on landmines. But is that my problem? Is Charlie my problem? Would I give a damn if Charlie was fifty and had five chins?*

If you wanna be some big-shot journalist, you can't give up easy. But you're fourteen. The helmet picture is everywhere. It'll be the first thing in your portfolio if you apply to journalism college. And you've already taken crazy risks for this girl.

This train of thought ran through the night. When sleep seemed impossible, Harry grabbed his laptop. He found stories about Charlie's family. *Court orders $6.9 million-dollar lifetime settlement for brain-damaged boy. Rock Springs mom of three found hanged. QB prospect steps out at Janssen Golf fundraiser.*

The last story was from the Facebook page of a local kids' hospice, and came with a photo. Harry had imagined Fawn Croker as an older, meaner version of Charlie. But she looked like a swimwear model, six feet tall in borrowed golf shoes, blouse tied at the waist to emphasise a huge bust. JJ had propped himself on a pricey Callaway driver and smiled with the easy confidence of a good-looking kid who'd won the lottery by being born.

JJ, aged 17, shot an excellent 79 off a five handicap, while companion Fawn Croker said she was 'thrilled' to break 100 for the first time . . .

Harry yawned, skimming the rest of the article, then moving on to research the Janssens. The Janssen Corporation website showed happy gamblers and mall shoppers. The Wikipedia page on Jay Janssen Sr had clearly been curated by a public-relations company, with lots of details on Janssen's business success and charity work, while cocaine dealing and jail time was kept to three short sentences under the *Early Years* tab.

But it didn't take much searching to find a darker side. There was a recent TV news story about Janssen casino workers complaining that they weren't being paid all their overtime and getting threatened if they spoke out or tried to join a union.

Harry read about a $30,000 fine for breaking hygiene regulations at a twenty-four-hour diner inside the Janssen Riverboat casino, a family-run construction company that went bust after Janssen's property business refused to pay bills and a senior employee who claimed staff were ordered to turn a blind eye to drug dealers.

Clearly the Janssens weren't the nicest people in town, but Harry couldn't see how any of these facts could be used to help Charlie. He tried to think of a strategy, but he felt as if he'd skipped ten chapters ahead in his math textbook, staring bleary-eyed at a problem he had no idea how to solve.

When Kirsten woke Harry up, he was sprawled bare-assed over his bed.

'School's closed,' he said, stretching into a yawn and knocking his still-open laptop off the edge of his bed. 'Shit!'

'Matt's in the kitchen. Says you arranged to go for a run before it got too hot.'

'Aww,' Harry said dozily. 'Forgot that . . .'

He slathered sunscreen, and rushed down to Matt with Nikes hooked over his fingers. They did some stretching outside in the courtyard, but Harry would never normally run in the evening and straight away the next morning. His tanks were empty and after less than a mile he faked an injury.

'I'm slowing you down, mate,' Harry told Matt. 'Thigh is really tight. I'm sorry . . .'

Harry's head was full of the stuff he'd been thinking about through the night. He wanted to help Charlie, but self-preservation had blossomed with the new day. The kid who'd flushed explosives and wiped the gun seemed like an aberration.

Harry walked stiffly through the Sinatra's main gate. He'd gone past reception and was waiting for the elevator up to four when a fist smashed the back of his head.

His brow smacked the metal elevator door and two guys bundled him into a side room. It had originally been the sales team's office when the Sinatra was first built. Now the windowless space had two parked housekeeping carts and stacked drums of bathroom cleaner and pool chemicals.

'Harry?' one guy asked, throwing the teenager's slender body over a cart, as a much bigger dude with a man bun elbowed him in the back.

'Friendly warning, kiddo,' the first guy said, grasping Harry's hair and yanking his head back.

Man Bun punched him again.

'We know Croker called you last night,' Man Bun shouted, sliding his hand between Harry's legs and grabbing his balls. 'What did she say?'

'Nothing,' Charlie groaned.

'Don't lie to me,' Man Bun shouted, squeezing Harry's balls. 'She asked for help, didn't she?'

'We heard the recording,' the smaller guy added. 'Lying to us is not a good idea.'

'Please,' Harry begged. 'I barely know her.'

'Keep your nose out and keep your balls,' Man Bun said. 'And your auntie, the la-de-da chef? We'll work her over too. Understood?'

'Understood,' Harry moaned as Man Bun let go and the little guy shoved him violently off the cleaning cart.

The goons backed out as Harry crashed into empty chemical drums, tears streaking his face, sure he was about to pass out from the pain.

• • •

Harry snuck into the apartment, back pain, rib pain and half doubled over. Kirsten would freak if she knew he'd been beaten up, so he was grateful that she was up in her room, and that she'd left for a meeting at her restaurant when he emerged from a hot soak.

The pain was mild as Harry hobbled downstairs, but his nerves were fried. He half expected the goons to crash through the door, and jerked with fright when a kid squealed in the communal pool outside.

Harry strapped an ice pack to his back and listened to a message Ellie had left while he was out. The take from the video and photos was now thirty-one grand, but thinking about his share made him feel shitty because it was earned at Charlie's expense.

There was another call as he read the instructions on an Ibuprofen bottle.

'Harry,' Charlie said.

The phone felt like molten lava.

'Harry, are you there?'

What if this is a test. Will the bad guys come back if they know I spoke to her?

'Hey,' Harry said warily.

'You sound off,' Charlie said.

'I'm good,' Harry said, unthinkingly trying to sit on a kitchen stool and getting a jolt of pain.

'My call last night? It doesn't matter now. I signed my life away. Felony assault and two charges of manufacturing an explosive device. I'll be out in two years if I behave. JJ gets to be quarterback, Fawn gets her annoying sister off her back. At least I'm not one of the poor saps who got half their skin burnt off.'

Harry acted like he was speaking to bad guys listening to a recording, instead of to Charlie. 'I didn't take any steps to investigate,' he said stiltedly.

Charlie sounded sore. 'Thanks for the sympathy, pal.'

'I . . .'

Harry's head was all over the place. He was keen to help Charlie, but getting jumped had turned him into a wreck.

'I'm sorry this is so messed up,' he said.

'I should never have dragged you into this,' Charlie said slowly. 'I just wanted you to know it's over. Have a nice life, Harry.'

'Wait,' Harry said. 'Don't go.'

Part of him was terrified of what might happen if he stayed involved, but Charlie needed him. And though they'd never had a normal conversation he'd felt a connection when they hugged.

'Yesterday, you said you didn't have a single real friend,'

Harry said. 'I'm not exactly fighting pals off since I moved here. So, I could write you, or send stuff you need like chocolate, or deodorant?'

'Are you saying I stink?'

'No,' Harry blurted, but then Charlie laughed and he realised she was messing. 'I don't know how this stuff works. Like, what I'd be allowed to send, or how far away you'll be. And visits. Is it only family members that can visit?'

'Could you bake me a cake with a gun inside?' Charlie asked dryly.

Harry's balls throbbed when he laughed. 'I'm sure they'd never suspect that . . .'

'I've spent too much time with Ed to make many friends and Fawn's a total bitch. So, it might be nice to hear that British accent occasionally.'

'Cool,' Harry said.

'I think my three minutes are up,' Charlie said. 'I'm being moved out of the police precinct soon, I think. So I'll try and call when . . .'

The phone went dead and Harry stood still for ages, holding the ice pack against his back and thinking about Charlie's giant blue eyes.

PART TWO
TWO YEARS LATER

13 SNor

A brief history of the SNor outbreak
By Charlie Croker (Inmate B3790)

Synthetic Norovirus K (SNorK) was originally developed as a treatment for stomach cancer by scientists at the University of Zurich.

While regular norovirus breeds in the human stomach, causing diarrhoea and vomiting (commonly known as stomach flu), the Zurich scientists used gene-editing techniques to create a modified virus that would only attack cancerous cells.

Early synthetic norovirus trials reduced levels of cancer, but most patients' immune systems destroyed the modified virus before it was completely effective. To combat this, scientists developed the 'K' version. In addition to the anti-cancer modifications, SNorK added genes from another virus capable of surviving in the human gut for up to two weeks.

In early trials, SNorK proved effective, surviving in the stomach long enough to completely cure stomach cancer in seven out of eight patients. All patients treated with SNorK had to stay under strict quarantine while undergoing treatment with the experimental virus.

This included the incineration of clothes, medical equipment and patients' bodily waste. All medical staff dealing with trial patients were inoculated against SNork, and all patients had to be clear of the virus for two weeks before being allowed to leave the research facility.

Despite the success of these trials, SNorK treatment was never licensed for general use. Medical bodies around the world agreed there was too much risk of the modified virus mutating, or that it would recombine with regular norovirus. This would risk producing a norovirus strain that survived in the gut for up to two weeks like SNorK, while producing the virus's normal symptoms of severe vomiting and diarrhoea.

The Zurich team published their results and drug companies began searching for ways to achieve the targeted cancer therapy without using a potentially dangerous virus.

Two years later, Chinese businessman Kenny Yo was diagnosed with stomach cancer. With a personal fortune of $11 billion and a life expectancy of less than one year, Yo offered Zurich University Virology Department $250 million to use their quarantine facility for his own course of SNorK treatment. The department said that using an unlicensed treatment was unethical, and illegal under Swiss Law.

But the determined billionaire found a group of Hangzhou-based genetic scientists who were seeking money to start their own gene-editing business. Most details of the Zurich University SNorK project had been published in a scientific journal, and they could use off-the-shelf gene-editing technology costing less than $10,000 to make a copycat version of SNorK.

Yo retreated to his country home, sealed himself away from friends and family and began dosing himself with SNorK. The treatment was successful, but while Yo kept himself isolated, the conditions were nothing like as secure as the viral containment lab at the University of Zurich.

It is believed that the first people to contract SNorK were Yo's cleaner, and two men who came to vacuum the septic tank at his country home. SNorK is highly contagious, but its symptoms are mild compared to regular norovirus and the SNorK outbreak went unnoticed. Most patients were not sick enough to go to a doctor, and those that did were assumed to have a minor stomach infection.

Norovirus thrives in cool temperatures (another name for it is 'winter vomiting bug') and as cold weather set in a typical winter outbreak of norovirus began in the area around Hangzhou. At first, everything seemed normal, but shortly after Christmas patients started showing serious symptoms.

Instead of lasting less than twenty-four hours, patients were often sick for a week or more and many weaker patients died through severe dehydration. Norovirus is extremely contagious. It is mainly passed by touch, particularly in public restrooms and food-preparation areas. This makes the virus prone to spreading in heavily populated environments such as schools, prisons, cruise ships and hospitals.

As the Zurich scientists had feared, SNorK and regular norovirus had swapped genes and formed a deadlier strain. The recombined synthetic norovirus – now commonly referred to as SNor – mixes the longevity of SNorK and the unpleasant gastric effects of regular norovirus. In the eight months since SNor was first detected, it has appeared in every country on Earth, and is estimated to have infected one billion people.

In most cases SNor causes three to seven days of painful vomiting and diarrhoea. Patients are advised to continually drink water, to stay away from others as much as possible and not to seek medical attention, because of the risk of bringing the virus into contact with people with other illnesses.

For a healthy adult, the risk of death from a SNor infection is less than 0.1%. However, this rises to more than 5% in children under two years old. Other groups who are seriously affected include the elderly, diabetics and people with immune system diseases such as HIV.

Deaths from SNor are now believed to be more than 2.5 million. However, cases declined sharply when summer hit the populous northern hemisphere and it has been shown that relatively simple hygiene procedures can greatly reduce reinfection rates.

The first inoculations against SNor have recently been released and are being given to high priority groups, such as hospital workers and children aged between six months and two years.

Grade A+++

Great Work!!!!

Charlie, this is well researched and structured. Hopefully this will be the last essay you write for me before your release.

It has been a HUGE pleasure teaching you English and science over the past two and a bit years. Although at times I can barely keep up with your thirst for knowledge!

If you can successfully put these difficult years behind you, there is no limit to where you can go in life!

All best!

Ms G. Higuain

14 GOOD LUCK, CHARLIE

Kirsten assuaged some of her guilt about not spending time with Harry by paying for him to attend Queensbridge Academy. The sixteen-year-old wore a shirt, tie and V-neck sweater as he strode a path between neat lawns, wary of a group of tenth-grade princesses in dark blue knee socks and tartan skirts.

'Harry Potter,' one of them shouted. 'Over here! Did you read my article?'

Esme was a Colombian fireball. Harry adored her athletic legs and chocolate-brown eyes, but was less impressed with the three hundred words of Christmas Gift Ideas she'd submitted for the Queensbridge online newspaper.

'I just left the fortnightly editorial meeting,' Harry explained. 'It's a good article, but the staff want articles about school life, sports matches and stuff.'

He wanted to say, *The school wants bland crap that makes it look good and I'm not going to use the trashy article you cobbled together in half an hour, because your homeroom tutor said you needed to start doing things that make you look less like a brain-dead mall rat on your college application.*

'You could try something less random,' Harry suggested.

'You'd understand what we're looking for if you sat in on the next editorial meeting and listened to . . .'

Harry's words withered under the gaze of scorn. Girls like Esme expected boys like Harry to kiss their asses, and she glared at him like he'd stamped on her toes. But even Esme's moody face was beautiful and Harry felt jealous of Cristiano, the beefy senior soccer goalie who got to see her naked.

'I get ten articles for every one we can publish,' Harry added. *And hassle for every rejection . . .*

'Zit faced prick on a power kick,' one of Esme's pals muttered, loud enough for Harry to hear as he backed away.

'It rhymes, it rhymes,' another one added, and then they were all squealing with laughter.

Harry's face turned red and he didn't dare glance back. His skin had been bad for the past few months, and beautiful girls calling him spotty was a slug in the gut.

Two hundred bucks for the dermatologist, ninety bucks for a pot of cream and my face still looks like a pizza . . .

Anita smiled as she ran the other way. Harry's deputy editor was skinny and had hands buried in her Queensbridge Athletic sweatshirt to fight the early evening cold. 'Left my poster tube in the meeting room . . .'

Anita was Indian-American, super smart, super blunt and had a filthy sense of humour. Harry still felt bad that he'd snapped a *no* when she'd nervously asked if he wanted to go to the Christmas formal with her.

Harry's phone rang before he found anything else to fuel his regret. It was the name he wanted to see and he trembled as he heard a familiar recorded message.

'*This is a collect call from White Boulder Juvenile Correction facility. If you wish to accept payment for this call, press one, followed by the star on your keypad.'*

'Charlie,' Harry said after a mechanical clunk that he'd always assumed was something to do with prisoner calls being recorded. 'How'd your hearing go?'

Charlie sounded like the whole world had landed on her head. 'Life sucks,' she groaned. 'The two guys on the early release panel were fine. But it was the same woman as last time. Said she wasn't comfortable. Because making alcohol showed I was still interested in chemistry, which showed I hadn't learned my lesson. Plus, the fight I got in last week didn't help.'

Harry shook his head. 'Seriously? You already did an extra two months for making that batch of hooch. And the fight wasn't your fault. Wasn't the whole thing on CCTV?'

'It has to be a unanimous decision to release me,' Charlie said.

'I'm *so* sorry,' Harry said, staring at a darkening sky and the light haze from the Vegas strip, four miles away. 'I wanted you to be out for Christmas . . .'

'Actually,' Charlie said, suddenly much brighter. 'I just made all that up.'

'Eh?'

'Everything went fine. They're releasing me to an Independent Living Facility in North Vegas on Friday!'

'Holy crap!' Harry gasped, punching the air with his free hand. 'Really?'

'I had you,' Charlie laughed.

'You're mean!' Harry said. 'You're *really* coming out?'

'Cross my heart and hope to die,' Charlie said. 'I had to sit through this big lecture about following the rules at Independent Living and how they could send me back for the rest of my sentence if I screw up once.'

'Friday!' Harry said, turning back towards his school. 'I've got lessons Friday. But you know what? I don't care. I'll bunk off and drive up to see you. Are you OK? Are you happy?'

Charlie laughed noisily. 'Of course I'm happy, dumbass. But don't bunk school. They're driving me and another inmate in a transit bus. Just as likely won't get there until two or three in the afternoon. Let me settle in, and you can drive up Saturday.'

'Makes sense,' Harry said, imagining a day with Charlie. 'All the hours we spent on the phone, I kinda forget that we've only met properly once.'

'You visited me four times.'

'Yeah, but in that dingy little room full of screaming kids . . . Only thing is, I can't stay late because I can't drive after sunset until I've had my licence for a year.'

'Any more crashes?' Charlie asked cheekily.

'My driving's OK,' Harry said. 'I just clipped that kerb coming out of the filling station. And then the cop pulled me over cos I was driving home with my fender hanging off.'

'You can laugh at me when I start drivers' ed next year,' Charlie said. 'But God knows how I'll ever afford a car.'

'So how's everyone been about you getting out?'

'They had a girl with SNor arrive on block C on Sunday,' Charlie said. 'So we're officially back on full quarantine. Only allowed to eat and use the toilet in our cells, and no close contact with other inmates. But a few of my girls have snuck in my cell for goodbyes and I've started giving my toiletries and stuff away. But you can't be over-the-top happy cos there's noobs who just arrived and are broken hearted. And bitches doing life who'll batter you if you rub in that you're getting out.'

'I actually need to go,' Harry said. 'It'll be dark soon, and I'm still at school.'

'Detention?' Charlie asked.

'Worse: editorial meeting for the school news website.'

'Life must be *sooooo* hard at your ten-thousand-dollar-per-term school,' Charlie teased. 'But, seriously, I have *no* idea how I'd have survived if you weren't around, Harry. Can't wait to hug the hell out of you on Saturday.'

'Day after tomorrow,' Harry said, saying the words like he didn't believe them before cracking a big smile. 'Let me know if there's anything you need me to pick up.'

Harry smiled up at the sky as he dropped his phone back in his pocket. *Probably past sunset, but home is only a ten-minute drive and there's no bus out here . . .*

Anita came running in the other direction, now carrying her art project in a plastic tube almost as tall as she was.

'Got there just before the caretaker locked up,' she huffed breathlessly. 'What are you looking so cheerful about?'

'Charlie's getting out Saturday,' Harry explained.

Anita nodded. 'Your girlfriend, the mad bomber!'

He didn't like the *mad bomber* comment, but he preferred Anita's bluntness to people who gossip behind your back.

'Not my girlfriend,' Harry said firmly.

'Could have fooled me, Haribo,' Anita teased. 'You're always talking about her, or calling her, or taking the three-hour bus ride to White Boulder.'

Harry liked Anita's jealousy, but this didn't sustain him for the walk across the parking lot to his Mini. He hoped Charlie was going to become his girlfriend, but had no clue if her feelings went beyond friendship.

15 BEEF AND COKE

Charlie wasn't much taller than when she'd arrived at White Boulder, but she'd filled out and the T-shirt and denim shorts she'd put into storage the day she'd arrived now looked like doll's clothes.

Her fake Ray Bans and a Raiders cap she'd stolen from JJ still did their job, but the cell with the cracked screen was flat and she had no idea if the battery would revive after more than two years. Besides the clothes, Charlie's mesh storage box contained two keys for a trailer where someone else now lived, an expired Rock Spring Middle School ID, a five-dollar bill and three more in change.

Since her clothes were too small, the officer handling Charlie's release let her keep the prison issue sneakers, tracksuit bottoms and undershirt she stood up in, plus one spare set of underwear. She also got a sixty-dollar release grant and a care package, containing anti-viral hand gel, a pack of condoms and leaflets on sexually transmitted diseases and dealing with depression.

After twenty-seven months on a fifty-acre prison lot, it seemed weird to be on the move. Charlie stared out the bus at new shops and ads for movies she'd never heard of. Cars were mostly electric and every inch of roof packed solar panels.

There were SNor warnings, and shopfront posters advertising virus-destroying UV lamps: *$299 FINALLY BACK IN STOCK*. About one person in four wore an anti-virus mask. These looked sturdier than the ones issued to White Boulder inmates, which split, crumbled and never got replaced.

The Barack Obama Independent Living Unit was in North Vegas, less than three blocks from open desert. There was a 7-Eleven next door and suburban houses sprawled in every direction. The building had been open less than two years, and made Charlie think of an alpine lodge, with exposed timber joists and black-framed windows.

Her whole life fitted in three trash sacks, which she unloaded from a cage in the rear of the prison bus, while its driver charged inside to piss. The guy behind reception showed no desire to help as Charlie dragged her stuff through an automatic door and into a double-height lobby area.

A bright yellow dispenser filled with anti-viral gel stood by the reception desk, along with a sign saying all visitors and residents must use it every time they entered. Charlie had a small cut, which stung as she slathered her hands and inhaled a mixture of eucalyptus and chlorine.

'You Croker?' the guy behind the desk asked, his masked face barely moving from the email he was typing. 'Can you read?'

'Yes.'

'This is your envelope. Its contents should answer *all* questions. If you come back here and ask me a question that is answered on a piece of paper inside this envelope I shall not be happy. Is that clear?'

What a dick.

'Clear as new-laid snow,' Charlie said, a set of keys rattling as she grabbed the big envelope.

He searched her face for sarcasm. Then grunted before continuing the spiel.

'Read the rules and regulations. *I didn't know* is never an excuse. Lunch has finished, but there are cookies if you're hungry. Becky will be back from her break shortly. She'll get your school electives sorted, answer any questions and hopefully dig something better than that prison issue out of our spare-clothes closet.'

It was school time, so there was peace in the short hallway leading to room 16a. The room's contents looked newish, with a stack of bedding sealed in polythene and a wardrobe with lockable blue doors. The only sign of the previous resident was remnants of white sticky pads where they'd removed posters.

The bathroom was small, with a powerful UV bulb and a smell of disinfectant. A clear box stood inside the shower tray containing four towels plus a sealed pack of toiletries and a giant yellow bottle of anti-viral gel. The mirror over the sink was half covered with a sticker giving instructions on the proper way to wash your hands after using the toilet.

The disinfectant stuck in Charlie's throat, but she felt good. It was way nicer than her tiny room in the trailer home, or the cell she'd had to share with another inmate at White Boulder. But while the building had a cosy vibe Charlie reckoned some residents in Independent Living would be light fingered, and dashed to grab her stuff from the lobby.

Charlie took the first two bags together, but the third was heavier. As she got out of reception, the bottom tore out of the black sack and books spewed over the hallway. She was on one knee, piling up some of the larger books, when she sensed movement.

'Little help?' a guy asked.

Charlie was startled when she looked behind. She hadn't been around many men in the past two years, and this one was *exceptional*. He looked about eighteen and he'd strode from his room in CK briefs that left little to the imagination. He had a square jaw, black hair still damp from a shower, huge hairless chest and biceps like giant mangos.

'I'm Brad,' he said. 'Need a hand with those?'

'I'll manage,' Charlie said, going red because his bulge was right in her eye line.

But he grabbed a book anyway and read the title aloud. 'Elementary principles of Aeronautical Engineering.' Brad studied more titles before making an observation. 'These are college level, but you don't look much over sixteen.'

'I'm almost sixteen,' Charlie said awkwardly, feeling like her tongue had swollen. 'My teacher at White Boulder got me permission to do some online college-level courses. I'm basically a total science geek.'

Brad shrugged and looked thoughtful. 'Why apologise for being smart?'

Charlie noticed how he got a six pack when he bent over. *I bet he could throw me in the air with one of those big arms. I spend half an hour looking in the mirror worrying that my butt is a weird shape, but this confident ass steps up to a stranger in his CKs.*

Is he hitting on me? I'm nearly sixteen, so I'm not a kid any more. But why would someone this good-looking want me?

Brad carried a dozen textbooks books down the hall to Charlie's room. 'Sixteen A, right? We're neighbours!'

Brad made another trip, before Charlie dumped the last books on the bare mattress.

'I know where to come if I need a math tutor,' Brad said as he waggled a *Get Set For College* math primer.

Charlie smiled. 'I helped a couple of girls at White Boulder.'

'You're sweating,' Brad observed. 'Would you like a cold Coke?'

Charlie nodded. 'Proper Coke? You don't get that inside.'

Brad's room was across the hall from Charlie's. She stood in the doorway nosing as he opened a mini-fridge covered in rock band stickers. It was a typical boy's room, strewn with dirty socks, barbells, a guitar amp and a picture on the wall showing Brad with two younger girls.

'My twin sisters,' Brad explained as he threw the Coke.

Charlie noticed trays of meat crammed in the bottom of Brad's fridge. 'Is that, like, protein for bodybuilding?'

Brad shook his head. 'Comes off my uncle's ranch in California. I work up there sometimes. He raises cattle. All organic. Mostly sells to restaurants in LA, or here on the strip.'

'I *love* steak,' Charlie said. 'But we could never afford it back home, and the only meat you get inside has been through a grinder . . .'

'Tell me 'bout that,' Brad laughed as he opened his cupboard and miraculously retrieved a dented frying pan and a stand-alone induction ring.

'The lady wants steak?' Brad said, grabbing a tray of meat out of the fridge. 'Two minutes per side, medium-rare?'

'No!' Charlie said, covering her face and laughing noisily. 'You don't have to.'

Brad plugged in his cooking ring, shoving coins and a wallet aside to make space on the corner of his desk.

'Sixty-day dry-aged rib eye,' Brad said, glancing around until he found a little bottle of oil on the window ledge. 'Cost you seventy bucks in a restaurant on The Strip.'

After putting some oil in the pan, Brad reached up and stretched a shower cap over his smoke detector.

'Stop lurking in the doorway,' Brad said. 'Have a seat.'

The bed looked grungy, and Charlie flicked grass-stained shorts out of the way before straightening the duvet and perching on the edge.

'So you don't go to school any more?' Charlie asked, but felt dumb because he'd mentioned math tutoring.

'Only work for my uncle weekends and holidays,' Brad said, unwrapping the steak as the pan started to sizzle. 'I landed a three-day suspension from school for fighting. Guy riding my back all day because they don't like OIL kids.'

Charlie looked confused. 'OIL?'

'Obama Independent Living,' Brad explained. 'Not proud I lost my temper, but I couldn't take his shit.'

Charlie nodded sympathetically, though it was the kind of line people always used to justify fighting. She thought no more, because Brad dropped the steak into the pan and started yelling.

'Jesus, holy mother of . . .'

Charlie was baffled as Brad hopped into the bathroom and blasted cold water.

'What happened?' Charlie gasped, standing up.

'Hot fat spattered my chest,' Brad explained, emerging from the bathroom smirking and rubbing beautiful abs with a damp towel. 'Wow, that hurt!'

'You want to put this on?' Charlie asked, laughing as she picked a balled-up Barcelona soccer shirt off his bed.

'That'll do, sure,' Brad said.

Charlie caught a whiff of BO as she threw the shirt. It was a smell that would be gross if it came off some old guy on the bus, but sexy coming from Brad.

'Steak for madame,' he said, presenting the meat one-handed on a cardboard plate, with a knife and fork he'd retrieved from a manky coffee mug and rinsed in the bathroom.

Charlie didn't give a damn about SNor prevention as she balanced the plate on her knees and started to cut. It was bloodier than expected, but she smiled when she tasted it.

'Good?' Brad asked, a touch anxious.

'Best steak ever,' Charlie said.

She wouldn't have been rude if it had tasted rank, but it was genuinely amazing.

'When you hang beef for two or three months, all the proteins start to break down and it gets super tender,' Brad explained.

'Murr eeee yum mar,' Charlie said, then swallowed and tried again. 'Melts in your mouth.'

'Any plans for tonight, Charlie?'

She shook her head. 'My friend Harry is coming tomorrow. I guess I'll sort out my books, read the rules and stuff.'

Brad shook his head. 'On your first night of freedom? No way! There's a group of us here. We head out most Fridays.'

'Where do you go?'

'Weekend curfew is eleven strict and none of us is rich,' Brad said. 'But we usually find a way to have fun. Are you with us?'

'I guess,' Charlie said, nodding as she swallowed another mouthful of steak and gave a thumbs-up. 'Dead cow and Coca Cola. This is what freedom tastes like!'

16 CHEF CHANNING

Kirsten had bought a seven-bed house in Jaguar Heights, one of Vegas's poshest developments. Set on a three-acre hillside lot, there was a four-car garage, basement home cinema and an infinity pool jutting over the hillside, giving clear views towards Charleston Peak.

Harry often felt the contrast with the little three-bed terrace he'd shared with his aunt in London. Especially when he remembered a sleepless night, a couple of weeks after his eleventh birthday.

He'd come downstairs at 3 a.m., trembling from a nightmare where he'd been trampled by a bull. He'd found Kirsten wrestling her accounts at the kitchen table, with tears streaking her face.

Kirsten Channing's restaurant in London's Primrose Hill had won awards and was always busy, but the sums didn't add up after the landlord hiked the rent. Harry overheard talk of Kirsten selling her house to raise money and of having to go live with his grandparents in Devon.

Then Kent Clark stumbled into Kirsten's restaurant on a trip to London. The Vegas-based billionaire liked the food so much he bought a half share in Kirsten's business, on condition that she moved to Vegas and opened a restaurant inside his new casino.

Kirsten's old London restaurant sat twenty-eight guests; Channing's at the Algarve Casino Las Vegas cost $14 million to fit out and could seat four hundred. It won Best New Vegas Restaurant the year it opened and Best Overall the year after that.

While many tourists never left the mega-casinos and tourist traps on the gridlocked four-mile stretch of Las Vegas Boulevard known as The Strip, locals steered clear. But Harry and Matt decided to drive The Strip a couple of days after Harry got his licence and he welled with pride when he saw a glammed-up version of his aunt on the Algarve's two-hundred-foot-tall video billboard, dressed in her chef whites and tossing a pan of fancy seafood.

After three years in Vegas, Kirsten had started building an empire. There was Channing's English Pub, for casino guests with more modest budgets, a copycat Channing's in Kent Clark's Macau casino, while her original London restaurant had reopened inside a five-star Chelsea hotel.

Plans for a fourth Channing's in New York had been put on hold, because fear of catching SNor had dented the restaurant trade, but Kirsten regularly made TV appearances on *Chef Challenge* and *Gourmet Chef Secrets* and had signed a deal for three recipe books.

When Harry came home early Friday evening, he had three bags from the shops at Summerlin. Kirsten was barefoot in the kitchen, wearing a sequinned black dress and a chunky gold neck chain worth a stupid number of dollars.

'I thought you loathed that necklace,' Harry said, striding

across an enormous black quartz floor to raid a $30,000 Sub-Zero refrigerator.

'Kent Clark bought it for me when we won Best Overall,' Kirsten explained. 'It's too bling for my tastes, but it's his seventieth birthday, so I've gotta wear it . . .'

'Have they fixed the pool?' Harry asked, grabbing a dish of shepherd's pie. 'Is this still OK?'

Kirsten nodded. 'It's today's batch from my pub. Pop it in for thirty-five minutes. Please *try* to eat the vegetables with it. And the pool guy says they don't have the parts in stock to fix the filter.'

Harry turned his nose up at a dish of cauliflower and broccoli, then shut the fridge and turned on the oven.

'Is Chopper Bill going with you?' Harry asked, smirking because his aunt's latest boyfriend was a perma-tanned tourist helicopter pilot twenty years her junior.

'You *like* Bill,' Kirsten reminded Harry sharply. 'He'll be here to pick me up in a bit. *Why* have you bought girls' knickers?'

Harry looked round, and saw his aunt nosing inside his shopping bags.

'Charlie messaged me her size,' Harry explained. 'All she's got is manky prison issue.'

Kirsten had a special look of disapproval for when Charlie's name got mentioned.

'Is that a laptop?' she asked, peeking inside a Fry's Electronics bag.

Harry tutted and spoke in a mocking tone. 'Thank you *so* much for asking, Auntie. My friend Charlie got out of prison today. I spoke to her after school and she seems to be doing great.'

'Was that expensive?' Kirsten asked, ignoring the sarcasm.

'Like, three fifty,' Harry said. 'And it's *my* money, from *my* job that paid for it.'

Harry showed his anger by making the shepherd's pie crash on to the oven rack.

'The top won't get crispy if you don't pre-heat,' Kirsten warned.

'Don't care,' Harry sulked.

'So where are you driving off to see her tomorrow?'

'North Vegas,' Harry said. 'When you meet Charlie, you *might* find that you like her.'

Kirsten opened her mouth like she was going to say something, sighed, then said it anyway.

'I know you don't want to hear this, Harry. But I *worry* about you doing so much for Charlie. I mean it's cool that you've taken an interest in this poor girl's life. But, let's face it, you're almost seventeen and you've not had a proper girlfriend. I'm worried that you're heavily invested in a girl with a troubled past, who you barely know.'

'That's the whole problem,' Harry said sourly. 'People like you *never* give people like Charlie a chance.'

Kirsten scoffed. 'People like *what* exactly?'

'Oh, you know,' Harry said, holding his arms out to the designer kitchen and the twinkling infinity pool out through the sliding doors. 'The six-million-dollar house. Your Bentley. Flying to publishers' meetings in New York in Clark Corp's executive jet.'

'Hard work got me where I am,' Kirsten said irritably as she fiddled with an earring. 'I've employed young offenders and drug-rehab kids in my restaurants. Dealing with people like that can be rewarding, but a lot of the time it's bloody hard work and they throw everything back in your face. So I don't think I'm crazy to worry when I see you running her errands and buying expensive gifts.'

'She's a science geek,' Harry explained. 'She'll need a laptop for schoolwork. If people help Charlie, she could get into an Ivy League college.'

'You've got a good heart, Harry,' Kirsten said as she cracked a slight smile. 'And I guess some girl's gonna break it sometime, no matter what I say.'

17 MAD BOMBER

After more than two years inside, everyday details felt like strange adventures. Pulling on a skirt, paying for Snickers ice cream and sunscreen in 7-Eleven, crossing a road, plugging her cell into a charger and seeing long-forgotten apps and games when it fired up.

Obama Independent Living was eighty per cent boys. Some released from lock-up, but mostly sixteen- to eighteen-year-olds who'd been booted by parents, or caused trouble in foster homes.

Charlie was one of the youngest, and felt intimidated when the high-school bus dropped off, filling her eight-room corridor with Friday-happy lads blasting tunes, banging doors and mercilessly tormenting a kid called Jamal who had a club foot and a stutter.

Brad introduced the only other girl on the corridor. Juno was black, with a stocky build and neon nails. She donated Charlie a couple of tops to go with the stuff she'd rummaged from the unit's spare-clothes cupboard, and a pair of cheap beach sandals that still wore shop tags.

Charlie felt a connection when she spotted Juno's shelf of

high-school math and science books. Juno was seventeen and explained that her plan was to join the US Navy scholarship programme to pay for college. She'd already had the interview and passed the academic requirement, but was swimming regularly and dieting to lose fifteen pounds, because she had to retake the physical.

'Just naturally got a big fat ass,' Juno said, laughing noisily as she slapped a thigh.

Charlie decided it was time to share some of her story. 'I was up at White Boulder,' she began.

'Everyone knows who you are,' Juno cut in, smiling. 'The shit you did was on every news back in the day. People said you was probably coming here. I even googled Deion Powell. He's started playing college ball, but his face is *wrecked . . .*'

Charlie twisted uncomfortably. On her first day at White Boulder, an inmate warned her not to go around claiming she was innocent, because the staff will write it on your file and the early release panel might say you're in denial and not truly sorry for what you've done.

It felt like yet another way the system was rigged against the innocent. But, over time, Charlie got used to having friends and cellmates who thought she was guilty and she got bullied less than most, because even the baddest girls feared making the Mad Bomber snap.

But while Charlie could handle nicknames, or friends speculating that Deion must have raped or beaten her to push level-headed Charlie over the edge, she detested people thinking she'd done something so cruel.

Deion had lost over seventy per cent of the skin on his face and torso. The other victim's burns were less serious, but she'd lost sight in one eye and endured painful operations to rebuild a shattered jaw and cheekbone.

'Got no family?' Juno asked.

'Just a twelve-year-old brother,' Charlie said, which wasn't a lie because Fawn was dead to her. 'He had a brain injury in childbirth. He's in an institution.'

'Gonna visit?'

'My friend Harry found where he's at,' Charlie explained. 'I left messages saying I wanted to see him, but nobody called back.'

Brad knocked on Juno's half-open door and poked his head round without waiting for a response.

'Everyone's heading out,' Brad said. 'You sluts ready?'

Juno flipped Brad off and mouthed something foul. It was past seven, but it was December, so it was already dark with a bite in the air. Charlie stared at the full moon in the lot out back, realising it was the first time in two years that she'd been outside after dark.

The ride was a mangled GMC pickup, driven by an older guy. Brad and their driver's younger brother filled the cab, leaving Charlie, Juno and a muscled little black guy nicknamed Dodge to ride on the open rear platform.

'Hang tight back there,' the driver yelled as he set off, then deliberately slammed the brakes.

Charlie's elbow scraped the rusty pick-up bed as Juno pounded on the cab's rear window. 'You do that one more time and I'll cut you!' she yelled, as the guys seat-belted inside the cab laughed hysterically.

Charlie felt cold and none too safe, linking arms with Juno so that they didn't get thrown about. The ride was too scary to be fun, but the dark sky and the blast of cold air was exhilarating.

There was a stop for booze. A hobo-looking guy behind a gas station took sixty-eight bucks. He had his underage drinking system all worked out, with clients calling orders in advance and the goods distributed from numbered Walmart bags in the back of an ancient station wagon.

Standing on a vacant lot with several hundred dollars' worth of booze wasn't without risks, and Charlie spotted the gun under the man's grubby overcoat as two dozen cans of Miller and a giant bottle of no-brand bourbon crashed into the pickup bed in front of her feet.

This is dumb. Two and a half years fighting to get out, and on my first night I'm driving to a place I don't know, with people I don't know . . .

'Nobody touch my bottle of Jack!' the driver ordered as Dodge passed beers into the cab.

'Here,' Juno said, handing Charlie a beer, before sucking the foam bubbling out of her own just-opened can.

Riding in the back of a pickup is probably illegal, drinking beer in a moving vehicle is definitely illegal. Juno isn't on early release. She'll get driven back to OIL by a cop; I'll get bounced back to White Boulder for three months' minimum. But it's dark, and I don't know my way back if I bail . . .

The pickup rattled over a pothole as it turned back on to the highway. Charlie tentatively sucked her first ever mouthful of beer, and while she didn't exactly like it, it was liquid velvet compared to the potato-and-orange-peel hooch she'd brewed with two pals at White Boulder.

Juno twisted the cap on the whisky bottle, sniffed, sipped and screwed up her face in disgust.

'Didn't he say not to drink that?' Charlie asked, starting to like the malty beer taste.

Juno smiled as she offered the bottle. 'He said don't drink my *Jack*,' Juno grinned. 'But this ain't Jack Daniels – it's store brand!'

If you can't turn back, you might as well try having fun . . .

Charlie grabbed the two-litre bottle, tapping a front tooth as she tipped it up and used the technique they used for the hooch at White Boulder: neck it fast, then flush the taste.

'Whoa!' Dodge roared as Charlie downed four big gulps.

'Holy shit!' Juno added while Charlie swished out with beer.

Less than a mile from where they'd picked up booze, the creaky pickup rolled into a parking lot. There were a few dozen cars, mostly old and tatty, and groups of teenagers vanishing into moonlit parkland.

'You gotta see this girl drink,' Dodge whooped. 'My God!'

Charlie felt the heat from the whisky in her throat as she jumped off the truck, still holding the bottle. 'It's not *that* strong,' she said. 'Not compared to prison hooch, anyway.'

Realising she was the centre of attention, Charlie proved her point by taking another slug. There was a roar of approval. Juno and Brad clapped, and a couple of randoms getting out of a car laughed too. The only disapproval came from the driver, who snatched his bottle and checked the level.

'Give you a ride and you drink my liquor,' he moaned.

'I'm sorry – I'll pay,' Charlie said, reaching down her skirt pocket and pulling a crumpled ten-dollar bill.

But Brad knocked her hand down and scowled at the driver. 'Joe's a tight ass. Charlie just got out of juvie, bro. It's her night.'

Charlie felt a glow of approval and wobbly from booze as she followed bodies moving into the desert park. The destination was a large outdoor pool, which had officially closed two hours earlier. Charlie guessed she was committing another crime as she walked over a section of wooden fence that looked as if it had been torn down deliberately.

There were at least sixty kids around, aged thirteen to eighteen. There were skaters doing tricks over the far side, some dripping from tumbles into the water. A few people sat on loungers poolside, while others paddled in shallow water, surrounded by bobbing beer cans and Pringle tubes.

'I haven't been in a pool for years,' Charlie said, abandoning her sandals amidst dozens of others and holding her beer high as she waded out until her skirt almost touched the water.

'It's freezing,' Brad said, splashing out behind, as Dodge gave Juno a massive shove that left her soaked and screaming.

'You're dead,' Juno screamed, trying to push Dodge back, but just bouncing off his muscly little body.

Charlie dumped her can and some random guy waded off to get her another. Someone parked a car with a big sound system outside the fence and started blazing EDM. There was drama as a girl cut her foot on broken glass in the bottom of the pool and Charlie got a damp butt as she sat poolside with her feet dangling. She was properly drunk, giggling helplessly as the skateboarders at the far end gave up on staying dry and started riding boards off the diving platform.

An hour passed. As younger kids drifted home, the crowd got drunker and hornier. None of the attempts to break into locked pool toilets were successful, so Charlie had to squat and pee behind an ice-cream stand. On her way back, two young teens groping passionately made her think about all the stuff she'd missed. She felt like she'd made the leap from ice cream and sleepovers to beer and blow jobs in a single night.

Charlie wobbled drunkenly as a hairy ginger guy told her she had a nice ass and asked if she wanted another beer. She felt nauseous, and worried that she'd lost everyone. It was less than an hour till the eleven o'clock curfew and she didn't know the way home.

Then she spotted Juno necking an Asian guy. The distraction made her trip on the leg of a sun lounger and somehow Brad was in Charlie's face when she straightened up. His shorts were dripping, but he'd ditched his T-shirt and swiped some other dude's plaid shirt. He wore it with the buttons undone, so you could see his perfect chest.

'Fun, fun, fun?' Brad roared, sounding as drunk as Charlie felt.

'Babies making babies back there,' Charlie said, outraged but laughing too. 'Little bare ass, pumping in the moonlight.'

'That's poetic,' Brad said.

'Uh?' Charlie said, vision blurring as she moved her head too fast.

'Moonlight,' Brad slurred. 'Words of poetry . . .'

There was a drunken pause when Charlie and Brad realised they had no clue what the other was saying.

'You're really sexy,' Brad said as he closed in.

Charlie smiled. She knew he was wasted, but nobody had told her she was sexy before and it was good to feel like she was worth something.

'You've got . . .' she began, thinking of complimenting Brad's abs, but unable to hold the thought. 'I want you to . . . I don't know the way home. I don't want to lose you again.'

A sun lounger sploshed into the pool as Brad moved closer. Charlie's eyes were level with his chin and his breath tasted of a joint he'd puffed. Charlie didn't know what she wanted, but Brad's face was right there and it seemed easier to kiss than back away.

But Charlie was off balance and after the barest touch of lips she stumbled. Brad thought he'd scared her off and his wounded look made Charlie smile. She stepped forward, and after a couple of seconds of drunken bafflement they started kissing properly. Or they tried, because Charlie didn't have a clue.

'Relax your mouth,' Brad said softly. 'Let me do the work.'

Charlie had imagined a first kiss to be some Disney thing, but it turned out to be a guy she didn't know very well sticking booze-tongue in her mouth and it just felt weird.

It got sexier when he grabbed her butt and lifted her up slightly. Charlie tipped her head back and shuddered as Brad pushed two fingers between her thighs. With her head back, he could only kiss her neck and she liked it when his nose tickled her ear.

'You're amazing,' Brad purred.

Charlie realised Brad would take this as far as she let him. She groaned with satisfaction – *this amazing-looking guy wants me* – but at the same time she wanted a pause button. Charlie was about to tell Brad to stop when one of the skateboarders over the far side yelled.

'Cop cars!'

'Pigs are coming.'

'They'll send me back,' Charlie gasped as Brad let her go and glanced behind.

Kids were streaming through the torn-out section of fence, but cops with flashlights picked some of them off.

'Try this way,' Brad yelled, bumping panicked kids as he grabbed Charlie's wrist.

Behind the changing rooms, the skateboarders had pushed a stack of loungers up against the fence, making an easy climb.

Brad lifted Charlie on to the stack. The loungers wobbled as she hesitated over the eight-foot jump.

'Jump or get out of the way,' a panicked kid shouted, the pile of loungers shifting precariously as he pushed past.

As Charlie dangled and dropped on the outside, Brad was fearless, placing his foot on the fence and landing with a parachute roll. The cops and their flashlight beams were closing, but as Charlie found her feet the next person to jump caught her ankle and sent her sprawling.

'Look where you're going,' Brad shouted.

'Up your mother,' the skinny kid shouted back.

'What you say?' Brad shouted, grabbing him by his hood.

He was properly weedy and no more than fourteen, but Brad punched him viciously in the face.

'Hey!' Charlie yelled, her ankle in excruciating pain as she tried to walk.

'I'll stomp you into the ground,' Brad shouted, kicking his much smaller opponent, who already had hands cupped over a bloody nose.

Brad's eyes were manic as he turned to Charlie. 'Come on.'

'My ankle's twisted,' Charlie gasped, almost falling as she tried putting weight on it.

The first cop had arrived, but went for the dazed kid Brad had thumped.

'Piggyback,' Brad said, crouching down. 'Put your arms round my neck.'

'I'm gonna puke,' Charlie said, close to tears.

Brad backed off as Charlie lurched forwards and sprayed the dirt. He looked around, clearly thinking about abandoning her.

'I don't know the way,' Charlie said pleadingly, her mouth strung with vomit.

Brad sounded angry. 'Get on my back. Stop dicking around!'

'I can't help feeling ill,' Charlie whined.

'You drank half a pint of whisky before we even arrived,' Brad said, as he lifted Charlie up and started a wobbly run. 'And you'd better not spew on me.'

18 BLOODSHOT

Pungent anti-viral gel evaporated from Harry's hands as he rapped on the door of 16A.

'Charlie, it's me. Are you awake?'

'Door's open,' she groaned.

Harry smiled when he set eyes on Charlie. Her smell, her hair all scruffy. Her big toe slightly shorter than the one before it. But the big blue eyes were framed in red, and the dressy purple top on the floor had an obvious puke stain.

'Have you been ill?' Harry asked anxiously as he put down the gift bags. He caught his reflection in the window as they hugged, hating the zit cluster on his chin and unpleasantly surprised by her booze-infused sweat.

'Got wasted,' Charlie confessed, backing up to the bed. 'There's a family of hippos disco dancing inside my skull.'

Harry felt deflated. He'd spent ages planning their day together and Charlie didn't seem up to it. 'This place looks OK,' he said weakly.

'Grab the seat,' Charlie said, pointing at the chair under a little desk.

'I got the underwear you asked for,' Harry said. 'And

there's a couple of other bits.'

Charlie reached for the bags as Harry settled into the school-style plastic bucket chair.

'Does it smell in here?' Charlie asked, sniffing her wrist.

In prison, she'd always worn a T-shirt, sweat pants and sneakers, so Harry was fascinated by her cleavage as she peered into a bag.

'Can't smell much of anything,' Harry lied. 'Who'd you go out with?'

Charlie didn't answer, because after briefly inspecting two packs of H&M underwear she saw the bag with the Dell laptop inside.

'No way!' Charlie gasped, as she lifted the box out. She looked excited, but then straightened up and pushed a hand through her hair. 'I can't accept that, Harry. It's *way* too much.'

'You need a laptop,' Harry said firmly. 'It's not amazing, but it'll do for internet and typing essays. And the screen flips behind, so you can stand it up to watch movies, or use it as a tablet.'

'But . . .' Charlie said, certain the gift was over-the-top, yet still wanting it badly.

Harry held up both hands. 'I'm doing well out of Vegas Local. Ellie's got local news sites in ten cities now. But he's always half broke, so I bought twenty-five per cent of Vegas Local with some of the money I made from the bombing footage. I also curate the home page and I get one third of the ad revenue. It's six times what Matt earns doing Saturdays at Five Guys.'

'So you write articles and stuff?'

'Sometimes,' Harry said, 'but most of the content is created by local people. Bake sales, school sports, retail coupons, restaurant and show reviews. Anyone can post a notice or an article. I'm more of a curator, making sure there's always something fresh on the home page. I bump the best stories people have submitted.

'Videos are super popular. We had a burst water main washing cars down Koval Lane a few months back that got over two million hits. The construction worker bit my hand off when I offered him three hundred bucks for his video and it's earned twelve times that in ad clicks.'

Charlie did the math in a flash. 'You made twelve hundred bucks from someone else's video?'

'Eleven after paying for the video,' Harry explained. 'It's the biggest site for local information. I get invites to grand openings, shop vouchers and tons of other freebies from people who want me to plug stuff on the home page.'

'Smart,' Charlie said admiringly.

Her favourite thing about Harry was that while most teenagers were all bravado and half-baked ambition, he was an unassuming guy who'd achieved more at sixteen than most thirty-year-olds.

'A laptop is important,' Charlie said thoughtfully. 'The only way I can realistically afford a top college is with a scholarship, which means top marks in *every* subject. Plus a ton of extra-curricular achievements to make me stand out from the herd.'

'Maybe stop erasing that big brain with booze,' Harry teased as Charlie used a thumbnail to pop the seal on the laptop box. Then he turned serious. 'I've also been keeping my ear to the ground on the Janssens. They're running dive casinos and half-empty strip malls, but their business finance records show profits of fifteen to twenty million a year. They're laundering drug money or something, but the cops don't seem to care.'

'They've certainly got powerful friends,' Charlie said, more interested in her new laptop.

'Did you hear that Fawn and JJ got married?' Harry asked.

Charlie reared up on the bed. 'I don't give a shit about Fawn,' she snapped. 'And you need to steer clear of the Janssens.'

'They destroyed your life,' Harry said furiously.

'I've had a lot of time to fantasise about revenge,' Charlie said, narrowing her bloodshot eyes. 'But they're powerful, Harry. You'll get steamrollered.'

'The only thing necessary for the triumph of evil is for good men to do nothing,' Harry said grandly.

'Who said that?' Charlie asked.

'Edmund Burke.'

'Who was he?'

'I have no clue,' Harry admitted.

But Charlie looked worried. 'Fancy quotes are great, but I want to forget my old life and start from scratch.'

'I get it,' Harry said. 'You've been through hell.'

Then he changed the subject. 'You know what you were saying about extra-curriculars? I knew you didn't have regular internet access at White Boulder, so I asked on the Vegas Local forum about charity work and stuff that might interest you in North Vegas. There's a maker space fifteen minutes' drive from here.'

'A what?' Charlie asked.

'A maker space is like a big workshop that's open to anyone. This one is called Maker's Yard. They have tools and workbenches. Everything from hammers and chisels, to fancy stuff like laser cutters, oscilloscopes and 3D printers. Some people rock up and work on their own projects, like making robots, automatic garden sprinklers, or whatever. They also have classes. There's an eco-thing, where a guy teaches people how to fix broken electrical goods rather than tossing everything in landfill.

'There are also more advanced classes. A practical robotics class taught by some retired UNLV professor, and this woman who teaches coding to seniors. If you got involved in something like that, it could be the difference between being a regular underprivileged brat going for a college scholarship and someone who stands out for doing some interesting projects.'

Charlie smiled. 'Besides making explosives . . .'

Harry laughed. 'If your hangover isn't too terrible, I thought we could drive up there.'

'I'll live,' Charlie said, her face brightening. 'Do you have to pay to join?'

'Only twenty bucks if you're in full time education. The classes are free, but you must provide materials, like computer boards, or whatever.'

Charlie nodded. 'It's cool knowing I've got you looking out for me.'

'It's in this ritzy gated community called Swallow Park. It's also got a café-restaurant type place, run by a chef who used to work with my mum. I had an email when they first opened, offering me a free lunch.'

Charlie laughed, leaning across her bed to plug the laptop charger. 'Look at Mr Vegas with all his connections.'

As the laptop booted, she hopped up and gave Harry a peck on the cheek. 'I can't believe we're hanging out, like two normal humans . . .'

She laid chest down on the bed as the laptop booted for the first time, flicking black-soled feet in the air and giving him a smile that made Harry feel like he was floating.

19 MANSPLAINING

Life had been slow at White Boulder. Lessons, free association, meals. Locked up with your cellmate by seven thirty and the electronic bolt releasing eleven hours later. Outside news and minor rebellions were the only thing to crack monotony.

Now Charlie's life was gaining speed. Hanging with Harry. New laptop, new clothes, new friends, new place to live. *Last night I had my first kiss and let a guy feel me up. Drank too much, took idiotic risks. Never again. And on Monday a new school. And this damned menu. I don't know what half of this stuff is . . .*

The restaurant's setting was beautiful. A table with a view over reed beds, swans gliding on a lake and rich folks' houses beyond.

'Walnut and olive bread,' the waitress said, her voice muffled by an anti-viral mask.

Vinyl-gloved hands set down the bread bowl and a compartmented dish, filled with vinegar, olive oil and pâté.

Charlie felt out of place as Harry casually dipped bread in the treacly balsamic.

'I've never been anywhere this fancy,' she whispered, not wanting the saggy-necked ladies at the next table to overhear.

'This menu's full of weird words. What is a tapenade?'

'Stewed cow's eyeballs,' Harry said.

'Eww . . . Wait. You're messing, aren't you?'

Harry laughed. 'It's a pesto. Mashed olives, anchovies, herbs and stuff. Do you like olives?'

Charlie shrugged. 'Never tried them.'

'Never?' Harry gawped.

Charlie looked a touch wounded. 'My mom had this truck-driver boyfriend for a while. He'd take us to IHOP for pancakes and I'd get *stupidly* excited. After Ma topped herself, I mostly ate with Ed, who only liked five things. And there wasn't much *baked red mullet with citrus jus* at White Boulder.'

One of the old birds at the next table glanced over at the mention of White Boulder. Harry glowered back until she started pretending she'd been looking for her napkin.

'So you ain't spawned from fancy-eating folk, then?' Harry smiled, accidentally touching Charlie's hand as he reached across and tapped her menu. 'This lamb burger is supposed to be really good.'

Charlie looked wary. 'It's twenty-six dollars and I'm not that hungry.'

'The man from Vegas Local doesn't pay,' Harry reminded her. 'And greasy food lines your stomach after a hangover.'

Charlie laughed. 'Is that official surgeon general's guidance?'

But she felt better once she'd scraped most of the mint foam off her burger and tucked in. After the main, the chef came out of the kitchen with some banana-and-honey crêpes. He asked Harry how Kirsten was doing, told him what a great website Vegas Local was. Then he went on about how his eighty-year-old grandma was on Vegas Local every day, reading gossip and printing off grocery coupons.

'That's Ellie's goal,' Harry told the chef, as he realised his crêpes were microwaved and rubbery. 'We do what local newspapers did before they all went broke. Vegas Local gets over a quarter million unique visitors per day, a lot of them tourists looking for insider tips.'

'This has been a tough year,' the chef said. 'People are getting out more now, but SNor cut our takings by half.'

'Brutal,' Harry said, 'but our lamb burgers were great and I'll make sure you get a feature review in the next few days. I'll get Sue-Ann to call. Maybe we can fix a deal for a coupon.'

'Anything that gets bodies through the door,' the chef said eagerly.

'You ain't got a bad life,' Charlie told Harry as they headed outside into a breeze coming off the lake. 'Cruising around picking up free food in restaurants.'

Harry admired Charlie as she walked ahead. Little ears, nice butt and legs that had been starved of sunlight.

'Not forgetting your wheels,' Charlie said, twirling as she got near his British racing-green Mini, with a Union Jack flag across the roof.

'I do OK,' Harry said humbly, unplugging the Mini. 'And grub like this is a treat. I burn heaps of calories running, but rich food is terrible for my skin.'

Maker's Yard was a two-minute drive on a road with speed humps that ran round Swallow Park's manmade lakes. Charlie wowed as they passed an ultra-modern house with a white Ferrari on the driveway.

'You're good at making money,' Charlie observed. 'This is where you'll end up.'

'You'll do OK with that big brain,' Harry told her.

Maker's Yard was an aluminium-sided building at the edge

of Swallow Park. It was screened behind a fifteen-foot hedge, next to recycling bins and a garage that housed the little carts used by security patrols.

It took a while to find the unassuming entrance. The yard was the size of a basketball court. There was a whiff of burnt wood and motor oil. The décor was trendy industrial, with a bare concrete floor, stripped walls, particle-board benches and some pricey-looking machinery along the edge.

An elderly woman was gluing a vintage record player in one corner, but the main action centred on a pre-teen gang building little carts, covered with stick-on solar panels and powered by repurposed washing-machine motors.

'Can I help you?' their pink-haired, heavily pregnant teacher asked.

'I messaged Steve,' Harry told her. 'We came to check this place out, and maybe for my friend here to join up.'

The punkish teacher explained that Steve had gone out to buy materials for another class later that afternoon. They waited on ancient comfy sofas in a lounge area. Besides the sofas, there were shelves of old technical manuals, a bright green coffee machine that hailed from the 1970s and some homemade cakes next to a donation jar.

Charlie laughed when she saw a motion-sensing camera rigged up to an old-fashioned police siren. She couldn't figure out how it worked, but the flashing blue light was clearly designed to shame anyone who didn't pay for their cake.

Moms of the kids doing the go-kart building sat on the sofas. There was also a beard-and-beer-gut in paint-spattered dungarees. He leaned on the back of a sofa, addressing the women like he was the world authority on everything.

'All this talk about mutated virus, designer babies and this whole gene-editing show like it'll be the end of days,' he said in a booming Texas drawl. 'But there's always been scaremongering. It's like this global warming. Been talking 'bout it for years, but I still ain't seen Manhattan under twelve feet a water.'

Three moms nodded, while the fourth built blocks with a toddler sat on a sterile play mat.

'Sure hope you're right,' one of them said.

'I worry about school bathrooms,' another commented. 'That's how those poor second-graders died in Miami. Thirteen in one year group.'

The drawler resumed his lecture. 'We heard it all before with nuclear proliferation,' he said, shaking his head slowly. 'Everyone saying the terrorists would get a nuke. But detection systems were in place. SNor caught us with our pants around our ankles, but governments are on red alert now . . .'

Charlie had always seemed shy, so Harry was surprised to hear her butt in.

'But the proliferation of nuclear weapons is difficult, because you need to enrich uranium ore into weapons-grade uranium,' Charlie said. 'Uranium enrichment requires a factory the size of three football fields, filled with thousands of gas centrifuges, each one more complex than a jet engine.

'But I could go online and buy all the equipment I need to do gene editing for the price of a second-hand car, and the equipment would fit in a regular garage. So, you're comparing two *very* different technologies.'

'They're clamping down on the sale of chemicals and equipment,' the Texan said.

'But tens of thousands of sequencing and editing machines have already been produced,' Charlie pointed out. 'And when all the rich countries ban the sale of gene-editing machinery, there will be dozens of poor ones, who either don't legislate or don't have the money to police it.'

One of the moms nodded. 'It's terrifying. I think about my three boys, and when I see it on the news . . . I know it sounds weak, but I turn it off because it's so horrible.'

The Texan hated Charlie undermining his authority. 'I'm sixty and I spent my whole life listening to people talking about threats. The communists were gonna wipe us out, then it was the AIDS, global warming, terrorists with nukes, terrorists with chemical weapons. All I know is I ain't dead yet.'

'SNor killed more people in six months than have ever been killed by terrorists and nuclear weapons,' Charlie said. 'I just researched it for my end-of-term paper.'

Now the guy roared with laughter, clutching his big gut. 'Well, I gotta change my mind if you wrote it in your school pro-ject, sweetheart . . .'

A couple of the moms smirked too, and Charlie turned and scowled at Harry. 'Screw this place. I'm outta here.'

'He's a pig,' Harry whispered, grabbing her arm anxiously as she stormed away. 'It's nothing.'

But Charlie didn't think so and headed for the exit. Luckily, a slim guy with a bouncy walk and a pocket full of pens blocked her path.

'Welcome to Maker's Yard. I'm Steve,' he said, offering a hand to shake. 'You must be Harry and Charlie. I'm sorry I had to pop out, but you didn't say exactly what time you'd be dropping by.'

'No probs,' Harry said.

Charlie shook hands, but kept sulking.

'Join me at my bench,' Steve said, then waved at the moms and told them. 'Your kids are doing so great over there,' which made the quartet crack proud smiles.

Steve's bench was back by reception and he looked across at Charlie as he led the way. 'I agree with what you said about the virus situation. The problem with setting up any open maker community is you can't tell big mouths like Jerry McLeod to go eff themselves.

'And mommies would rather have a good-ol'-boy telling them *I'm still standing*, than deal with the reality that the children they adore might soon die from a synthetic virus made in a suburban garage by couple of college dropouts.'

Charlie enjoyed Steve's bossy-but-cynical vibe and reluctantly cracked a smile. His desk was a particle-board workbench, covered in circuit boards, chocolate-bar wrappers, half-drunk Starbuckses and a soldering station.

'A lot of eggheads come here and sneer at my Wednesday-night appliance-repair workshop,' Steve told Charlie. 'They'd rather build killer robots than fix a suction chamber on a ten-year-old Dyson.

'But the wannabe robot builders get frustrated when they realise how complex it is, while my appliance fixers build up a skill set – learning how everyday things work and what tools you need to repair them. It makes a starting point for more ambitious maker projects. There's also satisfaction, when a struggling family gets their air-conditioner fixed, or we fit new batteries inside old iPads, load them up with educational apps and send them off to a school in Mozambique.'

'Sounds amazing,' Harry said, giving Charlie a nudge for encouragement.

'And before you ask in a sly and embarrassed fashion, yes Steve will write a reference for your college application stating that you're a wonderful young human, who repaired lots of computers for poor kiddies.'

Charlie seemed to have forgotten her humiliation a few moments earlier and looked hopefully at Harry. 'You could join too.'

'I do running club with Matt on Tuesdays,' Harry said, shaking his head. 'Plus it's dark way before nine, so I'd never be able to drive home.'

'Aww,' Charlie said, then smiled at Steve. 'You've sold me. How do I sign up?'

20 NAPALM DROPS

After leaving Maker's Yard, Harry and Charlie strolled around Swallow Park's lakes, talking about London, pets, White Boulder, bad music, apps they played when they were kids and funny shit that had happened at school.

They watched cute toddlers in masks feeding the water birds, got honked by an old coot in a golf buggy and watched a girl get screamed at by a spectacularly pompous dad, after she'd piloted his model boat into a tangle of reeds.

'I can't make it up here on school nights,' Harry said, 'but maybe you can come to my place next weekend? Matt will tell you all kinds of embarrassing stories about me, and you can meet Kirsten if she's not at work.'

It was just before five and the Mini was parked on the brick driveway in front of OIL.

'Sounds great,' Charlie said. 'I'll let you know how school goes, and if I hear anything about Ed.'

'You know what Vegas traffic is like on a Saturday evening,' Harry said. 'I'll pop in and take a leak before I head home.'

As Harry peed in Charlie's bathroom, a guy said something from out in the hallway. Harry aimed his stream down the side of the pan, so he could overhear.

'It was insanity last night!' Brad told Charlie, grabbing the top of the door frame with his big hands and smiling. 'Where you been hiding all day?

Charlie felt wary. Was Brad the sweet guy who'd cooked steak and told her she was sexy? Or the snarling drunk who'd smashed some kid's nose and accused her of drinking too much?

'Swallow Park, with my friend, Harry.'

'Schmaltzy,' Brad sneered. 'Bunch of us are seeing a movie tonight if you're up for it?'

Harry awaited her answer before flushing.

'I'm hungover,' Charlie said, shaking her head. 'I'd like to settle in. Sort my room out, watch some bad TV.'

'On Saturday night!' Brad said, outraged. 'C'mon! I'll let you share my popcorn.'

'Some other time,' Charlie said, a touch firmer.

Harry came out of the bathroom and hated Brad instantly. Handsome, hunky, confident. Harry would have given anything to be like him.

Charlie introduced the boys to each other.

'Hey,' Brad said grudgingly, narrowing his eyes like Harry was gum stuck on his shoe.

'Guess I'd better shift if I'm gonna get home before sunset,' Harry said. Then awkwardly added, 'Good to meet you, Brad.'

Brad snorted, but Charlie cracked a smile and put her arms out for Harry to hug.

'It's been such an awesome day,' Charlie said as she squeezed. 'Thanks for everything.'

Harry couldn't enjoy the hug with Brad staring.

'I'll be in touch,' he said, then checked the time on his phone.

He needed to leave, but Brad kept holding the door frame and only backed up six inches, making Harry duck slightly and almost have to stick his face in Brad's armpit.

That meathead lives right across the hall, Harry thought jealously as he walked towards his car. *He'll see Charlie six times a day. He's got moves; I've got acne. Why didn't I put my arm round Charlie at the lake when she was laughing at everything I said? Such a great day, but now this Brad prick is all I'm gonna think about . . .*

• • •

'Do you have earplugs?' Charlie asked, standing at the counter in 7-Eleven next morning.

When Charlie was ten, she'd stolen foam earplugs from CVS and dissolved them in gasoline to make her first tiny batch of napalm. The YouTube clip of her using the sticky explosive to melt a Barbie had resurfaced in the days after she'd confessed to the locker bombing, and she worried that an onlooker would make that connection as the store clerk shook his head.

'You'll get them at Walgreens, six blocks up.'

Charlie walked the six blocks to clear her head. She'd hardly slept. The guys in her corridor had yelled through the night, banged doors and lobbed a firecracker into Jamal's room at 2 a.m. At four, a pair of cop cars rolled up the driveway, their lights flashing up the walls of Charlie's room.

They had an arrest warrant for some kid from a room upstairs, and he wound up climbing OIL's steeply sloped roof and screaming that he *hadn't done nothing*. The guy on the roof's girlfriend came from somewhere and persuaded him to come down. By the time the sun came up, Charlie felt like she'd slept about fifteen minutes.

Charlie had just walked out of Walgreens' automatic doors when her phone buzzed. She didn't recognise the number, or the woman on the other end.

'My name is Dr Raphael,' she began. 'I received the message you sent regarding visitation for your brother, Edward.'

'Oh,' Charlie said, as she eyed a bench then sat down.

'Is now a good time to talk?'

'For sure,' Charlie said. 'Have you been working with Ed? How is he doing?'

'I'm an administrative director,' the woman said curtly. 'I have encountered your brother on several occasions, and taken part in clinical meetings where his case is discussed, but I'm not involved in his day-to-day care.'

'Right,' Charlie said.

'I received your request to visit Edward. It was discussed with the nursing staff, and I've spoken to your sister, Fawn, and your brother's independent trustee at the law firm Troughton and Oliver.'

Charlie shook her head. 'Troughton and *what*? Ed's trust money is administered by Care Nevada.'

'It was until the beginning of this year,' Dr Raphael corrected. 'I believe there was a legal dispute between your sister and Care Nevada. Your sister won the legal right to control Edward's settlement money, shortly before Edward was resettled here at Care4Kids.'

Charlie couldn't believe it. 'My sister has control of Ed's money?' she blurted.

'I believe that is the effective result of the legal dispute.'

'But it's Ed's,' Charlie said anxiously. 'It's his legal settlement from the hospital. He's got to survive on that money for the rest of his life.'

Dr Raphael sounded weary. 'A Nevada State court has deemed your sister fit to manage Ed's affairs.'

The hell she is . . . Charlie thought. *Probably cooked some scheme up with the Janssens' smartass lawyers . . .*

'If you wish to discuss your brother's financial arrangements, you'll have to contact your sister or Desiree Troughton at Troughton and Oliver. I called exclusively to discuss your visitation issue.'

'Yes,' Charlie said. 'Care4Kids doesn't have a website. I couldn't find any information with your visiting hours, or anything, but I'm eager to see my little brother.'

The doctor cleared her throat. 'Unfortunately things aren't that simple.'

'What do you mean?'

'Edward is a demanding resident, with strict routines. Your sister, and the nursing staff, have told me that Ed was attached to you. When you were first imprisoned, he was extremely distressed. Crying night after night. Asking where you were.

'But he's adjusted to your absence now. Your sister feels strongly that your reintroduction into Edward's life could cause a major setback. Someone with your volatile history is unlikely to be able to provide the emotional stability that a vulnerable young man like Edward needs.'

Charlie felt like she'd been punched in the head. 'He's my brother. Surely I have a *right* to see him?'

'You absolutely do not,' Dr Raphael said firmly.

'I looked after Ed,' Charlie protested. 'Washed his clothes, hugged him to sleep, made his food . . .'

'I suggest you speak to your sister. Perhaps Fawn will reconsider when you've demonstrated that your anger issues are behind you and your lifestyle has stabilised.'

Charlie didn't know how to reply. Saturday had felt like a fresh start, but now she'd barely slept and Fawn was messing with her again.

'Your sister's attorney will be sending a letter to you at Obama Independent Living. It will explain that there could be serious legal repercussions – including the possibility of arrest – if you make *any* attempt to contact your brother.'

Charlie's brain turned somersaults. She rested the phone against her thigh and stared at the sky with a huge lump in her throat.

Why does Fawn hate me so much? What did I ever do to her?

Living the high life at the Janssen house and dipping into Ed's money every chance she gets.

That girl's evil. That's all there is to it . . .

• • •

'How'd everything go yesterday?' Kirsten asked.

She'd been reading a book on the balcony and stepped inside as Harry spooned foamed milk on to two mugs of coffee.

'Good,' Harry said, shrugging.

'You seem grumpy.'

'We had a good day,' Harry said, resenting his aunt's intrusion.

'You can talk to me,' Kirsten said. 'I was a teenage girl once. I know how their brains work.'

'Matt's waiting upstairs,' Harry said dismissively as he picked up the coffees.

'Use a tray or you'll spill.'

Harry grabbed a tray and tried not to see Brad's smug face as he walked upstairs.

Why would Charlie want my skinny legs and spotty face when a guy like that is sniffing around?

'Just like Starbucks!' Matt said brightly as Harry stepped into his bedroom.

Harry's room was at the back of the hillside house, huge windows facing a rocky slope planted with cacti. Matt wore black, as always, and sprawled over Harry's leather couch, with his laptop resting on his belly so that it wobbled with each breath.

'Have you seen this insane dog video?' Matt asked.

Harry pointed at his own laptop on his desk. 'I don't mind you hanging out, but I seriously have to crack on with this history assignment.'

'Your fancy school gives way too much homework,' Matt said as Harry gave him his coffee. Matt turned his laptop towards Harry and tapped play. 'It's eighty seconds – you *have* to watch this.'

Harry tutted, but was immediately drawn into the CCTV footage. It was an alleyway. Two cops in full protective gear used a door-breacher to smash open a fire exit. Two more cops rushed inside, but within seconds they burst back out, chased by huge brown animals.

'Are those dogs?' Harry gasped, watching a second animal bound out. It was three feet high, almost as wide, and it hit the cop so hard he flipped like a bowling pin. 'Jesus, how strong is that thing!'

Two animals pounced on a female cop and started biting. There was a gunshot as another animal dragged a cop, leaving a streak of blood. The chaos lasted another fifty seconds, ending in a bloodbath, with more officers moving in and shooting the animals.

'They're calling them Nightmare Dogs,' Matt explained. 'The cops thought they were raiding a lab doing human gene editing. But the owner had a sideline producing nutty dogs for drug dealers. They're saying these beasts have got traces of DNA from tigers and bulls and all sorts. Twice the weight and four times stronger than an unmodified Dobermann.'

Harry gawped. 'I wish that had happened in Vegas. I could make a mint out of a video like that.'

'Dude,' Matt said, bursting out laughing. 'One cop is dead, the woman is critical. And you're worried about Vegas Local!'

'Just saying . . .' Harry said, shrugging defensively. 'A video like that will get a hundred million hits.'

'World's starting to scare me,' Matt said, shaking his head, then getting a milk moustache from his first mouthful of coffee. 'Why am I working my guts out at school and spending evenings flipping burgers if we're all gonna get wiped by mutant viruses or eaten alive by nightmare dogs?'

Harry saw Matt's point. 'History sucks,' he said, snapping the lid of his laptop shut. 'I'm sick of homework and I already make more money than most of my teachers. Do you wanna go downstairs to the cinema and play a video game or something?'

'I'm up for that,' Matt agreed. 'Just let me send this video to some of the guys first.'

21 BETSY & MEL

'Betsy is my one true love,' Brad told Charlie as he fondly slapped the roof of a petrol-powered Subaru. 'She's eighteen, same age as me, and almost as beautiful.'

'Obviously,' Charlie said, managing a smirk, but churning thoughts of her first day at school in over two years.

Betsy was born red, but the old Subaru now had a green door, a dented blue hood and several patches of dark grey Rust-Oleum. The passenger mirror was cracked, and the rear fender held in place with a web of plumber's tape.

'There's a knack,' Brad said when Charlie tried opening the front passenger door.

Brad hopped round from the driver's side. He pushed his knee against the door and strained until the latch popped.

'Voilà!'

The inside smelled of mould and beer. As Brad settled into a preposterous orange-and-black racing seat, Charlie lobbed a girl's leather jacket and a half-drunk bottle of vodka into the back, before bedding down on sticky green velour. She almost wished she'd taken the school bus, though Juno said they were the first stop on the route and it took half an hour longer than a car.

'Be nice to me, Betsy,' Brad pleaded, turning the ignition and bouncing like he was geeing a horse. He gave a whoop, followed by, 'Good girl,' as the engine clattered to life.

Charlie had warmed to Betsy's charm as they rolled out of the OIL parking lot, with dark grey smoke billowing behind.

'I think Betsy might struggle to pass her next emissions test,' Charlie noted.

'It's just oil,' Brad said. 'Once she warms up, she's golden . . .'

Every warning light on the dash lit up and the speedometer needle didn't move as Brad hurtled past another car.

'First day of high school,' Brad said dramatically. 'Nervous?'

'I guess,' Charlie said, staring at the near-empty backpack between her legs and realising that it still had the $7.99 tag from when she'd bought it at the mall the day before.

As Charlie ripped the tag, Betsy rolled into a side street and straight on to the driveway of a small-but-neat house. Brad blasted the horn, though his passenger was already halfway out the house. She was a Filipino-American, dressed in gold Adidas sneakers, rainbow-striped leggings and an oversized US Army jacket.'

'This is my girl, Mel,' Brad introduced.

Mel crouched by the passenger door, scowling at Charlie as she spoke with a thick New York accent. 'Who's this bitch?'

Charlie felt uncomfortable as Brad pushed the button to drop Charlie's window.

'Charlie, Mel. Mel, meet Charlie,' Brad said warmly. 'It's her first day of high school, so be nice.'

But Mel kept scowling. 'She's in my seat.'

'Seriously?' Brad said, shaking his head. 'It's a five-minute ride.'

'I get carsick in the back,' Mel said, but in such a way that it was obviously a lie.

'I don't care if I ride in the back,' Charlie said, popping the door open.

As Charlie settled into the back, pushing beer cans, a deflated football and greasy KFC packaging out of the way, Mel leaned across the front passenger seat and gave Brad a short, noisy kiss, followed by a hands-off-he's-mine glance at Charlie.

Charlie felt a touch of jealousy, but also relief. She had a whole new life to sort and *Brad the friend* was a simpler proposition than *Brad the potential boyfriend*.

'So who you fighting today, Tiger?' Mel asked as they set off. And now she'd marked her territory, she looked back at Charlie and smiled. 'This goof has been in so many fights they're sending him to anger management.'

'They made me do that at White Boulder,' Charlie said.

'Did it help?' Brad asked, sounding like he wanted it to.

'I guess,' Charlie said. 'They give you techniques to put the current situation in perspective. So, if you're about to kick off, they tell you to stop for three seconds and imagine yourself in the future. Then ask yourself if the consequences of what you're about to do are worth it.'

'Hope the other dude doesn't knock your ass out while you stand there gawping,' Mel said sourly. 'When I lose my shit, ain't nothing gonna stop me.'

'I don't like backing down,' Brad admitted. 'But at least I don't blow my enemies up.'

Charlie knew she was being teased, but Mel and Brad were facing the wrong way to catch her wounded expression. When Mel did look round, she'd cracked a big smile.

'You're *that* girl?' Mel asked admiringly. 'Bombed the

quarterback, over at Rock Spring. That was some dark behaviour! How'd they let you out so fast?'

'She's a white girl with sweet blue eyes who blew up a big ugly black dude,' Brad said. 'Now, if that was the other way round . . .'

Charlie resented the implication that she'd got off light, when all she'd actually done wrong was not disposing of explosives she'd made when she was eleven. But that was a big can of worms to open, so she stared out of the window until Betsy came to a smoky halt in the parking lot of Clayton Street High.

They were parked between a Mercedes and a Lexus convertible, and Charlie noted plenty more expensive metal and kids dressed in designer everything, as Mel made another big show, hugging Brad.

'I guess I'll go find the office,' Charlie said, backing away. 'I have to register.'

'I'll roll with you,' Brad said. 'Gotta do my post-suspension interview with the vice principal. The office you need is right next door.'

As they entered the school, three bulky hoods came over to Brad. A fat one in a Yankees baseball shirt bumped fists.

'Welcome back, bitch.'

'You hear about Mayhew?' another added. 'Wrecked his car Saturday night.'

Charlie stood by awkwardly as Brad smiled and said, 'Mayhew can't drive when he's sober.'

'His grandma cracked him up the side of the head. His eye is puffed up out to here, bro!'

The four boys erupted in laughter.

'So, who's this blue-eyed honey?' the Yankees-shirt guy said as he gave Charlie a creepy grin. 'Bit young, even for you, Brad.'

Charlie felt her face turn red. She wanted to storm off, but the hallway was packed with bodies and she hadn't read any signs because she'd been relying on Brad.

'Charlie's my neighbour at OIL,' Brad said strongly. 'And acting like dicks isn't compulsory, you know?'

Brad turned to Charlie, but kept his voice low, as if he didn't want the guys to hear. 'Gotta catch up with my boys, OK? Main office is straight down, third on the right.'

Charlie rolled her eyes to show she wasn't impressed, but cheered up as she made her own way, surrounded by school life. Stoners, losers. Musical instruments in big black cases. Backpacks and ring binders, locker doors slamming. False laughs and tangled voices.

For the first time in two and a half years, Charlie wasn't inmate B3790, or the mad bomber, or the suspect in handcuffs. She was a nobody in a school hallway, and that made her feel truly free.

22 TERRIBLE TRIO

Harry called after school on Monday and Charlie told him her first day had been fine. The locker they gave her was busted and they'd started her in a low-ability science set. But she'd spoken to her teacher about the college-level courses she'd done at White Boulder and he said he'd try to get her moved up.

The afternoon was theatre arts. Charlie was embarrassed when they split into pairs and she wound up standing alone, but the teacher pushed her into another group to make a trio, and had a laugh with two loud Latina girls, who messed around so much they had nothing to show at the end.

'Glad you survived,' Harry said cheerfully, though he hadn't liked hearing that Brad had picked her up and dropped her home.

Tuesday ticked by, but Wednesday turned out to be cursed. Betsy had a leaky fuel line and the school bus had already left by the time Brad found out. Charlie wound up taking a city bus and arriving twenty minutes late. She sat through three classes where nobody spoke a word to her. At lunch she found a table on her own and picked at her pizza slice and baked potato, until three ninth-grade girls came over.

Clayton Street had a broad mix of kids, from OIL dropouts and offspring whose parents came to North Vegas for the cheap housing, to rich brats who lived behind the security-patrolled walls of Swallow Park.

These three had the designer labels and fussy hairdos that come to girls with moneyed parents, but there was also an awkwardness about them. One was a giant with a huge onion-shaped ass, there was a ghostly redhead with beaky nose and a birthmark stretching from cheek to neck. The third wore an Armani tracksuit over a boyish frame and had one eye that never quite opened.

'Charlie Croker, isn't it?' the giant asked.

'Sure,' Charlie said, set on edge by an exchange of knowing glances.

'Blown anything good up lately?' the beaky one asked, earning noisy laughs from her two friends.

Charlie didn't rise.

'So, what's it like in White Boulder?' the girl in the tracksuit asked, sounding friendlier.

'Fine,' Charlie said, resenting the question as she unconsciously hid her face behind her pizza slice.

'Did you turn lesbian living with all those girls?' Tracksuit asked. 'Or do you still crush on big black quarterbacks?'

Beaky made a honking laugh, like she had a peg on her nose. Charlie decided to stay quiet, hoping they'd get bored if she offered nothing to feed on.

'It's nasty what you did,' the giant said. 'All the pictures with the skin burnt off that poor girl's face.'

'Sixteen skin-graft operations,' Beaky added.

So much for blissful anonymity, Charlie thought, standing up and grabbing her tray.

'Aww, that's so rude!' Tracksuit said, smirking. 'Walking off when we came here for a chat.'

'I didn't say you could leave,' the giant hissed, grabbing Charlie's wrist.

Charlie broke free and backed away, tipping her leftovers in a bin and slotting her tray into a metal rack. But as she headed for the closest door, the terrible trio were a few steps behind.

'Did you have sex with Deion Powell?' Tracksuit asked as Charlie started a brisk walk. 'You were only thirteen, you dirty girl!'

If Charlie had known the school better, she'd have walked towards the library, or a place where there was likely to be staff. But she'd never been through this door before and found herself walking down a long, deserted hallway. As she neared the end, the air thickened with humidity and body spray.

The male locker room was on the left, transgender right and female straight ahead. Charlie hoped to find plenty of bodies in the girls' room, or better still a member of staff to scare the terrible trio off. But this wasn't her day.

'A nice place for a pow-wow,' the giant carped, pounding locker doors as Charlie passed benches and lockers. She hoped the double doors leading to the gym would come open. But they rattled in their frame, locked.

When Charlie turned back, the three girls blocked her in. Although they were in the year below Charlie, the giant was taller, and the one in the tracksuit twice as wide.

'Our gardener's son was at the White Boulder Boys' Camp,' the beaky one said. 'He got in a fight and they sent him back for the rest of his sentence.'

'Is that right, Charlie?' Tracksuit asked, bunching a fist. 'We'll all say you started on us. Get you sent back to White

Boulder where your trashy ass belongs.'

'Don't you speak, Charlie Croker?' Beaky asked.

You've got the thing with the fire extinguisher, the locker bomb and three fights at White Boulder on your record. If you get caught fighting, you're screwed. Stay passive. Hopefully they won't get too far. You faced down worse at White Boulder . . .

Tracksuit threw a punch, but pulled it a half-inch from Charlie's face.

'Flincher,' she teased, then she fired a big glob of spit into her eye.

'Hey,' Charlie said, rearing up.

'Don't you like that?' Tracksuit mocked, spitting again. 'Why don't you do something?'

Charlie turned, so the next spit hit her earlobe. The giant had been gathering saliva in her mouth and shot a torrent into Charlie's face. Beaky pulled her phone to take a picture as foamy spit rolled into Charlie's eyes.

'Why don't you swing at me, Croker?' the giant teased. 'I can see you want to.'

Charlie tried pushing between Tracksuit and the giant as Beaky snapped with an iPhone.

'Make her kneel and kiss your Nikes,' Beaky suggested. 'That'll be a good Instagram!'

Charlie finally broke silence as she wiped her eye. 'You three had better watch your backs after this,' she snarled. 'Maybe I'll mix a nice batch of acid to throw in your ugly faces.'

At White Boulder, Charlie learned that a reputation for being vengeful made even the baddest girls think twice. She'd also picked up a couple of self-defence moves from an older cellmate, which had come in handy when fear wasn't enough.

As the terrible trio wondered if picking on a girl who'd done prison time for almost killing Deion Powell was a great idea, Charlie rammed Tracksuit in the solar plexus. As Tracksuit stumbled back in a choking fit, the giant tried to put Charlie in a headlock. But Charlie had momentum and charged into a gap.

Beaky was on the skinny side. Charlie caught her in the face with an elbow and sent her iPhone spinning. Charlie wanted to break free, but as the phone neared the tiled floor in front of her she succumbed to vengeance and caught the device with a volley that would have made a soccer player proud.

Beaky yelped as the iPhone hit the wall hard, and slid down, landing on a changing bench with a cracked screen.

Charlie thought she'd got clear, but the kick had slowed her down and her sneaker squealed as it hit a puddle. She started doing the splits, but managed to rebalance. As she tried pushing into a run, the giant got an arm round Charlie's waist.

The pocket on the back of Charlie's jeans ripped as the giant failed to hold on. Tracksuit had enough breath back in her lungs to launch a kick, but the giant started squealing like something out of a horror movie. One of the giants' manicured fingernails had snagged Charlie's T-shirt, and Charlie was horrified to see a tear in her shirt, filled with a bloody fingernail.

As Charlie tried to scramble up before Tracksuit could kick her again, the giant dry heaved, nauseated by the blood dripping from her fingertip.

Still half blinded by saliva, Charlie found her feet and scrambled towards the door. But the giant's screams had brought attention from across the hall and a hairy-legged gym teacher blocked the entrance.

'Ladies, ladies, what the heck?' the coach yelled, as he took in Charlie's gasping, spit covered face, the giant trailing drips of blood across floor and Beaky staring mortified at her cracked iPhone.

Charlie was breathless, tearful and hurt in at least four places. She'd been relieved when she first saw the teacher, but Charlie wasn't confident how things would pan out when it was her word versus the word of three best friends out of Swallow Park.

23 VICE PRINCIPAL

'I'm jinxed,' Charlie moaned. It was five in the afternoon, and she sat on the floor at the end of her bed with puffy eyes and her phone tucked between face and shoulder. 'Isn't luck supposed to even up? Because, if it does, I must deserve to win the state lottery by now.'

Harry was shocked hearing about Charlie's day and tried to sound soothing. 'So what happened after that?'

'This nice girls' coach came in. Luckily she knew what monsters those other three were, and she pointed out that this Meghan girl never could have got her nail ripped off the way she did unless she'd tried to grab me as I ran away. Then she got a wet towel from her office, so I could wipe the spit off.'

'But you still got in trouble?'

'It didn't look great when we got to the vice principal's office. One was sobbing over her smashed phone and there was Meghan with her finger bandaged up. The other girl was going for an Oscar. She had her inhaler out, saying I'd set off an asthma attack. All I had was a ripped shirt. It almost looked like I'd beaten the three of them up!'

'Where was the teacher who took your side?'

'I guess the coach was back teaching her lessons and the vice principal didn't care who'd done what to who. We got a lecture on Clayton Street High's zero tolerance stance on fighting and bullying. Her assistant had printed off the paperwork for us all to get two days' suspension before we said one word.'

'At least she didn't take their side,' Harry pointed out. 'And you get a four-day weekend . . .'

'I don't want a four-day weekend,' Charlie hissed furiously. 'I need good grades and I don't want *everyone* in my new life thinking I'm some mad bomber psycho freak.'

'Sorry, sorry,' Harry said anxiously. 'I was just . . . Well, being an insensitive dick, I guess. I'm sorry you've had a rotten day.'

'I've got an emergency appointment to see my support worker tomorrow lunchtime,' Charlie said, her voice wobbling. 'When I left White Boulder, they told me not to assume I had a free pass to mess up once or twice before they sent me back. *Any* breach of the rules can get my ass busted, and I think getting suspended for fighting on your third day back at school is about as bad as it gets.'

'Have you met this support worker?' Harry asked gingerly.

'I was supposed to, but there was some mix up last Friday. The guy was off sick or something . . .'

'Maybe they'll understand how tricky it can be settling into a new school.'

'With my luck?' Charlie sighed.

'I hate people who give cheesy clichéd advice, but try to stay positive.'

Charlie laughed. 'Look on the bright side. Take things one step at a time. Don't be a Debbie Downer.'

'There's always light at the end of the rainbow,' Harry said, joining the laughter. 'Or is it light at the end of the tunnel?'

'Long darned tunnel I'm in,' Charlie said, sighing as she rubbed her eyes. 'But talking to you always cheers me up.'

Harry felt a glow from the compliment. He hated having to wait until the weekend before he could see Charlie again, and the chance of her being sent back to White Boulder and not seeing her for months was appalling.

'I'm happy to come and be with you,' he said. 'It's too late for me to drive, but I could jump in a cab and be with you in fifty minutes.'

'You've got your running,' Charlie said. 'And a cab to North Vegas and back will cost a mint . . .'

'It's an after-school club – I'm not training for the Olympics . . .'

Charlie cut him off. 'Harry, *no*,' she said firmly. 'Just . . . I'm a mess. It's been a long day. It's sweet of you to offer, but I feel like I need to be alone. Get my head straight.'

'If you're sure . . .' Harry said, not entirely hiding his hurt. 'What about Makers Yard?'

'Oh, that . . .' Charlie said, thrown off balance. 'I was looking forward to it. But I've had so much going on today I've hardly thought about it. Maybe I'll go next week, if I haven't been booted back to White Boulder by then. I haven't even worked out how to get to Swallow Park.'

'It's not far,' Harry said. 'Maybe seven bucks in a cab.'

'I won't be focused with all this going on.'

'But you're meeting your support worker tomorrow. All you'll be able to say is that since your release, you've got trashed, hung with me, gone to the mall with Juno and been in a fight at school. It might make a difference if you have something you can big up and sound positive about.'

The last thing Charlie felt like doing was going out and

141

interacting with a bunch of strangers. But Harry had made a good point, and there'd be plenty of time to catch up on sulking if she didn't do all she could to avoid getting sent back to White Boulder.

24 HOT OR NOT

Betsy was back to her smoky best, and the sun was setting as she cruised the boundary of Swallow Park golf course, with Brad at the wheel and Charlie using her phone for directions.

'It says point-four of a mile, then left at the stop sign.'

'Aye-aye,' Brad said, then glanced across at Charlie. 'So that English kid, is he your boyfriend?'

'Just friends,' Charlie said, shaking her head.

'How'd you meet him? At school?'

'Long story,' Charlie said. 'Harry was awesome after I got busted. Wrote me, visited me. Paid money into my commissary account at White Boulder, so I could buy treats and toiletries.'

'And he don't get nothing out of that?' Brad asked.

The way Brad phrased it made Charlie feel guilty. 'He'd just moved from England and he was lonely.'

'You find him attractive?'

'He's a nice guy.' Charlie squirmed.

Brad laughed. 'That's not what I asked.'

Charlie realised she didn't exactly know the answer to that question. She was tempted to tell Brad to mind his own business, but he'd been sweet, offering a ride after she realised she'd spent most of her money on leggings and a school bag at the mall and didn't have enough for a cab both ways.

'I guess he's more like an older brother,' Charlie answered finally. 'He's my best friend, but I don't really think of him like ... *that*.'

Betsy misfired as she turned off, then rolled to a halt at a striped barrier, with a rock fountain and Swallow Park signs either side of the road. Harry's flash Mini had been waved through on Saturday, but two guards came out of their booth to inspect Betsy. One crouched and made a signal for Brad to lower his window, as the other went behind to inspect the smouldering exhaust.

'Sir, is this a zero-emission vehicle?'

Brad smiled, and dabbed the gas pedal so that the guy up the back got smoked. 'Does it look like one?'

As the guy behind started coughing, the one squatting down pointed at a zero-emissions sign next to the gate. 'Non-residents can only enter Swallow Park in a non-polluting vehicle. You're gonna have to turn about.'

Brad looked pissed. 'Are you telling me my car's not good enough for your snooty-assed—'

Charlie brushed Brad's shoulder and interrupted. 'It's three minutes' walk from here, so don't worry. Thanks for the ride.'

As Charlie ducked under the gate and started walking, Brad did a U-turn. Then he furiously revved Betsy, before blasting the horn as she shot off. Charlie smirked, seeing the entry booth and fountains obscured by a silver-grey haze.

After a wrong turn, which led to a row of tennis courts, Charlie hurried into Maker's Yard, conscious that she was a few minutes late. But that was the least of her problems.

It was like in an old movie where the baddie walks into a

bar. People doing personal projects at the benches stopped stapling and gluing. The pink-haired teacher who'd been there on Saturday was finishing a class with an all-girl group, and tween mouths froze like they'd sighted the devil. Steve was at his messy bench, facing a skinny ginger guy in a striped suit and the big-mouthed Texan.

'Charlie, welcome,' Steve said, voice wavering with stress. 'Can I talk to you for a moment?'

'This doesn't feel welcoming,' Charlie noted, as a chill went down her back.

'There have been some discussions regarding your attendance,' Steve said quietly. 'I've always felt that this maker community should be open to *everyone*.'

The big Texan interrupted with a grunt, and Steve scowled at him.

'Unfortunately not everyone shares my view and objections have been raised to your membership.'

'What have I done?' Charlie asked indignantly.

'Nothing,' Steve said, louder so that people could hear. 'You've done *nothing*.'

'Would you say that to the little girl she left half burnt to death?' the Texan bawled, shaking his chunky arm. 'And you wanna let her come here to learn all the skills to make bigger and better bombs?'

'I said *I'd* handle this,' Steve snapped. Then looked back at Charlie, shaking his head apologetically. 'Makers Yard has an inclusivity policy. We encourage people of all ages, races and genders to join. However, these premises are provided free of charge by the Swallow Park Community Association, which retains the right to exclude anyone if they choose to.'

The skinny ginger guy stepped round the desk and

handed Charlie a printed letter on Swallow Park Community Association letterhead.

'This notice excludes you from all communal facilities and from entering Swallow Park, unless you are an invited guest of a property owner visiting their private home. Failure to respect this notice will result—'

'Why?' Charlie yelled. 'What did I ever do to *you*?'

A mom in yoga pants came storming across from the lounge area, wagging her chubby finger. 'You got suspended from Clayton Street after less than three days. You smashed *my* daughter's eight-hundred-dollar phone and ripped out her best friend's fingernail like some savage beast!'

'Ask the school for the CCTV from the lunch room,' Charlie spat back. 'Look and see who was going after who.'

'We want that phone money,' the mom added. 'You'll be hearing from our family lawyer.'

'Sue me,' Charlie said, disgusted. 'But I don't have a cent. And when your darling daughter's phone gets fixed, be sure to look at the last photo she took. The one where her two pals smile while their spit runs down my face.'

'If they spat in your face, you gave them reason,' the mom snarled.

'Ya don't gotta to listen to this brat's nonsense, Terri,' the big Texan said cheerfully. 'It's time to shut her up and ship her out.'

Charlie looked around, to sour faces and jeers. She felt sorry for Steve, who was the only one taking her side.

'I'm friendly with the guys who run two other maker communities in Las Vegas,' Steve said as he led Charlie away. 'I'm going to call them on your behalf, because this is not the spirit in which maker communities are supposed to operate.'

Charlie was angry, but knew she'd book her one-way ticket

to White Boulder if she kicked off and the cops showed up.

'I'd resign my position if I thought it would make a difference,' Steve said.

'Might vote you off at the next committee meeting anyway,' the Texan sneered from behind. 'You're making a fool of yourself.'

'Vote me off, you dumb redneck,' Steve said, grinning like a loon. 'Take my unpaid job. See what it's like when you're the one who locks and unlocks, sterilises bathrooms, mops floors and unblocks the dust extractors. And I'll carp over the way you run things.'

As Steve and the Texan shot daggers across the room, Charlie shook her head and backed away.

'You don't know anything about me,' she said, fighting tears as she headed out the door.

25 JUICE JET

Charlie walked fast in the dusk. The road out of Swallow Park had no sidewalk and she had to hop into a rocky embankment whenever headlamps bore down. She couldn't face calling Harry or Brad. Part of her wanted to crawl into a hole and never come out, but a bigger part felt vengeful.

Go back with a gun. Shoot the big Texan first, then the lanky guy, the soccer moms and their sweaty brats. Burn Swallow Park to the ground and give everyone a real reason to send my ass back to White Boulder ...

But it was just a crazy fantasy and Charlie felt shaky and tearful as a single light closed from behind. She moved on to the verge as the electric motorbike passed, then felt angst as it slowed.

A shiver shot through Charlie as the rider set down a boot. The moonlit figure was wasp-like, in black riding leathers and a bright yellow helmet. Charlie backed up and glanced behind, worried about having to escape over jagged rocks in the dark, as the rider flipped their visor.

'Hey!' she yelled.

The rider made a huge groan as she stepped off and Charlie's nerves eased as she realised the riding leathers were stretched over a pregnant belly.

'I'm sorry if I startled you. Are you OK?'

When the rider removed her helmet, Charlie recognised the cropped pink hair of the woman who'd been teaching at Maker's Yard.

'Am I still inside Swallow Park?' Charlie asked warily. 'I'm moving as fast as I can.'

The woman shook her head as she stepped up. 'The security gate is the boundary – you're fine. But you're staying at Obama, right?'

'Sure.'

'Long walk,' the rider said, stopping three paces from Charlie and fighting for breath.

Below the pink hair, she had a pierced nose and half a dozen rings in each ear. She looked around thirty, some Latin blood, advanced pregnancy forcing her to stand with feet far apart.

'I'm sorry about what happened back there,' the rider said. 'Seems like there's more assholes in the world every day.'

'For sure,' Charlie said, appreciating the sympathy, but miffed that the woman had kept quiet at Maker's Yard.

'I'm Mango,' she said, reaching out to shake hands.

Charlie raised an eyebrow. 'Like the fruit?'

Mango nodded. 'My older brother's called Tomato, but at least that shortens to Tom.'

'Certain names are borderline parental cruelty,' Charlie said, smiling slightly.

'Steve's a diamond,' Mango said. 'I felt bad letting him hang, but I'm seven months gone, and my blood pressure is stratospheric.'

'I was looking forward to a new start,' Charlie confided. 'But it seems not to work like that.'

'Marc was ranting about you when I arrived to teach my lesson . . .' Mango explained.

'The big Texan?'

'Who else?' Mango said, shaking her head. 'I don't know what you did to tick him off but he had all his guns set on you. I Google-stalked you. You've led an interesting life.'

'A boring life would suit me fine.'

'You're looking at a forty-five-minute walk back to the Obama,' Mango said. 'I'm not even sure you can get across the two-fifteen, unless you play chicken with eight lanes of traffic. Have you ridden on the back of a motorbike before?'

'Never.'

'It'll be a squeeze with my big belly. But I can take it gentle. I need to get my blood sugar up, so I was planning to stop at Juice Jet up the road. I can fix you an Uber home from there.'

'I've got twelve dollars on me,' Charlie said. 'I think that should cover it.'

'Cab's on me,' Mango said. 'It'll burn some guilt for not sticking up for you.'

Mango didn't have a spare helmet and Charlie's fears swung between falling off if she wasn't holding on, and squashing the unborn if she held too tight. But the ride was over in five, and Charlie got the same confused vibe she'd had with Harry in the posh restaurant as she read the menu of the bright orange Juice Jet counter.

Wheatgrass Wings, After Gym and Tonic, Raspberry Ketone Tipple, Kale Blast, Honey and Ginseng Hangover Blitz . . .

Charlie was about to offer to pay when she realised that the cheapest blend was nine bucks.

'What can I get you?' Mango asked.

'I'm good,' Charlie said, freaked by the prices. 'Maybe just get me the Uber if that's OK.'

'Chill,' Mango said, firm but smiling. 'Keep me and Junior company until you've calmed down.'

'Is there, like . . . Regular juice, or something?'

Mango pointed at the menu. 'Almond Sunset is a good one. It's a creamy almond milk base with orange, coconut and cocoa. Most of these drinks have more calories than a Snickers bar, but us moms like to dress in sportswear, load an all-terrain stroller in the SUV and come here to pretend we're healthy . . .'

'What's the worst that could happen?' Charlie asked warily.

Rather than join the six-strong queue, Mango led Charlie to one of the few empty tables and pulled out her phone.

'Check this app,' Mango said, moving her chair round the table so Charlie could see.

'Is it like McDonald's, where you order from your phone?' Charlie asked.

But it wasn't an online ordering app, with the bright colours and corporate branding. The screen was black, and covered with tiny lines of code and a hash prompt, like an old-school computer.

'Staff take the orders on the left,' Mango explained quietly, pointing to the line at the register. 'Everything on the payment side is secure. One-twenty-eight-bit encryption, credit card and NFC data handled securely. But you see that other terminal, that shows the drink orders to the mixers? It links to the register using WiFi. There's no encryption whatsoever.'

To make her point, Mango tapped a code into her phone and the screen split.

'The top half shows the current queue of customer orders. You're seeing exactly what the two staff mixing drinks see.

Now, all I do is tap an order number and two product codes, and . . .'

Charlie saw an order for Almond Sunrise and Maternal Bliss appear as order seventy-three in the drinks queue.

'Neat,' Charlie said, wary, because trouble seemed to seek her out. 'So you're a hacker?'

'I hoped I'd catch you with my bike, because you remind me of myself as a teenager,' Mango explained. 'You made explosives. I worked out how to clone my seventh-grade gym teacher's cell phone and credit card. Then I went online and arranged to have all kinds of crazy stuff delivered to his house.'

Charlie smiled. 'Did you ever get caught?'

Mango nodded. 'Things got heavy when I was seventeen. I helped an environmental group find and release a secret Department of Energy report on fracking. I had FBI agents raiding my parent's house at 3 a.m. We were well off. My dad fixed up a great attorney and I pled down to a misdemeanour charge. I was sentenced to two hundred hours teaching computer skills to San Francisco homeless. It was in one of the first maker spaces, and that's how I got into teaching kids coding and engineering.'

'Do you work in IT now?'

Mango shook her head. 'My wife and I have a baked-goods business. We do specialist cakes and breads. And we have vans that we send out to music festivals and big public events.'

'Sounds like hard work,' Charlie said.

'I've had a lot of fun teaching kids over the years,' Mango said. 'We did a battle robot course with ten- to thirteen-year-olds at Maker's Yard this summer. I had a team, and your Texan friend Marc ran the opposition. We didn't officially split boy-girl. But you know how kids are: all the boys went with good ol''

Marc and the girls with me and my pink hair.

'Each team built three robots, and we smashed the boys! We had a robot with a hydraulic hammer. One hit and the boys' robot disintegrated. Some of the kids were mortified, but it was worth it for the look on Marc's idiot face.'

Charlie laughed noisily.

'Some of the girls who were seven or eight when I first moved to Nevada are at college doing programming or engineering now. I'm really proud of that.'

'Sounds awesome,' Charlie said, enjoying the story, though it made her feel worse about being kicked out of Maker's Yard. 'So is Junior your first?'

'I've got a boy and a girl, three and five,' Mango explained. 'And, as a matter of fact . . .'

'Order seventy-three,' a guy behind the counter shouted.

Charlie felt edgy as she walked to the counter and grabbed the illicitly ordered smoothies. Mango kept talking as Charlie dug in a straw and sucked her first mouthful of Almond Sunset.

'I'll need time off when the baby comes,' Mango said thoughtfully. 'We could probably use someone like you, if you're looking to earn some cash.'

'Baking cakes?'

'We're not exactly the Sara Lee Corporation,' Mango said. 'Everyone does a bit of everything.'

'I could certainly do with some extra cash,' Charlie said, but then her voice dropped. 'But I got suspended from school, three days in. I might be back at White Boulder this time tomorrow.'

'Harsh,' Mango said, between sips of juice. 'How's Almond Sunset?'

'Quite gritty,' Charlie said. 'Nice, though.'

'Tell you what, Charlie, how about I give you my cell number?

If things *do* go your way tomorrow, we could find you a part-time job ...'

'That's kind,' Charlie said as she pulled out her phone to take the number. 'I guess you never know ...'

Mango's offer reminded Charlie that there were decent people in the world, and she felt less desperate on the Uber ride back to OIL. A pint of Almond Sunset had worked through by the time she reached the automatic door and she dashed for her room.

'Hey!' the woman behind reception shouted, leaping from her seat. 'Croker, get back here!'

'Sorry, I'm busting,' Charlie said, assuming she was going to get told off for not using the anti-virus gel.

'Ken Kleinberg was looking for you,' the woman said, from behind her desk.

'Who's that?' Charlie asked, slathering her hands in gel from the dispenser.

'Your support worker,' the woman explained, peering over her glasses as if Charlie was a fool. 'He's been getting it in the ear from some lawyer up at Swallow Park. You're supposed to register your cell number with your support worker before going out after 5 p.m. And you can't join non-school groups or organisations without his permission.'

'How was I supposed to know that?' Charlie said, as the woman peeled a sticky note off the frame of her monitor. 'Ken was off sick when I arrived. Should I call him now?'

'Ken said you're confined to this building until he's seen you. And I wouldn't want to be in those grubby little sneakers when he does.'

26 LANA'S TINY FEET

Harry went back to Matt's house after running club. It lacked the spectacle of his aunt's mountainside home, but Harry's best friend did have the twin advantages of a giant video projector screen that filled an entire wall of his bedroom, and Lana, his beautiful girlfriend, who sat scoffing Pringles in a swing chair anchored to the ceiling.

'So, this is the voicemail I was telling you about,' Harry said, pressing play to set off a terse, gravelly male voice. 'Tell me what you think.'

'*Mr Smirnov, you don't know me, but I've heard things about Vegas Local, including the fact you don't take ads from Janssen Group. I can give you a huge story about the Janssens' Fremont Street casino. It could blow a big hole in their operations. I'm not looking for money, just someone who can give the story the airing it deserves before the Janssens get wind and shut it down. I might not be in town for much longer, so call me on this number as soon as you can.*'

'He sounds *really* frightened,' Lana observed.

Harry nodded in agreement. 'When I called back, the number was dead. I know a guy who knows a guy who can get details out of cell-phone companies. He said it was a twenty-dollar burner phone, purchased at an Exxon station last week.'

Lana seemed intrigued. 'Can the journalists at Vegas Local track him down?'

Matt laughed. 'Harry *is* the journalist at Vegas Local.'

'Most of our writers are local people, who get a cut of the ad revenue if their articles get more than five thousand views,' Harry explained. 'There's my co-owner, Ellie, but he's based in San Francisco. Ads and coupons are sold by two ad guys who work from home and our app and website development is done by Ngoc and Thanh in Hanoi.'

Lana looked surprised. 'I thought a popular site like Vegas Local would have an office, and full-time journalists.'

Harry shook his head. 'Ellie calls it the Super-Lean Business Model. The trick to getting people to keep visiting the site and clicking ads is lots of coupons and discounts, plus curating the homepage so that there are new stories twice a day. A mix of upbeat news, scary crime and funny pet videos seems to work best.'

'Pure exploitation,' Matt said mischievously. 'Harry funds his lavish lifestyle with cheap labour and locals writing articles for a few dollars.'

'Up your hole,' Harry said, giving Matt the finger, while simultaneously feeling guilty because his friend was close to the truth.

'It's amazing, though,' Lana said. 'Sixteen and you own a chunk of a super-successful website.'

'Evil capitalist!' Matt said, laughing and making whip-cracking sounds.

'Mind if I grab a Coke?' Lana asked.

'Help yourself,' Matt said.

'Anyone else want anything?'

Lana was also a member of the running club. Her little feet were red and chafed, and Harry decided they were cute as she padded off to the kitchen.

As soon as Lana was out of earshot, Matt crawled across his bed towards Harry and spoke words of warning.

'Remember what happened to your balls the last time you pissed the Janssens off.'

'I know,' Harry said, not enjoying the reminder, 'but I'm way more experienced now. I get a lot of crank tips and calls, but that guy sounded properly scared and too many people in this town turn a blind eye to all the shit the Janssens pull . . .'

Matt shrugged. 'If I were you, I'd stick to Ellie's money-making formula. I know you're after your Pulitzer Prize, but my burger-flipping ass wouldn't be making waves if *I* was taking seven big ones a month from traffic accidents, girl-scout fundraisers and coupons for ground beef.'

'I've told you before, if you give Fatburger the elbow, you can have a job helping me out.'

'Couldn't handle having you as my boss,' Matt said. 'And if you wouldn't mind making your excuses when Lana gets back.'

Matt made a sex gesture with his fingers. Harry nodded like it was no big deal but felt crazy jealous. Matt's moody-Goth act and soulful green eyes had brought him to a point where he'd switched from boasting about sexual conquests to downplaying them to protect Harry's feelings.

'It's all about confidence, buddy,' Matt said soothingly. 'Just be cool when Charlie comes to your place on Saturday.'

Harry had opened the Uber app to book his ride home when Lana stepped back in and yelled.

'Oh, that is so gross!'

Matt had his projector set on Cox Sport's news, and despite the picture stretched from skirting to ceiling, the sound was down to a murmur and neither he nor Harry had noticed the horribly snapped leg of the college football player onscreen.

A slow-motion replay showed a defensive mix-up, enabling a gigantic middle lineman to plough through a gap. The quarterback's cleat dug into soft ground as he threw a short pass, which meant his leg didn't give as the four-hundred-pound lineman hit it hard.

'That must be so painful,' Matt gasped. 'The bone's sticking out.'

'Is that Texas Midland?' Harry said excitedly. 'Turn the sound up.'

Matt was already going for the remote on his bedside table and wound back forty seconds.

'I don't want to see it again, you sickos!' Lana protested, shielding her eyes as Matt hit play.

'It's JJ Janssen,' Harry said, reading the name on the back of the quarterback's shirt, as Matt turned up the volume.

'Viewer discretion is advised for the following images, which come from our live Wednesday game currently showing on CS3. Texas Midland's rookie quarterback, JJ Janssen, was on an excellent six and zero start to the season. But this freak injury in the derby game with Austin Roadrunners will end his first season as starter.'

'How can you look at that?' Lana moaned.

Matt and Harry ignored the protest as the story went past the point where Matt had rewound.

'After the incident, there was a bizarre twist. Midland fans took offence at four-hundred-and-thirty-pound lineman

Perry Addison high-fiving team mates, while JJ Janssen was given oxygen and placed on a stretcher. Among those offended was Janssen's wife, who decided to take things into her own hands . . .'

Matt, Harry and Lana all gawped as they watched a tall woman stagger on to the muddy football field with a folding chair held above her head.

'Charlie's sister, Fawn!' Harry blurted.

'It's like WWE!' Matt howled, laughing hard.

Despite high-heeled boots on a muddy field, Fawn got close enough to swing the chair at the 400lb lineman, glancing the back of his head, before getting tackled by security staff in fluoro-pink jackets. Fawn's Midland shirt got ripped at the neck and her face hit the mud as the crowd went bananas.

Lana had uncovered her eyes and joined Matt, laughing at the footage of Fawn being dragged away. But Harry had stopped laughing, because JJ and Fawn were Vegas natives, and he had a hot story.

Licensing the clip from the National College Football Association would cost thousands of dollars, and Vegas Local would get sued if they used it without permission. Harry's task was to make a front-page article for Vegas Local which looked official, but opened the video of the incident in a window from another website.

'This could be the biggest story of the year,' Harry said happily, logging into the Vegas Local content-management system with his phone. 'Plus, it's an out-of-state game, so with any luck nobody else is watching and I can have this on Vegas Local ahead of all our rivals. Should easily clock half a million article views, which is a minimum three thousand dollars of ad revenue . . .'

Lana was impressed, watching over Harry's shoulder as he rapidly tapped a four-paragraph story, embedded a link to the horror-tackle video on Cox Sport's website, added keywords for search engines and coupons for a local sporting goods store and a solar-energy installer.

'I can improve the story and maybe buy some photos later,' Harry explained to Lana. 'Right now, the job is to get this online fast, so that people who see the story go to our site, not someone else's.'

'If you ever need an assistant,' Lana suggested brightly. 'This stuff is so cool!'

'But you have to leave now, don't you, Harry,' Matt said with the subtlety of a truck crashing through a storefront. 'Isn't it easier to polish this up at *your* place, on *your* laptop?'

'Uber's almost here,' Harry said, standing up. 'I'll wait out front, give you two peace and quiet.'

'I'm frazzled after that 10K run,' Lana said, stretching into a yawn as she pushed a foot into an Asics running shoe. 'I'm gonna walk home and hit the sack.'

'What about your Coke?' Matt asked, looking distraught as Harry tried not to smirk. 'It's dark. Shall I walk you?'

'It's one block,' Lana said. Then asked Harry, 'Are there ever jobs at Vegas Local?' and followed him down a short hallway to the front door.

'Send me a few samples of stuff you've written,' Harry said. 'There are definitely times when I could do with a day off, or a bit of help. Ellie used to cover, but he's busy running sites in sixteen other cities now.'

'I'd be up for anything,' Lana said.

She gave Matt a kiss on the doorstep, but there was more gusto in the smile she gave Harry.

'See you guys at school, and don't forget to message your girlfriend, Charlie,' Matt said, putting emphasis on *girlfriend* for Lana's benefit. 'She'll enjoy seeing Fawn looking like an asshat.'

27 SEXY TOAST

Charlie laughed like everyone else when someone said their goodbyes to White Boulder, only to violate early release and bounce back a few weeks later. But she couldn't think of anyone who'd bounced in one week.

I'm gonna set a world record.

There's only a one-in-four chance I'll go back to my old unit. So it'll be a new roommate. New pecking order. Please don't let it be block C with crazy Phyllis starting fights and screaming all night . . .

How can I ace a college-level statistics module in three weeks, but crash and burn in the real world? It can't all be someone else's fault. There's got to be something wrong with me. Something obvious that I'm too stupid and pathetic to see.

The door of the next room slammed hard, making Charlie shoot up in bed, tearful and angry with herself.

None of the boys on Charlie's hallway had shown her any disrespect, but they were mostly a couple of years older and their slams, shouts and the ruthless bullying of Jamal set her on edge, even after she'd shut the bolt inside her door.

Charlie realised she was thirsty as she tried to lie down,

and since she was failing at sleep she decided to fetch chilled spring water from the cooler at the end of the hall, rather than warm and chlorinated from her bathroom faucet.

As Charlie pushed the lever to fill her glass, Brad leaned out of a communal kitchen area, holding a slice of toast.

'How much toast do you eat?' Charlie said, smiling, but conscious that she looked a mess. Barefoot, baggy nylon shorts and one of Juno's old Gap tees, with no bra underneath.

'Been up playing pool on the mezzanine,' Brad explained. Charlie realised he was still in the clothes he'd worn when he'd dropped her off. 'Want some jelly toast?'

'Why not,' Charlie said.

She was too stressed to be hungry, but preferred chatting to Brad to going back to her room.

'They put fresh bread in here every day,' Brad complained, opening an overhead cupboard mounded with half-eaten loaves. 'But nobody ever cleans out the old stuff. This is green!'

Brad dropped the mouldy bread into a trash can.

'And the cleaners . . .' he moaned, tailing off as he placed two fresh slices into the toaster and pushed the lever down. 'So how was the Maker's Yard? Got back OK?'

Charlie couldn't face the humiliating details.

'It wasn't what I expected,' she said understatedly, before changing the subject. 'Do you know Ken Kleinberg?'

'The support officer?'

Charlie smirked. 'How many Ken Kleinbergs do you know?'

'All right, Miss Smartass,' Brad said, making Charlie flinch with a flicking gesture. 'He used to be my support officer, but he's been off sick a lot. I wouldn't say Ken's a bad guy, but he's moody. One day snapping and snarling, another he's so wrapped in his own problems you could probably rape a nun and get away with it.'

'A nun!' Charlie said, shaking her head and laughing. 'It's dark in that head of yours, Brad.'

But she was laughing, and she'd stepped slightly closer.

'You look cute with your hair all mussed,' Brad said, then bit his toast.

The compliment seemed ridiculous, but Charlie didn't care. Brad swung his toast in front of her mouth.

'Crunchy peanut, chocolate spread and lime jelly,' he said.

Charlie took a bemused sniff. 'Kinda gross . . .'

But Brad's smile was infectious and after a pause for thought, Charlie went on tiptoes and took a cautious bite.

'Tastes better than it looks, doesn't it?' Brad said, before putting a sticky hand on the back of Charlie's neck and gently kissing her lips. She loved his confidence, and the way he tasted like chocolate instead of beer and weed. Charlie considered Brad's girlfriend. But in this moment there were only two places to go: forward with a guy who turned her on, or back behind her bolted door, sleepless and tormented.

Brad grabbed her butt and lifted her easily on to the kitchen worktop. The back of her head hit a cabinet, but that didn't stop him pushing up her shirt. Charlie rubbed against Brad's chest, but she really wanted to see it.

'Take your shirt off.'

Brad took a step back and Charlie was scared that she'd done something wrong.

Do guys not like it if you tell them what to do?

'You don't have to take your shirt off,' Charlie said nervously as Brad swept a hand over his greasy brow and stared down at floor tiles.

Brad shook his head and breathed deep. 'It's not about the shirt.'

Charlie felt like a germ. 'Is something wrong with me?'

'You're awesome,' Brad said softly. 'But I'm guessing you're new at this . . .'

'I'll be sent back to White Boulder tomorrow,' Charlie pleaded. 'My whole life is shit. I might not be alone with a guy again for years.'

'You don't *know* you're going back,' Brad said.

Charlie slid off the cabinet, looking tearful. 'With my luck, you can bet the farm.'

Brad surprised Charlie by closing again. He pushed her back on to the worktop and stood between her legs, teasing them apart.

'Do you like that?'

She shuddered with pleasure as he kissed her neck.

'It'll hurt if it's your first time,' Brad said. 'Tell me you *really* want it.'

'I want you,' Charlie gasped, scared of what she was getting into, but surprised by a lack of doubts. Even a painful escape seemed better than reality.

28 COLGATE CHEST

Charlie sat on Brad's toilet and felt spaced out as she peed. *So, that was sex then . . .*

Brad reached from under the covers when she came out and picked her shorts off the floor.

'Come back to bed,' he said softly.

Charlie liked being spooned, with his hand on her belly and his breath spreading around her neck and down her back. Brad fell asleep quickly, but Charlie couldn't get comfortable without waking him up and found herself staring into the gloom, somehow comforted by the photo of Brad's twin sisters at the end of the bed.

She hadn't expected to sleep, so it was a surprise when Brad woke her, stroking her cheek with his little finger and kissing softly as she opened her eyes.

'Another day,' Brad said ruefully.

Hazy light breached a crack in the curtains as he climbed over Charlie, scratching his butt as he padded to the bathroom.

Charlie rolled to the middle of the single bed, finding Brad's heat and realising that his sheets were disgusting. She liked Brad's smell, but there were dried-out noodles stuck to the duvet and the thought that other girls had been here made her feel itchy.

Brad spat toothpaste in the basin, then leaned out of the bathroom door, his perfect chest blobbed with Colgate.

'Sleep good?' he asked.

'I guess,' Charlie said, yawning as she instinctively pulled the covers up to her neck. 'It's only twenty past seven.'

'I have to leave earlier when Mel's staying at her dad's,' Brad explained.

The girlfriend's name made the bed even less comfortable.

'I need a blast in the shower,' Brad said. 'Might be an idea to hop back to your room, before too many people are up and about.'

'Makes sense,' Charlie said weakly.

Brad moved towards Charlie as she swung her feet out of bed. She let covers drop around her feet as Brad pulled her into a hug and followed with a toothpastey kiss.

'Hope you're still around when I get home from school.'

'So do I,' Charlie replied, managing a slight smile.

• • •

Charlie panicked when she saw five messages on the phone plugged in beside her bed. Harry calling was no surprise, but there were *have you seen this video* messages from two girls she'd known at White Boulder, and her old schoolmate Trish, who'd moved to San Diego when they were in sixth grade and who barely looked recognisable in her avi picture.

The final message was from OIL's reception desk, reminding Charlie that she wasn't allowed off premises until she'd seen Ken Kleinberg at noon.

The WiFi at OIL wasn't great and the video buffered for ages before Charlie got to see JJ's horror leg break and Fawn making an ass of herself. Fawn looked older, but her snarling muddy face gave Charlie chills.

It was the expression Charlie had seen when her sister screamed and kicked and threw stuff around the trailer. It was hard to enjoy slapstick from the person who'd steamrollered her life to enable her boyfriend to play college ball, and now had her paws in their disabled brother's trust fund . . .

Harry and the others had sent the clip to cheer Charlie up, but seeing Fawn filled her with dread. *Why does she hate me so much? Why have I messed my life up so fast? Does Brad care about me? Where will I be sleeping tonight? The meeting with Ken isn't for four hours and time's gonna drag so bad . . .*

Charlie had showered by the time Juno came into her room, giving her a hug and wishing her luck. She only managed fruit for breakfast, and when everyone had left for school Charlie went up to the mezzanine floor and guilted herself about all the positive things she could be doing, instead of guzzling Pepsi and aimlessly blasting balls around the pool table.

'Apologies for being late,' Ken Kleinberg said, settling in front of his desk when he finally arrived.

Charlie felt like her insides had shrunk to a tangerine as she settled in a metal-framed chair, gripping both arms.

If Brad was a god in human form, Ken was his opposite. Crooked posture, shaving rash, snub nose and grey teeth. He had a shabby briefcase open on the desktop. Besides several files, it contained a model-railway magazine, a boxed lunch and a compartmented pill case.

Ken had a fresh cup from the water cooler, and he kept Charlie in suspense as he necked two red pills, a lilac triangle and a brown-and-red capsule.

'I'm keeping big pharma profitable all by myself,' Ken joked, seeming nicer than the ogre she'd imagined. 'How are you finding Obama?'

'OK,' Charlie said. 'My room is nice. And I'm sorry about what happened yesterday.'

'You've certainly caused a ruckus. One of the reasons I'm late is that I've been taking calls from several parties about your case.'

'Swallow Park?' Charlie asked warily.

'Amongst others,' Ken explained. 'I'm obliged to follow a set of rigid guidelines. The zero-tolerance policy for newly released offenders exists because we can't create the impression that someone can get away with staying out after curfew once, or puffing a joint, or skipping a couple of lessons at school.

'However, one of your friends pointed out that you are younger than most people released into an environment like this. I'm also supposed to evaluate any positive efforts you've made since your release.'

'My friends?' Charlie said curiously, thinking of Juno and Harry.

'Steve Malbrouck at Makers Yard has known my wife for many years and he called me this morning,' Ken explained. 'Steve tells me that you're a fine young person, and that the situation at Swallow Park was wholly unfair. I also had a conversation with Mango Kowalski-Clark at the Radical Cake Collective, saying that you've shown an interest in baking and that she'd like to offer you a part-time job.'

'Oh,' Charlie said, trying not to look as surprised as she felt.

'Have you always been a baker?' Ken asked.

'I didn't have much chance at White Boulder, but I've always loved it,' Charlie lied.

'I'm a bread maker,' Ken said, smiling. 'It never ceases to

amaze me that water, flour and yeast can make something that tastes and smells so wonderful.'

'I know.' Charlie nodded, wary of saying too much and exposing the fact that the only things she'd ever baked were Ed's frozen chicken bites.

'So, with a community figure like Steve speaking highly of you and a job lined up to keep you out of mischief, I'm willing to overlook yesterday's unfortunate incident at school.'

'Thank you *so* much,' Charlie beamed. 'That's awesome.'

'But . . .' Ken said firmly, resuming after a dramatic pause. 'It will look bad on me if you mess up again, so expect *zero* sympathy next time around. I also want to know where you are at all times. That means strict 6 p.m. curfew, except for pre-approved adult-supervised activities. Do not go out without your cell phone fully charged because a dead battery is not an excuse, and do not travel more than two miles from here without getting my permission in advance. Is all of that acceptable?'

'Very,' Charlie agreed.

The restrictions were a pain, but a thousand times better than getting sent back to White Boulder. Charlie's face was alight as she walked out, pulling her phone to call Harry. She'd hoped she might catch him before the end of his lunch break, but had to settle for voicemail.

29 TEACHERS ARE DICKS

The buzzer had gone for Queensbridge Academy's first afternoon lesson, but Harry was desperate to return a call. The school's darkroom hadn't been used in years and he glanced over his shoulder before unlocking the door.

The windowless space had a lingering smell of photographic chemicals. He flipped a switch, illuminating three deep-red bulbs, relocked the door from inside and propped his ass against a steel sink with a dripping faucet.

His phone's screen made more light than the bulbs. Harry made sure his call-recording app was enabled, dialled the number of a missed call and waited several rings before a man answered.

'Who's there?'

'Is that Earl? This is Harry Smirnov from Vegas Local. I'm returning the messages you left, about a possible story.'

'I'm Earl,' he said, halfway between confused and scared. 'Sorry about the other phone. I started getting weird calls and had to ditch it. What's your beef with the Janssens, Harry?'

'I don't have a beef,' Harry lied.

'But I've read that you don't take their advertisements.'

Harry didn't want to go into personal stuff about Charlie and getting his nuts wrung, so he waffled. 'Vegas Local depends on a strong relationship with the community. We select our advertising partners carefully and Janssen Corp put a lot of noses out of joint.'

'You mean they're a bunch a dirty crooks,' Earl croaked, then broke into a rasping laugh.

Harry smiled. 'I couldn't say that, sir. Especially online, cos the Janssens can afford to sue my ass.'

'The local TV stations swim in Janssen dollars,' the old guy said, a touch suspicious. 'I admire your decency, but how old are you, boy?'

'Twenty,' Harry said.

'You're all so young these days,' Earl snorted. 'Drop out of college and a billionaire by twenty-five, eh?'

'I live in hope.'

'Got quite an accent there, son. You Australian?'

Harry avoided answering. 'I'm under a lot of time pressure,' he said – not admitting that the pressure was fourth-period chemistry. 'I understand you have a story.'

'If you've got balls big enough to run it.'

'OK,' Harry said, preferring not to think too much about balls.

'You know about SNor?'

Harry laughed. 'Hard to miss.'

'What about HHD, the Hotel Hygiene Directive?' Earl asked.

'Nope.'

'At the height of the SNor epidemic, the Center for Disease Control in Washington issued cleaning guidelines. They focused on schools, prisons, retirement homes, cruise ships and hotels, because those were the places where the biggest outbreaks were happening. The HHD gave strict guidelines on how hotel rooms had to be cleaned, from towels being laundered at higher temperatures, strong chlorine bleach being used in all cleaning sprays, UV sterilisation, disposable gloves and masks for staff, disposable toilet brushes for each room and so forth.'

'Right,' Harry said. 'I remember all the hotels on the strip had to close their buffets, and there was no traffic in town, even Friday and Saturday.'

'The Hotel Hygiene Directive wasn't legally binding, but every big hotel operator agreed to follow the procedure, including the four Janssen Corp casinos that have hotel rooms. It was expensive to implement, but it was a way to rebuild customer confidence.

'HHD doubled the time it took to clean a hotel room. And you can imagine how hard it was trying to recruit minimum-wage hotel cleaners to do the dirty work during a virus outbreak. The Janssens had empty hotels and casinos losing money, while their cleaning and laundry costs spiralled. Their solution was to bend the rules.'

'Sounds like Janssen Corp,' Harry said, intrigued but not terribly excited. 'Trouble is, there have been a ton of stories about stuff like this, Earl. The corporations put it down to teething problems with new procedures, and say that they've got things sorted now. Plus, people have lost interest in SNor scare stories. Once you've had a dose you're immune and everyone has had their week on the toilet now.'

Earl sounded irritated. 'Seventeen people died after being infected at Janssen Island Casino in Fremont street. I've spoken to a few people who worked there. The hygiene was horrible. Cleaning staff quit. The rooms haven't been refurbished in twenty years and they keep Janssen Island busy on weekdays by offering twenty-dollar rooms and free bus rides to seniors from California.

'They were old and vulnerable, and they dropped like flies. The Island should have been shut down for two weeks and deep cleaned, but Janssen kept bussing seniors in. Because they were mostly one-night stays, most of them were home before they got sick. Cleaning staff who could see what was going on were scared to speak up because the Janssens are thugs. Quite a few people did wind up dying or getting seriously ill while they were still in Vegas, but the source of all the cases was never identified.'

'Why not?' Harry asked.

'Hospitals and doctors must notify every fatal case of SNor to the Center for Disease Control, including the likely source of infection. But not a single case was registered as being picked up at Janssen Island. The patients' hospital records were accurate, but when the hospital data got uploaded to the CDC, all reference to Janssen Island vanished.'

Seventeen deaths and a cover-up *was* a story and Harry was intrigued.

'How do you know this?' he asked.

'I worked at Clark County medical records department for over twenty years,' Earl explained. 'The major hospitals and clinics all use our centre. SNor created extra work, so I came out of retirement on a twelve-week contract to help with an administrative backlog.

'I thought something was peculiar when I had to track down a patient record with a wrongly entered insurance number. I noticed that the source of infection was Janssen Island Casino on the hospital record, but shown as "Out of State" on the stats uploaded to the Center for Disease Control.

'So I called up all SNor deaths in the hospital nearest Fremont Street, and found sixteen more records that had been changed from *Janssen Island* to *Out of State*. When I showed my line manager, she said she'd look into it. When nothing happened after two weeks, I made a fuss and got rebuked for ordering dead patients' records without authorisation.

'Two days later, I arrived at work and my swipe card was dead. I got told I was being dismissed for breaching patient confidentiality, but they said they'd pay the rest of my twelve-week contract if I signed an agreement not to speak out.'

'Did you sign?'

'I needed the money,' Earl said. 'But it's gnawed at my conscience ever since . . .'

'Did you think about going to the cops? Or the CDC?'

Earl snorted. 'I've lived in this town long enough to know better than to go to the cops complaining about the Janssens. And I called the CDC, but their manpower is focused on preventing the next synthetic-virus outbreak. The guy I spoke to was sympathetic but blunt: they've dealt with a major disease crisis and they don't have resources to send a team to Nevada to start digging around a hospital records department.'

Harry sighed. 'So the Janssens win again.'

'I'm being followed,' Earl said nervously. 'My daughter says I'm senile. But he's a big fellow, with his hair in a ball . . . I forget what you call that.'

'A man bun,' Harry said, shuddering.

'They came inside my house while I was bowling. They didn't take squat, but I live alone and I could tell things had been moved around.'

'What about evidence?' Harry said, knowing that one old man whose own daughter accused him of being senile wouldn't count for much. 'Do you have printouts of the records?'

Earl sounded outraged. 'Medical records are sensitive documents. Removing them would be a gross breach of patient confidentiality. But I am willing to give you names of the people whose records were changed. If you tracked down their relatives, they can legally request to see their deceased relative's medical records.'

This could be a huge story, but I'm a sixteen-year-old, who has school and homework and twice daily Vegas Local updates. The earliest I'm going to have any chance to consider this is Saturday, and that's when Charlie is coming. Unless I bunk off school. But I'd get suspended for sure and Kirsten will ground me, and take my driving privileges away and then I'll be more screwed . . .

'Earl, I appreciate you calling me,' Harry said. 'But this is a complex investigation. Have you thought about contacting one of the local TV stations? Or the *Vegas Mirror*?'

'Janssen is the third biggest advertiser in this state,' Earl said, sounding a little desperate. 'The money men will squash the story. I've never liked what the Janssens have done in this town, and seventeen seniors dying to keep dollars flowing into a rundown casino is sickening . . .'

'I agree,' Harry said, but he felt burdened by Earl's expectations and part of him wanted to fess up to being a schoolboy without the time or backup to run a real investigation.

Ellie might help, but most likely he'll tell me to drop it. And chances are, when we get to the medical records, the Janssens will have covered their tracks.

'How long do you think it might take?' Earl asked hopefully. 'Ain't sleeping right with people in my house and tailing me.'

Harry pounded the sink with frustration. 'Best not to think about it,' he said, unable to come up with anything more

reassuring. 'I can't ... ry looking
into t...

Ha... ...nessage
from C... ...o hear
her new...

'I fina...

Harry ... the
rest a key t ...ck
who taught ... ...n.
He'd never li... ...y
athletics team...

'Smirnov,' B... ...ng like
a git. 'Thought ... ...s eleven minutes
past.'

'Yes, sir,' Harry said. 'I'm sorry.'

'And the door was locked. Give me the key.'

Harry pulled a pair of keys out of his trousers. Mr Bowers
snatched and jangled them.

'Pupils do not have keys. Do you know how serious this is?'

'It unlocks the room we use for school news meetings,' Harry
explained. 'Vice Principal Presley always gives a set of keys to
the news editor. I guess the darkroom key is a relic, from when
they used film.'

Bowers didn't like being wrong, so he grunted and jangled
the keys again. 'Then you have abused the trust VP Presley
put in you, which is worse. Smirnov, you need to focus less on
outside interests, and engage fully with your education.'

Harry thought of a million answers he'd like to give, but
rolling his eyes was the most dissent he dared show. 'Yes, sir.'

'Phone,' Bowers snapped. 'Collect it from the front office
at the end of the day. And I'll be seeing you in the hall at

zero-eight-thirty Saturday for detention.'

'Aww, come on,' Harry begged, feeling like his head would burst from stress. 'Besides, I'm busy Saturday.'

'If you bring a parental note, the detention can be deferred until the following Saturday.'

Kirsten's gonna love hearing that I got Saturday detention. And she's no fan of Charlie, so she won't write a note so she can visit . . .

'Ugh!' Harry groaned, convinced that school was a waste of his valuable time. To make it worse, Bowers clearly enjoyed busting a kid he didn't like.

'Your attitude stinks, Smirnov,' Bowers said, then raised his voice significantly. 'Now march to class, double quick!'

30 DEVELOPMENT KITCHEN B

Ken gave Charlie permission to go out after the meeting, and she rode a 119 bus for half an hour, then made a short walk to an aluminium-clad industrial unit with four zebra-striped trucks out front and a sign bearing the giant punkish logo of the Radical Cake Collective.

It wasn't exactly the *little bakery where everyone mucks in* that Mango had described the night before. After making her don a hairnet and polythene shoe covers, an assistant led Charlie through an oppressively hot space, passing lines of giant ovens, waist-height mixers and a packaging area where brightly coloured cakes were iced by hand and slid into boxes that matched the zebra-striped vans out front.

Mango's office was up a set of metal stairs, painted pastel pink. Awards and photos were hung along the hallway wall and while Charlie didn't like the idea of working somewhere so hot, she felt super emotional when she stepped into Mango's office and accepted a hug.

'You are *so* awesome,' Charlie sniffled as she stretched over Mango's pregnant belly. 'You barely know me, but you really put your neck out.'

Mango shrugged as if she hadn't done much. 'I had a battle with Ken Kleinberg,' Mango said. 'But his daughter's getting married in the spring, so I offered him a six-hundred-dollar wedding cake, and here you are.'

'Really?' Charlie said, outraged. 'There I was thinking Ken had done the decent thing.'

'Have a squat,' Mango said. 'Would you like tea and cake?'

The office was done out in mid-century modern. There was a variety of cakes laid out on a wooden serving trolley with breads and croissants on the shelf beneath. Charlie went for a frosted lime muffin as Mango buzzed her assistant and asked for a pot of tea and two cups.

'This tastes *so* good,' Charlie said, as she bit the muffin and got moist lime sponge and tart raspberry cheesecake frosting. 'It's so fresh it's still warm.'

'I have to say I'm confused,' Mango told Charlie as a bearded man put down a pot and two cups with saucers. Then to the assistant, 'Close the door on the way out.'

There was something a touch sinister about the door closing, and the clack of a spoon as Mango stirred the teapot.

'What's confusing?' Charlie asked, the tea and cakes making her feel British.

'Your ingenuity reminds me of a younger version of myself,' Mango began. 'After I got home, I sat in bed reading a bunch of old news articles about the Rock Spring High bombing.

'Some things didn't make much sense. For instance, why would a smart individual like you make a bomb, but make no attempt to destroy the explosive residue or hide the rest of the explosives? And why bother slashing someone's tires to make them late for school, so that you – a smallish thirteen-year-old – can sneak into a high school and place explosives inside a locker . . .'

Charlie finished Mango's thought. 'Why plant the bomb in Deion's locker in a busy high school hallway with CCTV cameras, when it would have been easier to place a bomb under his car?'

Mango shook her head. 'You got framed?'

Charlie was so used to not being able to protest that she shuddered and went on a tangent. 'You said the FBI busted you for hacking. So, you know how it is: they put you in a room. You've hardly slept. You're scared witless. Then they tell you you'll get two years if you confess, and thirty if it goes to trial.'

Mango looked slightly tearful. Charlie was impressed by Mango's intelligence and liked having one more person in the world who didn't believe she'd half burnt two people to death.

'The Janssens?' Mango asked.

'Who else,' Charlie said. 'My friend Harry – the skinny guy you saw me with at Makers Yard on Saturday – wants to go after them. I just want to put the crap behind me and start fresh.'

'My wife, Veryan, and I started Radical Cake Collective in a unit in one of the Janssens' strip malls,' Mango explained. 'Their property manager was awful. Extra charges for lighting improvements that didn't happen, a leaky roof that damaged a four-thousand-dollar oven, cockroaches and mice coming through from the unlet unit next door.

'When Veryan was pregnant with our oldest, the site manager said we were troublemakers. She grabbed Veryan and threatened to push her down the stairs leading to her office. I took photos of Veryan's bruises, but the cops couldn't have been less interested.'

'Your wife could have miscarried or something,' Charlie said, horrified.

Mango nodded, then strained as she pushed against the desk to haul herself up.

'Do you need an arm?' Charlie asked anxiously.

'Could you rescue my shoes from under the desk?'

Charlie leaned under the desk and flicked two worn pool shoes, which Mango struggled to put on.

'Everything's swollen,' Mango said, holding her back. 'My feet look like footballs.'

'When are you due?' Charlie asked.

'Nine weeks, and twins for my sins,' Mango rhymed, as she headed for the door. 'Now I know you're more into science than cake-making. So I'd like to show you something.'

Mango held on to both handrails as she led the way down to the first floor. They rounded the end of the stairs, and Mango unlocked a door signed DEVELOPMENT KITCHEN 2.

'Hope you can keep secrets,' Mango said cryptically, and led the way in.

'Is this where you . . . ?' Charlie asked, but was struck dumb by what she saw.

The brightly lit counter along one wall had everything you might expect of a space where cake recipes got tested: sinks, mixers, microwaves, weighing scales and metal shelving with commercial-sized tubs of icing sugar and colourings. But the opposite cabinet was obscured by some much more advanced gear, mounted on wheeled trolleys.

'You know what this is for?' Mango asked.

'Gene editing,' Charlie said, feeling tense, as she racked her brain to think what use this gear would be in a bakery. 'Do you use genetically modified yeast?'

Mango smiled. 'Yeast was one of the first things to be genetically modified; most bakers have been using it for more than a decade. But we buy that in big tubs, off the shelf.'

'So . . .' Charlie said, warily inspecting a large gene-sequencing machine. 'Is this legal?'

'For now,' Mango said. 'Because of SNor, Congress is rushing through legislation that will require sales and ownership of sequencing and gene-editing equipment to be registered. But, as we stand here, the only thing that's illegal is unlicensed editing of human DNA.'

'So you could make something like SNor, in this room, with this equipment?'

'Easily,' Mango said. 'One of the scary things about synthetic viruses is that they're relatively simple to create. I could swab samples of SNor from public restrooms all over town. Then I could alter a few genes to reshape the outer proteins and make a new SNor strain to which nobody would have immunity.

'I'm no virus expert, but there will be websites and published scientific papers with all the technical information I'd need, and forums on the dark web where people have already posted prototypes and ideas for new SNor strains.'

'This is hidden at the back of a bakery,' Charlie said. 'So the gear may be legal, but I guess what you're doing with it isn't . . .'

Mango smiled as she propped her bulk against a counter. 'I originally trained as a physician,' she began. 'I drifted into genetic medicine, working on trials of skin cancer therapies in Boston and London. But at the same time the technology that enabled same-sex couples to produce viable embryos was starting to become reliable. So, instead of lesbian partners having to use a male sperm donor, or gay men having to use a woman's egg, I could fertilise one of Veryan's eggs using my own DNA.'

'Pseudo sperm and hijacked eggs,' Charlie said. 'I've heard

about them in the news, but it's still illegal, right?'

Mango nodded. 'It remains illegal in the United States, much to the chagrin of same-sex couples who feel it's their right to mix their genes and produce true offspring the same as everyone else. After Veryan gave birth to our older son, I repeated the procedure for a couple of close friends.

'Over a couple of years, that developed into a successful, if illegal, business. Besides producing offspring for single-sex couples, I've diversified into other genetic modifications. For instance, embryos can be given additional traits, so that children have a certain eye or hair colour, or you can determine a child's sex, or eliminate single-gene defects that cause serious illness.

'There's also gene therapy, which modifies genes in the cells of living humans. Some gene therapies, such as regenerating macular cells to cure some types of blindness, are now routinely performed in hospitals. But less essential treatments, such as those that alter melanin production to give someone a permanent tan, reduce strong body odour, or increase muscular strength or lung capacity in athletes are still illegal.'

'So you do all that stuff?' Charlie asked. 'Super athletes, designer babies . . .'

'I started doing extra projects to finance expansion of the Cake Collective,' Mango admitted. 'We've created a lot of jobs in the community. Veryan and I are proud of Radical Cakes, but it has never made huge profits. We'd never have expanded to premises this size, or moved to our nice house, without the extra income.

'I have a small, affluent client base. All my patients come through personal recommendation. An actress who wants a permanent perfect tan, or a teen basketball player who wants to be three inches taller and thirty per cent stronger will happily pay twenty to thirty thousand dollars for a personalised course of gene therapy.

'There are labs in India and China that charge a tenth of what I do, but I have a reputation for excellent work. Botched gene therapy runs a high risk of tumours and other complications, and I'm sure you've seen online pictures of designer babies gone wrong.'

'Horrific,' Charlie said, curious but also a little scared. 'Have you ever had any kind of ...'

Mango shook her head. 'I use the latest equipment and do all my work twice over. If two altered DNA samples aren't a perfect match, I start the entire job from scratch. Even the latest Gen-9 equipment doesn't eliminate minor errors when you splice DNA, but the chances of the same error occurring in two consecutive samples are thousands to one.

'But if you send your DNA off to some dark lab in China, pay with Bitcoin and get your gene-therapy drugs back in a padded envelope three weeks later, how can you be sure they've done the work properly?'

'I can't believe people would take that risk with their bodies,' Charlie said. 'What about the moral side? Like, it's basically cheating if an athlete has their genes enhanced? Or cultures where everyone wants male babies, and you end up with an entire generation of horny single men?'

Mango laughed. 'I like the way you phrase that! I'll do anything a client reasonably asks, except for z-mods,' Mango said.

'I've not heard of those,' Charlie admitted.

'Z-mods will be huge,' Mango predicted. 'They're a range of gene therapies originally developed to alter brain chemistry in bipolar and severely depressed patients. However, they effectively make a person permanently high. The Z stands for *zombie*, because that's what you turn into if you're always happy.'

'I'm so out of touch after being locked up,' Charlie admitted. 'You can only use the web in the White Boulder library, and only for life skills or a specific school project. And because I was in for bomb-making they let me do college-level math and language courses, but the warden banned me from advanced chemistry or biology.'

'The genetic patterns for z-mods were only leaked on the dark net six weeks ago,' Mango explained. 'They were designed to help people who are institutionalised by mental illness, but I suspect a lot of people will pay a few thousand bucks to live in a permanent state of bliss.'

'So why are you trusting me with all this?' Charlie asked.

'You drifted on to my radar, but I've been seeking someone like you for months,' Mango said. 'Gene modding work requires precision and intelligence. Pregnancy messes with your body and your brain. Right now, I'm a swollen mess, who gets hot flushes, leaves instant noodles to go cold in the microwave and forgets where she parked her car. And when that's over I'll have two tiny humans that will wreck my sleep patterns for years. So, Mango needs a lab assistant who learns fast.'

Charlie felt wary. She'd always loved anything to do with science, and gene editing was the most dangerous and exciting stuff out there. But she'd face years in White Boulder if she was caught.

'I *have* to stay out of trouble,' Charlie said after a few seconds' thought. 'From my life so far, I want to be the most boring, ordinary, well-behaved kid. I want to work hard, get top grades and earn a scholarship to a top college.'

Mango nodded. 'I don't want to pressure you,' she said. 'You've not seen anything illegal. You can't prove any of the things I've said I've done. And you're the last person who'd go running to the cops.

'But if you come aboard, the risk will be well rewarded. I'll pay a hundred and fifty dollars an hour. Maybe one evening per week, and five or six hours every Saturday or Sunday. That will give you twelve hundred a week, tax free. That's enough to buy a car, to have nice clothes and build a nest egg so you can study at college, rather than kill yourself working two jobs.'

'I've never had nice stuff,' Charlie admitted. 'But I've never studied synthetic biology. I don't know anything about designer babies, or gene therapy.'

'I can teach you, and for the first few weeks I'll be right alongside you. It's more complex than teaching a new employee to make an lime muffin, but it's a laboratory process that can be broken down into simple steps.'

'Can I think this over?' Charlie asked.

'For sure,' Mango said. 'But I know how curious minds work. You'll get back to OIL, log on to the WiFi and start reading articles on human-gene editing, then you'll look up the new laws going through Congress to see what the punishments are. Am I right?'

'Obviously,' Charlie said.

'Well don't,' Mango warned. 'The CIA uses a deep learning AI system that can scan a billion pieces of unencrypted web traffic per second. Even in privacy mode, your searches can easily be linked to you, and if the system links someone with your criminal record reading papers on human gene editing, it'll get flagged up to a human intelligence agent.'

'Really?' Charlie said.

Mango nodded. 'The government has had satellites and monitoring stations for decades, but in the last few years computer power and behavioural recognition tech has improved to the point where they can analyse *everything*. If you want to be a bad guy, data encryption is no longer optional. But I can loan you a quantum encrypted tablet, with a 5g hook-up and location masking.'

'Is that legal?' Charlie asked.

'First amendment says it is,' Mango said. 'So you're welcome to think, but there's a guy who works in the bakery. He's got an engineering degree. I've been considering approaching him for a while now. I think you have greater potential, but someone has to be trained in all the basic techniques before Junior is born, so I can't wait forever.'

'What if I let you know by Sunday evening?'

'Of course,' Mango said, smiling. 'And don't feel I'm forcing you. I'd much rather you said no than agreed to do something you're not comfortable with.'

31 D IN MATH

Harry's day went from bad to worse as he got collared by his homeroom teacher, Mrs Scott, on the way out of school. It was a repeat lecture about outside interests and *making best use of the many opportunities Queensbridge gives to pupils*, but Harry struggled to keep a straight face because his pal Anita stood behind Mrs Scott, flicking her tongue and making obscene gestures.

By the time Harry walked out, everyone else had had a five-minute start and he knew he'd be at the back of the line to get out of the student lot.

'Want to study for the math quiz at my place?' Anita asked, walking a couple of paces behind.

'I've got a million things to do,' Harry said grumpily.

'You got a D last Friday,' Anita said.

'Don't remind me,' Harry groaned, which made Anita spread her arms and break into song.

'D, dee, dee. Dee, D, D, dee, D, dee.'

'You're not funny.'

'I'm hilarious,' Anita contradicted. 'How's your Mad Bomber doing? Have you stuffed your hoo-hoo-dilly in her cha-cha yet?'

Harry stopped walking and spoke sharply. 'Look . . . we're cool, Anita. But sometimes you're too much . . . I've had a crap day and I need peace.'

'Sorry,' Anita said, staring at the gravel, hurting. 'But math is a core subject. They'll boot you out of Queensbridge if you keep getting Ds.'

'Is that a bad thing?' Harry asked.

Anita gave a wonky smile and backed away. 'We'll talk when you're in a better mood, Haribo.'

Harry grunted and gave Anita a wry thumbs-up. By the time he got in his Mini, traffic stretched from the street in front of Queensbridge Academy, down a curving lane and back to the edge of the parking lot. It would take at least ten minutes for the traffic in front to clear and the most annoying part was a second, completely empty exit lane that was for staff only.

'Autodrive, destination home,' Harry told the car.

The map on the centre console showed the route. Harry pressed the handover button on the steering wheel, and the car rolled itself a couple of feet before slowing to let Anita shoot past in her Mazda convertible.

'Call Ellie Gold,' Harry said.

The phone rang on a speaker in the centre console. Ellie's voice came through as the Mini joined the line of traffic.

'Wassup, champ?' Ellie asked.

'The universe sucks,' Harry said, half smiling. 'Is your boy Christian OK now?'

'He's fine, but Woody stuck a Lego brick in his ear. So that was another five-hundred-dollar trip to the emergency room.'

Ellie had four sons under seven. Harry had never met them, but Ellie's home life always sounded like a sitcom.

'Did you get my message about the tip off?'

'I tried to call you straight back,' Ellie said. 'Janssens are scumbags. But that story needs a heap of work to be publishable and they'll sue for sure.'

'But they won't have a leg to stand on if we do it right,' Harry said.

'The Janssens will find something,' Ellie said. 'Even if it's just an exchange of legal letters, it's a couple of thousand dollars in lawyer bills. If it gets to court, you're looking at twenty large.'

'I was thinking—' Harry began.

'Sounds dangerous,' Ellie interrupted.

'Let me finish,' Harry told him. 'The Fawn Janssen chair-whack video has already brought in four grand. I don't have time to go to California, but what if we used some of that money to hire a PI?'

'A private investigator?' Ellie blurted, outraged. 'Why are you so keen to spend my money today?'

'Nobody does proper journalism any more,' Harry protested. 'Twenty years ago, Vegas had three local newspapers, with teams of writers who'd have bitten Earl's hand off to investigate a juicy story about the Janssens. Now, it's all about scraping content from other sites, click-bait adverts and hoping some fat lady gets videoed hitting a wasps' nest with a broom.'

'It's not my fault people are cheap,' Ellie said. 'They'll eat ninety-nine-cent burgers with meat from God knows where. They pirate their favourite TV show, then complain when it gets cancelled. And they don't want to pay for quality news. The newspapers with proper journalists died, or got bought by billionaires, to go with their sports franchises and hundred-foot yachts . . .'

'My mum would spin in her grave if she saw the trash I put on the Vegas Local home page,' Harry reflected. 'And people like the Janssens are bribing every cop in town and *literally* getting away with murder.'

'Have I explained the super-lean business model?' Ellie asked.

'Three thousand times,' Harry groaned, knowing he was about to hear it again.

'We keep costs down by encouraging user-generated content. Elliegold Media will build a portfolio of profitable local news sites in the fifty biggest media markets. If we stick to my super-lean business model, in five to seven years I can have profitable local news websites in America's biggest advertising markets and a media company worth half a billion dollars.

'And, don't forget, when you bailed me out with the money from the Rock Spring bombing footage, your auntie's clever lawyer made sure that your one-third share of Vegas Local is convertible into five per cent of the parent company so that's . . .'

'Twenty-five million dollars,' Harry said as his car advanced out of the parking lot. 'But, apart from Vegas Local, how many of your other sites are currently profitable?'

'Palm Springs and Orlando are making money.'

'Retired folks love their e-coupons,' Harry laughed. 'What about the big markets? Washington, San Francisco, Chicago?'

'New York is close to breaking even,' Ellie said. 'And the super-lean model means that when we open a site in a new city our costs are less than a thousand dollars a month.'

'So what about Earl's story?' Harry asked. 'Can I at least make some calls and find out how much a private investigator would cost?'

'Harry, I need every penny right now.'

'You're broke *again*?' Harry said, sighing. 'I wish you'd focus on making our original, ten-grand-per-week-profitable Vegas

Local website great, instead of living in San Fran and trying to take over the world.'

'I'll ask if you still feel that way when you cash your cheque for twenty-five million,' Ellie said.

Harry tutted. 'I'm not holding my breath on that.'

'I'm truly sorry,' Ellie said, sighing. 'I value the work you do, Harry. You got that Fawn Janssen story up before anyone else in Vegas. It's making a ton of money.'

The ton of money hung in Harry's ears as Ellie hung up.

I don't care about money. But I guess that's easy to say when you live in a house the size of an aircraft hangar and your super-chef auntie buys you a $33,000 car the day you get your learner's permit.

Kirsten's gonna blow when she finds out I'm failing math. And Anita is ace at maths. When she asked if I wanted to study with her, she had nothing to gain. She was offering to help me out and I was rude. Why did I act like a grumpy dick?

Harry pounded the Mini's central armrest, then cursed when he realised that a car had broken down. The single-lane exit road was blocked, and idiots were honking, as if that was going to do any good.

In the end, Harry's ten-minute drive home from school took an hour. Kirsten's electric front gate opened obediently, but the roll-up door to the underground garage just made a weird grind and clunk sound. When Harry looked, he was baffled to see a hand trowel wedged in the door frame. The resistance was enough to trigger the safety mechanism and stop it from going up.

Why would the stupid gardener do that? Everything is shit today . . . Except that Charlie got a break, which is awesome . . .

Harry unbuckled and flung his door open. The fork was

wedged in hard and flakes of paint lifted off as he yanked the trowel and tossed it into a planting.

'All right, Harry,' a deep voice said, closing fast.

Harry sprang round, seeing a hulking, overcoated figure with wrecked army boots and a greasy man bun. He tried to scramble, but Man Bun had him cornered, yanking Harry's spindly arm behind his back, then crashing his forehead into the metal door.

'How are your balls?' Man Bun growled, dousing Harry with rancid breath. 'What's happened to your skin lately? I've seen leopards with less spots than you.'

As Harry squirmed, Man Bun located a big zit on the back of Harry's neck and popped it.

'You're like human bubble wrap,' Man Bun teased, squeezing another. 'I could spend all day popping these.'

'Piss off,' Harry moaned, twisting his head and getting his forehead bounced against the door again for his trouble.

Man Bun wiped pus and blood on Harry's school shirt, then tightened his grip until Harry's legs buckled.

'Sit,' Man Bun ordered, letting Harry go. 'Face me, legs crossed, hands on head like a good Queensbridge schoolboy.'

Harry shuddered and did as he was told.

'Lucky for you, the boss told me to take it easy,' Man Bun said. 'You're a man of influence, with your job at Vegas's number-one locals' website. I've brought you a nice juicy story as a peace offering.'

Harry peered up as Man Bun unlocked his phone. Man Bun tutted as he searched for something, finally flipping it round to show Harry a picture of an old Ford sedan with the front end obliterated.

'Happened a couple of hours ago. Some poor old guy. Truck

coming the other way swerved into his lane as he made his regular trip to the local bowling alley. Shattered pelvis, broken legs. Not sure if he'll live. You might have spoken to him. Went by the name Earl Everard?'

Harry closed his eyes and gagged.

32 BLOODY LOVE SCIENCE

Charlie spent the afternoon on her bed with the tablet Mango had given her. The unit was a brand-new $600 Vault Tab. It looked like a regular no-brand tablet that you could pick up in Walmart for fifty bucks, but it had hardware encryption chips and ran a version of Android designed for anonymous messaging and browsing.

Mango had sent through a bunch of links, and Charlie got sucked in as she read. Science had always been her escape. When Ed was screaming and Fawn was being impossible, when the trailer stank of unwashed laundry and there was no food in the cupboard.

Charlie would spend entire school holidays hiding in dens reading books and doing crude experiments. Getting top marks in school was the one thing that made Charlie feel that she counted for something, even if the other kids called her a geek.

Her first pre-teen fascination was dinosaurs, then space travel. She experimented with rockets, but when Charlie realised she had as much chance of saving $279 plus tax for a rocket-making kit as she did of being selected as the first woman on Mars, she became captivated with the idea of blowing stuff up with items she could buy for a few dollars, or shoplift from CVS.

For the first time in two years, Charlie had a free afternoon and unrestricted web access. Starting with links Mango sent, she read and watched videos on gene editing, scribbling notes, and struggled to finish anything because every topic threw up three more questions.

SNor had been a wake-up call to the world, but new infections had now dropped close to zero. The public had mostly decided they preferred not to dwell on something so depressing, but scientists realised it was the start of something much bigger.

Charlie read an article by a pessimistic virologist, who said that the ease of gene editing meant that some experimental accident or mad individual would wipe out the human population within fifty years. Others said simple hygiene procedures like hand-washing and UV sterilisation can make it very hard for viruses to spread, and there were optimists, pointing to the way that genetically modified tsetse flies had been used to eliminate malaria in parts of western Africa.

It remains a little-publicised fact that gene editing has already saved ten times more people from malarial deaths than were killed in the SNor outbreak.

Charlie read about governments panicking, banning all gene editing and forcing the registration of equipment and chemicals. Cynics said they'd have about as much success as governments had in their wars on drugs, and that it was more dangerous to have illegal underground labs than legal ones that could be monitored.

And while synthetic human viruses could be massively reduced with good hygiene, many scientists pointed out that viruses carried by birds, insects or rodents were much harder to control. Then there was the possibility of genetically altered bacteria, and a rumour that a Russian weapons lab had already developed a genetically modified fungus with reproductive spores that caused a severe allergic reaction and suffocated anyone that inhaled it.

Beyond the apocalyptic visions there were trashier stories too. Was a formerly pale TV star's perfect olive skin the result of illegal gene therapy? Had the athlete who broke the hundred-metre sprint record at the last Olympics used gene therapy after a tendon injury? Then there was the eccentric Indonesian cult leader who'd cloned himself six times and claimed that one day each of his children would rule a continent.

'I got your message,' Brad said cheerfully, when he stuck his head into Charlie's room, just after seven. 'Glad you're still with us.'

Charlie had been on her bed for three hours, and was surrounded by notes and the crumbs of three Radical Cake Collective muffins. Brad had done an after-school gym workout and wore black Nikes, and grey shorts. His T-shirt was balled up in his hand, and his torso glazed with sweat.

'What you studying?'

'Cake recipes,' Charlie lied, gathering her notes and hoping Brad couldn't see what was on them.

'Great idea to get some cash behind you,' Brad said encouragingly. 'And a bakery is a better way to earn than wading through slurry on my uncle's farm.'

Charlie hadn't a hundred per cent decided to accept Mango's offer, but the science fascinated her and the money would be life-changing. There was still part of her that wanted to be an ordinary teenager and stay out of trouble. But the odds were stacked against kids like her, and having a pregnant pink-haired lady for a boss, who ran a company that made trendy iced muffins, made the dark path seem less intimidating.

'Didn't you shower at school?' Charlie asked, feeling obliged to complain about Brad's funk, while actually being quite turned on by it.

'Betsy wouldn't start again this morning,' Brad explained, as he eyed the muffins. 'Just ran from school.'

'You can have one. Mango gave me the whole box and I've already made a pig of myself.'

'I saw these in a shop. They're seventeen bucks for four,' Brad said, outraged at this until he took a bite and moaned. 'Papaya and passion fruit . . . There's a party in my mouth!'

'Best muffins ever,' Charlie agreed.

'You'll wind up hating the sight of them if you're making them all day,' Brad pointed out.

'Let me taste a tiny piece of the papaya one,' Charlie said. She put the tablet and notes on her bedside table and knee-walked across the bed.

Brad broke off a piece of muffin, making sure it had plenty of the gooey passion-fruit filling, before holding the sticky blob at the end of two fingers a half-inch from Charlie's lips. She'd wondered if the night before had been a one-off, but this was clearly more than an offer of food and she craned slightly, biting the muffin, then gently sucking his fingertips.

Charlie wondered if she looked sexy or gormless as she stared up Brad's arm at pumped veins and boyishly hairless skin. Her breathing sped up as Brad put a hand on her leg.

'Gotcha now,' he said, smiling as he pulled the front of her T-shirt and sprinkled muffin crumbs down her cleavage.

'You dick!' Charlie protested, squirming as Brad pinned one arm, leaving the other free. She gave him a gentle slap. 'Big bully!'

Charlie liked his weight pressing on her, and the sense that he was messing about but strong enough to do anything he wanted. He looked down, keeping eye contact until it got uncomfortable and she laughed.

'You're crazy, Brad.'

'Shall I go back across the hall?' he teased.

Instead of answering, Charlie leaned back and relaxed her body. Brad got the message, and closed in for a kiss.

• • •

Harry stumbled to the shower, crying as he stripped off. The water washed blood off his neck. After his previous encounter with Man Bun, he'd had nightmares and spent days jolting at every strange noise. This time he was more angry than fearful, thinking how pathetic he must have looked, cross-legged at the garage door and too puny to stick up for himself.

Harry hated his skinny limbs and blotchy red skin. He hated his D in math, his Saturday detention, Queensbridge Academy and being too chicken to put his arm round Charlie's back when they'd strolled the Swallow Park lakes.

Dad said I could live with him now he's back in London. But I'd lose Matt, and Kirsten, and Vegas Local. And didn't someone famous say running away just moves your problems to a different place?

The fancy house had CCTV, but Harry wasn't surprised when he logged into the monitoring app on his phone and got a green SYSTEM INTERRUPT – DRIVE MISSING screen. He knew he ought to be studying for tomorrow's math quiz, but could barely understand it even when there weren't six other thoughts screaming for attention.

So Harry froze on his bed, staring at a cobweb on the ceiling. He tried to calm his breathing, but thoughts fluttered between wishing he'd never existed, wracking his brains trying to think of ways to destroy the Janssens and visions of beautiful girls who'd never go near him.

Harry's cell was next to him on the bed, ringing, but he didn't feel like talking to anyone and only weakened on the fifth ring, answering without looking at the display.

'Yeah,' Harry said, a touch surly, predicting Matt or Charlie and not feeling strong enough for either of them.

'Hiya, Harry,' a woman said brightly. He didn't recognise the voice, but it had a quality that was eerily familiar. 'This is Fawn Janssen.'

Harry shot up and got this creepy feeling, like his bedroom walls were about to get hauled up, revealing a studio audience that was laughing at him.

'Need a favour,' Fawn said. 'Been having a spot of bad publicity . . .'

'It's too late to take the story down,' Harry said warily.

'You sound scared of something, Harry,' Fawn teased. 'And I'm not dumb – I'm not asking you to undo the undoable.'

Harry wanted to tell her to get screwed and cut the call. Just thinking what she'd done to Charlie made him sick.

'What *are* you after?'

'Good publicity,' Fawn said. 'JJ's at our house, resting after his operation. I thought Vegas Local could run a nice puff piece, where you come along and interview us.'

'I can put that on the home page, but nobody will read it,' Harry said bluntly. 'I've run hundreds of different stories on Vegas Local and I know what doesn't click with the punters.'

'Don't you want to be nice to me, Harry?' Fawn purred menacingly.

I'm never going to beat the Janssens in a fight, but what if I could get them to trust me?

'I didn't say I wouldn't do it,' Harry said sourly. 'I said, nobody would read it. People can sniff out a bland puff interview. You need a hook to draw them in.'

'Then find a hook,' Fawn snapped.

Fawn crushed her own sister. Fawn can squash me like a bug. What the hell do I say . . . ?

'People love seeing inside their rich neighbour's houses,' Harry blurted finally. 'That way you sneak your wholesome message in. I can do a short interview, pictures of your chandeliers and fancy stuff, pictures of you looking nice. If you or JJ have any swanky cars, park 'em in front of the house and you'll draw in clicks from men too.'

'My yellow Lamborghini?' Fawn suggested.

'That'll work,' Harry said, hooked on the idea of photographing a fancy house, until he remembered who it was for and why he was doing it.

'It's a neat idea,' Fawn said. 'I'd heard you were smart. And how's my kid sister faring?'

'Not bad. She'd really like to see Ed.'

'I'll think about it,' Fawn said, though her tone made it clear she wouldn't. 'I'll look at my diary and message you some possible dates for the photo shoot. And be sure to give my best regards next time you hang with Charlie.'

Harry heard a sly cackle as Fawn hung up, and the image of Cruella de Vil in the old *101 Dalmatians* cartoon came into his head. He realised how tense he'd been when he saw the back of his phone smeared with sweat.

'Bastard Janssens,' he shouted, throwing a big punch at his mattress. Then Harry muttered under his breath, as if he was trying to convince himself, 'Nobody's unbeatable. There's *got* to be a way to get them.'

33 EARLY BIRD

'You normally need an atomic blast to get you out of bed,' Kirsten told Harry. 'What happened?'

Kirsten was dressed in a silk Algarve Casino-branded robe, holding her first coffee of the day. It was only a quarter past seven, but Harry had his school uniform on, and stood at the counter checking his bag.

'English lit, English lit textbook, Spanish, math, clean gym kit.'

'Earth to Harry?' Kirsten said. 'Come in, please.'

'Ellie called me,' Harry explained. 'He's on a super-early flight from San Francisco. He wants to meet me before school.'

'When did that happen?' Kirsten asked.

'Midnight.'

'You're spending so much time on Vegas Local and talking to Charlie,' Kirsten said, keeping her tone bright so that Harry didn't accuse her of repeating her usual moan. 'You'd better not be letting your schoolwork slip.'

'Would I, Auntie?' Harry charmed, smiling guiltily as he dashed round the counter and gave Kirsten a goodbye kiss. 'Love you, gotta dash.'

Harry wondered why Ellie had called him in a late-night panic as his Mini shot down the Beltway, with the sun low on the horizon and barely a car in sight. Ellie had made the midnight call with a bawling toddler on his lap. He'd refused to go into detail, but he told Harry to make sure he was on time and that it was regarding a business deal that would *make all our lives easier.*

Huddy's was a popular diner, close enough to McCarran International Airport to be populated with the high-vis jackets worn by aircraft mechanics, ground staff and in-flight caterers. Harry had to circle twice to find an empty bay, something that hadn't troubled the huge Rolls-Royce Phantom blocking three disabled spots in front of the main entrance.

Harry's morning appetite was tempered by angst as he pushed through bodies queuing for breakfast bagels and take-out coffee. The air was dense with talk and hissing deep-fat fryers as he cut between busy tables, his youth and Queensbridge Academy blazer drawing glances as he picked out Ellie's thin white shirt, yellow tie and shocking dispersion of red hair. An older, somehow familiar man sat facing him.

Harry wasn't late, but empty breakfast plates and half-drunk coffee mugs suggested that he hadn't been invited to join from the start.

'Here's my boy wonder,' Ellie said, sliding into the booth to make space.

Harry felt like he'd been kicked as he linked the man to the Rolls out front. *I'm gonna open my eyes and Kirsten will shake me awake.*

'Jay Janssen Senior,' he said, stretching out to shake Harry's hand. 'Heard you're a young mover and shaker, Smirnov.'

Harry felt queasy, crunched by a big old hand as he settled

on the bench. Janssen was seventy-six, sporting a denim shirt and bolo tie, his ink-blue cowboy hat on the table beside him.

'I . . . Umm, hello,' Harry said, realising that Ellie knew nothing about Earl's accident, or Man Bun's visit.

'I admire someone like you,' Jay told Harry. 'World's full of kids expecting everything on a plate, my two boys included. When I was your age, I was buying and selling cars. Making more money than my old man by fourteen. School was a drag, so I stopped going. When my pa whipped me and made me go back, I got myself expelled.'

Harry smiled uneasily. He sensed he was being softened up. Ellie must have told Jay that he was earning good money and didn't like school.

'You can relate to that, can't you?' Ellie asked.

Harry looked over at Ellie as he noticed the two hulking figures at the table behind. Apparently, the elderly tycoon had too many enemies to go out unaccompanied.

'So what got you rushing here on a 5 a.m. flight, boss?'

Harry had asked Ellie, but Jay answered. 'The *Vegas Mirror* is the only newspaper left in town, and it's owned by that streak-a piss Kent Clark. It tramples my family name every chance it gets. But, thanks to you guys, *Vegas Mirror* only has the second-biggest Vegas news website.'

'Mr Janssen has offered a long-term deal, for Janssen Corp to become Vegas Local's biggest advertising partner,' Ellie explained, his voice wavering because he knew Harry would be furious. 'The money will fund Vegas Local and Elliegold Media for the next five years, at the end of which Jay will have an option to buy Vegas Local outright for twenty-five million dollars.'

My one-third of twenty-five is . . . Well, three eights are twenty-four, so it's eight point something . . .

'But won't it affect our independence?' Harry asked, riled. 'We'll lose credibility if we're taking Janssen money.'

'Credibility?' Ellie said, smirking. 'We're hardly *The New York Times*.'

Harry realised that wasn't a strong argument, and stabbed anxiously at another. 'I thought you were talking to venture capitalists about investing money.'

'Cool down, Harry,' Ellie said, smiling awkwardly and making an *it's fine* gesture at Jay Janssen. 'If I take money from outside investors, I must give them shares in the company, and I have to clear all the big decisions with them. If I make this advertising partnership with Janssen, you can carry on running Vegas Local and I can build Elliegold Media without interference.'

Harry narrowed his eyes and decided to be bold. 'Except I get my head kicked in if I say anything about Janssen Corp?'

Jay grew larger in his seat, but Ellie spoke before he got to say anything.

'I've got four kids,' Ellie said, raising his voice, then lowering it because there were people all around. 'Your deal gives you a generous cut of the advertising money from Vegas Local, and it's basically pocket money. All I'm taking is a small salary, so that Elliegold stays afloat. I don't have health insurance; six of us live in a tiny two-room apartment. My car is eleven years old. I have one pair of sneakers and my only pair of dress shoes leak when it rains.'

If I get into bed with Jay Janssen, Charlie will never speak to me again ...

Jay cleared his throat and sounded stern. 'Mr Gold owns a majority share in Vegas Local and its parent company,' he began. 'The contract your family lawyer drew up when you invested in Vegas Local gives you a right to a share of all advertising revenue if you run the site, and a right of *reasonable consultation* over any change of ownership. But you are only a minority shareholder...'

Harry got where this was going. 'So you got here before me, you had breakfast, made a deal and Ellie can outvote me no matter what I say.'

'I want you to stay on the team, Harry,' Ellie said. 'You have an instinct for great stories. If I could click my fingers and make money rain from the sky, I would. But I have to make a deal with someone, and this is the best on the table.'

Ellie's always been good to me. It must be tough raising four kids with no money. I don't agree with his business-model bull crap and national expansion plan, but he works seven days a week and deserves financial security . . . But why did it have to be Janssen?

'Ellie tells me you're one of the biggest factors in Vegas Local's success,' Jay said, dabbing his mouth with a napkin. 'But I can get someone in to take the strain off if you like.'

'Or you could take on a different role,' Ellie suggested, trying a reassuring smile that came out creepy. 'You may be young, but you know what people want to read. The start-up sites in other cities need that.'

Jay nodded. 'My daughter-in-law, Fawn, thought your idea for a photoshoot at their house was genius. And I remember the frustrations of being a sixteen-year-old. Tell me what kinda girl floats your boat and we'll make sure your new assistant makes you a *very* happy boy.'

Harry felt patronised and shot out of his seat. His first instinct was to tell everyone to go to hell and storm out, but Harry was too placid for tantrums and he knew Ellie was just putting his family first.

'The world is full of lives that don't matter,' Janssen said, jabbing a fat pointing finger towards Harry. 'Things have happened in the past that you don't like, but I'm as loyal to my friends as I am ruthless in dealing with my enemies. So why don't you sit that ass back down and see if we can work things through?'

Harry thought of Earl and Charlie and seventeen seniors dying in hospital.

'Ellie, it's your company,' Harry said, shrugging and starting a turn towards the exit. 'You need to do whatever's best for your family and I need to get to school. I've got a math quiz to flunk.'

34 PATIENT Q

Charlie felt helplessly smiley as she jumped off the bus and headed towards the giant sign over Radical Cake Collective's main entrance. Brad had made her happy. She didn't love him, and with his girlfriend in the picture things would probably get complicated. But the attentions of a guy who could be a model, and prospects of work and money made Charlie feel like she mattered.

After donning a hairnet and face mask, Mango met up with Charlie in Radical Cake's employee break room. Since her fresh start was underway, Charlie decided to be adventurous and try black coffee. But even with three sugars it still tasted like battery acid. She thought throwing it away might offend and hid a grimace every time she swallowed.

Mango had made Charlie a series of lesson plans, like the ones she did for her groups at Maker's Yard. After ensuring Development Kitchen 2 was locked from inside, Mango showed Charlie a printed copy of a case file from which she'd blanked the names.

'Patient Q is thirty-two years old,' Mango began as she sat at a table facing Charlie. 'To help maintain security for my operation I don't meet clients directly. I use a retired nurse, who consulted with him in Anaheim a couple of weeks back. Patient Q is a single man who's made a lot of money with an online food business. But he lacks confidence and feels that his body isn't attractive. He's got pale skin with almost no pigmentation; he's also a classic ectomorph. Do you know what that is?'

'Scrawny?' Charlie said.

'Basically,' Mango agreed, smiling and nodding. 'An ectomorphic person is characterised by a slim body with little muscle mass. Most ectomorphs don't bulk up when they do strength training. So, after some discussion, I've agreed to edit two gene groups.

'One set of changes will affect melanin production and darken patient Q's skin. The second will change muscle fibres and increase muscle mass. It's a good example of a therapy that requires skilful patient matching. People with heavy musculature have also evolved heavy bones and strong tendons. But if you add Olympic muscle to a ninety-pound weakling, they end up with joint pain and injuries.'

'But most gene therapies are reversible?'

'They are,' Mango agreed. 'But every alteration carries a chance of a mistake, and increases the risk of mosaicism.'

'Oh, I read about that yesterday afternoon,' Charlie said.

Mango smiled. 'Show me what you've got, then!'

Charlie felt the pressure and turned a touch red. 'Each course of gene therapy targets and alters cells using a transmission vehicle such as a targeted E. coli virus, or stem-cell injection. But even after several courses of gene therapy, a tiny percentage of your original DNA will probably remain. Having two variants of the same cell type in the body can confuse the immune system into thinking one type is a disease, and the body starts attacking its own cells. Also, for reasons nobody understands yet, it gets more likely when you switch genes back and forth.'

'Not bad,' Mango said, satisfied with her recruit.

'I was looking for information on how these gene-mods are tested,' Charlie said. 'I can see that someone would be willing to try an experimental treatment that might cure terminal cancer, but there are hundreds of gene-therapy mods. Who tests the long-term effects and how can you know they're safe?'

'I'm very conservative,' Mango said. 'There are tens of thousands of gene-therapy templates that you can download and synthesise. I only do mods that people I trust in the online modding community have already tried, and I make it clear to my patients that even the best mods carry a one-in-four-hundred risk of autoimmune disease, or tumours.'

'So have any of your patients ever got sick?' Charlie asked, uncomfortable with the idea that a mistake might kill someone.

'All my patients get a sixty-day cocktail of autoimmune drugs. Mild side-effects are common after gene therapy and I know of a few that have got sick while the modified cells took over, but my only really bad result was an anti-obesity mod.

'It was designed to affect the hormones that create hunger. It was tested successfully by a Danish university. Unfortunately, all the test subjects were Caucasian and it turned out that it triggers cancer in some racial groups.

'I did it on a woman born in Peru and within weeks she started passing blood. She got rushed to hospital. The surgeon who cut her open said it was like she had thousands of tiny white teeth growing inside her digestive tract. There was nothing they could do.

'I felt awful and considered quitting the business. The family weren't wealthy and we offered to refund my fee to pay for the funeral. But the husband and daughter were very understanding. The woman was desperate to lose weight and my associate in California spoke with them before the treatment and carefully explained that gene therapy carries a chance of unexpected results.'

'I didn't realise a mod can affect different ethnicities differently,' Charlie said.

'When they first mapped the human genome back in the nineties, scientists thought genes were like rows of switches. A switch for blue eyes, or being short, or being autistic. There are a few genes that work like that, but most influence more than one thing.

'For instance, twenty genes have been identified that influence how tall a person could be. Then there's gene expression – which means different genes get switched on and off in the womb and early childhood. That's why some identical twins look different, though their DNA matches perfectly. Then there's the junk DNA every human carries. They named it that because it didn't seem to do anything, like corrupted files on an old hard drive. But it turns out it does influence certain things.'

Charlie's science-geek brain was ticking happily. 'So editing genes is easy, but you can't be sure what it will do, and the same treatment might do different things to different people?'

Mango nodded. 'The more we play around with DNA, the less we seem to know for sure.'

'So would *you* risk having gene therapy from an underground lab like this?' Charlie asked.

Mango liked the thoughtfulness behind this question and paused for a few seconds before answering.

'The risk of severe complications of a well-understood gene-therapy procedure done with proper safety precautions is less than one per cent. That's lower than the risk of a life-threatening infection after surgery in a hospital. So if I was like Patient Q and I suffered from depression, hated my body and was crippled by a lack of confidence I'd probably spend my twenty thousand dollars and take the risk.'

'Not sure I would,' Charlie said, shuddering. 'But then I don't even like going to the dentist.'

'Getting back to Patient Q, I do every procedure twice and if the two samples match I know that no random errors have crept in during gene editing,' Mango explained. 'So my plan is I'll do Patient Q's first sample and explain as I go. Then you can take over and do the second sample while I look on.

'Provided the two samples match, we'll grab lunch and when we come back I'll show you how we insert the altered DNA into an E. coli virus, and turn that into a stable solution that will infect the patient with his perma tan and manly physique.'

35 ALL A BIT CRUMMY

The plan had been for Charlie to ride a bus to the transit terminal. Harry would pick her up after his detention and they'd drive to a movie theatre, meet with Matt and Lana, catch an early showing then hang out at Harry's place until Charlie had to get home for her 6 p.m. curfew. But Ken Kleinberg had to approve any trip Charlie made, and he either didn't like the idea of her spending the day on the other side of town, or wanted to show who was boss.

Either way, Harry had to go to North Vegas again. He wanted to make the most of the day, so he set a 7 a.m. alarm and sat up in bed doing updates to Vegas Local, then he sorted books for his schoolbag, hoping to get most of his weekend homework done during the detention.

After a shower, Harry dressed in casual clothes, bagging his school uniform because Kirsten would realise he had detention if she saw him wearing it on a Saturday.

Things ran smooth until Kirsten knocked on Harry's door. He was on the end of his bed, battling a sock that had shrunk in the wash.

'Are you decent?'

'Yeah, come on in.'

Kirsten often came knocking to ask what food Harry fancied, or just for a chat. But her face wasn't friendly as she crashed the door and stormed in.

'I got an email from Mrs Scott at Queensbridge,' Kirsten said, shaking her tablet furiously. 'What the hell, Harry?'

Harry tried to play it cool, not sure if she'd found out about the detention, the D in math or both. 'What?' he asked dopily.

Kirsten's eyes bulged. 'I asked about your grades yesterday. Now Mrs Scott's saying that you're getting Ds in maths, and Cs in four other subjects. They want us to go in for an urgent academic review, and she's sent me a list of tutors.'

'The teacher's a dick,' Harry said. 'I'm usually good at maths, or above average at least. But this term . . .'

Kirsten riled up. 'If he's so bad, is every other kid in the class getting Ds?'

'Not exactly.' Harry squirmed. 'But . . .'

'Everyone has ups and downs at school,' Kirsten said, placing hands on hips. 'It's the lying that ticks me off.'

'What lying?'

'I asked yesterday morning, and you said your grades were fine.'

'I was in a rush to meet Ellie,' Harry said. 'I didn't have time to open this whole can of worms.'

'You're always in a rush,' Kirsten said. 'Charlie gets priority. Vegas Local gets priority. Hanging with Matt gets priority. But according to Mrs Scott your schoolwork is down the shitter.'

'Was that her exact phrasing?' Harry smirked, zipping his jeans and pushing his feet into sneakers.

'Don't get cute,' Kirsten warned. 'And don't think you're

rushing off across the city to see Charlie before we talk about this.'

Harry grabbed his bag, and the carrier with his uniform balled inside.

'Did you buy her more gifts?' Kirsten asked.

'I'm not going to Charlie till later. And the gifts were a one-off, because she's one of my best friends and she'd just got out of the joint.'

Kirsten backed up, blocking the door. 'You're not leaving until we've talked this through.'

'I have to,' Harry said firmly.

'No you don't,' Kirsten said.

Harry cast a downward glance. 'I have Saturday detention,' he admitted. 'Starts at eight thirty, so I need to leave now.'

Harry stepped back as a vein pulsed in Kirsten's temple. 'What for?'

'I was late for class,' Harry said, deciding not to lie outright, but be economical with the truth. 'I was in a side room doing stuff for the school newspaper and somehow I missed the bell.'

'Mrs Scott will confirm that when we have your academic review?'

'Don't you believe *anything* I say?' Harry moaned. 'I've been at Queensbridge two years and this is my first Saturday detention. It's not a huge deal.'

'All right,' Kirsten sighed. 'Go to your detention, then come back here.'

'That's when I'm driving to Charlie's.'

'You think?' Kirsten asked. 'Call Charlie and tell her you'll be an hour late. Then you're gonna drive your ass back here, and we're going to talk about this properly, before I go to work.'

Harry hated how his Saturday with Charlie was getting

more and more squeezed. 'She's got a 6 p.m. curfew. It'll hardly be worth going.'

Kirsten smirked. 'Don't go, then.'

'Bloody hell,' Harry said, looking hurt, as Kirsten let him out of the door.

'It's your own fault for lying to me,' she yelled, as Harry ran downstairs and scooped his keys off the kitchen countertop.

Since Kirsten now knew about the detention, Harry could have changed before leaving, but he wasn't thinking straight so he wound up in the school parking lot, sitting with his legs out of the car, switching trousers and buttoning his shirt.

Harry had forgotten his tie and gasped with relief as he sprinted to his locker and found a spare. It was 8.29 as he skidded through the door of a basketball court, settling behind a folding desk, as Mr Bowers locked the door to keep out latecomers.

Harry's hopes of catching up on homework were dashed. He had to spend the first twenty minutes in silence, filling a form with answers to questions like *Explain why you received a Saturday detention,* and *What are three steps you can take to modify your behaviour to ensure that this does not happen again?*

Once that was done, the teens were split into two groups of six. One half was given black bags and grabbers and sent on litter patrol. Harry was in the second group, dispatched to Queensbridge's theatre to sweep up the auditorium after the previous night's performance of *Cats*.

When Mr Bowers finally set Harry free, he jogged back to his locker, replaced the spare tie and squirted deodorant before hopping back into jeans and polo shirt in the deserted hallway. After the mad dash, Harry found himself buckled into the Mini's driving seat, locked in thought.

Kirsten will ground me and take the Mini away if I don't go home now, but she's probably gonna do that anyway . . . If I go see Charlie, she'll have gone to the restaurant before I get home, so I won't have to deal with her tonight, and she might have calmed down by then . . . Or she might go bat shit crazy . . . But I need to hear Charlie's voice. See her smile, catch her smell. And the way she sits with her head tilted and one eyebrow slightly raised . . .

Thinking about Charlie gave him a warm tingle as he spoke to the car. 'Autodrive, set destination Obama Independent Living.'

He ignored a call from Kirsten as the Mini headed north and defiance felt worthwhile when he pulled into the little lot behind OIL. Charlie had seen him arrive and dashed out for a tight hug. She looked so sexy it blew Harry away: lacy white mini dress, a brand new pair of white Converse and her hair was cut in a bob with bangs.

'Love the hair,' Harry said, grinning as they hugged.

'I got a hundred-dollar advance from Mango at the bakery,' Charlie explained. 'Juno took me to this place she knows and I got it done this morning.'

But it wasn't just hair and clothes. From the first day they'd met, Charlie always had a downtrodden wariness about her. Her smiles always cautious, her walk hunched. Now she was upright and bouncing in her dazzlingly white All Stars.

'You seem happy,' Harry noted, contrasting his own crummy day.

'Getting a grip on life,' Charlie said as she led the way in through OIL's back door.

They ignored the anti-virus gel dispenser and Charlie got a compliment on her new hair from one of the girls who lived upstairs.

'The only thing is my support officer, Ken, rolled up. He says he wants a five-minute catch-up, so if you don't mind waiting in my room?'

'Sure,' Harry said. 'I need a pee anyway.'

'It's not locked,' Charlie called, starting up the stairs.

Charlie's room looked more settled. The laptop he'd bought was on the desk alongside a neat stack of school books. He was surprised to see she'd got a tablet from somewhere and there was a bag with some just-purchased clothes at the end of the bed.

Charlie's bathroom was in a state, with balled-up underwear and the smell of lime shampoo. Harry kicked a soggy towel out of the way and imagined Charlie stepping from the shower as he saw little dried-up floor marks in the shape of her toes.

He washed his hands after peeing, but the only towel was the soggy one on the floor. Harry pulled a Huddy's napkin from his pocket and used it to dab them dry.

'Ken just wanted to check my movements over the weekend,' Charlie explained, stepping into the bedroom as Harry stepped on a bin pedal. 'Don't know why he was a pain about me coming to visit you. He's been OK apart from that.'

Harry felt like he'd been shot as he looked down to aim his soggy napkin into the tiny chromed bin. Amidst cotton balls, a toilet paper core and a pair of holed White Boulder-issue socks was a strip of golden foil Trojan wrappers and a used condom stuck to the can's liner.

36 SAMURAI COP II

'You gotta try these muffins,' Charlie said, taking a striped Radical Cake Collective box from the shelf above her desk. 'They're fifteen bucks a box in the shops. I'll be a whale if I keep eating them.'

'Had a big breakfast,' Harry said, trying to act normal while a hot poker charred his soul.

Brad? Who else could it be? Bet it was right there on the bed. Bet he had a big smile on his face. After everything I've done, she sleeps with someone else.

How pathetic am I? Skinny, spotty. Crushing on her for two years. Telling myself I'm giving her space and doing the right thing, but really just scared to make a move in case the answer is no.

'How was detention?'

'Two hours of my life wasted,' Harry said. 'Nice sneakers.'

Two years of my life wasted. How could Charlie do this? She must have known I have feelings . . . Or maybe she thinks I don't because I dicked about for so long.

'My hair feels so weird,' Charlie said. 'I catch myself in the mirror and I'm looking at someone else! Sit on my bed. Do you want a drink? I bought some of that English tea you like at Walgreens.'

She bought me tea. She cares about me. Maybe it was a one-time deal . . .

'I hope you don't mind, but Brad said he'd like to see *Samurai Cop II*. He's gonna come along, and Juno's seeing her dad now, but she's gonna meet us at the theatre. And Juno said there's a great taco place we might go to after.'

This sucks so hard. I can't breathe.

'Can I just get some water?' Harry said.

'Are you OK?' Charlie asked. 'You look hot.'

'Stressy day,' Harry said. 'Kirsten's not happy about the detention.'

And I blew Kirsten off, to come here for this . . .

'Harry,' Brad said cheerfully, coming in the half-opened door without knocking. 'How's life?'

You could have any girl you want, so why muscle in on mine? You're laughing at me, aren't you? I bet you've had a hundred other girls too. Charlie probably doesn't even mean that much to you, but you've stomped my life.

'Could be worse,' Harry said, wondering if Brad was going to kiss her or something. But there was just a glance between them, so clearly they were keeping it under the radar.

'I figured we'd take Betsy,' Brad said. 'Harry's Mini only has two doors, and there'll be four on the ride back.'

Harry felt like the walls were swaying as he stumbled into the hallway and placed a cup under the water cooler. He felt like running. *If I make an excuse now, I might get back home before Kirsten goes to work and I can beg for forgiveness. But imagine what she'll say if she finds out. The I told you so she's been waiting to dish out since the day I met Charlie.*

Harry ploughed on. He rode in Betsy's back seat, while Charlie sat next to Brad. He got introduced to Juno and her cousin in the lobby of a grotty fifteen-screen multiplex, bought his ticket and a stupidly large Coke. He sat next to Charlie, with Brad on her other side and when Charlie reached across to offer her bag of Hershey Drops, Harry caught her shampoo smell again and felt his eyes go blurry.

And, to cap it off, the movie sucked for two hours and forty minutes.

'We should get a ton of booze tonight,' Brad told everyone as they headed out. 'It's been a while since I got properly wasted.'

'You got a fake ID?' Juno asked.

'Confiscated when I was out with Mel,' Brad said. 'But the homeless chick behind Walmart is platinum. Give her ten bucks and she'll grab all the booze you can buy.'

'She ain't always there, though,' Juno warned as they exited the multiplex into a haze of rain.

'My curfew's six,' Charlie said, checking her phone and seeing that it was already almost four. 'And Harry needs to get back to Summerlin before sunset.'

'It's dark by six thirty this time of year,' Harry said. 'With Saturday traffic, I need to leave by ten past five.'

Brad gave Harry a patronising *calm down* gesture as they neared Betsy.

Die with a big spike up your rectum, you handsome dick hole ...

'Snacks,' Juno said, adding a clap. 'We need snack-a-dee-doodles.'

'You can buy snacks anywhere,' Brad said impatiently. 'There's a 7-Eleven next door to where we live.'

'Walmart's way cheaper,' Juno said.

'All right, we'll get snacks,' Brad said, tutting. 'As long as Betsy's a good girl, we've got plenty of time to get the hobo chick to buy us booze, beat Charlie's curfew and get Harry home before he turns into a pumpkin.'

It took less than ten minutes for the old Subaru to reach a small lot. It had a doughnut shop and an Italian restaurant that had both gone bust after the SNor outbreak. The restaurant's covered dining deck now housed four tents and a couple of scrap-built shelters. Electricity had been pirated from the nearest pole and the parking bays closest to the tents had scorch marks where residents had lit bonfires.

'Gimme money,' Brad said, turning to the three passengers in the back as he pulled Betsy's handbrake. 'Tell me what you want and keep it simple.'

Charlie handed Brad ten dollars and asked for some beers. Harry was in the middle seat, squashed between Juno's bulk and her ample cousin. As the cousins asked for the biggest, cheapest bottle of Vodka they could get, Harry pulled out seventy dollars.

'You're going home,' Charlie said.

'Might as well get booze in while I have the chance,' Harry said. 'I'll have some beer, plus a bottle of whatever vodka and a bottle of Jack Daniels.'

Brad laughed as he snatched the money from the driver's seat. 'Charlie said your auntie was rich!'

'Well, he drives a forty-grand Mini Cooper,' Juno pointed out as Harry flushed red.

'Are you rich, Harry?' Juno's cousin smirked, grabbing his knee. 'Please tell me you're single.'

Harry turned redder as Brad got out with the money and the three girls howled with laughter. Rain streaked down Betsy's windows as they watched Brad lean into a tent. A top-heavy woman in torn leggings came out, giving Brad a hug and a kiss on the lips that meant more than hello.

'Oooh,' Juno purred, her throbs of laughter rocking Harry. 'Dirty boy, Brad! I'd bet you my last dollar he's tapped that girl.'

'She looks at least thirty,' her cousin added. 'Bet she's on drugs or some shit.'

Juno shook her head. 'How does Mel stand his nonsense?'

Harry looked between the front seats and drew some satisfaction from Charlie's pained expression.

'Is he really that bad?' Charlie asked, looking round, trying to sound casual.

Juno and her cousin spoke in unison, 'Worse!' then cracked up laughing.

Serves you right, Harry thought.

The laughter died off as Brad got back in the car. 'I'll drive across to Walmart. You can buy your snacks and we'll meet Emily when she comes out with our booze.'

Juno and her cousin took ages wandering around Walmart and it was close to Christmas, so the queues were epic. The sun was precariously low as they got back to OIL. Harry got out of Betsy, and grabbed his carrier bag of booze from the trunk.

'Sorry my choice of movie sucked,' Charlie said, giving Harry a goodbye hug. 'I'm gonna keep working on my support officer. I'd really like to meet Kirsten, and your friend Matt.'

'Sure,' Harry said weakly. 'Maybe next weekend.'

37 DIRTY SHAKE

Harry felt mournful watching Charlie and the others head inside to get drunk as he buckled up and told the car to drive home. Kirsten would be at work and the only thing he wanted less than their inevitable confrontation was an evening alone with his thoughts. He pressed a button on the central display to call Matt, who answered after a couple of rings.

"Sup, you big homo?' Matt asked cheerfully.

'Not much,' Harry lied. 'Just heading home from seeing Charlie. I scored a ton of booze if you're interested in coming to mine later.'

Matt laughed. 'Do you *ever* listen to a word I say?'

'Mostly,' Harry said.

'Lana's birthday? I've been talking about it all week. She thinks we're going bowling with her sister, but I've—'

'The fancy restaurant,' Harry remembered. 'I forgot. I've had a ton on my mind, with math, and Janssen, and . . .'

'Don't drink all the booze on your own,' Matt said. 'I've gotta dash. I'm at the cleaners picking up my suit.'

'Have a good night,' Harry said, looking at the road, then at the bag of booze down in the footwell.

Although the car was on auto, the law said drivers had to watch the road and react in an emergency. A siren sounded as Harry took both hands off the steering wheel, growing louder as he grabbed the bag and snatched the Jack Daniels.

The siren stopped as he looked back out at the road. Keeping one hand on the wheel, Harry clamped the bottle between his thighs, twisted the cap, then took a big slug. It burnt his throat and made him cough, but when his eyes stopped watering he saw a neon Shake Shack sign a couple of blocks ahead.

Arguing with Kirsten had nixed breakfast; the condom shock had crushed his appetite for lunch and the planned stop to get tacos had been replaced by the booze stop at Walmart. Harry realised that the only things he'd eaten all day were a few of Charlie's Hershey Drops in the cinema.

He double tapped the handover button to take back control, pulled off the road and joined a queue at a drive-thru window. He decided to pig out, ordering a large salted caramel shake, cheese fries and a double bacon burger. It took a while for the order to come through, and as Harry waited he realised there was no way he'd get home before sunset.

Driving while eating would mean getting home faster, but it was a big shake and a messy burger. He wanted to enjoy it, and he'd heard a bunch of people at school say that cops let you off with a warning if they stop you after dark, and you act respectful and say you felt ill and had to use a restroom, or got stuck in traffic.

So Harry rolled into a parking bay. The world still felt like a crappy place, but the hot food was comforting, and the shake soothed the burn from the Jack Daniels. It soothed it so much that he experimented, tipping his fries out of their paper cup, and replacing it with a half inch of whiskey and a scoop of milkshake.

He loved the sweet shake mixed with the heat of alcohol, and made himself another, this time half filling the cup with whisky, topping with milkshake and stirring. Harry ate the last of his burger, watching people coming in and out of the restaurant as the light faded and drizzle trailed down his windscreen.

'I love you, Charlie,' Harry told nobody, necking more whisky milkshake and sniffling loudly. 'I love you so much.'

'Calling Charlie,' the car said.

Harry knocked fries out of his lap as he reached for the centre console and cancelled the call.

'Bad car,' Harry said, stuffing escaped fries in his mouth as his eyes rolled. 'This milkshake is strong.'

Rather than mix more in the little French-fry cup, Harry took the big shake cup and glugged in a quarter bottle of whiskey. This mix was stronger than before and the first gulps left him bloated and a touch queasy.

'Why don't you want me, Charlie?' Harry sobbed, his head slumped on the steering wheel. 'Why am I such a loser?'

Harry dripped tears and felt sorry for himself, until he got a call. Ellie's name flashed on the centre console, but he was still suspicious. Kirsten might have asked him to call . . .

'Answer,' Harry sniffled after several rings. 'Hey, Ellie.'

'Harry, are you crying?' Ellie said, worried.

'All good,' Harry lied, fighting to sound normal. 'Good, good. I'm in the car, it's probably a weak signal.'

'I can't stop thinking about our meeting yesterday,' Ellie said. 'I feel pretty bad. The way Janssen treated you was patronising and I was an ass to join in.'

'And the fact you had the *real* meeting and ate breakfast before I got there,' Harry said acidly.

'I founded Vegas Local,' Ellie said. 'But it's your nose for a story that gives the site its voice.'

'Cheers,' Harry slurred, wiping tears out of one eye.

'I was blinded by the money,' Ellie said. 'I've been thinking about Janssen. Five rundown casinos and a bunch of strip malls doesn't add up to the kind of influence he's got.'

'You just worked that out?' Harry said, managing a laugh.

'He's definitely a drug dealer,' Ellie said. 'I hear he's into prostitution. And are you flunking math?'

'Maths,' Harry said irritably, hissing the S. 'In the UK we call it maths.'

'Harry, are you drunk, or crying, or what?'

Harry ignored the question. 'How do you know I'm failing maths?'

'I had this jokey message from Janssen this afternoon. He said he enjoyed meeting us yesterday and yada-yada. But he made a remark that he'll be more than happy to send one of his boys to have a word with your math – *maths* – teacher.'

'How does he know stuff like that about me?' Harry said, shuddering.

'He knows my wife's birthday too,' Ellie said. 'That's what I've been mulling, Harry. I want to put food on the table for my kids. But do I want a sociopath as a business partner? If we have a major disagreement, does Janssen back down, or do I find myself being dangled from a third-storey window by one of his goons?'

'Take his money, kiss his ass for a couple of years, then bail,' Harry slurred. 'The people you think are your friends betray you. Even the ones you think care about you.'

'And what he did to Charlie and Deion,' Ellie said, disgusted with himself.

'Charlie's a slut,' Harry shouted.

'Harry, I'm *really* worried about you,' Ellie said softly. 'Are you driving right now? What happened.'

'I'm pathetic,' Harry sobbed. 'I'm a loser.'

'I'd say the exact opposite,' Ellie said firmly. 'Harry, I want you to be safe. If you're driving, pull over.'

'I'm parked.'

'Great,' Ellie said, gasping with relief. 'But I want you to keep talking to me, and I'm going to get my wife to call your aunt, or someone else who can come and get you.'

'Kirsten will want to say *I told you so* and Charlie's probably got her legs wrapped around Brad as I speak.'

'Stay on the line, Harry,' Ellie said. 'I've been dumped by enough girls to know it's brutal. But if all those girls hadn't broken up with me, I never would have met my wife and made my four beautiful kids.'

Harry sniffed and laughed at the same time. 'You're *always* moaning about your kids.'

'You've got me there, buddy,' Ellie said. 'Now tell me where you're at.'

'I don't want Kirsten to come,' Harry said, pushing out words between sobs. 'Can you come?'

'I'm six hundred miles away in San Francisco. I'll call Sue-Ann, or if she's not home . . . I'm not exactly sure, but I'll find someone.'

'I'm at the Shake Shack in North Vegas.'

'All right,' Ellie said, before repeating the location to his wife.

'I really need to pee now,' Harry said, realising how drunk he was as he reached for the driver's door handle and missed. 'I love Charlie so much, Ellie. I should have put my arm around her last week . . .'

'Go inside and use the restroom if you need it,' Ellie said.

'Don't wander anywhere else, though. Someone will be there soon.'

Harry had to hold the door frame with both hands as he stumbled out of the Mini, then he cut through two rows of parked cars. As he neared the restaurant entrance two big guys in golf clothes were coming out. One said goodnight, and the other turned and walked backwards, making a phone gesture with his right hand.

'Golf, Tuesday. Tell that beautiful wife I said hi.'

The guy backed into Harry, stumbling drunkenly in the other direction. He was twice Harry's weight, and the skinny teenager stumbled and bashed his hip on a concrete trash can.

'Are you blind?' the big golfer roared.

Harry reared up, way bolder than if there hadn't been a pint of Jack Daniels in his bloodstream. '*I'm* not the brain-dead moron walking out of a restaurant backwards,' he shouted back.

The guy had psycho eyes and bunched his enormous fists. Fear sobered Harry up as he backed towards the restaurant's plate-glass window, with diners inside looking his way. Harry put his hands over his face, but the guy punched him ruthlessly in the side of the head. As Harry slammed into the glass, a left hook smashed his face.

'Any more names you wanna call me?' the guy roared.

But Harry didn't hear. He was out cold, with a broken nose and three loose teeth.

PART THREE
TWO YEARS LATER

38 FREE FLOOR MATS

Vegas Local

FRIDAY'S HOT STORIES

WORLD NEWS – West backs UK
government stance on LHV.

At his weekly White House press briefing, President West repeated his support for the British government's position on the London Haemorrhaging Virus.

Despite nine thousand deaths in the two weeks since the synthetically engineered Ebola-like virus first appeared in the British capital, the UK government has refused to pay the £1 billion ($1.45 billion) the MGB group has demanded for the genetic template of a full antidote.

West said, 'The only thing more dangerous than a world filled with synthetic viruses, is a world where the people who make them can earn billions of dollars through blackmail.'

The president said sixty laboratories around the United States are working with the British on a vaccine, and that the CDC had robust systems in place for the manufacture and rapid deployment of 350 million anti-viral doses.

FULL STORY AND LONDON VIRUS LATEST

EXCLUSIVE VIDEO – Angry Minnesota woman smashes car through dental clinic after cancelled appointment.

SPORT – QB Janssen upbeat on NFL draft prospects.

Former Rock Spring High and Texas Midland Quarterback JJ Janssen says he remains optimistic about his prospects of being an early pick in next week's NFL draft.

Janssen's performances have been under scrutiny, with college coaches and former NFL players claiming Janssen's astonishing performances since his return from a horrific leg break are 'too good to be true' and may be a result of gene doping.

MORE, INCLUDING JANSSEN'S COLLEGE HIGHLIGHT REEL

VEGAS BUSINESS – Resorts braced for another quiet weekend.

The transatlantic flight ban is expected to result in another slow weekend on the Las Vegas strip.

Hotel bookings are down 30% on the same weekend last year. Resorts have slashed last-minute room rates by more than half. Along with the collapse in European visitors, fears that the London Haemorrhaging Virus may have already reached the US have led many to steer clear of airports and other busy locations.

A Las Vegas Hotel and Conference Association spokesperson said, 'Las Vegas is super safe and open for business.'

FULL STORY

COUPON DEALS – EXCLUSIVE Taco Ranch 30% off ALL food.

Come for hottest local news; stick around for Vegas Local's legendary coupons!

RED-HOT WEEKEND DEALS

VEGAS BUSINESS – Judgement leaves Elliegold Media clear for NASDAQ float.

A Nevada State judge ended a two-year spat between embittered casino moguls Kent Clark and Jay Janssen.

In a written verdict, Judge Marian Sanchez said she saw no wrongdoing when Kent Clark and British-born chef Kirsten Channing made an investment in Elliegold Media (the parent company of this website).

Janssen claimed that Ellie Gold reneged on a prior agreement to sell to Janssen Corporation.

Elliegold Media now outputs its successful blend of local news and discount coupons in 54 US cities and recently expanded into Mexico and Canada.

The business last reported quarterly profits of $6.2 million. The judgement clears the way for next month's share flotation, which could value the company at more than $800 million.

In an angry statement, Jay Janssen said, 'Kent Clark's control of the *Vegas Mirror* and Vegas Local gives him a monopolistic grip on Las Vegas media, which he has used to mercilessly batter the good name of my family and the Janssen Corporation.'

VEGAS HEALTH – Keeping kids safe from synthetic nasties.

As summer returns, the threat of lethal purple wasps, itchy neon mites, poison-claw rats and other genetically modified critters is set to peak. But experts say your kids can still play outdoors, if you stay vigilant and follow a few simple rules.

FULL ARTICLE

WEATHER OUTLOOK – Downtown Las Vegas

Saturday	Sunny.	High 97°	Low 68°
Sunday	Some cloud early on.	High 95°	Low 70°
Monday	Turning hotter.	High 104°	Low 83°

FULL 7-DAY FORECAST

39 BREAKING BAD

Charlie came down the steps of a thirty-nine-foot recreational vehicle, parked beneath the aluminium roof of a storage unit. She was seventeen now and wore blue nitrile gloves, jeans and a lab coat as she followed a thick yellow cable from the rear of the RV to a rusted electrical panel. Water dripped from a pipe above and Charlie feared a shock as she stepped tentatively into the puddle beneath.

'Can you believe this?' Charlie shouted, looking back at Juno's chunky frame in the RV's open door. Charlie found it hard to trust people after everything she'd been through, but she'd stayed friends with Juno, even after they'd both moved out of Obama Independent Living.

She took a rubber-handled electrical screwdriver out of her coat pocket and touched it against the fuse box's metal door. The bulb in the end of the screwdriver didn't light up, but she was still wary as she used the metal tip to open the fuse-box door.

The inside had a couple of dead spiders bouncing in cobwebs. Charlie checked carefully for live bugs before tapping the electrical screwdriver in several places to ensure she wasn't about to get electrocuted.

The metal cabinet had a main power switch, three high-voltage sockets and a row of fuses. A drip hit Charlie's arm as she studied the fuses. None were labelled, but the power sockets were linked to a bank of three switches along the bottom row. Two were on green, but one had blown out and flipped to red.

'OK,' Charlie told herself, nervously approaching the red switch and resetting the fuse by pushing the switch with the tip of the screwdriver.

'We have light,' Juno announced. But before her words were out, the fuse clicked back to red and the bulbs inside the RV died. 'What about the diesel generator?' she asked.

'It's not enough juice when all the equipment's running,' Charlie said. 'I'm gonna try another socket.'

Charlie pulled the high-voltage RV hook-up, then locked it into another socket. The lights behind Juno wobbled, but this time they stayed on.

'All righty!' Charlie said, jiggling her ass as she shut the fuse box. 'I didn't die!'

She felt drained and frustrated as she headed back into the RV. She'd done a full day at high school, followed by baseball training, a supermarket shop and a microwaved dinner. Then, while most seventeen-year-olds headed out for Friday-night fun, Juno had picked her up and they'd driven out to the remote storage warehouse for a lab session that would last into the early hours of Saturday.

'What was I doing when the lights went out?' Charlie asked herself as she peeled off her disposable blue gloves, dropped them into a trash can, then grabbed a clean set out of a wall-mounted dispenser.

Mango had moved her gene-editing lab out of Development Kitchen 2 a few weeks before the law made it illegal to own unregistered gene-editing equipment. Over the following year and a half, Charlie had worked in a variety of homes and shuttered retail units, before Mango came up with the idea of using an RV.

The vehicle had been purchased new, its double bed and TVs replaced by refrigerators, storage cupboards and an extra sink. Oak kitchen cabinets and homey décor in the main cabin had been retained so, when the lab equipment was stowed, anyone peeking inside saw nothing but a vehicle in storage, awaiting its owner's next expedition.

'Six jobs, two complete,' Charlie sighed, looking at rows of trays and bottled solutions.

Before Mango trained her, Charlie envisaged gene editing being done with a giant microscope and a miniature knife, slicing strands of DNA like a microsurgeon. In reality, once a client's DNA was extracted and modified genes printed, the chopping and cutting was handled by enzymes and involved nothing more glamorous than mixing two clear solutions in a test tube.

The creation of edited gene sequences required concentration and the mastery of some temperamental machinery, but once Charlie had done it a few dozen times it felt no more exciting than flipping burgers, except she earned twenty times as much money and faced serious jail time if the FBI burst in.

'When's Mango getting our new machines?' Juno asked irritably as she loaded a tray of glassware into a dishwasher and began wiping her workspace down with chlorine to avoid sample contamination.

'She says good gear is getting harder to find,' Charlie explained. 'Illegal equipment manufacturers used to get around it by adapting stuff used in other fields. But now a lot of that gear must be registered too. Printers and sequencers have to be smuggled out of China or built from scratch. Plus, the people manufacturing zombie drugs and non-targeted mods have the big bucks.'

'I thought we were getting two state-of-the-art eleventh-generation doodahs,' Juno said. 'This equipment is at death's door.'

'I complain every time I see Mango,' Charlie said as she dropped a bone-marrow sample into a DNA-extraction unit and locked down the lid.

Juno huffed. 'I bet Mango would shell out for newer equipment if she ever came and worked here herself.'

Charlie shared Juno's frustration but liked Mango and was willing to defend her.

'Mango does all the treatment plans and research on safe techniques,' Charlie said. 'And she's got the twins and two older ones to look after.'

'I've got a baby younger than her two,' Juno pointed out. 'If the power goes down again, I have to bounce no matter what. Patrick's sitter can't stay no later than one.'

'I'll finish and clean up,' Charlie said, loathing the prospect.

'You can't drive after dark yet,' Juno said. 'Paying taxis all the time ain't right.'

'I take the cab out of expenses. We both make good money.'

Juno worked slower and made mistakes when she was in a mood, and lately she was always in a mood.

When Charlie first met her, Juno was a straight-A student going for a Navy scholarship. But when that fell through Juno spiraled down. Dropping out of school and hooking up with Seth, a small-time crook with a violent temper.

Charlie cared about her friend, but she hated that Juno had

become the teen-mom cliché that people expect from girls who grow up in state care.

'You didn't put the music back on after the power went,' Charlie noted, hoping it would help Juno focus. 'I need noise to stay awake.'

Tunes helped an hour pass. Charlie got knocked out of her groove when she picked the wrong sample out of a warming cabinet. Getting a sample mixed up could have horrific health consequences and Mango had trained Charlie and Juno to follow strict labelling and task-separation protocols. But the screw-top bottle in Charlie's hand had no label at all.

'What's this, Juno?'

Juno looked up from a spinning centrifuge and seemed startled.

'Oh, that's mine,' she said, reaching out to grab.

Charlie would have accepted a labelling error, but they were almost out of syringes and a short time earlier she'd noticed there was only one sterile pack left in the cupboard, when there should have been two. She'd also noticed extra glassware in the dishwasher.

Charlie jiggled the sample, refusing to hand it over. 'What is this?'

'I had a sample jam in the sequencer. So I started from scratch, rather than find out it had gone wrong after I'd done another two hours' work.'

It was a credible excuse, but Charlie didn't buy it.

'If the sequencer had cooked one of your samples, you'd have moaned like hell,' Charlie said.

'OK, it's off the books,' Juno admitted. 'A private job.'

'Pardon me?' Charlie said, eyes growing wide. 'A job for who?'

'A guy Seth knows.'

'Some guy your boyfriend knows? Do you even know what you're making?'

'He's a personal trainer,' Juno admitted. 'It's a non-targeted therapy that boosts muscle and endurance.'

'There's a reason people save for months and pay ten grand for individually targeted therapy,' Charlie spat. 'Broad-spectrum gene edits have a massively greater risk of tumours or other long-term damage. And if they don't take auto-immune drugs and there's a reaction . . .'

'I'm making enough E. coli for a thousand doses,' Juno said. 'They sell for a hundred bucks a pop. Mine and Seth's half share comes to fifty grand. It's enough to get the deposit for a nice house, for my son, *your* godson. And this one job makes more than Mango pays me in three months.'

'I've been to prison once,' Charlie said, shaking a fist. 'Do you want to go too? Do you want to see Patrick dragged off by social services?'

'Mango is ripping us off,' Juno spat back. 'Two hundred fifty an hour for you, one fifty for me. Sounds like a lot when you compare it to working a register at K-Mart, but I'll bet she's making eighty or ninety thousand dollars from the six treatments we're doing tonight. We're doing all the hard work, and we're getting less than ten per cent of the money.'

'Mango's a qualified doctor. She pays all the expenses and you just got a five-thousand-dollar bonus,' Charlie pointed out. 'Most importantly, Mango shields us. She's our only point of contact. We never see clients. Mango and her wife were the only people who knew I was doing this work, until I told her I couldn't cope without an assistant and brought you in.

'Mango also encrypts everything she does online. Does this

random guy Seth met at the gym do that? Or did he download the gene sequence at home and bounce it to Seth's regular Gmail? It only takes one tiny slip for the Feds to sniff out a lab.'

'I don't know if he uses encryption,' Juno admitted. 'But Seth has kept my name out of it. He told his client that stuff is made by a guy he was with at Arizona State. And the previous two batches didn't cause any problems.'

'Previous two?' Charlie blurted. 'Juno . . .'

'I want a nice place to bring up my kid,' Juno interrupted. 'Somewhere in a gated development, with a good pre-school and full biosecurity, so Patrick can play outdoors when he starts walking.

'I was going to do a couple more batches to see how things went, then I was going to tell you about this and offer to bring you on board. You've said you're quitting this racket when you leave for college. But why not bank a couple of million, instead of a couple of hundred thousand?'

'Mango's been decent to me,' Charlie said.

Juno snorted. 'Mango just moved to a six-million-dollar house. Do you think muffins paid for that?'

'I trusted you,' Charlie said. 'Now you've made me feel like an idiot.'

'So, am I fired?' Juno said, dramatically ripping off one disposable glove.

'You're my friend,' Charlie answered, angry but with no idea how to deal with it. 'Patrick's my godson – I love him to bits. You're a great lab partner, but you *lied* to me. And you've put *my* freedom at risk without consulting.'

'You've got a blind spot where Mango's concerned,' Juno said. 'You should be on a percentage . . . And . . .'

'And what?' Charlie asked.

Juno sighed. 'I don't know why Mango's so tight about buying us decent equipment. Seth and I have been putting feelers out. There's gene-editing equipment available. The good stuff's not cheap, but after a couple more batches I'll have enough to buy a set-up better than the junk we're using here.'

'You want your own lab?' Charlie gawped. 'You've only been doing this for a year.'

'We could be partners,' Juno said. 'And you don't need to be a genius to do this. The patterns for every popular mod can be downloaded. We're lab monkeys, doing the same tasks, over and over.'

Charlie shook her head. 'I don't want to go back to prison. Maybe Mango could have paid me a fatter share, but she's shielded me from the risks that you're now taking. And I never wanted millions, just enough to pay my way through college.'

'So what now?' Juno asked.

Charlie looked at the unlabelled sample bottle she'd been holding the entire time. 'I suppose your personal trainer is expecting his delivery. Take it, finish the batch. But if you've got time to do extra jobs under my nose, you can damned well stick around and help me clean up.'

Juno looked remorseful as she took the sample. 'What about long term? Are we still friends?'

Charlie's vision blurred as she tipped her head back and looked at the ceiling.

'I've been at school all day,' Charlie said, sighing deeply. 'Right now, I need the energy I have left to get through this job list. Everything else can wait.'

40 LOVE SHACK

Harry's bed sheets were tangled and sweaty as he peeled them back. He kissed Gemma's shoulder and the pretty teen rolled over and whined.

'My uncle's barbecue wouldn't be so boring if you came.'

Harry flashed a cheesy smile. 'Harry would come, but he can't be bothered.'

'You're an ass,' Gemma said, grabbing and flinging a cushion.

Harry ducked and kept teasing. 'Will your hot cousin Cari be there?'

Another cushion flew and this time Harry caught it and flipped it back.

Gemma rubbed the bed. 'If you go to my family party, I'll make it worth your while.'

Harry wasn't tempted. 'Matt's on his way here,' he told her. 'Gotta shower and make myself beautiful for Axl's party.'

Harry stepped naked into his bathroom. His apartment was on the forty-third floor and the window over his jet tub had a prime view towards the Las Vegas strip. After peeing, Harry checked himself in the mirror.

Gemma had an annoying habit of clawing Harry's back

when they had sex and he turned round to inspect a bloodied, slightly stinging right shoulder blade. But these scrapes and a few acne scars from spottier days were Harry's only major imperfections.

After Charlie broke his heart, Harry used $26,000 from his Vegas Local earnings to have gene therapy on an epic scale. Seven changes to Harry's genome had more than doubled his muscle mass, strengthened tendons, enhanced respiration, subtly darkened the pallid complexion he'd inherited from his Russian father and reduced the output of the hormone that caused his acne.

The therapy came from a respected underground lab. On their doctor's recommendation, Harry had additionally paid for longer term enhancements that would reduce his chances of going bald, improve memory, eliminate susceptibility to several viruses, reduce the risk of early-onset dementia and – most crucially – repair a faulty section of his genome that gave him a one-in-four chance of developing bowel cancer by age sixty.

Harry did the whole thing behind Kirsten's back. She only found out when an auto-immune reaction made him pass out in school. She broke down in tears and grounded Harry for a thousand years, but Harry was fine after three nights in hospital, a change in auto-immune medication and a couple of weeks' bed rest.

He began outrunning Matt with ease, hit the weights to max his enhanced physique and started catching the eye of some seriously fit Queensbridge girls. Around the same time, Kirsten sheepishly asked Harry for the clinic details. She had the same cancer-causing defect as her nephew and while that got fixed she had a few other mods, including a controversial one that was supposed to slow down the ageing process.

Harry stepped out of the shower and kissed Gemma before she hopped into the cubicle to clean up. He was towelling off in his bedroom as Matt strode through the open door.

While Harry's fragile ego had led him to gene therapy, Matt had registered his unaltered DNA with the United States Athletic Federation and stood to lose a USC athletics scholarship if he had any mods done.

'Have you spent the whole day in bed?' Matt asked as he mischievously hooked Gemma's panties on the end of his pool shoe and flicked them deep under the bed.

'Not all day,' Harry grinned. 'I went to the kitchen and made grilled cheese.'

'I sent you a message after training,' Matt said. 'I changed the top story on Vegas Local and Reno Local to the Chinese soldier thing.'

Harry looked baffled as he took briefs out of a drawer. 'What Chinese soldier thing?'

'Your back's bleeding,' Matt pointed out. 'How can you not have watched it?'

'You said you'd handle this morning's updates,' Harry said defensively. 'I didn't get home from the house party till three. I've not seen the news all day.'

'Matilda,' Matt said, addressing their apartment's AV system. 'Open the Vegas Local home page on Harry's bedroom screen.'

The web page popped up on a big projector screen.

'Matilda, play the video at top right, full screen.'

The clip began after a *WARNING: Graphic Content* banner. It was taken from a surveillance camera in a bleak sports hall, draped with banners written in Mandarin. A time code in the top corner of the screen suggested the clip was a couple of years old. The video quality was excellent, but there was no audio.

Two outrageously broad-shouldered men in army camouflage were doing exercises, lifting giant tractor tires over their heads, while a tracksuited trio looked on.

'Where's this from?' Harry asked, as he squinted and saw that the men exercising had boyish faces and small heads.

'Remember that giant Chinese intelligence leak a few months back? When sixty million Chinese military files got dumped on a public server? Most were encrypted, but hackers have been crunching away and they've decoded videos and paperwork from an enhanced warrior programme.'

Genetically enhanced soldiers had been in the news a lot. The US government claimed to have only done theoretical research into the possibilities, but Russia had openly announced an enhanced soldier programme, and other nations were suspected of doing so in secret.

The subject was controversial, because a lot of voters and religious groups said altering human DNA was against God's will and should be banned. But pragmatists pointed out that the US Army would be in trouble if they went to war against a nation whose soldiers were seven-foot-tall hulks who could flip a car and run fifteen miles without breaking a sweat.

'Here comes the juicy part,' Matt warned, pointing to the bottom right corner of the image.

A small tracksuited woman holding a computer tablet was giving the two muscle men instructions. But something upset one of them. He set the five-hundred-pound tractor tire rolling violently towards a wall and approached the instructor. The clip had no audio, but it didn't take a genius to see that she was ordering the giant to return to exercising.

'If she's five feet tall, that monster must be close to eight,' Harry calculated.

'You certainly wouldn't want to shoot hoops with him,' Matt observed.

After a brief face-off, the pin-headed hulk grabbed the woman by the shoulders and yanked the arm holding the tablet.

'Oh!' Harry winced, as he watched the monster tear the woman's arm off.

'He rips it off like a chicken wing!' Matt said, smirking. 'They're calling him Chinese Chewbacca.'

'Matilda, go back fifteen seconds,' Harry said, so that he could watch and gasp all over again. 'Play at one third speed.'

The clip ended as the monster chased several other officials out of the sports hall, while the one-armed woman lay spasming in a pool of blood.

'Best of all, the Chinese government are saying the video is a fake created by Taiwanese agents,' Matt explained. 'So there's no copyright. We get to keep *all* the ad revenue.'

'Could it be a hoax?' Harry asked.

'Nobody seems to think so,' Matt said. 'The hackers have decrypted hundreds of other files relating to this warrior programme. You can't see what the warriors look like on that video, but they've released photographs that show how young those hulks are. Kids make the best subjects, because their bodies regenerate faster and soft bones adapt more easily to large scale genetic changes.'

'So that monster was a kid?' Harry gasped.

'Thirteen or fourteen. There are genetic templates in the decrypted files, which suggest they're experimenting with gorilla DNA. Apparently, gorillas are nine times stronger than men, and their genetic make-up is near identical.'

'Where does all this craziness end?' Harry said, mostly to himself.

'Too much scary shit going down,' Matt agreed. 'Did you hear from your relatives in London?'

'I Skyped with my granddad in Devon. He says everything is locked down. Everyone is supposed to stay at home apart from key workers like cops and medics. He was all stiff-upper-lip *don't worry, Harry, we'll all be fine*, but you could tell he was scared. And my nan came on and kept saying how much she loved me and that it was the first time she'd ever been glad me and Kirsten are so far away.'

'And your dad? Isn't he in London?'

'I've tried, but his phone's dead and he didn't answer my messages.'

'Bummer,' Matt said.

Harry shrugged. 'If I couldn't get through to my grandparents and cousins I'd worry. But my dad's shady. He goes off radar for months even when things are normal.'

Gemma stepped naked from the bathroom and yelped when she saw Matt.

'Jesus!' she squealed, hopping back into the bathroom and slamming the door. 'You could have warned me, Harry.'

Harry laughed as he grabbed a T-shirt, pulling it over his head and following Matt across the hallway to his bedroom.

He'd bought the swanky apartment with money he'd made selling some of his five per cent stake in Elliegold Media to Kent Clark. After a few battles, Matt's parents reluctantly agreed to let the besties live together for their last year of high school.

'Is your girl Lana coming to Axl's party tonight?' Harry asked Matt.

'I got *sooo* lucky,' Matt said cheerfully. 'Lana apologised to me, because she's got this girls'-night-out thing. I was all, like, *oh, that's so sad*. But inside I'm smiling my ass off, because Axl's big brother's party was total depravity and people are saying tonight is gonna be worse.'

'A ton of people who know Lana will still be there,' Harry noted. 'And you sobbed your little heart out the last time she ditched you.'

A shout came from across the hall. 'Harry, did you see where my underwear went?'

'Matt kicked them under the bed,' Harry called back.

'Tell your boyfriend he's a jackass,' Gemma yelled irritably.

'I didn't cry,' Matt lied, shaking his head. 'And at least I don't sleep with random girls who wait till you fall asleep and steal your Mini.'

Harry was enjoying the banter. 'At least I still have my licence, Mr Ninety-Miles-Per-Hour-Through-a-LIDAR-Trap.'

'I'm outta here, you guys,' Gemma said, sounding ticked off as she came out of Harry's room.

'Pat her down for car keys,' Matt joked as Harry stepped into the hall to say goodbye.

Gemma's hair was combed straight but still wet, and she wore denim shorts and a red sports tank with a big Nike tick stretched over her chest.

'Be cool to hook up again some time,' Harry said, making it sound like that wouldn't be a big deal.

He moved for a goodbye kiss, but Gemma stuck her hand in the way.

'I first met you when you were going out with Anita, and you were a nice guy,' Gemma said. 'But the muscle and the money have gone to your head, Harry. Acting like a sleazy jock doesn't suit you, and you're smart enough to know better.'

'Women be crazy,' Harry told Matt as the front door slammed.

But Harry was a lot less sure of himself as he strode on to his balcony. He felt dead inside as he leaned on the hot metal railing and looked at the sun fading behind The Strip's giant hotel towers.

He was eighteen years old. He had a sweet apartment, a lively sex life, an orange Porsche and a place on New York University's renowned photography course in the fall. But Gemma's words stuck in Harry's throat, because none of that stuff had made him happy.

41 INDUSTRIAL RELATIONS

Charlie had bought nice clothes and a few expensive things for her room, but, apart from Juno, everyone she knew thought she worked for the Radical Cake Collective, so she couldn't go flashing big bucks around. She'd bought a two-year-old Volkswagen after she'd got her licence and the car felt especially small as it approached the giant arched gates of Highgrove, one of Vegas's oldest and most prestigious gated developments.

After passing the gate, a black man in a breathing mask came out with a pressure hose, spraying Charlie's car with insecticide, then going down on one knee to blast the tires and the underside. As Charlie watched the milky solution drain down her windows, a call rang through the centre console. *Unknown number.*

'Charlie? It's Owen. I was at the Science Outreach day last week.'

'Oh, hey,' Charlie said, remembering giving her number to a tall ginger guy with a cuddly-mad-professor vibe.

'There's a place called Tenders downtown,' Owen said. 'It sells vinyl and coffee. My friend Seb is playing there tonight. I thought, maybe, you'd like to come by.'

'Ahh,' Charlie said as the masked man wiped insecticide

smears off her windscreen. 'It's kinda short notice, Owen. Maybe another time.'

'When are you free?' Owen asked.

The masked man waved Charlie's VW forward. As she gently pressed the accelerator, he started blasting a big Range Rover with dogs in the back.

'I'm not sure,' Charlie said, looking across at a huge three-storey house with fountains along the driveway.

Owen cleared his throat. 'It's no biggie. But you said you weren't seeing anyone, and you gave me your number. Just say if you want me to quit bugging you.'

Owen was cute, but Charlie was always busy, studying, and working, and visiting Ed. Dating was a hassle, but she hadn't kissed a guy since Christmas. School ended in five weeks, and a summer fling had a certain appeal ...

'I think I'm free Thursday night,' Charlie said impulsively. 'I'm driving so I can't check my calendar. Call me Wednesday and we'll meet up for coffee.'

'Awesome,' Owen said happily. 'Enjoy your weekend, whatever you're up to.'

'I'll try,' Charlie said. 'Hope your pal's set at Tenders goes well.'

Charlie drove slow, reading the numbers off stone plinths at the foot of each grand house. Number twenty-eight was a colonial-style monster, but one side was covered in blue tarps, with an extension being built beneath a scaffold.

Mango's oldest, Josh, raced to the door and gave Charlie a hug. Charlie said hello to Mango and her stand-offish wife, Veryan.

'You have to see my new bedroom,' the seven-year-old said as he tugged Charlie's arm.

After climbing a curved marble staircase, Josh showed

her several huge, bare rooms and took her to the edge of the construction zone, which was going to be a pool and a large indoor garden. Then Josh showed Charlie his room. He had a bed shaped like a racing car, and Lego sprayed over the floor. Josh proudly held up a Lego box and told Charlie he could build it easily, even though the box said age eleven plus.

Mango and Veryan's five-year-old daughter trailed Charlie and Josh for the last part of the tour and both kids looked sad when Mango said she needed to talk to Charlie in private.

'They've grown since I last saw them,' Charlie said as Mango led her into a library.

The room had a sneezy sawdust smell from newly installed shelves, but the books remained in moving boxes and there was a brand-new desk still covered in polystyrene blocks.

'The indoor garden will be amazing,' Charlie said.

'The kids can play out here now,' Mango explained. 'But who knows what the situation will be in a year?'

'They reckon LHV has hit mainland Europe,' Charlie said. 'The first case was detected in Calais yesterday; by this morning there's over three hundred reported cases, as far south as Milan.'

'Scary,' Mango said as she moved a box file off an armchair so that Charlie could sit down. 'As soon as that antidote gets released, I want to go straight to the lab to make our own batch. Even if you're in school.'

'Absolutely,' Charlie agreed. 'Hopefully it'll be a couple of weeks before it crosses the Atlantic.'

'I wouldn't bet on that,' Mango said. 'Judging by the symptoms, LHV is a modified Ebola virus. That's a tropical virus, so chances are it'll be suited to hot climates like this and much harder to kill than SNor . . . So, how did the lab session go last night?'

Charlie didn't like lying, but she'd decided it was too risky to tell her boss about Juno's private job.

'The power supply in that storage unit scares me. It blew twice. The second time the fuse panel was hot to touch. We finished up using the diesel generator in the RV, but it's noisy and it doesn't power everything at once.'

'I'll get an electrician down there before your next lab session,' Mango said.

'When are we getting the new equipment?' Charlie asked. 'You said it would be two weeks over a month ago. It's getting to the point where something jams, or has to be repeated every time we're in the lab.'

'Juno's heavy handed,' Mango said acidly.

Charlie knew there was some truth to this, but she was fed up with her boss failing to bring in more reliable equipment. And while Charlie had saved a decent nest egg for college, Mango's enormous new home and Juno making fifty grand from one batch of an easy-to-produce muscle mod made her feel short changed.

'I've been thinking,' Charlie said, a nervous edge coming into her voice. 'I'm taking a lot of risks for a small share of the money we make. I'm getting four to six hundred dollars for complex mods you're charging fifteen thousand for.'

Mango leaned forward in her armchair and narrowed her eyes. She employed eighty people in the bakery, so she was used to dealing with people asking for a raise.

'What rate were you thinking?' Mango asked.

'I don't want a raise – I want a percentage,' Charlie said. 'I know you have a lot of expenses, but I thought fifteen per cent would be more than fair.'

Mango smiled and shook her head, like Charlie had made a joke.

'Charlie, you earn seven hundred and fifty dollars for a three-hour shift. You'd be lucky to earn sixty in a shop or a restaurant.'

'The restaurant doesn't sell hamburgers for fifteen grand,' Charlie pointed out. 'And I wouldn't go to prison for grilling meat.'

'Fifteen per cent is over two thousand dollars per job. You did six jobs last night.'

'I think you can afford it,' Charlie said firmly.

Mango tutted. 'Everything costs, Charlie. Three years ago, I could buy a hundred bone-marrow extraction kits for seven hundred bucks. Now they're a registered product. Decent ones have to be smuggled in from Mexico and they want ninety dollars per pack. Same goes for proteins, enzyme packs and auto-immune drugs.

'You walk in the RV and it's all there waiting, but it takes careful planning to keep everything in stock without tipping off the cops.'

'You're not doing badly, though,' Charlie said, sweeping her arm out at the rows of freshly built shelves. 'How much is your indoor pool and garden. Two million? Three? I could set up my own lab and do one job a week, and make more money than you pay me to work three long shifts.'

'Nobody knows who you are,' Mango said tartly. 'I can charge fifteen grand for a procedure because I'm a qualified doctor, with hundreds of satisfied clients and a reputation for excellence. I never tout for work; every job comes through personal recommendation.

'If you set up your own lab, you'd have all the stress and the risks, but you wouldn't be competing with me. You'd be competing with Chinese labs that people find on the dark web.

They charge five hundred dollars per mod, which wouldn't cover the cost of base enzymes and auto-immune drugs.'

'I don't want to be your competition,' Charlie said sharply. 'I appreciate all that you've done for me, Mango. But the laws keep getting tougher. I'm risking serious jail time every time I step into the RV.

'My plan was always to quit when I started college. But I've already saved enough to make college life bearable and it's not worth risk and stress all through my last year of high school just to make a hundred grand or so.'

'When things have gone well, you've had generous bonuses,' Mango said. 'When you asked for help, I took on your friend and paid her well too.'

Charlie got out of the armchair. 'I don't want to fight with you. I've said what I came here to say. And it was nice to see your six-million-dollar house.'

Mango was irritated by the sarcasm as Charlie stood and marched between boxes on the way to the library door.

'I'm not prepared to offer you a percentage,' Mango yelled after her. 'But I do value your work, so I'll discuss with Veryan, and we'll see what we can squeeze out of the budget.'

42 ONE-ONE-SEVEN

Steak and Eggs was a sprawling pool deck and club on the roof of downtown's trendy Red Spot Casino. The Nevada drinking age was twenty-one, but Axl Darmon was a spoiled Queensbridge senior, whose something-big-in-solar-energy father had spent thirty grand hiring the entire rooftop club for his son's eighteenth-birthday bash.

Harry and Matt's Uber dropped them in an underground car park, and scarily huge bouncers scanned barcodes on their invites before letting them ride a glass elevator up the side of the building to the twenty-third floor.

'Those doormen were all natural,' Matt joked as downtown's glitz reflected on the elevator's polished surfaces.

They were sharing the elevator with two Queensbridge girls, who both wore Ralph Lauren polos and short skirts over their swimming costumes. A girl with huge teeth gave Harry a smile.

'Who's your friend, Harry Potter?' she asked.

Matt didn't seem eager as the girl began flirting with him. The elevator doors opened to a wave of party noise and a tower of champagne glasses. As Harry grabbed a glass of bubbly, a pool attendant stepped up and apparently knew who he was.

'Your cabana is prepared, Mr Smirnov.'

Matt gawped as the pool attendant led them past ordinary partygoers fighting for space on plastic loungers to a swanky poolside cabana.

'Big shot,' Matt teased as Harry smirked. 'I'll never hear the end of this, will I?'

Harry barely knew Axl Darmon, but Axl's dad's energy business advertised on Vegas Local, and everyone in town knew Harry and his aunt were friendly with Kent Clark, whose casinos and hotels used more solar panels than anyone else in town.

The cabana's interior had six chairs round a circular table, a full bar and a bed behind sliding doors at the back. Outside, Harry had eight poolside loungers with cards saying *Reserved for Guests of Mr Smirnov* on the neatly rolled towels, while nozzles overhead countered smouldering heat with a mist of water.

'This is the bees,' Matt said.

By the time Harry gave the pool attendant a ten-dollar tip for an overlong demonstration of a tablet for ordering free food and cocktails, several girls hovered in the shallow water by the cabana's steps.

For Harry, the greatest prize was Lupita Diaz, dripping in a black bikini. A few years earlier, princesses like Esme Diaz had been an impossible dream; now her equally beautiful kid sister was practically begging for attention.

'Step up,' Harry told Lupita before offering her a cocktail.

Matt invited more beautiful girls up the steps as Harry finished his champagne, drank a Long Island Iced Tea and flirted with Lupita on a double-width lounger.

The next cabana was packed with beefy dudes being loud

and annoying, and there seemed to be a Roman orgy taking place behind the cloth flaps. Harry was startled when one of them crossed to his side and offered a vast hand.

'JJ, wow!' Harry said, forcing a smile, even though the Janssen family stirred unsettling memories. 'NFL big shot now! I saw a mock draft predicting that you'll get picked by the Lions.'

'I hate Detroit,' JJ said. 'The Texans would be nice. My offensive coordinator from Midland took a coaching job there. But *don't* put that on Vegas Local.'

'No fear,' Harry said as Lupita smiled and bumped JJ's fist.

The pool attendant put two platters of canapés on the bar and everyone dived in. JJ's buddies had interpreted their main man stepping across to Harry's cabana as an open invite and suddenly all the girls were getting hassled by loud college-age guys. Harry decided to escape, stripping off his tank top and swaying from the booze as he waded into the pool.

It wasn't even nine, but Steak and Eggs was popping. Kids of sixteen and seventeen were wasted and JJ's pals were sneaking inside to snort cocaine. Lupita wanted to make out, but Harry was too trashed and she bounced to another cabana.

He wound up beached on the big lounger, a touch queasy, tapping to pounding music and occasionally getting jolted when someone squeezed past.

'Awesome party,' Matt said, gesturing towards a girl on his arm. 'I'm taking Hermione to our apartment to show her the view,' Matt said. 'I'll see you back home.'

'It's *so* cool that you guys don't have to live with your parents,' Hermione said. 'I can't wait to get to college.'

Harry wished he hadn't drunk so much as he watched Matt head to the elevator. But he didn't hold the thought, because

Fawn Janssen was striding towards the cabanas with purpose.

'JJ,' she barked.

Fawn was twenty-nine and the fact that every other girl was ten years younger and dressed for the pool made her seem gigantic in her tight purple dress and high-heeled boots. Harry had met Fawn when he'd photographed her house, and she shot him a fierce glare of recognition as she crossed in front of his cabana, then up the steps and through the flaps into JJ's.

'Rooster in the hen house,' one of JJ's mates boomed. 'Feathers gonna fly!'

Harry was drunk and knackered, but his instinct for a story trumped both handicaps. He pressed the record button on his phone as Fawn started yelling.

'You dirty cheat! Get these tramps outta here.'

Harry recognised a pair of eleventh-grade Queensbridge girls. The first stumbled through the flaps into the arms of a huge, guffawing jock. The second was propelled by the sharp heel of Fawn Janssen's boot, crashing into an empty lounger, followed by the top half of her bikini.

'You paying someone to stalk me now?' JJ shouted from inside.

Then he gave a deep groan and Harry winced at the thought of what Fawn had just kneed.

'Show me up in front of the whole city!' Fawn screamed.

'Who are you to talk?' JJ shouted back. 'I know you've been sniffing around my dad.'

Holy shit! Harry thought.

'Your father showed me some kindness while you were strutting the TMU campus like a horny bull,' Fawn shouted. 'But I've never cheated on you.'

'Yeah, you're a saint,' JJ taunted, grabbing Fawn and pushing her out through the cabana's flaps. 'If you don't like it, divorce me. But you signed a pre-nup, so you won't get one damned cent.'

'Won't I?' Fawn teased, wagging a finger. 'You think I'll go down without a fight?'

JJ was six-five, but Fawn's four-inch heels made her a match as they stared off.

'You were born trailer trash and you'll die trailer trash,' JJ taunted.

Fawn swung, drawing blood as she scraped purple nails across JJ's cheek. 'You'll see what I'm capable of,' Fawn threatened. 'You wait and see.'

'All you do is make my life miserable,' JJ shouted.

Fawn tried to claw again, but JJ saw it coming. He snatched his wife's wrist and bent back her fingers.

'You like that?' JJ shouted, making Fawn whimper. 'Show me up some more – I'll break 'em.'

JJ released his wife's hand and shoved her hard. Fawn's heels weren't designed for wet tiles and she skidded on her front foot, grabbing the bar to save herself. She almost did the splits, but carried enough momentum to spin and crack her head against the wall-mounted TV.

JJ's crew erupted in cheers and applause as the screen cracked and Fawn slumped to the floor.

'Quit filming,' one of JJ's pals demanded, stepping in to block Harry's shot. 'Gimme that camera.'

Harry had spent so much of his life as a skinny dude that his instinct was to back off. But though the guy had a couple of inches on Harry, he was flabby, while Harry was all muscle.

'Or what?' Harry said, shooting the guy daggers. 'Touch my phone and I'll rip your head off.'

'Press assholes,' the guy spat. 'I know who you are, big shot.'

Harry was worried JJ's pals would turn on him, but they were more concerned about getting JJ away from his semi-conscious wife in case the cops showed.

As JJ and his crew grabbed their stuff and rushed the elevator, a giant bouncer hefted Fawn over his shoulder. He was tailed by a much smaller guy, who spoke into a radio, asking someone to make sure a casino limo was on standby to take her to hospital.

Harry wasn't the only person who'd filmed the incident, though he'd had the closest view. He considered uploading straight to Vegas Local, but the two Queensbridge girls were under eighteen, which meant he had to blur them in post-production, or risk getting sued by their undoubtedly wealthy parents.

Harry decided it was safest to edit the video when he had a clear head, even if it meant someone else got the story online first. The TV breaking had tripped a fuse, wiping out the lights in Harry's cabana and the nearest set of loudspeakers.

He grabbed a can of Blue Moon from his bar and enjoyed the gloom as he settled back on his lounger. JJ's crew had bounced and the partying teens didn't want to be close by if the cops showed, so Harry found himself alone on his double lounger, detached from dancing, splashing and the laser show coming out of the DJ booth. He thought about going home and catching some sleep, but he lacked energy, and figured the decent thing was to give Matt and Hermione a clear hour at the apartment.

But no cops showed. A guy in a suit barked orders as pool attendants swarmed JJ's cabana, gathering towels and drinks, mopping tiles, covering up the bar and placing fresh cushions and rolled towels on each lounger. As the clean-up crew left, an electrician came along with a TV balanced on his shoulder.

He whistled cheerfully as he placed the screen face down on the bar. Then he opened a little tool bag and started unscrewing the broken set. Feeling wasted and watching the party from a distance had made Harry grumpy, but he was captivated by the happy little man in his beige shorts and Red Spot-branded polo.

'Can I ask you something, sir?' Harry said politely, sitting up.

The man turned and smiled. 'Depends what it is, I guess.'

'Have you got a one-one-seven?'

The psychiatrists who developed and studied Zombie mods as a way of combatting mental illness catalogued hundreds of genetic modifications that might affect brain chemistry and alter a person's mental state. Most z-mods were still known by these catalogue numbers.

'How'd you work that out?' he asked.

Harry smiled. 'Guys with sixty-eights and one-seven-nines are more jittery,' Harry said. 'But one-one-sevens are chilled.'

The electrician strained as he lifted the broken TV from its wall mount.

'May I ask why you had it done?'

'Wife dumped me,' the electrician explained. 'Lived with my daughter for a while, but there wasn't a lot of space in her apartment. Wound up drinking more and staying out later every night. I'd wake up stinking of booze and aching like the world was ending. I thought about killing myself. Got as far as buying a handgun, then I met a guy in a bar selling mod kits for eight hundred bucks. Took me out back to show me how to do the needles and the rest is history . . .'

Harry was fascinated. 'So now you're happy all the time?'

'Not happy exactly,' the electrician answered. 'You feel sad but it don't matter.'

'Isn't it flat, though?' Harry said. 'Like, does anything matter, if you're happy no matter what?'

There was a pause as the electrician lifted the new TV on to the bracket and reached behind the bar to plug cables.

'You reach a certain age and you realise life doesn't amount to much,' the electrician said. 'I'm no philosopher. I don't know if being like this makes my life less meaningful. But I wake in the morning and don't dread the day in front of me.'

'So you'd recommend it?' Harry asked. 'Because I don't have much to complain about, but most of the time I feel empty.'

The electrician stepped out of JJ's cabana. Harry watched as he twisted a key in an access panel at the base of a metal post with a circle of Bose speakers at the top.

'Well,' the electrician said as he flipped a fuse switch, making the cabana lights and water mist come back on. 'Maybe you should live a little longer before you start messing with your brain. What are you, a college freshman?'

'High school senior.'

'Just a kid,' the electrician said, grabbing the remote for the TV he'd installed and flipping channels to make sure they were all tuned. 'You have a good night. Go easy on the free liquor. That's one thing I know won't solve your problems.'

'I'll drink to that advice,' Harry joked.

'Enjoy your night, son,' the electrician said. His permanent smile niggled Harry as he strode peacefully away.

43 KILLER-T

Charlie had moved out of Obama Independent Living when her supervised release period ended. She now lived with Iranian-American foster parents Navid and Jan Rahimi and their two tween sons.

Charlie's room was an extension built over the garage, with its own shower room and kitchenette. Since she'd never given her foster parents cause to think she was anything other than a model student, Charlie came and went as she pleased.

It was the closest she'd come to normal family life. She ate with the family most evenings, helped with grocery shopping, drove the boys to Ju Jitsu and occasionally got drafted as the ten- and twelve-year-olds' tutor.

When Ken Kleinberg retired with health problems, Charlie got assigned to an energetic young welfare officer, who bugged Fawn until she agreed to let Charlie visit her younger brother. It was officially restricted to once a week, but Charlie made friends with the nurses and they let her visit Ed on Tuesdays, Thursdays before school and first thing on Saturday. Fawn didn't visit, so was none the wiser.

The fifteen-mile ride from the Rahimis' modest home to

the irritatingly named Care4Kids was mostly freeway, taking twenty minutes in light traffic. Charlie usually let the car drive and tried to kick-start her day with perky tunes and a travel mug of black coffee.

She'd lain awake most of the night, worrying about Juno, Mango and the LHV situation, and the 7 a.m. radio headlines didn't help her mood.

'President West has urged people to stay calm and prepare for a possible quarantine order after it was confirmed that LHV has been diagnosed in three patients in the San Francisco area. Two have been confirmed as a pilot and co-pilot who flew a private jet from London hours before transatlantic flights were halted. The four passengers on the flight, which include the tennis player Lee Rosenwein and his wife, have been placed in quarantine, but authorities in Winnipeg are still trying to track down two cleaning staff who boarded the plane during a refuelling stop.

'In other news, the death toll in the United Kingdom is said to be over twenty thousand, with the National Health Service on the brink of collapse. The British parliament held its first ever session under quarantine protocol yesterday, with Prime Minister Lawrence taking questions over a video-conferencing system. Leader of the opposition New Labour Group made an unexpected call to pay the $1.5-billion-dollar ransom, and then "hunt the culprits without mercy to the ends of the earth".

'Meanwhile, a team of virologists at Britain's Defence Research Authority, DefRA, have announced that LHV appears not to be related to the Ebola virus, as had been previously thought. Although the symptoms of massive internal bleeding and rapid physical collapse are similar to Ebola, scientists now say the virus is either completely synthetic, or derived from an as-yet-unidentified animal virus adapted to infect humans.

'The group's initial finding is that the virus appears to work by taking control of so-called Killer-T cells that produce antibodies. This effectively turns the human immune system into a massive virus factory and leaves the body with no means of defence. Although global governments have poured over one hundred billion dollars into anti-viral research since the SNor outbreak, even the most optimistic scientists say trial vaccines will take months to develop from scratch ...'

Charlie felt grumpy as her car reached the Care4Kids lot. It seemed deeply unfair, having some bunch of nuts in a lab on the other side of the world, determining whether she got to fall in love, get a doctorate, have a family and grow old, or die coughing up blood in two weeks' time.

'Down in the dumps today, Charlie,' Joyce the Jamaican nurse said as Charlie scrubbed her hands in reception.

'It crossed the Atlantic,' Charlie said.

Joyce put her palms together. 'May our Lord protect us,' she said as Charlie donned blackout goggles. She stepped into a plastic cubicle, spreading fingers and raising her arms over her head as Joyce activated the dazzling bluish light of a UV sterilisation booth.

Charlie's phone and the contents of a small bag rolled through a more powerful steriliser before Joyce opened the electric gate to let Charlie inside. The first time Charlie had visited Care4Kids, she'd been reduced to tears by the yelling and droning, and a whiff of urine and disinfectant that lingered after you left.

But Charlie barely noticed this now, instead admiring the patient work of mental-health nurses, who got punched and screamed at by their mostly teenage charges. Ed was one of the most able residents, and one of the few who attended a special education unit at a nearby middle school.

'Guess who,' Charlie said as she rapped on Ed's door, which had his name along with a picture of his face superimposed on a *Star Wars* movie poster. He was easily upset and sensitive to other people's emotions, so Charlie shook her arms and tried to relax as she stepped into his room.

Ed was fifteen and close to six feet tall. Handsome, but borderline obese. He wore grubby white soccer socks into which he always tucked his tracksuit bottoms because he had a phobia about things crawling up his leg.

Charlie caught a strong whiff of BO as Ed's arms locked round her back. His first hug always predicted how the next hour would go. If it was stiff and rushed, it meant he was fretting about something, usually about a lesson at school or his constant nagging fear that he'd forgotten something. But today's hug was lengthy and relaxed.

'I love you so much, Charlie,' Ed said, slurring slightly.

'Aww,' Charlie said, suddenly feeling better about the world. 'You haven't told me that for *ages*. I love you too, Ed.'

'I got a new book from Amazon,' Ed said. 'It's true stories about Arctic explorers. I read a hundred and three pages already.'

Ed's slurred speech and emotional outbursts meant people thought he was stupid. But while his damaged brain struggled with spatial tasks like tying laces or putting on a T-shirt the right way round, he was an average ninth-grader in most school subjects, and he loved to read. Especially biographies of astronauts and explorers, and books about wars.

'So,' Charlie said, speaking slowly because she knew the confusion could tilt Ed into panic. 'Today is Saturday so we don't have to go to school. How about I help you in the shower?

Then we'll get some breakfast. Then we can play a video game, or watch one of your shows together.'

'I don't need a shower,' Ed said.

'You certainly do,' Charlie said firmly. 'You'll never get a girlfriend with smelly armpits and dirty socks on your feet.'

Ed picked up one of his feet and seemed proud of how black the sole was.

'Come on, pilgrim,' Charlie said firmly. 'I'll go and set the shower at the temperature you like. You take off those nasty clothes and drop them in the laundry hamper.'

44 SPOILED BRATS

Harry opened his eyes slowly. His brain throbbed and his vision blurred as he tried to raise his head. The sun was coming up and a sharp breeze rattled the rooftop palms.

There was puke sprayed the other side of the double-lounger and a sparrow pecking at it. Harry didn't think he'd been sick, but most of what happened after Matt left was a blur.

'Time you got your ass home,' a cleaner said irritably. She wore a chequered smock, thick rubber gloves and had faded tattoos down her arms.

Harry felt like his brain would rupture as he sat up, rubbing his face and planting his feet down. The pool shoes on the floor weren't his, but they'd do. He looked around for his tank top.

'You seen a blue-grey tank?' Harry asked, then started coughing.

'Ya ain't supposed to be here,' the woman said sharply. 'And we ain't gonna start looking for your shit.'

Harry tapped his back pocket, relieved to feel his phone, house key and money clip zipped inside his swim shorts. It was a $90 Lululemon tank that he looked good in, but his thirst and a need for the toilet overrode any desire to start searching.

The deck swayed as Harry stood and steadied himself on a post. The scene across the pool reminded him of a news item he'd seen about kids who lived on landfill sites. There was tons of litter, sticky cocktail spills and lounger cushions floating in the pool.

Harry stumbled round the pool towards the glass elevator, straddling half-eaten nachos, beer cans and dried blood.

A guy in the pool wore rubber waders, using a giant boom to scoop litter off the surface. When Harry caught the cleaner's eye, he got a look of pure hate. He realised he was the hungover spoiled brat, loathed by people on minimum wage who had to clean up after him.

Harry drank from a water fountain outside the restrooms. A smell like a rotting carcass turned him off the gents.

'Hello?' he yelled, making sure there was no answer before cutting into a stall in the ladies. He kicked a dead lip gloss across the floor, then walked into a stall and lifted the seat.

Harry was halfway through a much-needed piss when he noticed a wasp on the wall, the stripes on its back a shimmering metallic purple. He hadn't noticed with his blurred head and desperation to pee, but someone must have spilled something sugary in the next stall because the synthetic wasps were coming under the partition and a few fizzed up near the ceiling.

'Christ,' Harry gasped, spraying his shorts as he backed out frantically.

The University of Chicago biology student who'd engineered purple wasps was serving fifty years in federal prison, but his genetically altered creatures had spread across North America. Besides their dark metallic stripes, purple wasps produced a much more potent venom than regular wasps. It could kill an untreated child in twenty minutes, or an adult in three agonising hours.

Harry had peed over his feet, but the shock boosted his energy. He checked all over his body, making sure there were no wasps, then jogged to the elevator, only to find it shut down, with the car open and a woman inside polishing the glass.

'Service elevator, at back,' a cleaner said, aiming her pointing finger behind the main bar.

'*Gracias*,' Harry mumbled.

The service elevator had scuffed plastic walls and a whiff of burnt rubber. Harry rode it down twenty-three floors, expecting to emerge inside the casino, or the taxi lobby where he'd been dropped off the night before.

But he exited into a deserted underground loading area with a strong smell of trash. He pressed the button to try riding up, but a red light flashed, indicating that he needed to swipe an employee card in the control panel.

Harry cursed, then walked around trying to find someone who could tell him the way out or swipe the elevator so he could get up to casino level. But the hot basement was dead and his only option was to follow a narrow vehicle ramp towards chinks of sunlight.

The heat was oppressive and the stench churned Harry's weakened stomach. After a couple of hundred yards he was out in warm morning air and able to draw a full breath. He glanced around and realised he'd reached street level, with a bunch of tacky Fremont Street casinos visible at the end of the access road. Fremont was pedestrianised, but Harry knew there were taxi ranks in the side streets.

Since it was too early for traffic, he reckoned he'd be home inside twenty minutes.

'Can you spare a few dollars, bud?' a young male zombie said, as he stepped out of an alcove into Harry's path.

There were two girls as well. Neither were much older than Harry, but their top halves were filthy and their legs caked in dried excrement. One hadn't taken well to her mod, with a tumour the size of a tennis ball closing her right eye.

Permanent diarrhoea was a sure sign of a one-zero-six zombie mod. While their bodies went to hell, their brains had been tuned to a state of bliss that the few people who'd had a one-zero-six reversed described as like having the greatest moment of your life stretched out forever.

One-zero-sixes weren't capable of work, or any other task that required concentration, but they retained enough of a survival instinct to stick together, either stealing or begging for food.

'Heavy night,' Harry said, holding his breath as he stepped off the sidewalk to dodge the zombie. 'I've got no coins.'

If he hadn't been so hungover, Harry would have seen the leg that tripped him up. And, even if he hadn't, he would have stumbled instead of sprawling and almost cracking his skull on the kerb.

'I'll kick all your asses,' Harry shouted, holding his face as he rolled out of the gutter.

But the healthier of the two girls had a little .22 revolver waving in Harry's face. This was scarier than a regular mugger, because most zombies had no fear of committing crime. Four walls, free healthcare and food pushed through a cell door was practically their idea of paradise.

'Give,' the male said, pointing to the obvious bulge of the phone and money clip in the inner pocket of Harry's Vilebrequin beach shorts.

Harry didn't want to lose his phone or house key, so he pulled out his money clip. His hands trembled as he freed seventy dollars in small bills and threw them in the air. The girl with the gun looked up at the money as the male zombie snatched two twenties and a ten before breaking into a clumsy run.

'Hey!' the girl with the gun shouted, shifting aim towards her disloyal partner.

Harry saw his moment to escape, leaping to his feet and sprinting towards Fremont. There was no gunshot and he wondered if the gun wasn't loaded. Or fake. Or jammed up, given how filthy its owner was. The casinos on Fremont Street paid for private security patrols, and Harry passed one of them riding a Segway down the pedestrianised street.

But seventy dollars was no fortune, and Harry was exhausted. The last thing he needed was to explain everything to some dumbass private security, then sit in an office waiting for real cops to show and having to write out a bunch of statements.

There were four cabs ranked in the street running between the Lucky Star and O'Malley's Gambling Hall. Harry jumped in the first one and fought an urge to spew as he told the driver to take him home.

45 BACK TAXIS

Ellie wouldn't get super wealthy until Elliegold floated on the NASDAQ stock exchange, but the company was now profitable, and his chief-executive salary covered the rent on a sizeable house in San Francisco's trendy Marina District, and paid for a Mercedes SUV big enough for his wife and five kids.

The stretch along Marina Boulevard was usually busy on a spring Sunday morning, but today there were no moms with jogging strollers, or father-son sailing partnerships.

Ellie took the Mercedes right, away from the ocean, and was surprised by the handwritten *We're Open* sign on a family-owned gas station. There was an old Nissan plugged into a rapid charger, its driver leaning against the hood, vaping.

Ellie glanced at his watch as he parked up, grabbing his anti-virus mask off the passenger seat and snapping the elastic straps behind his head. Then he fitted white sanitary gloves and stepped out. The shop was open, but it was in night-time mode, with the automatic doors bolted and the server picking items from behind a bullet-proof screen.

'What are my chances of size-two diapers?' Ellie asked.

He'd figured this was a long shot, but the assistant backed

into the store's mostly empty racks and returned holding a bulky pack in each hand. They were some weird brand Ellie had never seen, but it was still a miracle.

'Size two, ninety-two per pack,' the assistant said, holding them up to the glass. 'You want?'

'Yes I want,' Ellie said triumphantly. 'I ordered a super-jumbo pack online, but they're not gonna show until the quarantine ends. Do you just have the two boxes?'

'The only others I have are size four,' the guy said. 'Anything else you need?'

'All good,' Ellie said.

'The total with tax comes to one hundred and forty-eight, sixty-two. The credit-card system is down, so it's cash only.'

Ellie felt stung, knowing ninety Huggies cost twenty-eight bucks in Walmart. But he counted seven twenties and two fives and dropped them into a counter tray saturated in sterilising UV light. His change rattled down a plastic chute. He grabbed the diapers through a hatch and threw them on to the back seat, before settling back behind the wheel.

In the two years since SNor the US government had spent billions on planning for another synthetic virus outbreak, and three blocks down Ellie turned right into a checkpoint manned by National Guard officers in bright yellow biohazard suits.

A rubber-gloved hand made a halt signal and tapped Ellie's registration into a computer strapped to the opposite wrist. After a few seconds, the suited creature stepped forward and signalled for him to put down the window.

'Do you have an emergency travel authorisation?' she asked, a speaker on her mask giving a Darth Vader quality to her voice.

Ellie shook his head. 'I tried to submit an application, but the online system is swamped.'

'What's the purpose of your journey?'

'I'm picking up my mother-in-law from her apartment. She's sixty-nine and diabetic. Her carer can't get to her so she's going to stay with us till this blows over.'

Or we're all dead . . .

The hooded guardswoman nodded. Her colleague waved a police car and a couple of other vehicles through as Ellie handed over his licence and gave his mother-in-law's name and address. When this was done, the woman disappeared inside a truck and returned with a quarantine authorisation sticker, which she stuck to the windshield.

'Mr Gold, I'm giving you ninety minutes to collect your mother-in-law and return to your home address. I'm going to waive the six-hundred-dollar ticket for breaching quarantine, because we appreciate there have been problems with the trip-authorisation website. However, if you are stopped a second time, there'll be a twelve-hundred-dollar fixed penalty, and people who persistently breach quarantine regulations may be detained for an indefinite period.'

'Thank you kindly, ma'am,' Ellie said, shuffling to peel his sweaty back off his seat before rolling through the barricade and on down the deserted street.

46 DEAD BIRTHDAY

After a crazy Thursday house party and his Friday overnighter at Steak and Eggs, Harry's Saturday evening was more sedate, celebrating Kirsten's forty-seventh birthday at a creepily deserted tapas restaurant, with a bunch of her friends, co-workers and James, the latest in her line of much younger boyfriends.

There was talk of LHV, though Harry noted how fast the catchier Killer-T moniker had taken hold. Bleak conversation and the empty tables all around stifled any hint of celebration.

The quarantine around San Francisco had been extended to the whole of Northern California. One of Kirsten's guests had spotted Nevada State Guards preparing to block the I-15 freeway between Las Vegas and Los Angeles, and everyone agreed that Nevada and the rest of California would get locked down soon.

Harry was the only guest under twenty, and the gloomy conversation made him feel like he was dining on the *Titanic* as he got tipsy on red wine, flirted unproductively with one of Kirsten's junior chefs and made it home by ten thirty after saying that he had a ton of school stuff to catch up on in the morning.

Harry got woken by Matt and Lana fighting in his kitchen, just after nine on Sunday morning. He usually went to the fridge for juice when he woke, but he didn't want to go near Lana in case she tried interrogating him about what Matt had been up to on Friday night.

Instead, he filled a glass from his bathroom tap, sat up in bed and logged into the Vegas Local content management system. The site had 11,000 active users, double the average for a Sunday morning. Visitors would usually focus on local sports and downloading 2-for-1 coupons for Sunday lunch, but the stats screen showed eighty per cent of visitors were logged into the gossip boards, talking about Killer-T and the prospect of quarantine.

The news kept getting darker. Since Harry had left Kirsten's birthday meal the night before, the governors of California and Oregon had confirmed state-wide quarantines. Seventeen clinics had been constructed in the Vegas area, designed to prevent virus outbreaks ravaging regular hospitals. There were rumours that a family of visitors from San Francisco had been admitted with Killer-T style haemorrhaging. Four cases had been confirmed in Canada, at least five hundred in San Francisco and more than a hundred thousand in Europe.

Harry felt sick. Even the optimists were predicting thousands of deaths and he reckoned his readers might appreciate some light relief on the Vegas Local home page. Ellie had linked all his local news sites into a central database, and Harry trawled it, hoping to find a nice car chase out of Omaha, or a skateboarding pig in Philadelphia.

When his quest drew a blank, Harry decided to check the responses to Vegas Local's Send Us Your Story inbox. According to the blurb on the Your Story page, Vegas Local wanted to hear from you. In reality, Harry, Matt and Roberta the intern didn't have time to investigate daily reports of rat droppings in restaurant kitchens, or some old couple's complaint that the neighbouring motel had turned into a drug den.

But every so often there was a ready-made story, and out of sixteen unopened story tips, the one titled 'Help me bust Helen Back' stood out.

Back was a Harley-riding Goth magician, her stage name a play on Hell and Back. Her solo magic act had played in theatres up and down the strip for more than a decade, most recently in the custom-built Hell Arena at the Fontainebleau.

Harry clicked the header, opening a message full of dodgy spellings and swears.

Dear editor,

Helen Back real name Helen Margolis was my step ma until recenteley

She is a nastey manipulating **** who treated my mom like **** and my mom wound up in psychoatric hospital and Helen ran me down evree chance she got for two whole years until I got into fighting and staying out all hours of the night and got kicked outta school last term.

Helen got busted by IRS for not paying over $10 million in back taxis. But she has now got off prison with a deal. By snitching on the lab that did her gene mods to the FBI.

Just so you know I am not making things up, the dumb ***** gave me her old laptop and left her email on it so I can still see EVREYTHING

LOLS!! So dumb

So here is a letter with attachements out of all the most information that my step ma gave the feds.

I hope you can use this and do the nastey ***** Helen

Back a lot of damage and take her down a peg to her
suck-up fans.

Max Briston (Age 13)

'Good old vengeful stepkids,' Harry told himself, smirking as he
opened up the first of two attachments.

It was an accountant's report, more than sixty pages long,
with details of Helen Back's past earnings and a schedule for
paying a seven-figure fine and more than twelve million in back
taxes.

A major Vegas entertainer getting busted for tax avoidance
was a solid story, but the second document was the zinger. It
was a copy of a two-week-old statement that Helen Back had
made for the FBI.

It began with Back's real name and home address. Then the
document stated that Helen knew of a large-scale Las Vegas-
based human-genetic-modification operation run by her
friends Veryan and Mango Kowalski-Clark.

After details of several modifications that Helen Back had
paid for, there was a list of names. The first were two nurses
who Back claimed worked in Los Angeles dealing with patients.

*Mango never sees patients directly, but made an exception
for me as we have known each other for many years. Mango
was keen to impress me and often boasted that she has modded
famous film and TV personalities ...*

Harry was disappointed that there were no celebrity names,
because that would be enough to make this a national story. The
next couple of pages were dry, with long-winded details about
how long Mango, Veryan and Helen had known one another,
and a long list of details on dates when they'd met, both socially
and for Helen's treatment.

But Harry gawped when he read the last section, right before the box where Helen Back was supposed to sign her name.

In response to Agent Sander's final question regarding my knowledge of any other persons connected to, or working for, the organisation: last February I attended a children's birthday party at Mango and Veryan's home.

Their son Josh seemed fond of a girl in her late teens, who I assumed was a local babysitter. I did not speak to the girl, but later that evening Mango had drunk a lot and told me in confidence that the girl was her 'brilliant little lab rat', and was responsible for the lab work on all of my genetic modifications.

I did not catch the girl's last name, but her first name was Charlie. As always, Mango seemed keen to impress and boasted that Charlie was 'a bad girl, who had done time in White Boulder'.

47 TEAM MANGO

Charlie was sprawled on a wrecked couch, watching her two foster brothers playing a basketball game on their Xbox when her foster father Navid called from the kitchen.

'The British prime minister is about to make a statement.'

Charlie moved a bowl of M&Ms from her lap to a side table and hopped to the kitchen. Her step-parents sat at the dining table, looking worried as the screen on the refrigerator door showed Prime Minister Lawrence stepping up to a lectern outside 10 Downing Street.

It was past midnight in London, the weather was drizzly and dozens of cameras flashed as Lawrence spoke from behind an acrylic quarantine screen, while an aide sheltered him with a large umbrella.

'Ladies and gentlemen, the past week has unarguably been the most difficult of my career. I am now able to announce that shortly before 5 a.m. on Thursday a team of SAS soldiers and Special Branch officers raided an address in West London, following a tip-off from a member of the public.

'Three suspects were arrested, and a female suspect was shot and fatally wounded. The premises contained a laboratory, where we now believe the initial samples of the Killer-T virus were developed before release. Following on from this initial raid, a second home was raided nearby, and two more suspects arrested.

'Paperwork and computer files relating to the development of Killer-T were seized, along with samples of a vaccine. Preliminary tests at the Porton Down biocontainment facility indicate that the vaccine is at least ninety-five per cent effective and has no immediately obvious side-effects. A few moments ago, the DNA patterns and other details for manufacturing this vaccine were deployed to hundreds of vaccine laboratories around the world.

'I would like to personally thank the police officers, military personnel and scientists who have taken part in this operation. And to offer special thanks to the member of the public, who wishes to remain anonymous, but whose vigilance may save millions of lives.'

Shouts came from the gaggle of media the instant the prime minister stopped talking.

'Prime Minister, if the raid took place early on Thursday, why are you only announcing it now?'

'Couldn't the anti-virus samples have been released sooner?'

'How long will it take to manufacture enough of the vaccine for everyone?'

The prime minister cleared his throat. 'My scientific advisors are in a better position than me to answer detailed questions and will be available shortly. Given the sophisticated nature of the plot, we felt it was essential to conduct preliminary safety tests on the vaccine before releasing it for manufacture.

'Over the past two years, my government has put unprecedented resources into preparedness for another outbreak of a synthetic virus, and twenty-fold advances have been made in the speed with which vaccines can be manufactured, tested and deployed. The first batches of vaccine will be released to healthcare professionals and other essential workers within twenty-four hours.

'As with all vaccines, there will be a period of between twelve and twenty-four hours before a patient has a high level of protection from Killer-T. Given the rapid spread of the disease, and the time it will take for widespread vaccine distribution, we can still expect the number of cases and fatalities to increase sharply over the coming days. I must urge everyone in the United Kingdom to continue to follow quarantine rules and await announcements on the vaccination programme in their area.'

As the prime minister stepped back into number 10, Charlie turned and smiled at her foster parents.

'Looks like we got lucky this time,' Navid said.

Charlie nodded.

'But even with . . .' She paused as the phone in her pocket vibrated. 'Cases of Killer-T are at least doubling every twenty-four hours. So if it takes a week to vaccinate most people and another day or two for their bodies to develop immunity . . . That's two to the ninth power . . . Making five hundred and twelve infections for every one we have now.'

'But quarantines should significantly slow the infection rate,' Navid pointed out.

'True,' Charlie said, pulling out her phone, which now had Mango's name on the screen. 'Sorry, I'd better take this.'

Charlie's regular phone wasn't encrypted so Mango spoke cautiously.

'Have you seen the news?

'Just watched it,' Charlie said.

'I've seen the recipe,' Mango said. 'The techniques are complex, but it's doable. Can you get to the bakery straight away?'

Charlie's regular lab sessions were scheduled in advance and she'd tell her foster parents she was out at a party, or sleeping over at Juno's. But driving off when most people were scared to leave home would make Jan and Navid ask questions. Charlie decided the best course was to skip out without telling them anything.

The roads were quiet. Fast-food restaurants, cinema and casino parking lots were deserted and many smaller outlets shuttered. The US government had been running a quarantine preparedness campaign for over a year, urging everyone to keep a month's supply of bottled water, canned food and other essentials in case of a lengthy quarantine. But Charlie still passed a supermarket lot crammed with panic shoppers and Target had a big handwritten sign out front with a long list of items they'd run out of.

For security, Charlie always parked her VW a block and a half from the storage unit where the RV was berthed. Since cell phones are basically a big *here I am* sign to the authorities, she switched off her handset as she got out.

Juno was walking from the other direction. The storage unit and the RV's side door were already unlocked and Charlie was pleased to see that the nightmare fuse panel had been swapped for an entirely new unit.

'Hey, girls,' Mango said brightly as Juno clanked up the RV's metal steps.

Charlie was surprised to see Veryan there too. Mango's wife supposedly had a scientific background, but she was always prickly, and this was the first time Charlie had seen her near the lab.

'Got new toys!' Juno said, looking on the cabinet by the sink where three small machines were set up in a row. 'They finally came! This is state-of-the-art shit.'

'It's amazing how fast technology changes,' Charlie said as she admired the new machines, each with colour touchscreens and no bigger than an espresso maker. 'This whole set-up is smaller than the old sequencer on its own.'

'Faster too,' Veryan said, snapping on a nitrile glove. 'The printer can generate over ten thousand base pairs per minute. Which, given the complexity of what we're handling today, will be a big help.'

Besides the trio of new machines, Mango had bought a big box of sterile syringes and vaccine sample vials. There were also four much larger containers with the base compound for a vaccine and a number of chemicals that Charlie hadn't used before. Finally, there were bottles of Cola and bags of snacks.

'You've been stockpiling all this stuff?' Charlie asked.

Veryan nodded, and gave a loaded reply, 'There's a lot more work behind the scenes than *some* people seem to realise.'

Mango smoothed things quickly. 'I haven't worked on a vaccine since I was in graduate school, but the technical documents the British government have released are comprehensive and designed so that any competent genetics lab can produce a working vaccine. But even with four of us, and no major foul-ups, we're looking at a fourteen-hour shift.

'We can make enough vaccine for a thousand people, but I've only got enough vials and syringes for a hundred and twenty doses. There's no pecking order and no money involved. I want this to be about helping the people we love to stay alive. I want all disputes set aside and each of us will leave here with thirty doses to distribute as they wish. Agreed?'

'Agreed,' Charlie said as Veryan and Juno nodded.

48 TWELVE-PIECE BUCKET

The Helen Back story sat awkwardly in Harry's mind. He could have run the details by Vegas Local's media lawyer, typed a few hundred words and had it on the front page within a couple of hours. But Harry had done a lot of growing up since he'd last seen Charlie. The sexual jealousy over Brad seemed childish, and when he realised the hurt was no longer there Harry found himself feeling nostalgic for a friendship more meaningful than any he had now.

He'd left Charlie two phone messages, but she hadn't responded. Her email had bounced and she didn't do social media, because a lot of Rock Spring football fans still hated her guts.

Harry wondered if she'd changed her number as Matt stepped in the apartment's main door holding a giant bucket of fried chicken.

'Dig in while it's hot,' Matt said.

'Took you long enough,' Harry said, heading into their messy kitchen. 'I put out plates and shit.'

'The unit on Flamingo was closed,' Matt explained as he planted the bucket in the middle of the dining table.

'Beer or coke?' Harry asked, peering in the fridge, then laughing as he noticed Matt's swollen eye. 'Lana clocked you *good!*'

'Coke,' Matt said, ignoring the comment about his eye as he pulled off his gloves and virus mask. 'I got a call from Ethan.'

'Fat Ethan?' Harry asked. He popped the lid off the bucket and grabbed a pack of fries and two wings.

'Nah, big-ears Ethan,' Matt said, sitting down. 'His ma works at the emergency coordination centre. She says fifteen people who were staying at the Red Spot have been taken ill.'

'I didn't step inside the casino,' Harry said warily.

'Gets worse,' Matt said, popping a can of Pepsi and tipping fries on to his plate. 'They've tracked down the person who brought the virus to Vegas. It's Greg Rosenwein.'

'Never heard of him.'

'You've heard of Lee Rosenwein?'

Harry nodded. 'Sure, tennis player.'

'Rosenwein was in London for a veteran's tennis tournament. His private jet pilots were the first to come down with Killer-T in San Fran. Turns out his seventeen-year-old son, Greg, was at military school in Pasadena, back when Axl got his ass busted for meth and his ma sent him there to straighten out. So Greg Rosenwein was partying with us on Friday night.'

Harry felt like he'd been smacked. 'Well, that's put me off my fried chicken.'

'Greg's dead,' Matt said dramatically.

'No way!' Harry gawped.

'Same as in London,' Matt said. 'Killer-T's more potent in kids and younger adults. There's hardly any cases in people over seventy.'

'Was Greg near us?' Harry asked. 'Did you see him?'

'No idea what he looks like,' Matt said, greasy fingers and cheeks crammed with poultry. 'But everyone was around that pool, and given how infectious this is supposed to be . . .'

'How can you sit there eating?' Harry said as he walked to the fridge. 'This sucks.'

'Schools are closed until further notice,' Matt said. 'The governor's making a statement to the media at nine, which must be the full curfew announcement. And President West's supposedly gonna announce that no domestic flights can take off after midnight.'

'Look on the bright side,' Harry said, as he stuffed his face with fries. 'Neither of us is gonna live long enough for this junk food to make us fat.'

49 CLYDE'S DONGFENG

It was 6 a.m. when the lab rats finished work. Four Radical Cake muffin boxes stood on the RV's fold-out dining table, each containing thirty sterile syringe packs and thirty glass vials of Killer-T vaccine.

'Here's to a good night's work,' Mango said as she wheeled an office chair up to the table, ripped open a syringe pack and pricked the needle through the thin metal lid of a glass vial. 'I guess I'll go first.'

Before Mango could stab herself, Juno, Charlie and Veryan rushed up to the table, rolling sleeves and filling syringes. After a count of three, the four sweaty and exhausted women jabbed their arms with the fine needles.

The sun was creeping up as Charlie walked back to her VW, the little glass bottles chinking with every step. Charlie dry-heaved as she caught the smell of two zombies sleeping on the sidewalk. She upped her pace in case there were more in the deserted street and only felt safe when she'd shut her car door and pressed the lock button.

She switched on her phone. Her arm itched as she placed the vaccine in the passenger-side footwell, then grabbed a hoodie from the back seat and used it to cover the box.

'You have two new messages from Harry Smirnov,' the speaker in the centre console announced.

The name jarred, but her phone was old and she guessed it was an ancient message triggered by a bug when it switched back on. She was more concerned with where to drive. Mango had kept a radio on while they'd worked and the state of Nevada's full quarantine had been announced at midnight.

Under quarantine rules, people could make a single *final destination* journey for a further twelve hours, but were warned that licence-plate recognition systems would catch and fine drivers making multiple journeys.

Charlie opened up her navigation screen. She wanted to give Ed a dose of vaccine, but no matter how hard Charlie looked there was no getting around the fact that Care4Kids was eight miles north, while the Rahimi residence was a little under two miles east.

Working on the assumption that licence plate and speed radar were concentrated on major roads, Charlie plotted a route that avoided freeways and ran through a grid of residential streets. Once she'd drawn the route on her nav screen, and the car had told her that *based on current traffic patterns a faster route was available*, Charlie decided to check if there were any new messages on her phone before setting off.

She listened to a message from Navid, who guilted her by stating that he was concerned she'd gone out without saying where, and that he trusted her, but it was now midnight and everyone including the boys were worried.

'*Harry Smirnov called yesterday at 1637. Call back or play message?*'

Charlie pressed the button to play back as Juno drove past in a big Ford truck, giving a goodbye wave. Harry sounded older, but his voice still evoked the years in White Boulder, when his calls and letters kept her sane, and a flicker of the rejection she'd felt when he'd ignored her messages and stopped visiting a few weeks after she'd been released.

'Charlie, long time no speak,' Harry said, with an irritating casualness. 'I'd like you to call me back ASAP. Vegas Local has received an FBI witness statement. Helen Back turned snitch to get out of some tax beef. She claims that Mango and Veryan Kowalski-Clark run a gene lab. Your name crops up too, saying that you're their *best lab rat*. Even if that's not true, you're gonna have the Feds on your case. Call me back when you can. It's Harry . . . Harry Smirnov, obviously.'

Charlie felt a stab down one side as she breathed. She thought about calling Harry straight back, or talking to Mango. Mango might still be tidying up in the RV if she ran, but Charlie decided her priority was to give Ed his vaccine, then head home for a tricky conversation with her foster parents.

I know you thought I was a near-perfect foster daughter, but last night I ran off to go to the illegal gene-modding lab where I've been working since before I met you. And I'm telling you this now because I have four doses of Killer-T vaccine that might save you and your sons' lives . . .

But that was a bridge to cross later and Charlie hit the accelerator. Vegas was built on a grid system, so even minor streets were easy to navigate. She did the driving herself and kept the speed down, hoping it would give her a chance to spot road blocks and turn ahead of them.

At times Charlie felt she was the only car moving in the whole city. As she'd hoped, there were no patrols on the side streets and after six miles of suburbs and fifty stop signs, she rolled on to the Care4Kids lot, barren aside from three cars belonging to the night staff.

Charlie knew the unit would be closed to visitors, but reckoned she could twist the arm of Joyce, or one of the other nurses she'd got friendly with. Unfortunately, the front desk was manned by Clyde, a huge Chinese-American nurse who was always miserable. He had a reputation for being thick, and mostly did cleaning tasks and served as muscle when one of the teen residents got aggressive.

'Morning,' Charlie said brightly, stepping up to the reception desk in mask and gloves and taking her phone out to be sterilised, like nothing was out of the ordinary.

Clyde lowered a tablet on which he was playing a bubble-shooting game and made a grunt through his mask.

'You must be tripping.'

'I always come to see Ed on Monday mornings. You know how important his routine is.'

'Charlie, there's a state-wide quarantine. Did you just get in your car and drive here?'

'Obviously.'

'You're lucky you didn't get arrested,' Clyde warned, reaching for a phone. 'You can get in serious trouble. I'll call and say you've been here overnight and hopefully they'll give you a quarantine authorisation to drive home.'

'No,' Charlie said frantically. 'Can you *please* let me in to see Ed. Ten minutes tops. This might be my last chance to see him in weeks.'

Clyde shook his head. 'Letting someone in off the street during a level-one quarantine? Joyce would fire my ass in a heartbeat.'

'Come on,' Charlie begged.

I have to give Ed the vaccine. If I jumped the counter, this big lump would flatten me. He might take a bribe, but I only have thirty bucks in my wallet. But what if . . .

'You're a total dick hole,' Charlie screamed, as a better idea dawned. 'Why can't you let me see my brother?'

Clyde was used to being thumped and spat on, so he wasn't fazed by a girl having a hissy fit. He picked his tablet back up as Charlie slammed the door and stormed into the parking lot.

Charlie frequently arrived at Care4Kids around the same time that nurses on the dayshift clocked in. She'd often seen Clyde clambering out of a two-seat Dongfeng sports car, complete with a go-faster body kit and a pearlescent paint job.

Charlie passed the Dongfeng as she ran back to her little VW. It took a couple of minutes swiping through the car's menus to find the setting to turn off collision avoidance, a decision the car informed her was *Not Recommended and may invalidate insurance policies in some states*, before making her reconfirm.

After reversing around the lot, Charlie lined her rear up with Clyde's Dongfeng and backed into it at around eight miles per hour. She expected no more than a crackle of plastic and some scraped paint, but the rear fender of her tiddly VW managed to tangle with the Dongfeng's body kit, and a three-foot section ripped off as Charlie pulled away.

'You've gotta be kidding . . .' Charlie gasped as she looked behind from the driver's seat. She half expected Clyde to come charging outside, but Clyde's focus was on bubble-popping and Charlie meekly strolled back into the lobby.

'What now?' Clyde snapped, peering up from his game.

'I had a little accident,' Charlie said, holding up a chunk of pearlescent fender. 'Is there someone here who drives a weird-looking sports car?'

'My Dongfeng,' Clyde howled, putting his hands to his head as he charged around the counter and ran into the lot without mask or gloves.

'I'm really sorry.'

'This lot is empty,' Clyde shouted when he saw fender dangling off the front of his car. 'How did you manage to hit my car in an empty lot, you stupid little girl?'

'Dark cars are hard to see when you go backwards,' Charlie suggested. 'I'm sorry.'

As Clyde crouched down to study the damage, Charlie backed up towards the entrance. The instant she got inside, she twisted the bolt inside the door and had vaulted behind the counter before the hulking nurse realised what had happened.

An older nurse spotted her as she bolted down a short hallway to Ed's room. Injections were near the top of the long list of things that freaked Ed out and Charlie felt horrible as she stepped into his dark room.

'Excuse me, miss,' an angry voice was shouting, clearly getting closer. 'Miss!'

Charlie pulled a syringe pack out of her trouser pocket. Ed was bigger than her and she desperately hoped he didn't wake up and thump her as she pushed the needle into a vial of Killer-T vaccine, gently peeled back the bedsheet curled round Ed's back and jabbed his upper arm.

'You can't be in here!' the nurse shouted, bursting in as Charlie pocketed the evidence of what she'd done.

'Charlie?' Ed roared, sitting up in bed, clutching a pillow to his chest.

Clyde had used a key to let himself back inside. He furiously slammed Charlie against the wall. Ed didn't like seeing his sister manhandled and jumped out of bed, locking his chunky hands round Clyde's neck and giving Charlie a chance to break free.

'It's OK, Ed, but I have to go,' Charlie said, feeling horribly guilty as she abandoned her panicked brother to a pair of angry nurses and sprinted back the way she'd come.

Outside, Charlie quickly inspected her car to make sure it was drivable before jumping in. One of the rear light clusters was cracked, but everything else seemed fine.

I smashed up a car and violated quarantine at a hospital. Harry says the FBI are on to me. I'd probably be in an interrogation room already if the world wasn't focused on Killer-T. But I did what I came here to do. I need to get home and vaccinate Navid, Jan and the boys.

With good behaviour, I might be out by the time I'm thirty . . .

50 HAVING WORDS

'It's Charlie, returning your call.'

Her voice made the past erupt. From the desperate sweaty hug in the tire shop, to the morning Harry woke in hospital, with three loose teeth, crazy sexual jealousy and a vow never to speak to Charlie again. They were just kids. They'd never even kissed, but her voice still felt big. Like she'd grown roots in his brain.

'You sound upset,' Harry said as he stepped on to his balcony and looked at dead streets four hundred and fifty feet below.

'Just had my first ever row with my foster parents,' Charlie said in a dazed sing-song voice. 'And other crazy stuff happened. And I'm on my way back to jail . . .'

'Only if it's true,' Harry pointed out.

Charlie sounded wary. 'Am I talking to Harry my old friend, or Harry from Vegas Local?'

'Friend,' Harry said. 'There's no point running a story now anyway. Elvis Presley could land mid-strip in a UFO, take a crap and start singing "Viva Las Vegas", and Killer-T would still be all anyone talked about.'

'Focuses the mind when something could kill you,' Charlie observed.

'Helen Back's FBI statement is probably under some sort of legal protection,' Harry said. 'I could get into trouble if I sent it to you. But the gist is simple.'

'I've been running Mango's lab,' Charlie confessed.

'This call isn't encrypted,' Harry warned.

Charlie laughed. 'If the FBI have been on my case for two weeks, they'll have all they need to bust me. Mango's so cautious about *everything*. I can't believe she gossiped to a celeb like some star-struck teen.'

'You've got money, right?' Harry said. 'As soon as quarantine ends, you need to get lawyered up, big time. Cut the best deal you can.'

'I haven't got much info to give them,' Charlie said. 'Shoulda learned my lesson and taken a job at the mall . . .'

'Ambition is one thing we've always had in common,' Harry noted.

'But yours doesn't get you into trouble,' Charlie said, remembering how easily they'd always found stuff to talk about. 'Can I ask a question, if you're not too busy?'

Harry laughed. 'I'm holed up in this apartment with Matt until quarantine ends. There's nowt on Netflix and I've jerked off twice already.'

'I never figured out what I did to upset you,' Charlie said. 'I called. I sent a dozen messages. I even went old-skool and bought a card and a stamp and put it in the post. You were my best friend and you cut me dead.'

Harry considered lying, but after two years his ego could handle the truth.

'I was in love with you,' Harry admitted. 'There was a Trojan full of Brad's sperm in your bathroom bin and the thought of being anywhere near when he was around made me feel like firing a bullet through my acne-splattered temple.'

'Brad . . .' Charlie gasped. 'I didn't realise you found out . . .'

'Are you still seeing him?'

Charlie laughed. 'Brad had a girlfriend, and another girlfriend when he went to his uncle's farm, and other girls at school he was hooking up with. After a few weeks, I realised I was never gonna be anything more than the girl across the hall.'

'Seeing anyone now?'

'Not really,' Charlie said. 'I guess I should have realised you were crushing on me, all the time you spent talking to me, and the gifts. But for over two years you were my only friend. That meant *so* much to me.'

'The weekend before, I almost put my arm around you after we had lunch.'

'I had a lot going on back then,' Charlie said awkwardly. 'How about your love life?'

'Nothing significant,' Harry said, as he realised Charlie probably had no idea about his mods. 'My skin is better now. Went out with my friend Anita for a few months at the start of junior year.'

'You must be a senior now, right? Is college sorted?'

'NYU, Photography and Reportage,' Harry said.

'Living in New York will be *so* cool!'

'I've been so involved with trashy stories on Vegas Local and Ellie's *super-lean business model*. It's two years since I got my good camera out and did proper photography. And eighteen seems too young to be a sell out.'

'A bit,' Charlie said, and her laugh made Harry feel great.

'How about you? I'm assuming you've aced your SATs already.'

'I got a thirty-six in the ACT in my sophomore year,' Charlie said.

'Holy shit!' Harry said. 'I knew you were smart, but that's insane.'

'Yay,' Charlie chirped. 'I'll be the smartest kid in the whole damned jail.'

'You should call a lawyer now,' Harry said. 'It could make a huge difference to your chances.'

'I guess,' Charlie said.

'I've missed talking to you, Charlie.'

'Same here,' Charlie agreed. 'If we don't die horrifically from a virus that liquefies our internal organs and makes us drown slowly in our own blood, and I'm not in federal prison, we should totally do coffee.'

'Sounds like a plan,' Harry laughed.

'I need to call Mango and let her know what's going down,' Charlie said. 'But I'd like to thank you properly for tipping us off. I've got twenty-five doses of Killer-T vaccine, but no idea how to get one to you in Summerlin.'

'I don't live with Kirsten any more. I've got my own place in a high rise on Sammy Davis Junior.'

'North strip?' Charlie asked brightly. 'I'm at my foster parents' on Rancho Circle, maybe a mile and a half away. I drove north to give Ed his vaccine earlier. I stuck to back streets and I didn't get stopped.'

Harry didn't seem sure. 'The fifteen is closed and I can count three ... actually *four* checkpoints from right here on my balcony. But I might be able to run to you, after dark.'

'I don't want to put my foster family at any more risk than I have already,' Charlie said. 'They've all had jabs, but immunity will take a while to build up, and the Brits estimate the vaccine is only ninety-five per cent effective. So here's what I'll do:

'I'm messaging you my address right now. But you'll need to go down the alley between two wooden fences a couple of doors down. At the end of the alley there's a scrap of land where the local kids ride bikes and hang. I'll hide the doses there and message you a photo of the exact position.'

'OK,' Harry said, a touch wary.

'And this way you can still get hold of the vaccine if the Feds come knocking. How many shots do you want?'

'Me obviously,' Harry said. 'My housemate, Matt. Kirsten didn't like the idea of being alone at her big house in Summerlin, so she's with her toy boy. It's a fair distance, but if I can run to Rancho Circle in the dark I can probably get to them too. Is four doses too much?'

'I'll give you five in case you think of someone else,' Charlie said. 'Ed and my foster family have had their shots; my best friend and my godson have their own supply. I'd hand the spares out to my neighbours, but I had a nightmare convincing Navid and Jan that I wasn't trying to poison *them*.'

'I guess I'd think twice if some random girl came to my door with a hypodermic needle,' Harry said.

'Exactly,' Charlie said. 'It's been awesome talking to you again, but I need to let Mango know.'

'Keep my name out of it,' Harry said. 'Especially if you talk to a lawyer. I'm not sure what the laws are on distributing a confidential FBI witness statement, but it ain't gonna be legal.'

'No worries,' Charlie said.

'You keep safe,' Harry said soothingly. 'And try not to worry too much till you've had words with a decent lawyer.'

51 BOUNCING BOYS

The quarantine was barely twelve hours old, but Charlie's foster brothers were already bouncing off the walls and fighting downstairs. Foster mom, Jan, was a sweetie and she bought Charlie mint tea and cookies, gave her a hug and told her that everyone in the house loved her.

Charlie felt bad shooing her stepmom out, but she'd sent Mango a message straight after calling Harry, and Mango replied saying she was busy with the twins and would contact her on the encrypted tablet.

'Thought you'd be catching zeds after the all-nighter,' Mango said cheerfully as Charlie settled in a chair at her desk and angled the tablet so that Mango got to see her.

'Running on adrenalin, I guess,' Charlie said.

'Did you make it to Ed?' Mango asked.

'I did.'

'That's *so* great,' Mango said. 'My four all had a scream up about the injection, but kids' immune systems work fast. If it's like most vaccines, they'll have good protection in eight to twelve hours.'

'I called because I have bad news,' Charlie said. 'I can't tell you my source, but your friend Helen Back has given the FBI a statement . . .'

'Ahh, that,' Mango said weakly.

Charlie gasped. 'You knew already?'

Mango made a big sigh, followed by a yawn. 'Two Feds came into Radical Cakes, Thursday the week before last. They'd filmed me when I went to restock the RV. They knew about you, Juno and my contacts in LA. They had everything they needed to bust me on the spot.'

'So why didn't they?' Charlie asked anxiously. 'And why didn't you tell us?'

'I apologise,' Mango said. 'I've known Helen for a long time. I was pissed when I saw her statement describing me as star struck, and blabbing. But if I'm honest that's exactly what I did.'

'If they had so much evidence, why didn't they move on us?'

'I have desirable skills,' Mango explained. 'The FBI and CDC budgets have increased massively over the past few years. But people with medical degrees and experience with synthetic biology are in desperately short supply.'

'So you have to go to work for the Feds?'

'Not just that,' Mango said. 'The feds will take everything we've earned except one vehicle and one small home. We lose the cake business, all our savings and we must make full disclosure on every patient we've treated. Veryan must serve twelve to eighteen months in a minimum-security federal prison on money-laundering charges.'

'What about me and Juno?'

'I've tried really hard to help you . . .' Mango said, before halting.

Charlie shuddered. 'Tried really hard, but *what*?'

'You're not an adult, so you can't become an FBI employee. And with your past history, with the explosives . . .'

Charlie growled. 'So you get off, and I go to prison? Again!'

'You're seventeen,' Mango soothed. 'You worked in a lab. You didn't make Z-drugs or purple wasps, just designer embryos and high quality gene mods for people who wanted them.'

'Have they given a number?' Charlie snapped.

'One to two years for Juno. Three to five for you, because of your record.'

Could be worse, but it doesn't include breaking quarantine at Care4Kids . . .

Charlie closed her eyes and bunched a fist. 'Why do I always get shafted? You're treating me no better than the Janssens did.'

'That's not fair,' Mango said.

'No,' Charlie hissed, wanting to yell but aware of her foster family in adjoining rooms. 'What's not fair is you blab to your celebrity friends and I go to jail. I've saved money. I'm getting my own lawyer. A damned good one.'

'What have you got to offer?' Mango asked stiffly. 'You have nothing the feds don't know already.'

'But it all works nicely for you,' Charlie said acidly.

'I'm a mom. I get to keep my kids in a modest home and spend a minimum of eight years doing low-paid work in an FBI lab. You can blow ten grand on a lawyer, but you won't get a better deal. And I'm not even supposed to be talking about this with you.

'I'm closing the lab. You won't be hearing from me again, and if you make contact I'll pass the message to my lawyer. Goodbye, Charlie. I like you, and wish our friendship could have ended better.'

Mango closed the call window. Seconds later the tablet cut to black and a message popped on to the screen:

This device has been deauthorised and is now locked.

To reinstate access, contact your system administrator.

52 ZOMBIE SMASH

Vegas Local

SUNDAY'S HOT STORIES

LAS VEGAS – First Killer-T deaths confirmed at emergency clinic. Police warn of severe penalties for quarantine violation.

Deaths include 16yo violin prodigy. Toll expected to rise sharply as Las Vegas cases reach 150.

FULL STORY

CARSON CITY – SynthLab Inc. admits production delay.

The private contractor charged with rapid production of 3.3 million anti-virus doses for the State of Nevada has admitted a refrigeration fault will result in longer than expected lead times for vaccine production.

The Nevada Rapid Vaccine Production Target calls for 15,000 doses of vaccine to be prepared for emergency workers within ten hours. However, a worker inside SynthLab's Carson City facility has claimed that precursor compounds had spoiled inside damaged refrigeration units, and that vaccine production had still not begun fifteen hours after the British released the manufacturing process.

FULL STORY

Matt sprawled on a sofa, dressed in tie-dyed polo and camo shorts. Banners scrolled on a twenty-four-hour news channel, but the volume was off and he was studying a glossy book titled *Sara Channing's Photo Bombs*.

'I've never seen this before,' Matt said, raising the book as Harry strode in, wearing a black running shirt and boxer briefs.

The open page was a picture taken with a Congolese sniper, sixty feet up a tree.

'Your ma was hardcore,' Matt told Harry. 'It says she spent two nights up in the tree with this guy while he shot and killed at least six people. And they had to stay in position, not even coming down to use the toilet.'

'She was young too,' Harry said, still loving the shiner Lana had given his best friend.

'How come I've never seen this book before?' Matt asked.

'That's the first edition,' Harry said. 'They released an expanded edition after mum died, with more photos and a foreword by some BBC newsreader who Kirsten reckons my mum couldn't stand. But the original is worth a bit to photo-book collectors, so don't go getting the pages all sticky when you see the topless tribeswomen.'

Matt laughed. 'What made you get it out?'

'Puts our current situation in perspective,' Harry said, shrugging. 'Speaking of, you mostly wear black. Is there a long-sleeve black shirt I can borrow?'

'Several,' Matt said. 'Not sure if they'll stretch over your freakishly mutated body, but you're welcome to try.'

'Cheers,' Harry said.

'You're really going out there?'

'I often ask what my mum would do in certain situations,' Harry said. 'But I took one look at the photos in that book and I knew *exactly* what she'd do.'

Harry found a slate-grey shirt in Matt's closet that was only a little tight. Back in his own room, he put on black jogging bottoms and pushed his feet into Nike running shoes, on which he'd meticulously blacked out all the reflective parts with a Sharpie. Then he turned to the gear laid out on the bed.

He'd decided to take his cell in case of emergency, but would leave it switched off. The cops could easily track the location of a phone, and during a quarantine they might be hunting any device with a signal that moved around.

Then there was the camera gear. Harry felt ashamed when he got his Nikon out and found the battery dead and that the most recent pictures on the memory card were taken on a Queensbridge trip to Washington, DC over a year earlier.

The deserted city might provide interesting photo opportunities, and Harry hoped that if he got busted and used the excuse that he was out taking photos for Vegas Local he'd get off with nothing more serious than a warning and a ride home in a cop car.

'Best-a luck, guv'nor,' Matt said, mocking Harry's London accent.

Harry pulled a black pack with his camera gear up his arm, then put on a black baseball cap, the darkest pair of blue nitrile gloves he'd been able to find, and a yellow virus mask, over which he'd crudely stitched a rectangle cut out of an old black tank top.

The elevator came fast, because nobody else was using it.

Only a couple of emergency lights were on in the lobby, but Harry dipped his face because there was CCTV. He'd not expected to find anyone behind the concierge desk and the revolving doors didn't budge either. He could get out by pushing the bar on the fire door to the side. But he wouldn't get back in that way and he decided to iron out that niggle by going downstairs to the basement parking.

There were more parked cars than usual, though since many apartments were second homes it was still barely half full. Harry's building had installed full-height barriers on the vehicle entrances after zombies baseball-batted and robbed an elderly couple getting out of their car, so he had to grab an electronic remote control out of his Porsche to operate the rattling exit gate.

With his phone off, Harry had to memorise the route and the silence got eerie as he reached the point where he needed to cross the Interstate. Apart from The Strip and a few streets downtown, Vegas wasn't a walking city. The only way for pedestrians to cross the freeway was a network of run-for-your-life foot crossings over on and off-ramps and a stretch of graffitied footbridge.

Ignoring the yellow pedestrian arrows, Harry scrambled up twenty feet of gravel embankment to the barrier at the edge of the freeway. The I-15 through the centre of Las Vegas had six lanes in each direction, plus extra lanes for cars peeling on and off.

Harry cracked a childlike grin when he stepped on to the hard shoulder, catching a whiff of rubber in the warm evening air as he stared at fourteen lanes of nothing. Turning back gave a vista over the west side of the Vegas strip. The giant casinos' rear video screens usually enticed visitors arriving from

California with ads for their latest shows and restaurants. But tonight they were either dark, or said stuff like *Casino closed – We wish our guests the best of health and a safe journey home.* Most of the casino lights were off, but some rooms had lights on inside, and Harry got a tingle, imagining lonely souls who hadn't got home before the airport closed.

Velcro ripped as Harry pulled his Nikon out of the pack. The controls felt clumsy through gloves and his mask made it hard to get the viewfinder close to his eye. He photographed the rows of casino signs, then jogged to the central reservation, where he switched the camera into low-light mode and took several shots down the empty freeway.

The roar of a military truck sandwiched between a pair of cop cars blew up from behind an overpass, blue and reds flashing, but no need for sirens. Harry was out of practice with the camera, but he kept low, set a slow exposure and rested the camera on the central barrier so that the skimming cars turned into streaks of light.

He viewed the image. It wasn't great, but having a few shots on the memory card would help the photographer argument if he got busted. The ideal outcome was to not get busted at all, so Harry crossed the rest of the freeway, hurdled a low fence and found himself in an overgrown patch at the back of a souvenir store wrapped in bright yellow signage.

Don't pay crazy strip prices! Fridge magnets $3 for 4, smartphone cases $4, tees from $6 or 4 for $20.

There were some makeshift shelters in the overgrown scrub between the freeway and the back of the store. The tangle of plants would easily hide a flaked-out zombie and while Harry's virus mask filtered smells, hundreds of buzzing flies were a sure indicator of filth. It was a relief to reach the rear of the souvenir store without anything squelching underfoot.

'Down on the ground,' someone shouted.

Harry jolted and glanced both ways, before realising it came from the front of the store and wasn't meant for him. When he peeked round the side of the building, Harry saw the headlights of a Vegas Metro police car and a military truck with slatted sides, like the one he'd seen on the freeway.

Harry could make out zombies sitting on benches in the back of the truck. Up front two female zombies stood in the truck's headlamps, facing two large men armed with long cattle prods. Their bio-suits were made of extra-thick material and smeared with the body fluids of the zombies they'd thrown in the truck.

'Kneel!' one of the men ordered. 'Hands on heads.'

Harry still had his Nikon swinging in his right hand. He flipped to video mode, starting to shoot as a third rubber suit came round the side of the truck. This one was female and held a device that looked like a police speed gun, the screen at one end reflecting off her plastic visor.

'Can't you understand, zombie scum?' one man roared.

Harry had unconsciously edged along the side of the souvenir store to get closer to the action. He took a shot of the zombie's agonised face as she got dragged to the back of the truck by her matted hair.

He realised you couldn't have an effective quarantine while hundreds of people roamed the streets crusted in bodily waste. But, since most zombies were happy being locked in a cell with regular meals, the brutality of the roundup seemed unnecessary.

'Got one round the side,' the rubber-suited female shouted. 'Big heat signature. Gonna be a strong sucker!'

Harry panned his camera back from the rear of the truck

and realised two things. First, the weird detector thing the woman was holding was an infra-red body-heat detector and, second, it was being aimed down the side of the building, right at him.

53 OLIVE PALM DRIVE

The Nikon flailed from its strap as Harry spun and ran.

'We're not going to harm you,' a loudspeaker on the cop car announced. 'Step out with hands raised.'

Harry had made four steps before there was a pop, like a giant champagne cork. The rubber-suited woman had fired an electric stun bolt. Harry felt it glance the back of his calf, but it was at the limit of its range and what remained of its momentum wasn't enough for the barbed tip to hook his trousers and release its sting.

Rather than go back to the freeway, where he'd be exposed, Harry charged along the embankment until he reached the back of a mini-mall. He sprinted past a dry cleaner's, an attorney's office, a yoga gym and a dollar store with a zombie sprawled in front of its main doors.

Harry doubted the round-up crew could chase in their thick suits and rubber boots, but he was spooked so he kept running. After a left-right glance – seeing the cop car still parked a couple of hundred yards up the road – Harry sprinted across four lanes, then kept low as he cut down a suburban side street.

It wasn't the road he'd planned to use, but the streets were on a grid and having the casino towers at his back gave Harry confidence that he was moving west. A motorbike speared the silence, shooting down the empty road at more than a hundred miles per hour, closely followed by another.

Harry wondered if they had some mission, or had decided to use the empty roads as a racetrack. A right took him into Olive Palm Drive, a short cul-de-sac with houses fanning off a turning circle at the far end.

It seemed unusually bright, because everyone was home with the lights on. Harry spotted number eight and imagined Charlie inside, watching TV with her foster family. The front lawns didn't offer cover and Harry felt exposed as he saw the alleyway leading to a kids' play area.

Two masked sisters played catch in their back yard as Harry jogged, wooden fences tight on either side. The little park was shabby, with two out of three swings broken. He recognised the wood and plastic climbing castle from Charlie's photo. He ducked beneath a wooden ladder and reached into a gap, where a turret was bolted to a bright red tunnel.

Harry's gloved fingers touched a plastic food container and it took a hard tug to strip the plumber's tape holding it in place. The tub was slippery with condensation, and Harry popped it open and got splashed with melted ice, which Charlie had packed around the glass vials to keep the vaccine cool.

A scuttling sound came from Harry's left, making him back out and bash his shoulder on a wooden prop. As he glanced around, shocked and with water from the open box trickling inside his shirtsleeve, Charlie stood up at the end of the slide.

'You scared the tits off me!' Harry gasped.

She was dressed not to be seen, in dark purple leggings and a black hoodie.

'I was hoping you'd show,' Charlie said, grinning behind her mask. 'But when this big muscle guy arrived, I scrambled up the slide.'

'I started doing push-ups,' Harry joked, pulling his mask away from his face for a moment to catch fresh air.

Charlie stepped forward and held her arms out wide. 'I've missed you.'

'Me too,' Harry said, masked face to masked face, each wrapping gloved hands round the other's dark clothing.

'Crazy times . . .' Charlie said as she took a half step back. 'Everything happening at once.'

'For sure,' Harry said, nodding.

'Your mods look good. So many guys go overboard.'

'I get told that a lot,' Harry said, flattered. 'I mainly got it because of my acne. I'd look in the mirror and hate myself.'

Charlie nodded thoughtfully. 'You should inject your vaccine now. Full immunity takes at least a day to build up, but it should improve your ability to fight a virus within hours. I take it you know how to inject yourself?'

'I did four jabs every two hours when I started my mods,' Harry said, resting the tub on the edge of the wooden turret and rolling his sleeve.

Besides syringes and vials, Charlie had put five little alcohol wipes in the box. She tore one open, sterilised a patch of skin on Harry's upper arm, then gave him a jab.

'Nice one,' Harry said, wishing his mask wasn't blocking the expression on his face.

'I phoned that attorney, like you suggested,' Charlie said, as Harry buttoned his cuff. 'She was helpful. She agreed with Mango's assessment that I'm looking at three to five years, unless I can trade information on crimes they don't already know about.'

'Do you have any?'

'Kinda,' Charlie said. 'But she's my best friend, and the mother of my little godson.'

'Awkward . . .'

'The good news is, the attorney says there's a decent chance law enforcement is too busy with quarantine to arrest me any time soon. But there's a downside. Have you heard of SOPA?'

Harry nodded. 'The Synthetic Organism Protection Act. Basically, the destruction of all human rights during a quarantine period.'

'That's the one,' Charlie said warily. 'SOPA laws give law-enforcement powers to arrest and hold people in detention, even on the barest suspicion that a suspect is involved in unregistered genetic modification. While quarantine is running, they can charge me under SOPA laws and lock me in a quarantine centre for months, without having to charge me, question me, or allow me to see an attorney.'

'That's messed up,' Harry said.

'The attorney recommends I make myself difficult to find until the quarantine ends and the Feds lose their emergency powers.'

'You could stay with Matt and me,' Harry suggested. 'I can clear the junk out of the spare bedroom.'

'That's sweet,' Charlie said. 'But you'd be risking a charge of harbouring a fugitive.'

'Sounds like a story for Vegas Local,' Harry noted.

Charlie smiled behind her mask. 'I haven't laid eyes on Matt since he graduated junior high.'

Harry had been doing the handsome rich-kid thing, sleeping around, acting cocky and having a couple of short-term girlfriends. But none of them felt right like Charlie had. He wanted to pull down his mask and go for a kiss, but somehow he'd morphed back into the anxious fourteen-year-old who'd first met her.

'I've got our route home memorised,' Harry mumbled. 'It's longer, but I'm not covering the same ground twice, and I can drop two doses of vaccine at Kirsten's boyfriend's place.'

'OK,' Charlie said. 'Just let me go in my house and pack a bag. And there's a stop I have to make along the way.'

54 IGNITION

'Grab this,' Charlie whispered, her arm dangling a backpack out of her bedroom window.

Harry caught it and placed it in the back of the little VW, while Charlie straddled on to the roof. She crabbed over a few rows of roof tiles and Harry grabbed her legs as she dangled over the gutter.

'Can you drive?' Charlie asked, after he'd put her down. 'I've only had my licence six months, so I've never driven after dark.'

'I think we're better on foot,' Harry said. 'With my mods I can run fast. If you tell me what you want from this storage unit, I can go get it on my own.'

Charlie shook her head. 'It's too heavy and I drove all the way to Care4Kids in *daylight*. If we avoid main roads, things are fine.'

'They might be better organised now,' Harry suggested. 'And, no offence, but your car wouldn't outrun a shopping cart.'

Charlie tutted. 'I'm not forcing you to help me, Harry. You can take the vaccines to Kirsten. I'll grab what I need from the storage unit and we'll meet at your building later.'

Harry shook his head. 'I think we should stick together. So let's drive.'

'I don't want a scene with my foster parents,' Charlie said, glancing towards the house. 'We need to shift before they see I'm gone.'

Charlie looked back mournfully as her titchy Volkswagen rolled down the drive and on to the street.

'What's in this storage unit?' Harry asked, ignoring a red light at a junction that would normally be clogged with cars.

'Modding equipment,' Charlie explained. 'I trusted Mango with all my financial arrangements. I've got two grand in emergency cash, but the attorney said the Feds will seize every cent they can lay their hands on. Chances are, Mango has already given them my account details. So I'll be broke when I need money for a lawyer.'

'Don't they need to prove you're a criminal before they freeze your assets?' Harry asked.

Charlie shook her head. 'The attorney said the Feds can freeze any assets they believe are the proceeds of criminal activity. The onus is then on me to show a judge how I earned the money legally. Which, seeing as I'm a seventeen-year-old schoolgirl with no legitimate income, means I can wave my savings goodbye.'

'That blows,' Harry noted.

'Turn at the next left. I need the third storage unit, but stop by the main entrance so I can make sure nobody's around.'

As Harry pulled to the kerb, Charlie reached into the rear seats, unzipped her backpack and pulled out an automatic pistol.

'Where'd you get that?' Harry gasped as Charlie opened the clip to check that the gun was loaded, then clicked off the safety.

'My foster dad's dresser.'

'I thought this was an empty storage unit.'

'I doubt anyone will be here,' Charlie said, 'but better safe than sorry. When I give the all-clear, back the car in, so we can load up the lab equipment. I just hope Mango didn't take it home . . .'

'I don't like this,' Harry said, grabbing Charlie's arm as she opened the passenger door. 'Let's get out of here. I can pay your lawyer.'

'I'm not your charity project,' Charlie said firmly. 'The equipment gives me power. I could set up my own lab, sell the equipment, or surrender it in return for a lighter sentence. It's not too late if you want to run to your auntie's place.'

'Never a dull moment with you,' Harry joked.

Harry was scared, but now realised that the combo of brains and danger was why he'd always found her so attractive.

What's that thing they say about guys wanting a girlfriend who's just like their mum?

Harry couldn't take his eyes off Charlie's ass as she strode purposefully towards the locked door of the storage unit. She buried the gun in the front of her hoodie and pulled a set of keys. After unlocking, she rolled a big door far enough to let her car in, then opened the RV and flipped the light inside.

Charlie was relieved to see the three glowing touchscreens of the new modding machines. She leaned outside to signal Harry, and as he reversed the VW to the side of the RV Charlie unplugged the machines, then grabbed strong trash bags from under the sink and started filling them with glassware and lab equipment out of the kitchen cupboards.

'So this is a modding lab,' Harry said, poking his head in.

He'd have loved to take photographs, but Charlie was on a mission.

'Put the machines in the trunk of my car,' she ordered.

As Harry made three round trips, Charlie went to the refrigerators in the back room, returning with another trash bag full of chemicals and supplies. Then she plugged the sink and unscrewed the lid on a two-gallon bottle of pure alcohol. Charlie poured two inches of the alcohol into the sink, then worked her way around the RV, splashing the flammable liquid over the dining table, dashboard and driver's seat.

'Why are you burning it?' Harry asked.

'The less physical evidence, the more the FBI's case becomes Mango's word against mine,' Charlie said. 'Plus, this RV cost Mango a hundred grand, and I'm not loving her right now.'

Harry shook his head wryly. 'Most girls want dinner and a movie. With you it's *dispose of my homemade explosives, help me burn out a modding lab . . .*'

Charlie laughed and flipped Harry off, before her next set of orders. 'Drive the car out, then open the storage unit door fully, so that the oxygen doesn't run out when this burns.'

As Harry dealt with the car and the door, Charlie ditched the empty drum of alcohol and took a last walk around, opening the RV's skylights, windows and the driver's door. Finally, she reached into a cupboard and cut the rubber hose that ran from a propane cylinder to the hob.

After jumping the steps, Charlie made sure Harry was behind the wheel of her car.

'Open the passenger door for me,' she shouted. 'Ready?'

Charlie was alarmed by a growing whiff of gas as she pulled the gun out of her hoodie and aimed inside the door where she'd sprinkled alcohol on a nylon cushion. The bang made her jump. The heat of the bullet caused static, igniting the cushion and sending streaks of burning alcohol through the RV's interior.

'Drive, drive, drive!' Charlie screamed as she jumped in her car.

But the car decided to be bossy. *'Please ensure the passenger door is closed, and passenger seatbelt fastened before hitting the accelerator.'*

'Bastard!' Harry yelled, smashing the steering wheel as Charlie reached for the seatbelt.

Spreading the fuel through the cabin and opening doors and windows ensured that the RV burnt rather than exploded. But Harry was dazzled by the flames as Charlie's belt clicked.

'It's in!' Charlie shouted. 'Why aren't we moving?'

The accelerator was limp. Harry looked along the VW's dashboard as the flames coming off the RV began licking the wooden beams of the storage unit's roof.

'The battery light is flashing.'

'It was fully charged when we left!' Charlie protested.

'Must be the fire,' Harry said, his neck catching the intense heat radiating through the car's rear window. 'The car thinks the battery pack is overheating.'

'Are you kidding?' Charlie gasped.

'Get out and push,' Harry said.

But Charlie leaned over the centre console.

'It did this once before on a hot day,' Charlie said, scrolling through menus. 'You can reset the sensor, by going into . . .'

Charlie flipped on-screen menus as heat expansion blew one of the tires on the RV. The storage-unit roof was now ablaze, including a section directly above the Volkswagen.

'Go now!' Charlie shouted.

Harry pressed the accelerator and felt a satisfying whirr from the motor. The battery overheating light started to flash again, but Harry had enough momentum to clear the storage units and turn on to an unlit side road.

'If a police chopper spots these flames, we are *so* screwed,' Harry said.

'We're away from the heat source,' Charlie said as Harry turned the car off. 'Just give it a few seconds and we should be OK.'

A cop siren whooped in the distance while Harry gave the back of the car time to cool down. The flames behind had settled into a steady pattern, but a plume of smoke had erupted, suggesting a partial collapse of the storage unit's roof.

'Fingers crossed,' Harry said. He pressed the start button and felt a whirr. 'And off we go . . .'

55 BUST

Harry drove until the fire was just a plume in distant sky, sticking to side streets, passing the backs of industrial units and strip malls. Keeping slow meant Charlie spotted a checkpoint in time for Harry to avoid it, swinging across four empty lanes and down an alleyway between a motel and a Wells Fargo bank.

But their luck tanked a quarter-mile from Kirsten's boyfriend's place, taking a blind corner and finding a Metro Police car parked at the kerb while a bulky officer pissed in a storm drain.

'I'd hit the accelerator if I was in my Porsche,' Harry joked nervously as a female officer stepped into the road, raising a gloved hand.

'What's going on, kids?' she yelled through her mask, making a lower-the-window gesture as she crouched down. 'I need four hands where I can see 'em.'

The other officer shone a flashlight as he approached the rear of the car.

Harry had put some thought into how he'd act if he was stopped. 'Good evening, officer,' Harry said, laying on his politest English accent. 'Is there a problem?'

The officer acted sarcastic. 'Did you happen to notice a quarantine going down?'

'My girlfriend and I were at a friend's house. But there isn't enough food there, so I'm driving home to my aunt's.'

'You got a transit authorisation code?'

'Did we need one?' Harry asked innocently.

Charlie got goose bumps as the male officer shone his flashlight through the back window. Cops were trained to recognise gene-modding equipment, and the gear in the back wasn't even covered.

'We had a huge row with the guys we were staying with,' Charlie told the officer, trying to sound upset. 'I yelled at Harry to get in the car and leave. Are we in a lot of trouble?'

'Calm down, sweetheart,' the female cop said. 'You shouldn't have driven off without seeking authorisation. I'll need to take details of where you're from and where you're heading, and we'll sort it from there.'

But while the female officer bought the story of the teen couple leaving their friend's house after a row, her partner wasn't so sure.

'How come you're skulking down back streets at ten miles per hour?' he asked.

'I took a wrong turn,' Harry said. 'Shoulda pulled over and set the navigation, but I thought I knew where I was at.'

'What's that gear piled in the trunk?' the officer asked.

Charlie thought about the gun bulging inside her hoodie as Harry shuddered and thought about hitting the accelerator.

'Random junk,' Harry said.

The cop rocked his head knowingly. 'Mind if I look?'

'Sure,' Harry said, glancing anxiously across at Charlie. 'It's just school books, and a few clothes . . .'

'I'll need you both to step out of the car, keeping your hands visible at all times.'

Charlie knew they'd see her bulging gun as she stepped out, but as Harry opened the driver's door, the radios on the officers' lapels burst to life.

'All units, all units, we have a report of youths looting at the Fashion Show Mall. If anyone is in the area, proceed immediately.'

The woman snatched her radio, 'Car four-forty-one responding. We can be on scene in three to four minutes, over.'

The male cop scowled at his partner. 'There's more than school books in the back of this car.'

'Give me a break,' the woman yelled back, then looked in at Harry, wagging a stern finger. 'I'm gonna log an authorisation for your licence plate. You got one hour to get where you're going. If you're on the road after that, both your asses go to jail.'

'Thank you, ma'am,' Harry gasped, then spoke through gritted teeth as he put the window up. 'That was too close.'

'I feel *so* sick,' Charlie said, clutching her belly. 'But we've got an hour now. That's easily enough to get to Kirsten's place and drive on to yours.'

• • •

Kirsten's boyfriend was suspicious when Harry buzzed the intercom, and Kirsten reacted furiously when they reached the door of apartment 4C. She told Harry that they were crazy to be taking risks during quarantine, before shepherding them into the hallway.

'I don't care if you write me out of your will and never want to see me again,' Harry told his aunt when she finally stopped yelling. 'Just promise you'll use this vaccine.'

Harry hadn't realised Kirsten's boyfriend had a six-year-old son, which took care of his spare dose.

'I could make dinner,' Kirsten suggested diplomatically, once she'd calmed down. 'I've heard a lot about you, Charlie.'

'We've only got twenty minutes left on my travel permit,' Harry said. 'We want to get a dose to Matt as soon as possible.'

There were tears from the six-year-old as Charlie administered the jabs, then Kirsten gave Harry a stack of meals from her freezer and they hugged before jogging downstairs to the VW.

'I sense your aunt isn't my biggest fan,' Charlie said.

Harry laughed. 'She has this crazy idea that you'll make me do all kinds of illegal stuff that could get me into trouble with the law.'

'Me?' Charlie asked, smirking. 'I haven't committed a major felony in over an hour.'

The car was parked in front of the apartment block.

'These meals are freezing,' Harry said as Charlie opened the back of her car.

'Frozen meals are freezing,' Charlie mocked as Harry put them inside. 'Who'd a thought that? Kirsten offered you a cool bag . . .'

'I just wanted to get out of there,' Harry said, reaching out and dabbing two icy fingers on Charlie's neck.

'Buzz off!' Charlie yelped, stepping back and catching her sneaker on a jutting drain cover.

Harry caught her as she stumbled. Charlie showed a wounded expression as she looked up into his eyes and pulled down her virus mask. Harry's breath shuddered.

'Are you gonna kiss me or not?' Charlie asked.

Harry tore off his mask and closed in for a kiss. Gently at first, then pressing her against the car and sliding a hand down her back.

'I never thought this would happen,' Harry said hungrily.

Charlie enjoyed him kissing around her neck and biting gently on her earlobe, but pushed back when he started pulling her leggings down.

'Not here, you horny goat,' she said, pushing Harry away.

'I want you so much.'

'I'm not saying no,' Charlie teased, 'but what if your aunt looks out the window? And we should get Matt his vaccine.'

'At least there's no traffic,' Harry said, burning with lust as he rushed round to the driver's side. He kissed Charlie again, before reversing out of the spot.

She rubbed his thigh as they drove. A checkpoint officer scanned their licence plate and waved them through. Harry was so excited by the idea of seeing Charlie naked that he scraped her car roof on the underside of the rising barrier at his building.

'It's only paint,' Harry said, pulling Charlie's arm as she inspected the damage. 'I'll pay for the repair. Hell, I'll buy you a new car!'

Charlie shoved Harry against the back of the elevator and wrapped her arms round his neck. They made out from the basement to the forty-third floor. Harry trembled with excitement, fumbling the lock and dropping his key as he tried to get into his apartment.

'You are *such* a bad influence,' he said, feeling Charlie's hand between his legs as the pair stumbled into the hallway.

His mood was jarred by a shattered mug and coffee pooled across the lobby's tiled floor. It seemed odd that Matt hadn't cleared it up, but Charlie had his wrist and was leading him down the hallway.

'Where's your bed?' she said, pulling off a sneaker and flicking it into the air.

'Double doors at the end,' Harry said, wishing he'd changed the sheets after his Saturday romp with Gemma.

But Charlie screamed sharply as she glanced through an archway.

Harry reached for her arm. 'What's wrong?'

Everything fell apart when he looked into the living room. A tea-coloured rug had a huge splat of bloody vomit. Dark red spots formed a trail to Matt. He'd tried to make it to the couch but had collapsed, grazing his head on the corner of a glass table.

'Matt, buddy,' Harry said, racing into the room.

'Don't go near him,' Charlie shouted, the gun dropping out of her hoodie as she pulled up her virus mask.

'Matt, can you hear me?' Harry shouted. 'Are you there, mate?'

Matt wore the same shorts and polo he'd been in three hours earlier. Bloody, coin-sized blisters had erupted on the back of his neck and all down his legs.

'Stay away from him,' Charlie warned again.

But Harry had to know if his best friend was alive. Rather than get closer, he moved round to the other side of the coffee table and squatted. Clotting blood oozed from Matt's ear and his tongue had puffed up like a balloon.

'I think he choked on his swollen tongue,' Harry said. 'I read that it killed a lot of people in England that way.'

'Harry, please,' Charlie begged, fighting an urge to bolt for the door. 'It's super contagious.'

'He was my best friend,' Harry sobbed, finally backing away. 'I've been around him all day. If he's got it I've got it.'

'Not necessarily,' Charlie said. 'Viruses can be weird. You've had the vaccine and your mods might give you some protection . . .'

334

'What do I do now?' Harry asked, swallowing a sob. 'I guess I have to call quarantine to take the body away and decontaminate the apartment. And I'll have to call Lana. And Matt's mum and dad. He was fine when I went out. Not even a sneeze.'

Charlie felt terrified as Harry got close. *Harry might be infected, but he's taken crazy risks for me every time I've asked. So how can I run out on him now?*

'I'm really sorry about your friend,' Charlie said.

The words came out stiffer than she'd expected, so she stepped up to Harry and kissed him.

'I could be infected,' Harry said, backing off. 'You should get out of here.'

'To where?' Charlie said, looking up into Harry's eyes. 'I'm not going to put my foster family at risk. We'll call quarantine control to collect Matt.'

'Then what?' Harry asked desperately.

Charlie looked stunned. 'Since we've been exposed, they'll take us to a quarantine centre,' she said, then paused to think. 'We'll either be dead within forty-eight hours. Or the vaccine will kick in and we live to see whatever crazy virus they invent next.'

Harry pulled Charlie back in, closing his eyes and trying to imagine that her smell and her warmth were the only things in the universe. She nestled her head into his shoulder. She felt loved in Harry's big arms, and amidst tangled thoughts one rang shockingly clear.

I'd rather die here with Harry, than go on living without him.

PART FOUR
THREE YEARS LATER

56 DEAD BUGS

Vegas Local

HAVE YOUR SAY – Should Killer-T masterminds face extradition to the US?

Killer-T and its variants have directly caused 1.6 billion deaths, including 70 million in the United States.

Millions more continue to die from global food shortages and the political and economic chaos that has followed.

The three men and two women who created Killer-T were tried in Britain and sentenced to life in prison. They are unlikely to ever be released, but the British parliament will now debate special legislation that will enable extradition of the perpetrators to the United States, where they could face the federal death penalty.

Should the Killer-T Five face execution for perpetrating the greatest genocide in human history? Or is it better that they rot in prison for the rest of their lives?

Vote in our poll and post your comments below!

Poll Latest

Yes – The Killer-T Five deserve to die	84%
No – Let them rot in prison	16%

There are flies.

Dead ones dotted on the hallway floor like raisins. Live ones walking over the bodies. Eating blood out of the blisters on the dead nurse's arms. I'm getting out of bed, stepping over Stephanie in her neon top. Using the nurses' key to unlock the kitchen and opening a big can of pineapple. Swatting flies away as I tip the can and drink the juice.

The air-con stopped working and it's so hot. Everyone else is dead. The phone is dead. The faucets don't work and the toilets are dry. I drink more juice, drop a pineapple ring on the floor. And look down at the rattlesnake, crawling over the bug-covered floor. Its head snaps around. Jumping up and sinking its teeth into my ankle ...

'Charlie!' Ed shouted breathlessly as he shot up in his bed. 'Charlie.'

Harry came into the little bedroom first, dressed in his boxers, sitting on Ed's bed and squeezing his hand.

'Did you have a nightmare, big guy?' he asked.

'A big bad one,' Ed said, eyes glazed with tears. He was a bulky seventeen-year-old now, and his grip was close to painful.

'You're safe,' Harry soothed. 'I'm here. Charlie's just across the hall. Breathe in through your mouth, and out through your nose, like the therapist showed you.'

'It was Care4Kids,' Ed said, trembling as he took a big breath. 'Everyone was dead. The nurse left the door open and the snake got in.'

'But me and Charlie came and found you, didn't we?' Harry said. 'It was scary, but you're safe now.'

Ed got spooked if you touched him by surprise. So Harry held his arm up, and waited for Ed to nod before wrapping it around his back.

'You came in your orange Porsche,' Ed said, and Harry felt him tremble. 'There was no water, but I kept myself clean with wipes. And the snake part was only in my dream.'

'But that was three years ago,' Harry soothed. 'You live here now, with me and Charlie. And you're safe, aren't you?'

Ed nodded, then his head dropped. 'I wish I didn't get nightmares.'

'Sounds like you had a bad one,' Harry said as he craned his neck to look at the bedside clock. 'Why don't you take a shower and I'll mix you some space food for breakfast?'

'Peach flavour?'

'Sure,' Harry said. 'Don't use all the hot water. You know how mad Charlie gets when it runs out!'

Ed managed a smile, and he got off the bed and grabbed his towel from a hook. Harry started to cough as he crossed the hall and stepped into the room he shared with Charlie. Ed's nightmare had woken her too, and she sat up in bed, looking at the battered laptop Harry had bought her more than five years earlier.

'Ed OK?' Charlie asked as Harry gave her a good morning kiss.

'The Care4Kids nightmare again,' Harry sighed, hunting in a bedside drawer. 'He's *so* frightened when he wakes up like that. I told him to go shower.'

Charlie looked anxious. 'You reminded him not to hog all the hot water?'

'Sure,' Harry said. He grabbed a syringe from the drawer and settled on the edge of his bed. 'How are the threat forecasts looking?'

'There's a new strain of super-flu flaring in Melbourne,' Charlie said. 'It's winter down there, I guess. Killer-T3B is showing vaccine resistance in the Ukraine. I'll get you and Ed the latest vaccine shots in town today. It's been more than a week.'

Harry pulled the cap off the needle and injected a dose of steroids into his upper arm.

'Do you think they're helping?' Charlie asked. 'You were coughing half the night.'

'Did I keep you awake? I can always go down and sleep on the couch.'

Charlie shook her head. 'I want you here, beside me,' she said fondly. 'Cough or no cough.'

Harry smiled as he crawled over the bed towards Charlie and gave her another kiss.

'Ed woke us up early,' Harry said. 'You wanna fool around?'

'Depends what you've got,' Charlie teased, kissing Harry back as she set the laptop on her bedside table and kicked off the duvet.

Charlie had her legs hooked around Harry's back when Ed burst in.

'There's no hot water,' he announced, trailing damp footprints.

'I've told you to knock,' Charlie said, halfway between amused and irritated as she hurled a pillow at him.

'Did you adjust the middle tap?' Harry asked. 'If you push the lever too far, you just get cold.'

'The hot is only a dribble,' Ed said as Harry grabbed well-worn jeans off the floor.

Harry crossed to the bathroom. Ed loomed in the background as he stepped into the shower cubicle, turned the hot to full blast and got a dribble.

'Told you,' Ed said. 'I'm not stupid.'

'You look stupid,' Harry teased, poking his tongue childishly as he went back to the bedroom to grab a shirt.

'You're rude, Harry!'

Ed's emotional age was nine and he enjoyed gentle teasing if he was in a good mood.

'Water's hot, but there's no pressure,' Harry yelled to Charlie. 'I'll go outside and check the pump.'

Harry stepped out after grabbing a toolbox from the garage and slipping on some work boots. The modest, wooden-framed house was on high ground with a hilly four-acre plot. On a clear day, you could see Las Vegas thirty miles south, but right now all Harry got was a face full of rising sun, and a wave from Vern, his grey-bearded neighbour.

'Want some fresh milk?' Vern shouted.

'Always,' Harry said brightly as he waved back.

'Could Charlie pick up the latest anti-virus shots for me and Rosie if she's going into town?'

'No problem. She's got to get mine and Ed's as well.' Harry didn't stop because Vern would talk all day if you let him. 'I've got no hot water. I think it's the pump.'

'Let me know if you get stuck with that,' Vern said. 'Drop by for tea and cake, if you like.'

'Will do,' Harry said, now far enough away that he had to raise his voice. 'I'll bring some of my tomatoes over.'

DIY and yakking with the neighbours made Harry feel way older than twenty-one as he made the climb to the solar array, set on a natural slope thirty yards from the house.

He often wondered about an alternative history, where Killer-T didn't happen and he'd gone to college in New York. But Harry was as happy as he'd ever been.

His parents had offered no stability when he was little.

Kirsten had done her best, but was always busy with work and Harry rarely felt like the most important thing in her life. So, while it wasn't easy living in the desert, he felt as if he properly belonged somewhere for the first time in his life.

He pulled his cell and switched on Bluetooth to connect to the panel's diagnostic app. Four six-yard-long solar strips provided enough electricity for the house, two cars and a large backup battery. Their water was pumped from an underground well and directly heated by the sun for most of the year.

The energy app told Harry that all four panels were doing their job, and the water in the tubes was near boiling, though the sun had barely risen. The problem had to be the pump that sent pressurised hot water into the house.

It took a hex key to loosen the water pump's sun-warmed metal cover. The pump worked by spinning a little turbine connected to an electric motor and Harry saw that the drive gears were clogged with sand and grit. After switching the pump off, he blasted the dust with a compressed air cylinder, dripped in some lubrication oil and rolled the gears back and forth to spread it.

When he flipped the power back on, Harry was pleased to see the pump spin for around twenty seconds, cutting off when a gauge showed that the water flowing to the house had reached the correct pressure.

As he reattached the pump cover, a gust caught Harry by surprise and the grit he inhaled made him start coughing. He clutched his ribs and hacked violently, grabbing the toolbox and jogging back to the house.

Ed sat shirtless at the kitchen table as Harry rushed in.

'Is it fixed?' Ed asked, but Harry ignored him and leaned under the kitchen faucet to gulp water.

'This damned cough!' Harry rasped. He swallowed water, then hacked a big bloody glob into the sink.

'You OK?' Charlie asked as she stepped into the doorway wearing a robe. 'That cough's getting worse.'

'All good,' Harry denied, swallowing the taste of blood as he looked round and tried not to wince at the powerful ache in his chest.

'Is the water back on?' Charlie asked.

'Should be,' Harry said. 'I'm gonna ask Vern to look at that pump, though. I think we might need a bigger one.'

'I'll go for my shower now,' Ed said.

Charlie cracked a cheeky grin from the doorway. 'I'm nearest,' she announced. 'I'm gonna use all the hot water today.'

'Aww!' Ed shouted, knocking his chair back and charging after his sister.

But Charlie was already halfway up the stairs. 'I'm gonna take a looooong shower today,' she teased, reaching the landing and opening the bathroom door. 'You boys are gonna freeze your balls off!'

Ed slipped at the top of the stairs, then pounded the door as Charlie cracked a maniacal laugh from inside. He wore a huge smile as he came back into the kitchen.

'Charlie's a meanie,' Ed said.

'Peach-flavoured space food, coming up,' Harry told Ed as he opened a cabinet and took out a brown bag. It had simple black printing, *USDA Emergency Adult Nutrition 12lbs. Not for Resale.*

Harry scooped the powder into two breakfast bowls and added half a mug of water, which made it swell into a doughy, cream-coloured porridge. Space food could be baked to make a sweet, slightly nutty bread, or mixed with a range of synthetic flavours designed to make it palatable for kids.

'Breakfast for *monsieur*,' Harry said, hamming it with a French accent as he placed the bowl and flavour sachet in front of Ed. Then in his normal voice, 'Charlie managed to buy a bag of apples if you want one.'

Ed preferred the synthetic peach flavour and turned up his nose. 'What are we doing today?'

Harry crunched an apple. 'You need to go online and do some independent learning modules this morning.'

'Can't I go into town with Charlie?' Ed moaned.

'She's seeing a patient today,' Harry said. 'If there are no virus alerts, we might all go bowling together on Saturday.'

'Nice,' Ed said, beaming. 'I *smashed* you last time.'

'I've got jobs to do in the polytunnels and around the house. If my chest calms down, we can go for a run together after lunch.'

Ed liked this idea. 'And lift weights afterwards?'

Harry laughed. 'You're turning into a proper gym rat.'

Ed lifted his arms to show a chunky bicep. 'All natural,' he said. 'Unlike some people in this house . . .'

57 ONE-POINT-SIX BILLION

Fresh from her shower, and dressed in a business-like grey skirt and black blouse combo, Charlie rolled back a rug, exposing a circular metal floor hatch.

The house had been built in the 1980s, when nuclear fall-out shelters were all the rage. The underground space now served as Charlie's lab, and she clanked down a metal ladder, walked an eight-foot section of tunnel, then ducked through the frame of a metal door, the airtight rubber seals of which had long since perished.

The backbone of Charlie's lab was the sequencing, printing and replicating units she'd taken from Mango's RV three years earlier. To the best of Charlie's knowledge, Mango and her family were all still alive. Luckily for Charlie, the same couldn't be said for magician Helen Back, or the agents who'd been investigating Mango's operation.

Charlie's lawyer had advised that the FBI case against her would be on file somewhere, but the aftermath of Killer-T had left law enforcement with a depleted staff and a huge caseload. It was unlikely anyone would revive a case where lead investigators and the originating witness were dead.

After grabbing a foil-lined cool bag out of a benchtop freezer, Charlie took fifteen sealed glass vials from a refrigerator. She laid them carefully in the bag and topped it with protective foam to stop the contents rattling.

She lowered this gently into a drawstring bag she'd readied the day before. It contained sterile syringes and a memory card, on to which she'd burnt full details of a patient's original DNA, along with details of the modifications being made.

Techniques for reversing DNA alterations had advanced significantly since Charlie first started working for Mango, and the card contained a set of files that could be loaded into the DNA printer at any major hospital to create a safe reversal treatment.

'I'm heading out,' Charlie yelled as she exited the shelter and hid the door with the rug.

She got no answer. Ed was in the kitchen at his laptop, wearing headphones. He didn't even notice when Charlie peeked in to check that he was doing schoolwork rather than playing a game or chatting to his home-schooled pals.

Harry had gone out to the polytunnels behind the house, tending the fruit and veggies before it got too hot. Since Harry wouldn't be leaving home, Charlie took his Porsche for the first part of the journey into Vegas.

The penalties for running an illegal gene lab, or minor involvement in modding activity, now began with ten years' imprisonment. Though stiff sentencing and the creation of a lavishly funded Genetic Modification Enforcement Agency had done no more to stop people altering their bodies than previous generations of cops had done to halt the supply of illegal drugs.

After stopping at a drugstore to pick up five of the latest

vaccine needles, Charlie crossed a sunny parking lot towards a coffee shop.

Killer-T had wiped close to forty per cent of Nevada's population and small businesses had been devastated by a combination of supply problems, the death of skilled staff and a lack of customers. Charlie had bought the coffee shop's lease cheaply from the owner's surviving grandkids.

'Hey, boss,' a barista named Gwen said as Charlie went through the quarantine box. Gwen was one of the lucky five per cent who'd caught Killer-T and survived. But her arms and forehead bore deep blister scars, and her scalp had several bald patches.

All shops now had drive-thru or walk-up windows, where staff fetched online orders or grabbed what you needed. Entering any store, office or indoor mall meant a couple of minutes in a quarantine box. Besides powerful UV lamps, the box sprayed disinfectant on your shoes, scanned your body for a raised temperature and read the tag from your most recent vaccine update.

There were eight customers spread over sixty seats, but the drive-thru window had a healthy queue, and Charlie was pleased to see cakes and sandwiches shelved inside the glass counter, each individually packaged with their own sterile cutlery.

There was less variety than there would have been before Killer-T, and hyperinflation meant a choc-chip muffin cost sixty dollars, but things were improving. A year ago the only edibles would have been instant noodle packs and space-food biscuits.

'I've got something for you girls,' Charlie said as the quarantine box's acrylic doors slid open to let her in.

She reached into a bag and placed four small pints of strawberries on the countertop. 'We grew them in the polytunnels,' Charlie explained. 'Well, Harry did.'

'First strawberry I've seen since Killer-T,' Gwen said as another barista backed up from the drive-thru window to admire them.

'Anything else going on?' Charlie asked. 'Supplies?'

'No major problems, for once,' Gwen said. 'I can't get carbon dioxide cylinders, so drinks with whipped cream are off the menu for now. I called around the catering suppliers. Everyone's saying four to eight weeks until they get a delivery, and when they do it's not gonna be cheap.'

'I appreciate the work you put in to keep this place running,' Charlie said brightly. 'How about those zombies hanging around?'

'The two that kept banging the windows and harassing us when we locked up at night got picked up,' Gwen said. 'Put up a heck of a fight.'

'They didn't used to mind getting arrested,' Charlie said. 'But they know they'll get shipped to a reversal centre now.'

'Three times my neighbour's boy has been reversed,' Gwen said, tutting. 'Every time they reverse his z-mods, he cries and says he wants to kill himself. His poor ma is at her wits end.'

'Awful seeing kids like that,' Charlie agreed. She glanced at her watch. 'Can I grab a flat white, and a couple of the cinnamon chocolate sticks to take up to the office while I do the accounts?'

'Synthetic coffee?' Gwen asked.

'I'll go mad,' Charlie laughed. 'What's the point owning a coffee shop if you can't have a real one every now and then?'

58 PEER PRESSURE

Charlie had copied Mango's business model, doing genetic editing on clients who came by word-of-mouth recommendation and were happy to pay for quality work. While Mango had used Radical Cakes to launder the profits from her lab, Charlie used her income to buy up cheap leases and reopen bankrupt coffee shops.

After taking her real coffee upstairs to an office, and spending two hours doing bookkeeping and payroll for her employees, Charlie took a taxi to The Strip and used cash to rent one of the Algarve Casino's meeting rooms.

Her clients were fifteen minutes late. An apologetic woman, with greying hair and a formidable bust, accompanied by her thirteen-year-old grandson, Judah. He was a serious boy with a slender build and the type of curled black hair that always looks a mess.

Charlie tried to seem older than her twenty years when she met patients. Besides her sober outfit, she adopted a deeper voice as she went through the ritual of hellos, seat taking and offers of bottled water from the little bar at the back of the room.

'So, Judah, how's life?' Charlie said, reading anxiety in the boy's face and remembering how awkward being thirteen felt.

'Good,' he spat.

'Your general health?'

'Fine.'

The grandmother spoke. 'He had a temperature a couple of weeks back, after our first meeting. There were some weird modified ants around in the lockers at his school. Nobody quite knows what they were, but a few kids got sick.'

'Oh dear,' Charlie said. 'When did you last record an elevated temperature?'

'Seven days ago,' Judah said. 'The quarantine box at school rejected me and I had to go home.'

'I wouldn't start treatment if you're under the weather, but seven days is fine,' Charlie said as she pulled the cooler bag out and placed it on the oval meeting table. 'So I've done all your lab work. The bad news is we discussed thirteen modifications, but I could only do twelve.

'When I checked your DNA, I found that you have a fairly common genetic mutation that can cause complications with the memory enhancement you requested. The side effect is uncommon, but I always urge a conservative approach.'

Judah didn't seem too worried, but the grandmother looked flustered. 'Can we consider something else for his memory? So many other boys in his school have memory mods. It's hard to compete academically.'

'I did some research,' Charlie said. 'There are other modifications that improve memory, but none that I'd be happy to use until we have a better idea of the long-term effects. Judah is still having mods that will improve cognition and IQ.'

Judah sat forward. 'But all the physical stuff is OK, right?'

Charlie smiled. 'Absolutely. The mods will darken your skin, as if you have a good tan. Straighten that tangled hair. Improve muscle mass and bone density, and probably increase your eventual adult height by three to four inches. The mods will also give your immune system a boost, protect against depression and reduce your chances of many cancers and long-term obesity.'

'You modded two boys in my class,' Judah said excitedly. 'They're *so* ripped now. They can crush me!'

'That's David and Ben, isn't it?' Charlie asked, and Judah nodded. 'I'm glad they're doing well.'

'I have to say this makes me queasy,' the grandmother interrupted. 'But what can I do? He's surrounded by boys who are modded. They're faster and stronger. They do better than him academically and he comes home upset. Once a couple of boys get enhanced, they all want it.'

Charlie had no medical qualifications, but over time she'd realised that people liked her to act like a doctor and give words of comfort, even if she was only parroting information that could be found online.

'I think we all stress over modding teenagers,' Charlie reassured her. 'But the technology is far better than it was even a couple of years ago. Instead of injecting stem cells until modded cells outnumber the regular ones and start to take over, we can now actively destroy the original cells too.

'The transformation from your original genes to enhanced ones is faster and, whereas everyone used to take auto-immune drugs and three-quarters of people had some kind of unpleasant reaction to gene therapy, the immune drugs are now built into the treatment and less than five per cent get anything more than a slightly raised temperature. It's a lot more work for me – which is why other labs still use less sophisticated methods – but it's worth the effort.'

The grandmother managed a nod and a slight smile.

'If you're both happy, I'm ready to show Judah how to handle his injections. But I will need to take payment before beginning the treatment.'

'Can you run through fines and registration again?' the grandmother asked.

Charlie nodded. 'The government websites make it look scary, but, while gene modding is illegal, close to half the population now has at least one mod and they can't throw us all in jail. The best thing to do is wait a month or so for Judah's mods to bed in, then go online and fill in the Modification Declaration form. The fines are currently twenty thousand dollars, though with inflation they'll probably be closer to twenty-five by next month.

'You'll also have to register Judah's modified genome with his family doctor, and it's best to give them copies of my records. Your medical insurance won't cover complications related to Judah's mods and, lastly, you'll have to notify his school. Once Judah is modified, he'll no longer be eligible to play for school sports teams, or get an athletic scholarship to college.'

'I'm awful at sport anyway,' Judah said. 'But I'm gonna buy some weights, cos David and Ben look awesome. The girls are practically drooling!'

The grandma went a little thin lipped. 'There's more to getting a girlfriend than having abs and a big chest, Judah,' she said crossly. 'And you're only thirteen. You should be focused on your studies.'

There was a moment's awkward silence before the grandmother opened her handbag and pulled out two large bundles of $5,000 bills.

'One point two million,' she said, resting the bricks of money on the desktop. 'Which is ten times what I paid for my house. But with this crazy inflation . . .'

Judah mocked his grandma. 'I remember when you could buy a condo tower, three Bentleys and a slave plantation and still have change out of a dollar!'

'Don't be tiresome, Judah,' the grandmother snapped as Charlie concealed a smirk.

'I drank a three-hundred-dollar cup of real coffee this morning,' Charlie said. 'Hyperinflation is a crazy thing! Now, Judah, on a scale of one to ten, where ten is the worst, how scared would you say you are of needles?'

Judah shrugged casually, but she could tell he was worried. 'If my friend Ben can do it . . . Maybe a five, or six out of ten.'

'OK,' Charlie said. 'You're going to need three injections per day, for thirty days. Then you'll come back to me, and we'll do bone marrow and muscle tests. Hopefully all the mods should be locked in, and you'll be seeing new tissue types growing.

'Now, I'll do your first injection and you can do the second yourself while I watch. And remember it's *really* important to stick to the schedule and inject the doses in the correct spots. The good news is it's better than it used to be. When my boyfriend had mods done a few years back, he had to do eighteen injections per day.'

Judah looked anxious as Charlie ripped the plastic off a two-and-a-half-inch needle.

'It's a lot bigger than the ones used for vaccine updates,' Charlie warned, pushing the needle into a vial. 'And its intra-muscular, so I'm not going to pretend it isn't painful.'

Judah had started rolling up his T-shirt, but Charlie shook her head.

'Push your tracksuit bottoms down to your knees, and pull

your underwear up so I can see your thigh.'

Judah pushed his chair back and Charlie went down on one knee beside him. Kids were getting modded younger and younger, and Charlie felt a little guilty looking at Judah's hairless boy leg and Batman boxers.

But if I don't take their money, someone else will and they probably won't do half as good a job . . .

Charlie pushed the long needle into thigh muscle as Judah gripped the sides of his chair and teared up with pain.

59 GREEN FINGERS

In some developing countries, Killer-T had disrupted food production and transport so badly that famine had killed more people than the virus itself. The US had prepared for a more serious epidemic after the SNor outbreak, and while people got tired of sweet, claggy space food, no American went hungry.

The shortages made people want to become self-sufficient in food, and the government had helped, providing online education programs, free polythene greenhouse kits and genetically modified seeds designed to grow in a variety of climates and produce high yields.

Working in the polytunnels could be hard, especially since it was August and the outdoor temperature was in triple digits, but Harry felt a sense of accomplishment as he brought two large bags filled with potatoes, parsnips, tomatoes and beans into the kitchen. His jeans were grubbier than when he'd put them on that morning, and his polo shirt soaked in sweat.

The polytunnels were sealed, but nothing completely kept out synthetic nasties. Harry washed his haul in a solution of dilute chlorine and insecticide, then spread them out to dry on the countertop.

'How's school?' he asked Ed, who'd barely moved since breakfast.

'I got an eighty-two on my History module,' Ed said proudly. 'Now I'm playing Gretchen at chess.'

'Who's winning?' Harry asked as he wiped mud out of the sink.

'I've never beaten her,' Ed admitted. 'She's twelve; it's embarrassing.'

Ed had been much happier since they'd moved out of the city, but Harry and Charlie worried that he only had friends in the virtual world.

'Rosie and Vern invited us over for elevenses,' Harry said. 'Do you want to come?'

Ed shook his head. 'I've got a one-to-one tutorial with Miss at eleven twenty. And she said you haven't paid this month's tuition.'

'Charlie handles the money,' Harry said. He noticed that he'd dropped a small potato and picked it up to dry with the others. 'You know what Vern's like when he gets talking, but I won't stay over there too long. I've got a bunch of updates to make on Vegas Local this afternoon. If you get hungry, there's some of the strawberry-and-apple pie Charlie made yesterday in the refrigerator.'

'I'll have space food,' Ed said.

'Of course you will,' Harry said, smirking. He grabbed a clean polo shirt out of a basket of unfolded laundry and pulled it over his muscular chest as he crossed the two hundred feet of dirt to Vern and Rosie's place. Then he realised he'd forgotten the tomatoes he'd promised and doubled back.

'Hey, Rosie!' Harry said happily, taking off his boots before stepping through the insect screen over her back door.

It was one of those time-warp homes where people do a place up when they first move in, then leave everything to decay. The kitchen made Harry feel like he was on a sitcom set, with its yellowed Kenwood mixer and old-skool TV with a bulbous beige case and a plastic antenna on top. Rosie always watched a game show or nature channel, with the volume uncomfortably loud because she was going deaf.

'Afraid I'm grubby,' Harry said, settling at the table with his tomatoes as a quiz show buzzer ripped from the TV.

'I raised three boys,' Rosie said, bringing a clanking jug of iced tea to the dining table. 'A bit of stink won't shock me.'

She fetched a plate of cheese and homemade-pickle sandwiches, then showed Harry new pictures of her seven- and nine-year-old granddaughters on her tablet.

'The younger one looks a lot like you,' Harry said, noticing dirt packed under his nails as he bit a sandwich.

'Her father just got redeployed to become a flight-deck technician on the USS *Gerald Ford*,' Rosie said proudly. 'I helped design the electromagnetic catapults on that boat.'

'Really?' Harry said, surprised.

Harry saw Vern and Rosie as a couple of sweet seventy-somethings who pottered around on their farm, but they'd both been scientists at the Groom Lake research base a hundred miles north of Vegas – more commonly known as Area 51.

'I've soldered up another lithium battery pack if you want it,' Rosie said, holding her lower back and making a soft moan as she sat down.

'That would be fabulous,' Harry said. 'Plenty of cold nights at this altitude and I like to keep the polytunnels above sixty degrees. We'll have to find something to swap.'

'We're neighbours,' Rosie said warmly. 'I'm not keeping score.'

'Charlie said you were going to show her how to make them.'

'It's not hard,' Rosie said. 'Millions of cars with old battery packs get scrapped. The batteries are too weak to put in another car, but they still make low-drain backup batteries for solar-power systems. The scrapyards have to pay to dispose of the batteries, so they let me grab as many as I want.'

'We got lucky having you and Vern as neighbours,' Harry said brightly. 'I could barely change a light bulb when we first moved out of the city. You've taught us everything.'

'You help us too,' Rosie pointed out. 'Charlie takes our parcels and runs all our errands in town. You helped Vern lift the new air-conditioner on to our roof. And the people who owned that house before you were a nightmare. Growing weed and partying all hours . . .'

This jarred with Harry, because Vern and Rosie didn't know about the modding lab.

'Think I hear Vern,' Harry said as the garage door rattled.

Vern usually took a few moments to take off his boots, but he came straight through to the kitchen looking flustered.

'There's two pickups racing up the hill,' he said breathlessly.

Harry grabbed his phone to check the CCTV cameras they'd set up together.

'Already checked. The cameras are out,' Vern said as he picked up an old wall-mounted telephone with a long curly cord. 'Landline's cut too.'

Harry thought fast. *There's no phone signal out here in the mountains. The CCTV works on our shared WiFi network and Vern's landline phone is a different system. So two different systems have stopped working, and it isn't a power failure because the air-conditioning is humming . . .*

'Internet seems to be down too,' Harry said, looking at his phone.

'It's gotta be zombies in them pickups,' Rosie said, looking frightened.

'Cutting phone lines seems too organised for zombies,' Harry said.

'Now that the cops reverse zombies when they're caught, they're selecting mods that leave them with better survival skills,' Vern said. 'We watched a PBS documentary about it a few weeks back.'

'It's called a three-fourteen-B mod,' Rosie said as she checked her tablet to confirm there was no outgoing connection.

'Better gear up,' Vern said, leading a charge into the garage and unlocking a hefty gun cabinet.

As Vern, Rosie and Harry pulled on body armour and grabbed automatic rifles, Ed yelled from out front.

'There's two cars coming, Harry!' he called, as he came up the porch steps and into Vern and Rosie's kitchen. 'And my internet stopped working.'

Harry didn't want to spook Ed, but it was hard not to, dressed in a flak vest and holding an assault rifle.

'Is it zombies?' Ed asked.

'They'll be at the gate in under a minute,' Rosie said as she expertly loaded a clip into her assault rifle. 'I'll head upstairs and cover you boys.'

'Ed, I need you to be calm and sensible, OK?' Harry said.

Ed was trembling and Harry feared one of his panic attacks, or, worse, a full-on fit.

'Run back to the house, go down into the shelter and don't come out until one of us tells you to,' Harry said.

Ed was terrified of being left alone after the Care4Kids abandonment. He started rocking from side to side as Vern came out of the garage, fixing an ammo belt, then passing another to Harry.

'Can you come down to the gate with me?' Vern asked Harry. 'You look scarier than I do.'

'Sure,' Harry said, still wondering how to deal with Ed.

Telling him not to panic would have the opposite effect. But Ed could be distracted if you gave him a task.

'This is important,' Harry told Ed. 'Run back to our house, then go around very quickly. Take your laptop and any other expensive things that you can carry. Then take them into the shelter and guard them. You're a guard, OK? Your job is *really* important.'

Ed nodded excitedly.

'I know you'll do a good job,' Harry said.

Ed rushed out of the door, and Vern smiled and handed Harry an ammo belt.

'You've got a knack with that boy,' Vern complimented as Rosie ran to the top of the house. 'Give a man responsibility to stop the panic. Learned the same trick on survival training in the air force.'

Ed had reached the other house when Harry and Vern stepped out into midday heat.

'I grabbed a few of your girlfriend's homemade grenades,' Vern said, handing a pair to Harry. 'I made wire clips so they can hook on your belt.'

60 TERATOMA TUMORS

Harry felt like a cowboy, striding the desert in his flak vest and assault rifle. He thought about the contrast with the skinny English kid who'd landed in Las Vegas eight years earlier and, like always, wondered if his mum would approve of what he was about to do.

The two dust plumes from the pickups were close. The properties weren't fenced in, but the ground leading up from the highway was steep and bouldered. Even a powerful 4x4 would have to use the dirt road, and Vern had built a hefty steel gate between two boulders a hundred and fifty yards from the houses.

'If they cut the phone and the CCTV, they must have staked us out,' Harry said, checking that his gun was loaded as he followed Vern towards the gate.

'Possibly,' Vern said. 'But a wireless signal blocker isn't hard to make, and there's a telephone cabinet down by the highway. Just crowbar the door and cut the wires with a pocket knife . . .'

The giant rocks made natural cover, and the lead pickup's squealing brakes suggested the driver wasn't expecting the heavy gate. Harry stepped up into a foothold and peeked over the top of the boulder. The two pickups were modern, but wore a coat of desert grit. The lead unit was driven by a huge man, hunched over the wheel with a hairy forehead and vast woolly arms.

'Some kind of superhero,' Harry warned, using the popular nickname for anyone who'd been modded for extreme strength, using the experimental mods developed by the Chinese army. 'I think there's another superhero in the second pickup. The ones on the pickup beds are younger. Mostly girls.'

'Armed?' Vern asked.

'I can see knives and pistols for the girls. The superhero's got a machine gun.'

'Body count?' Vern asked.

'The first superhero's getting out,' Harry said. 'There's two guys in each cab. Four or five kids riding on the back of each one.'

Vern stepped out from behind the rock, his assault rifle aimed at the superhero who'd just got out of the main vehicle.

'You're on a private road and the police were alerted by radio as soon as the phone was cut,' Vern lied. 'I strongly advise you to turn back.'

Vern gave a signal for Harry to step out behind him. As he did so, sweaty zombie girls jumped down from the pickups, while a mean-looking Asian teen pointed an assault rifle. Harry looked left and right warily as the superhero spat in the dirt, then confidently chimed the muzzle of his MP7 machine gun against the barred gate.

The superhero was seven and a half feet tall and his T-shirt size must have included a dozen Xs. While modders like Charlie would only do therapies that used variants of human DNA, superhero mods included genes from powerful primates.

The results of non-human mods were unpredictable. Along with cancerous growths and sudden heart failure, the most common side-effect of mixing ape and human DNA were stem cells that produced the wrong type of tissue in the wrong location. So hard tissues like teeth and nails would grow in random spots through your body, or internal organs would get blocked by clumps of hair.

The superhero at the gate showed a particularly gruesome example of stem-cell confusion, with infected balls of milky-white eye tissue clumped on his hairy arms.

'If you pay us two hundred thousand, we'll go away,' the superhero said. 'Fifty thousand a month buys you protection.'

'Got my own protection,' Vern scoffed, raising his gun. 'I'm an old man. Inflation wiped out my pension. We live off what we grow.'

'I'll have your computers, phones and watches,' the superhero growled as Harry eyed the zombie girls moving further away from the pickups, some disappearing behind rocks. 'There won't be trouble unless you make trouble.'

'If I pay now, you'll be back for more,' Vern said, 'but the girls look dehydrated. I'd be happy to fetch some bottled water.'

A zombie girl shouted cockily from the pick-up's passenger seat. 'There's only two of 'em, Tony. Just kill 'em and get on with it.'

The superhero made an animal grunt and shook his fist at the girl. 'It's two-inch-thick steel,' he shouted, rattling the gate. 'Shut your hole.'

Suddenly a shot cracked. Harry flinched as the boulder splintered, less than three feet from the superhero's head. As he looked back, another bullet whizzed overhead, obliterating the door mirror of the lead truck.

'That's two warning shots,' Rosie yelled from her top-floor window. 'You got thirty seconds to clear out, or the next one cleaves your skull.'

The superhero shielded his eyes, looking into the glare to see where the shots had come from. He had greater numbers, but his vehicles were trapped behind a gate that hadn't figured in his plans, and Rosie's sniper position meant they'd take heavy casualties if they tried crossing the open ground between the boulders and the houses on foot.

'Back on the trucks,' the superhero growled to his crew. Then he fired a monstrous wodge of spit into the dirt between his boots and pointed at Harry.

'This isn't over,' he warned.

'We'll be waiting,' Harry said, shuddering as he looked the superhero in the eye.

61 WHIPPED CREAM

Charlie came out of the quarantine box inside her coffee shop, this time carrying a plastic bag full of little carbon dioxide cylinders.

'Ta-da!' she told Gwen cheerfully.

The barista was nearing the end of a ten-hour shift and disappointed Charlie with a tired, 'Where'd you get 'em?'

'There's a shuttered coffee shop over on Sands. I'll be reopening it in a couple of months, but I remembered seeing a box of CO_2 cartridges when I met with the construction manager who's gonna fix it up.'

'*Another* store,' Gwen said, managing a slight smile. 'You'll be running Starbucks outta town before you know it.'

Charlie ran up to the office and put a million dollars out of her $1.2 million modding fee in the safe. She split the rest, pocketing a hundred thousand for expenses back at the house, and the remainder into a cash register tray containing the shop's morning takings.

After a phone consultation with a potential modding client over her encrypted phone, Charlie headed down to the shop. She was in a decent mood and her plan was to catch a city bus back to where she'd parked the Porsche, then drive home and help Harry make dinner.

Her mood jarred when she noticed a black guy, sitting by the front window with an espresso. He was scruffy, with staring eyes, high cheekbones and plaited hair down his back. Gwen was serving a six-cup order at the drive-thru window, so Charlie had to wait before speaking to her.

'The guy at table three,' Charlie said warily. 'Have you seen him in here before?'

'Couple of times yesterday,' Gwen said. 'I know his eyes look zombieish, but he's never caused problems.'

'He looks familiar,' Charlie said thoughtfully. 'I'm half convinced I saw him at the Algarve earlier.'

The cops would never use someone so distinctive to tail me, but it could be someone who knows I do modding, looking to shake me down, or rob me.

But that face triggers something further back. Was he at Rock Spring High? Or in the visiting room at White Boulder?

'I've gotta grab something upstairs, then I'm gonna head home,' Charlie told Gwen. 'Can you give me a call, and let me know if that guy follows me?'

Gwen seemed alarmed. 'If you think something's wrong, I can call the security office. We pay enough money for them.'

'No need,' Charlie said firmly.

The face kept gnawing at Charlie's brain. *Was he at OIL? Did he hit on me at a house party? Was he the guy who delivered fertiliser to the house?*

'Where do I know you from?' Charlie asked herself irritably, seeing him on the CCTV in the office as she unlocked a desk drawer.

She took out an automatic pistol and checked that the

clip was loaded before wedging it into her handbag. Then she decided her smart seeing-a-patient shoes weren't the best option if she had to run and switched to a pair of battered Converse under her desk.

'I'm off now,' Charlie told Gwen, straightening her virus mask as she exited the coffee shop.

Charlie glanced over her shoulder as she headed out into blazing Vegas heat. Swapping shoes and grabbing the gun meant she only got to see the 15:15 bus as it rolled away from the stop outside Shoe Right. But there were a couple of taxis on the rank, so she grabbed one of those.

The driver had gone half a mile when Gwen called.

'He left a minute or so after you,' she told Charlie. 'He got into a beige BMW with a black rear spoiler. But I watched him drive out the back of the mall and turn on to the highway, so he can't have been following you.'

'Cool beans,' Charlie said. 'Sorry to waste your time, Gwen. I'll see you Friday.'

But I know that face from somewhere. It's gonna bug me till I work it out ...

62 LIVING HIGH

Charlie told the taxi to drop her behind a stationery store at the rear of the mall where she'd parked the Porsche.

'You know it's closed?' the driver asked as Charlie handed over three hundred bucks and told him to keep the change. 'Sure to have zombies out here.'

'I'm good,' Charlie said. 'I'm meeting someone around the corner.'

Charlie could have got the taxi to drop her in front of the mall, but she wanted to be sure no one was eyeballing the Porsche. After jogging up six flights, Charlie strode on to the rooftop deck of a parking lot. The only cars up here belonged to dead people who'd lived in an adjoining apartment block. A few were burnt out, while the rest had been ransacked.

She kept her handbag's flap open so she could grab the gun. When she reached the middle of the parking structure, she could see Harry's orange Porsche at ground level.

The stationery and pet stores at the back of the mall had gone bust, but the street-level parking was moderately busy, serving a food market, a discount designer-clothing store and a recently opened branch of Leo's Quarantine Supplies.

From the far end of the parking structure, Charlie got a vista down a line of parking bays running past the mall's shuttered cinema. In the first row was a camel-coloured BMW with a plastic spoiler, like the one Gwen had described.

The discovery was annoying, but at the same time Charlie was pleased to have outsmarted him. *Whoever he was ...*

The BMW was several hundred feet away and reflections on the windshield made it impossible to see inside. But Charlie reckoned the spot had been carefully chosen, enabling the driver to see anyone getting into the Porsche, and easily pull out on to the exit road to follow.

At least I'm not paranoid. He didn't follow the taxi so he must have known where I was going. I could jump in another taxi and arrange for Harry to pick me up somewhere, but I should try finding out who he is while I have the upper hand ...

The deserted multistorey parking lot gave Charlie a view of the outdoor mall's layout. She was glad she'd switched to comfy sneakers as she took a lengthy detour in the afternoon heat back round the stationery store, switching to a jog when she spotted a trio of zombies living out of a camper behind the pet store.

A right turn by the supermarket took her into the alleyway with the boarded-up cinema in front. Charlie now approached the parked BMW from the rear, shielding behind a couple of strength-modded construction workers walking the same way.

The BMW was old, with a dented rear fender. The bright red child seat visible through the back window jarred with Charlie's mental image of a bad guy, but a few steps later she recognised the woman in the passenger seat, and things fell into place.

Charlie felt more confident as she jogged up behind the car and tapped her pistol on the glass in the passenger door. Juno and her friend both jumped.

'Why are you tailing me?' Charlie asked angrily.

Juno looked different. After three years, it was no surprise she looked older and she had the kind of build that was always going to pile on weight. But glazed eyes and rigidity in the facial muscles hinted that Juno had taken one of the milder z-mods.

It matched the gaze Charlie saw in her coffee shop on the man who now sat in the driver's seat. He was Juno's cousin, Mikey. Charlie had met him a couple of times at her apartment, but his hair had been in an Afro.

'You dumped your phone and vanished on me,' Juno said as Charlie lowered the gun into her bag.

'Why make it easy for the cops to find me?' Charlie asked.

'I thought we were besties,' Juno said.

'You were doing lab work behind my back and mixing with a bunch of Seth's friends who I didn't like,' Charlie said. 'Frankly, I didn't trust you any more.'

Juno sounded cross. 'I made you my baby's godmother. And I was left with *nothing* when you burnt the RV and robbed the equipment.'

'I'm not here to rake the past,' Charlie said. 'Tell me why you're following me around.'

Mikey leaned forward and tried to sound authoritative. 'Why don't you ladies chill? Charlie, please get in my car.'

Charlie thought for a second. She had the gun and four-year-old Patrick was asleep in the back. The vibe was messed up, but she wasn't intimidated.

'If this car moves one inch, I'll shoot you both in the backs,' Charlie said firmly.

'I got no beef with yous, Charlie,' Mikey said as he pressed the button to unlock.

Charlie got in the back and felt a wave of affection as she looked at her sleeping godson.

Juno had designed her son using a mix of her own and her old boyfriend Seth's DNA, along with a bunch of mods that would ensure he was clever and strong, with a powerful immune system. She'd also followed a fashion that Charlie found creepy, combining his parents' dark skin with striking blue eyes that would never occur naturally.

'I've missed him growing up,' Charlie said, keeping her tone bright, but concerned by Patrick's filthy clothes and a urine smell.

'The noisy prick's best when he's sleeping,' Mikey said.

'Are you still with Seth?' Charlie asked.

'*Your* sister killed Seth,' Juno said acidly.

'Fawn?' Charlie said, shuddering at the name. 'Are you mixed up with her?'

'Me and the Sethster set up a lab for Juno to work in,' Mikey explained. 'Seth borrowed money from some Janssen associates to buy new lab equipment. Then he lost a bunch gambling and when you don't pay the Janssens back . . .'

Juno looked upset as Mikey made a throat-cutting gesture.

'You know Fawn's nothing to do with me,' Charlie said, 'but I'd heard the Janssens muscled in on modding labs when z-mods killed most of the narcotics trade.'

Juno sucked air between her teeth before telling the story. 'In olden days, you paid a lab for a z-mod. Zombie staggered around for a year or two, until they picked up an infection or something. They'd die blissfully happy, barely aware they're covered in tumours and caked in their own shit.

'Now the cops send zombies to a reversal clinic to set their DNA back to normal. But there's no psychiatric care. Going back to normal emotions feels like hell once you've lived high. They get depressed, steal a bunch of money and use it to buy the latest z-mod. The government reversing zombie mods just generates repeat business for the modders.

'And the Janssens own the cops in this town, like they've always done. So, if you wanna run a lab in Vegas, you pay tax to the Janssens. Else cops be tearing down your lab.'

'Fawn runs everything now,' Mikey added. 'Old man Jay is dead, along with JJ and his older brother.'

'Life expectancy plummets if you rub Fawn Janssen the wrong way,' Juno noted. 'Your sis is queen of the Vegas underworld.'

'I'd heard she'd been busy,' Charlie said warily. 'It's why I live out of town. I use precautions when I travel and nobody knows my real address. It's also why I *don't* appreciate people following me.'

'Why your sister got no love for you?' Mikey interrupted.

'I offended Fawn by being born, and it's been downhill ever since,' Charlie sighed. 'I guess some people are just born bad.'

'Bad to the bone,' Juno agreed. 'Sadistic.'

Talk of Fawn reminded Charlie of a childhood she preferred to forget. She changed the subject.

'So, how'd you find me?'

'Cole spotted you,' Juno said.

'Cole who?' Charlie asked.

'He was at OIL with us, but I mostly got to know him after you left,' Juno explained. 'Told me you were reopening a coffee shop under some fake name. Cole helped his uncle do painting and electrical work for you.'

'What was your plan?' Charlie asked. 'Kidnap me? Follow me home and rob me?'

'We're reasonable people,' Mikey said unconvincingly. 'You and Juno were tight for a long time. Patrick is your godson and we need help.'

'So why the cloak and dagger? Why not just come by and say, *Hey, Charlie, long time no see.*'

'We were about to,' Juno said, 'but we had to be careful. Fawn's your sister. For all we knew you're back on terms with her.'

Charlie wasn't convinced, but knew she'd learn nothing useful by calling them liars.

'So how can I help you?' Charlie asked, hiding her suspicions.

'We're riding a downward spiral,' Juno admitted. 'You and Mango taught me good and I ran a *tight* lab, until Seth gambled the money we needed to pay off the Janssens. I brokered a deal with some guys in LA to produce a batch of fighting-dog embryos. The plan was to do that and sell our lab equipment. We'd have had enough money to pay our debts and make a fresh start in California. But the cops raided my lab before I completed the work.

'We owe Janssen associates four-point-something million and we burnt through the deposit the guys in California paid us,' Mikey said, sounding super anxious. 'The only way we get out of this mess alive is if we can access a decent lab, finish the job and get paid.'

'I've got the embryos in the trunk,' Juno explained. 'You'd save our asses if you let me use your lab. We'd be out of your hair in a day if you helped.'

'I've seen videos of nightmare dogs fighting,' Charlie said, shaking her head. 'It's barbaric.'

'I know it's no picnic,' Juno snapped. 'But is your godson getting orphaned any better?'

'Nobody gets in my lab,' Charlie said. 'I have money set aside. What if I gave you some cash, so you could make a fresh start somewhere out of state?'

'Fawn's merciless – they'd *always* be looking for us,' Juno pleaded. 'I know we had our differences towards the end, Charlie. But we were good buddies. We had fun, back in the day.'

Charlie was torn. She did have fond memories of Juno. They'd been especially close the first year after she'd been released from White Boulder, when Harry had stopped talking to her. But Charlie didn't accept that they'd spent two days following her around just to ask for help.

Plus, they both had zombie mods going on. It was one of the milder ones, but Charlie suspected that Seth gambling and getting killed, the lab getting seized by cops and the angry California dog fighters were all linked with Juno and Mikey living in a permanently high state that made it near impossible to judge risks and make good decisions.

But then there was Patrick. If it wasn't for the four-year-old, Charlie would have bounced already.

'Here's the only deal on the table,' Charlie said quietly. 'I'm not getting involved with fighting dog breeders, or your debt with the Janssens. I'll give you a million dollars. It's no fortune these days, but it's enough to get you out of Nevada and cover rent and bills till you're back on your feet.'

Juno and Mikey looked at one another.

'I'll do all the work myself,' Juno begged. 'Just one night in your lab.'

'This *isn't* a negotiation,' Charlie said. 'Take it or leave it.'

'Do you have the money on you?' Mikey asked.

Charlie laughed. 'Sure, Mikey. I *always* keep a million in my purse . . . It'll take a day to get cash together, maybe two. Where are you staying?'

'We're flat broke,' Juno admitted. 'We slept in the car last night.'

'Has he eaten?' Charlie said, looking towards Patrick.

'There's space food, but the little prick's fussy,' Mikey said.

Charlie reached into her bag and peeled eighty thousand out of the hundred she'd taken at the coffee shop.

'There's a motel called The Paddler on East Harmon, by the Old Rock Casino,' Charlie said. 'I've used it for meetings. It looks dingy from outside, but the rooms are clean. They take cash up front, no ID, no questions asked, and there's a laundromat and a diner on the same block.'

'We can't be seen,' Juno said. 'Fawn's got people looking for us.'

'If you can follow me around town all day, you can wash your kid's clothes and buy him a decent meal,' Charlie snarled, and she pushed the bundle of five- and ten-thousand-dollar bills into Juno's palm.

Juno had always fussed over her nails, and it saddened Charlie to see them all chewed and broken. It was like her old friend's brain was running different software.

'You're a good girl, Charlie,' Mikey said.

'Someone will bring the money to you at The Paddler as soon as I can get it,' Charlie said as she opened the car door. 'If I catch you tailing me, or I get one sniff of anything else I don't like, the money is cancelled. Godson or no godson.'

Charlie felt awful about little Patrick as she gently kissed his food-crusted cheek. Then she jumped out of the car, keeping one hand on the pistol as she jogged towards the Porsche.

63 MONEY, MONEY, MONEY

Charlie didn't trust Juno and Mikey, but felt more disappointed in herself. *If those two half-off-their-head losers can track me down and figure out I'm running a lab, then anyone can.*

Don't I take every reasonable precaution?

None of my clients in Vegas knows where I live, but you only need to make one slip. Just a matter of time before I'm robbed, or blackmailed. I wish I could stop. But we used most of Harry's money to buy the house and inflation has wiped out the rest. Ed's home-schooling and medical bills cost a fortune. Both cars will need new battery packs soon . . . And an imported Porsche battery pack won't come cheap, if you can get hold of one at all . . .

To be extra safe, Charlie drove the Porsche out of the city, parked behind the restrooms of a long-abandoned gas station and switched to an old Chevrolet she kept there for an emergency.

She had to sponge six weeks' worth of desert grit off the Chevy's windows and, while the battery had been left plugged into a solar generator, the charge meter at the socket reckoned the car was only good for thirty miles.

Those gauges always underestimate by a few miles. I should just make it home ...

There was a maraca sound as Charlie grabbed the driver's door handle. She screamed and stumbled back as a rattlesnake sprang from behind the front tire. She grabbed the gun out of her purse, but the snake decided Charlie was more of a threat than a meal and flung itself energetically over the hot sand.

Charlie scrambled breathlessly into the car and listened to her heart drum. The air-con wasn't running, so it was unbelievably hot, but when she switched it on full blast, the dash flashed red lights like a downtown casino and the range meter dropped to fifteen miles.

'Today sucks,' Charlie screamed, pounding on the steering wheel as she switched the cooling off again. 'Screw it. Screw everything!'

She wanted to cry, but the thought of Harry and Ed waiting for her at home helped her keep it together.

I'll soak in the bath. I'm having wine with dinner. And Harry will hold me in his arms. I'll pretend I'm impressed by whatever veggies he's brought home and moan about my day. And things will be OK, because I love that boy.

The world is screwed, but if he's around I can take it.

The last stretch home was barren two-lane highway, rising into the mountains. Charlie kept the speed low to conserve the dodgy battery. Every couple of miles, someone swung into the opposite lane to overtake, including a Nye County Police cruiser. She felt sure it was going to pull her over, because she was driving so slow.

Charlie's mood lightened when she came round a corner and exited left. *Almost home. Get the sneakers off my feet. Harry will laugh when I tell him about the rattlesnake. But don't mention snakes in front of Ed . . . What's that at the top of the road?*

Charlie pulled to the side of the track as an ambulance came the other way. There were four cop cars and a pair of police drones in the sky.

Have they busted my lab? But it's Nye County cars, not FBI or GMEA. Who was in the ambulance? Should I turn and run? But I won't get far and it's been on the news that there's a big gang of zombies robbing . . . Oh shit. I bet that's what it is.

A police SUV blocked the gate, so Charlie pulled off track and saw Harry and a police officer come striding down to meet her.

Charlie recognised Officer Martinez. He'd gone to school with Rosie and Vern's kids and she'd met him at their Christmas party. He was the local patrol officer, though out here local meant eight thousand square miles of desert.

'What happened?' Charlie asked. 'Who was in that ambulance?'

'Zombie attack,' Harry said. 'We held 'em off at the gate, mostly thanks to Rosie's sniper skills. Ed's badly shaken. Vern started having chest pains after it happened. He wanted to go check on his cows, but the medic insisted on taking him to hospital to run tests.'

'We've seen this in a couple of places recently,' Martinez explained. 'Packs of thirty or forty zombies. They're well armed and coerced by superheroes.'

'Christ,' Charlie said tearfully. She moved closer to Harry and gave him a hug.

'The zombies attacked the Sanchez place up the hill at the same time,' Harry said as he engulfed her. 'Nobody was home, but their truck was stolen and the place is trashed.'

'We've got drones up looking for them,' Martinez said. 'We're doing all we can, but it's a big old desert and this rocky terrain makes it easy to hide.'

'The cops will stay here overnight, but they don't have the manpower to guard us after that,' Harry told Charlie. 'I've already spoken with the neighbours. Officer Martinez says he knows a reliable security company. They put up guard drones and patrol the area twenty-four/seven. It won't be cheap, but the cost will be split five ways and I don't think we have much choice . . .'

'At least until this gang is caught,' Martinez added.

• • •

Ed grew more childlike when something spooked him. While Rosie helped Harry make dinner, Charlie sat on the living room sofa with Ed's head in her lap, gently stroking his hair.

The phone company wouldn't repair the landline and internet until morning, but a young cop guarding the gate relayed a radio message, saying that Vern showed signs of a minor heart attack and would be kept in hospital overnight.

Rosie didn't like driving unlit desert roads after dark and, while Harry offered to take her to the hospital, they decided it was best to stick together until morning. Rather than spend the night alone, Rosie stayed in Charlie and Harry's spare bedroom.

Charlie sat by Ed's bedside until he fell asleep. Harry was frazzled and crashed straight away, but Charlie wasn't so lucky, staring at the ceiling, wide eyed and hearing everything at once: a police drone buzzing the house, the air-con, Harry's rattling chest and the tick of the vintage Mickey Mouse alarm clock he'd bought for her nineteenth birthday.

Money was Charlie's big worry. Many businesses had gone bust after Killer-T. The ones that survived had cut back on advertising, so Harry only earned a fraction of what he used to from Vegas Local. Modding work paid well, but the risks of a long prison sentence or a shakedown were real.

They'd been doing OK the past few months, but Charlie had promised money to Juno, their cars were on their last legs, there were medical bills, expensive jobs that needed doing on the house and now they'd agreed to pay for private security patrols in case the zombies came back.

Charlie and Harry had made a plan: become self-sufficient in food and energy, build a healthy financial nest egg, then quit the risky modding business. But that dream seemed further off than ever.

64 CARDBOARD THE PIG

'Boys and their toys,' Rosie smiled.

It was just after 8 a.m. She was behind the wheel of Vern's big Jeep as Charlie climbed in the passenger seat. Harry, Ed and a few neighbours from up the hill stood on a patch of relatively flat land inspecting a pair of security drones, and testing out the walkie-talkies they'd been given by just-arrived security guards, with a thuggish air and machine guns slung across their chests.

'I hope these creepy guards aren't around for too long,' Charlie said, buckling her safety belt as Rosie drove off.

'They can't be,' Rosie said. 'Unless they start accepting payment in green beans and milk.'

Down by the gate, the cops were loading their drones on to a trailer. As the Jeep reached the highway, they saw a phone-company crew repairing the cables, and Rosie lowered her window and introduced herself to a third security guard, who had waves of curly red hair coming out the back of her combat helmet.

Vern had spent the night at Clover Medical Center in North Vegas. The hospital operated permanent quarantine and only allowed one visitor for short-stay patients. While Rosie took a chemical shower and garbed up like an astronaut, Charlie told her to give Vern her love and grabbed a taxi off the hospital rank.

The coffee shop below Charlie's office was super busy, with most tables in use and a dozen cars queuing at the drive-thru window.

'It's bedlam,' Charlie told Gwen as she stepped out of the quarantine box and moved behind the serving counter. 'What's going on?'

With no access to vaccines or quarantine programmes, the developing-world farmers who grew most of the world's cocoa, tea and coffee had been devastated by Killer-T. Gwen explained to Charlie that she'd unearthed a supplier of fresh pains au chocolat, baked with real dark chocolate. Word had spread among local office workers and there was pandemonium whenever they got a delivery.

The busy store was the first good piece of news Charlie had heard in a while, and she also felt pleased with her own business brain: Charlie let managers like Gwen decide what to sell and paid a bonus based on how much profit each shop made. At a time when the supply of basic items like coffee and milk remained erratic, it meant managers went the extra mile to find local suppliers, while staff at the big chains put up out-of-stock signs and awaited delivery from a warehouse hundreds of miles away.

Charlie had no modding clients to meet. After scoffing two pains au chocolat, she grabbed a bundle of money from her office safe, then jumped into another taxi. First stop was her most recently reopened coffee shop. She'd hoped the location close to the University of Nevada's Las Vegas campus would be popular, but so far business had been underwhelming.

Two staff stood inside with hands in their apron pockets, jolting like anxious schoolboys when Charlie stepped out of the quarantine box. There was a studenty crowd at the tables, but most of them were chatting and not buying much. Some were blatantly scoffing cola and cheap space-food doughnuts that came from the supermarket across the parking lot.

'Where's Bill?' Charlie asked, squaring up to a bearded barista several years older than she was.

'He was here earlier, but he had to go run an errand for his girlfriend.'

'Oh, did he?' Charlie hissed as the barista got a *you-shouldn't-have-said-that* look off his colleague. 'When Bill gets back, tell him to call me. And when you get this crowd in, hogging the tables and not buying anything, here's what you do.'

Charlie reached under the counter and turned the music up loud.

'And how come I see you two standing around, but the floor's filthy and four tables need wiping? Also change the code on the bathroom lock. That guy just walked in off the street. If this place is still losing money in eight weeks, I'm closing it down.'

The two workers gave Charlie filthy looks as she stormed out to a waiting taxi. She told the cabbie to take her to The Paddler motel.

Before Killer-T, this stretch of East Harmon had been a lively strip of old-fashioned motels, wedding chapels, convenience stores and family restaurants, mostly frequented by tourists who couldn't afford fancier places on The Strip.

But with half the big resorts closed and tourists thin on the ground, Cleveland had a ghostlike air and The Paddler was one of the last places open for business. Charlie now resented agreeing to give hard-earned money to Juno, and the more she thought the more she suspected it would do little to help her godson.

Maybe if I sat down and spoke to Juno ... Instead of giving her money, try persuading her to get the zombie mods removed and be a better mom. But who am I kidding? People turn themselves into zombies because it makes them happy no matter what. Zombies lie and make bad decisions. Above all, they're selfish.

Juno had messaged late the night before, saying she'd checked into room eighteen and asking if Charlie knew when she'd get the money. With their internet down, Charlie hadn't picked up the message until she'd got to the hospital with Rosie, and its bluntness made Juno and Mikey seem more mercenary.

Am I being soft? Why don't I walk away? This million will pay Ed's medical bills for six months. But Patrick's my godson. The prospects aren't rosy for a kid with a dead dad and zombie mom, but I should try to help, shouldn't I?

Room eighteen was past an ice machine and up an outdoor staircase. It was near noon and the sun was blazing, but the room still had curtains drawn. Charlie checked her bag to make sure she had the gun close, before ignoring the *Do not disturb* tag and giving a knock.

'Juno, open up,' Charlie said irritably as a kids' show blared from the TV inside. 'It's the middle of the day.'

Mikey's BMW is here, so they can't have gone far. Maybe the type of z-mod they have makes them sleep a lot.

'I'm not coming back for this shit,' Charlie shouted, this time pounding hard on the door and getting a look from a guy stepping out five rooms down.

I've got enough on my plate. I've ...

Charlie noticed the door handle rattle from inside. There

was a little voice around waist height, but the TV blotted it out.

'Patrick, is that you?'

Charlie went down on one knee and put her ear close to the door.

'I can't open it,' the voice said.

'Push the handle.'

'I am,' Patrick said.

Charlie tried to think what the inside of a motel room door looked like.

'Is there a bolt, or a lever below the door handle?'

'I don't think so.'

Charlie wondered if Patrick understood what a bolt was.

'Patrick, is it a handle, or is it a knob, like a ball?'

'Like a ball.'

'Is there a button in the middle of the ball?'

'Yes.'

'Push the button,' Charlie said. The knob rattled, then there was a click. 'OK, now try turning it.'

The door cracked open and Charlie saw Patrick, bare legged and wearing the same striped shirt and stained briefs as the day before.

'Who are you?' Patrick asked, forced to step back as Charlie shoved the door.

A stink of unwashed everything got through Charlie's virus mask. She kept a hand on the gun and gagged as she stepped inside. There were two double beds. Juno was on the one furthest from the door, face down in socks and knickers.

'I ate the chocolate,' Patrick said, facing the wall guiltily and scratching one leg with his big toe.

Charlie trembled as she closed in on Juno. There was urine soaked into the bed. Juno showed no sign of breathing and a deep bruise·ran in a straight line across her throat.

'Where's Mikey?' Charlie asked urgently.

Patrick pointed into the bathroom. Charlie straddled dirty clothes, passed the blaring TV and leaned into the bathroom.

Mikey had been in the shower when the bad guys showed. He was face down, naked, with shampoo lathered through his long hair. The method of execution was identical to Juno, with the purple wound across the neck.

'Is my mom too dead for a doctor?' Patrick asked, pleading eyes making Charlie choke up.

'I think so,' Charlie said.

I feel sick. What do I do? What do I do? What do I do? What do I do?

Charlie's lawyer had said it was unlikely anyone would randomly dig up the old investigation into her work in Mango's lab, but the FBI file would still exist and it would surely surface if she reported the murder of her former lab partner . . .

I can't be linked to this, but I can't abandon the little guy . . .

Killer-T had created a thousand times more orphans than the child-protection system had been designed to cope with. Most kids got taken into good homes with relatives or friends, but thousands had vanished and there had been a ton of media coverage about paedophile abductions, grotty makeshift orphanages in school gyms and overcrowded foster homes.

The only way I can be sure Patrick doesn't get dumped somewhere awful is if I take care of him.

'OK, little man,' Charlie said, trying to sound confident and friendly. 'I think it's best if we leave. Where are your favourite toys?'

Gotta think about forensics. I'm wearing anti-virus gloves and the only thing I've touched is the door handle. The only people who

can link me to this location are the guy who came out of the room
down the hall and the taxi driver who took me here. Hopefully
the local cops will put minimal effort into investigating the death
of a couple of zombies . . .

Patrick climbed on to the empty double bed and grabbed a well-worn stuffed pig and a grubby fleece blanket.

'Has your pig got a name?' Charlie asked as she looked inside an open suitcase by the door.

'This is Cardboard,' Patrick said.

'That's a cool name for a pig,' Charlie said.

There were some of Patrick's clothes in the bag, but it was jumbled with dirty bras and Mikey's crusty boxers. After a rummage with her gloved hand, Charlie found a pair of green soccer shorts.

'Take those dirty briefs off and put these on,' Charlie said, flicking the shorts to Patrick as she spotted toddler sized Nikes with Velcro fastenings.

Patrick wore a serious expression as he sat on the floor, pulling on the shorts. 'Are you allowed to take me away?' he asked thoughtfully.

'It's just until we sort things out,' Charlie said, peeling back the Velcro tabs to open the shoes. 'You can't stay here, can you? There's nobody to look after you.'

Patrick considered this as he fully stretched the waistband of the shorts and let it ping against his waist.

Charlie changed the subject. 'I like these sneakers, Patrick. I bet you can run really fast in these.'

'Zoom!' Patrick said, throwing a hand into the air and stepping towards Charlie.

Charlie helped him put on the shoes. Focusing on Patrick's needs made her detach from Juno's dead body eight feet away.

But when she looked up she felt it: a little boy's dead mommy and a person she'd once considered her best friend.

'OK, soldier,' Charlie said, stifling a sob as she stuffed Cardboard the pig and the tatty blanket into her bag. 'Let's march outta here.'

65 BUBBLEGUM

Vern left hospital two days after the zombie attack. He'd been told to take it easy, but as soon as he arrived home he checked on his beloved dairy cows, then crossed the driveway to check on Charlie and Harry.

Patrick sat swinging his legs off a chair as Vern helped Harry replace a broken hinge on one of the kitchen cabinets. The four-year-old looked less babyish with his hair cut, nails clipped and smart new shorts and shirt. He was confused by what had happened, sometimes mentioning that his mom had died, but at other times asking when she was coming back.

'Mikey can never come back, right?' Patrick asked anxiously, for the third time in an hour.

'Never ever, ever, ever,' Harry said, smiling as he screwed a new hinge on the door.

'Good,' Patrick said, nodding.

Harry whispered to Vern, who insisted on helping by holding the door steady. 'Charlie almost cried when she took his shirt off. Whip and burn marks all over his back and buttocks.'

'What are you whispering?' Patrick asked. Then when he didn't get an answer: 'Where are Charlie and Ed?'

'Ed has to do schoolwork,' Harry said. 'Charlie is working down in the shelter.'

'Can we play catch outside again tonight?'

'Maybe,' Harry said. 'I have to start making dinner when we've fixed this cupboard.'

Vern cracked a warm smile. 'Maybe you can come across and meet my cows later, Patrick.'

Patrick acted shy. 'Will you come with me, Harry?'

Harry had seen horrible stories about the overworked child-care system on TV news and Vegas Local. He supported Charlie bringing Patrick home, but wasn't used to little kids and found the constant need for attention a strain.

'I'll be making dinner,' Harry said. 'But Ed might go with you.'

'What's the gooey stuff?' Patrick asked, sliding off the dining chair and moving closer to the epoxy filler that Harry had mixed to fill the screw holes where the old hinge had torn loose.

'Don't touch that,' Vern and Harry yelled in unison, just as the phone started to ring.

'Can you fetch that, pal?' Harry asked.

Patrick ran into the hallway, returning with the ringing handset as Harry wiped sticky hands on his jeans.

'Afternoon, Harry speaking.'

'Young Mr Smirnov,' the man on the other end said brightly. 'It's Dr Harkom. I've had your biopsy results back, and I was hoping you had a minute to catch up.'

Harry asked Vern to keep an eye on Patrick, then crossed to the living room and shut the door.

'How's the cough been since I saw you?' the doctor asked.

Harry settled into an armchair. 'It's manageable in the day, when I'm busy doing stuff, but at night it tickles like crazy. Sleeping propped on pillows helps.'

'Are you still bringing up blood?'

'Blood most days,' Harry admitted as he heard one of the patrol drones skim over the house.

'Better or worse since you started the steroid injections?'

'No difference so far,' Harry said disappointedly. 'You said you had the biopsy results?'

Dr Harkom laughed uneasily. 'My colleagues found your lung tissue interesting.'

'In a good way?' Harry asked nervously.

'The picture is complex,' Dr Harkom explained. 'For the first ten years I practised medicine, you looked at symptoms, compared them to a list of known ailments and diseases and decided which one it was.

'Now, we have patients altering their genes, synthetic viruses, mutant bacteria, purple wasps, neurotoxic dog bites and Lord knows what else. And, of course, all those things interact with one another, and the health infrastructure is overwhelmed with millions suffering the after-effects of Killer-T and superflu.'

'So we've not got anywhere?'

'Your lung tissue was sticky and inflamed,' Dr Harkom explained. 'Healthy lung tissue has a colour and texture similar to a fresh white mushroom. Under the microscope, your sample looked more like chewed pink bubble gum. I showed the pictures to some colleagues. One had seen similar tissue in a keen amateur cyclist, who had the same respiratory mod as you.'

Harry was surprised. 'But my respiratory mod is common. I've looked online and there's nothing saying it's dangerous.'

'It's clearly a rare complication,' the doctor agreed. 'The KL553 respiratory modification is now on the approved list of mods and can legally be given to severe asthma sufferers. It's hard to say what is causing your problems. It may be an infection that reacted badly with the modified lung tissue. Or an environmental factor, such as an allergy to something in your diet or workplace.'

'Will reversing the mod help?'

'It may stop things getting worse, Harry. But a proportion of your lungs is clogged and spongy already. Altering your genes won't make dead lung tissue grow back. In the long term, the only solution may be a double lung transplant, using a donor lung or synthetically grown lungs.'

'That sounds expensive,' Harry said warily.

'Donor lungs rely on the tiny number of people who die with young, healthy lungs. Primarily accident victims. Synthetically grown organs are a new technology. It's extremely expensive and with current techniques adult-sized lungs take four years to grow.'

Harry drummed anxiously on the arm of his chair. 'So, in the long term, this doesn't look good?'

'I won't pretend that it's great, but there are options. Reversing your respiratory modification will hopefully stop new tissue damage. If it's an allergy, we may be able to identify the trigger. Possibly a dust mite in your home, or one of the fertilisers in your polytunnels. Then we could consider surgery to remove the most damaged areas of your lungs. Of course, your lung capacity will be reduced.'

'By how much?'

'It would be proportional to the amount of lung tissue removed. You wouldn't be running marathons, but I've seen cancer patients who've had an entire lung removed who manage to live relatively normal lives.'

'I don't know what we can afford. Ed's medical bills are already killing us.'

'You'd be entitled to free medical treatment if you returned to the UK,' Dr Harkom noted. 'Though the system is under strain and you'd probably find yourself at the end of a long waiting list.'

'Something to consider, I guess,' Harry said, tipping his head back and feeling angry with himself for getting modded.

But would I be here with Charlie if I was still pale and spotty?

'I'm still talking over your options with a couple of colleagues,' the doctor said. 'We can decide how to progress when I see you in two weeks' time.'

'Sounds like a plan,' Harry said. 'One other thing. Charlie's got a ton of other stuff to worry about. If she comes in to see you with Ed, I'd prefer you didn't mention this.'

As Harry ended the call, he could hear Vern finishing off the door in the kitchen, while Ed horsed around with Patrick in the hallway. Harry sat still in the armchair, holding the phone and scared of the gunk that rattled his chest every time he breathed.

He stayed that way for a couple of minutes, until the guilt about leaving Vern fixing his kitchen won out. Patrick and Ed were mucking about with a set of juggling bags, and Patrick howled with laughter as Ed lobbed one at Harry's back.

'Go easy, Ed,' Harry warned. 'You're a lot stronger than Patrick.'

Harry was levelling up the repaired door when Charlie came up from the lab, giving Vern a welcome-home hug before grabbing a cold-water jug from the fridge. Her eyes looked glazed as she gave Harry a kiss, and asked Vern why he wasn't lying down.

'Went crazy cooped up in the hospital,' Vern said as he wiped dust and filler crumbs off the kitchen worktop. 'Not one for sitting still.'

Charlie looked at Harry. 'I got a call back from lawyer Sue. She said technically I need to file an adoption petition for Patrick, or hand him to the authorities. But in the real world it's only a problem if someone is looking for him, like a grandma or something.'

'Did Seth have family?' Harry asked as he spotted Rosie coming up their drive holding a plate of something she'd baked.

'Not that I know of,' Charlie said. 'And, judging by the filthy clothes and cigarette burns, they didn't much care if they were around.'

'Knock, knock,' Rosie said brightly, coming through the door holding a loaf cake sealed in an anti-virus bag. 'Have you stolen my husband?'

Ed had a nose for Rosie's cake and strode in, dragging one leg because Patrick was clamped to it.

'You two seem to be hitting it off,' Rosie said as Harry reached into a cupboard to grab a pile of plates.

Patrick let go of Ed's leg, then stood between Harry and Charlie and spoke quietly. 'My butt hurts again.'

'You mean you want the toilet?' Harry asked.

Charlie shook her head and squatted down. 'He uses the toilet by himself, but he keeps saying his butt hurts.'

'Where does it hurt, sweetie?' Rosie asked.

'Here,' Patrick said, squeezing his left buttock. 'The man who killed Mikey and mom did it.'

'I've looked,' Charlie explained to Rosie. 'I can't see anything except a tiny red mark.'

'Take him to the clinic,' Harry suggested.

'I'd love to get him checked out,' Charlie said. 'But if I rock up at a paediatrician's office, twenty years old, with a kid that isn't mine who's covered in bruises and belt marks and with no adoption paperwork, they'll call the cops on me.'

'True,' Harry said thoughtfully.

'I could take him,' Rosie said. 'I'll make sure it's Dr Laurel. She's partly retired now, but she still works three days a week and I've known her since my eldest was born.'

'That would be *so* great,' Charlie said. 'My lawyer said it's much better to wait a few weeks before filing paperwork. Adoption is tricky, but if a kid is settled and happy, and nobody else wants him, there's virtually zero chance they'll take him away.'

Rosie started slicing the cake and Harry felt like he belonged as he surveyed the scene. Vern cross-legged, Ed scoffing cake like a typical hungry teenager, Patrick insisting on dunking his cake in a glass of milk and making everyone laugh when he inevitably dropped a big bit in it. And Charlie, standing bare-legged by the fridge, making a pot of tea. Sweaty and tired from a shift in the lab, but still the most beautiful thing Harry had ever seen.

66 BIG ONION

Harry opened one eye and saw a bauble of snot on Patrick's top lip. They'd put Patrick to bed in the spare room, but if he woke up he'd lift the bottom of Harry and Charlie's covers and wriggle into the space between them.

Mickey Mouse said it was a quarter past four as Harry rolled on to one side and realised he'd been disturbed by a clank from the air-conditioner. The unit that cooled the upper floor was decrepit and the banging suggested that the outside fan had come loose from its cracked bearing for the second time in a month.

A replacement bearing was on order, but getting spare parts for an elderly Chinese-made air-conditioner was tricky. Vern said it could cause major damage if the fan blades shattered, so Harry decided it couldn't wait until morning.

When Harry sat up, he felt the ball of muck that had built up on his chest while he'd been sleeping. To avoid waking Patrick and Charlie, he held his breath as he grabbed his jeans off the floor, bolted downstairs and ripped into a coughing fit over the kitchen sink.

It took a couple of minutes to hack out a build-up of blood

and phlegm. As the fit died down, Harry filled a glass with iced water and caught his breath, propped against the dining table. He thought about the conversation with Dr Harkom, and the situation with medical bills.

Maybe it's best if I go back to the UK to get these lungs fixed ... But my US residency expired when Kirsten went home to look after Granddad. Charlie can't come with me because of Ed and Patrick, but I won't be able to return to the USA, unless Charlie marries me first ...

Keeping busy was the best way to stop coughing and troubled thoughts, so Harry threw the rest of his water down the sink, grabbed a ladder and toolbox out of the garage and spoke into the walkie-talkie the private security company had given him.

'This is Harry to the guard on duty, do you copy?'

He recognised the voice of the redhead with the amazing long hair. 'Copy, Harry. Is there a problem?'

'I'm going out back with a ladder to fix my air-conditioner. Just letting you know, so one of your drones doesn't shoot fifty thousand volts up my rear!'

'I'll program a buffer zone around your house,' the redhead answered. 'And you be careful – it's windy out here.'

The racket from the air-con meant Harry didn't hear the howling wind until it almost snatched the back door out of his hand. Harry isolated the air-conditioner with a switch at ground level, then rested the little ladder against the house and fixed on his leather tool belt and the elastic strap of a head-mounted lamp.

There were a bunch of weird-looking shell beetles crawling on the ground and Harry sprayed the area around the ladder with insecticide before climbing up. The storm was chucking up dust and he considered going down for a set of goggles as he loosened three screws on a safety grille and let it pivot down round the fourth.

He gave the fan blades a wiggle, confirming it was vibration from the cracked bearing making the blades rattle. But when he felt in his tool belt he realised he'd climbed up without the wrench he needed to tighten them.

'Dammit.'

Harry coughed into his virus mask as he went down the ladder and opened the expanding tool box. He found the wrench in the second layer of drawers, and was about to climb back up when he noticed moving white light.

Nerves kicked in as he looked round the side of the house and saw two panel vans at the gate. Harry charged into the house and roared up the stairs.

'Charlie, wake the hell up!'

She sprang up sleepily, accidentally leaning on Patrick's arm and making him yelp.

'I think the zombies are back,' Harry shouted as he reached the bedroom doorway. 'I'll grab my gun and go wake Vern. You get the boys down in the shelter.'

He reached for the assault rifle on top of his wardrobe, stuck two spare clips in his tool belt, then grabbed the walkie-talkie.

'What's going on at the front gate?' Harry shouted into the box. 'Front gate, do you copy?'

The redhead spoke. 'One of my colleagues isn't well. His replacement is arriving. No cause for alarm.'

But her tone was off somehow, and one sick guard didn't explain two vans. Back downstairs, Harry stepped out of the front door where he could see the front gate being opened by two men.

When the walkie-talkies got handed out, the guard explained

two buttons. One sent an emergency alarm to all the other radios on the circuit, while the other alerted the local police. Harry flipped a protective cover and pressed both buttons as Charlie yelled inside the house.

'Just this once, don't argue,' she begged Ed. 'Grab Patrick and lock yourself in the shelter.'

Harry looked at the radio. Its luminous blue display now read, *Error. No base station.* He pressed the buttons again, but just got the error message

I want Charlie down in that shelter too. I need to tell Vern and Rosie. But the vans will be through the gate any second.

Patrick was squealing and Ed defiant as Harry vaulted the rail at the end of his front porch. Rosie and Vern's place was less than fifty yards away, and he remembered how Rosie's sharpshooting had saved their asses during the previous attack.

'Eat this, zombie bastards,' Charlie shouted as she opened the kitchen window and lobbed several of her handmade grenades towards the vans approaching the house. 'And, Ed, I'm not telling you again. Get down that shelter NOW!'

Harry only made it a couple of paces from the porch before one of the guards he'd been paying for stepped from behind Vern's parked Jeep and tackled him. Harry tried to shove him off, but another guy loomed overhead and smashed his nose with a rifle butt.

It wasn't a zombie.

'Long time no see, Harry,' Man Bun smirked as the guard snatched Harry's rifle.

A pair of Charlie's homemade grenades exploded almost simultaneously. The lead van was too close to the house, but the blast threw up clouds of dirt and set fire to the underside of the second van.

Harry tried to scramble as Man Bun and the security guard shielded their eyes from a third grenade blast, but he was concussed and his limbs weren't following orders. Vern and Rosie's bedroom light came on as the two thugs dragged Harry through the dirt.

While several armed men jumped out of the burning panel van, a four-man squad who'd come from higher ground approached the rear of the house.

Dressed only in one of Harry's T-shirts, Charlie kept screaming at Ed to get down to the shelter as she heard footsteps in the back yard. She spun, shooting the lead man in the face as he booted the back door, which Harry had left on the latch when he went out to do the repair.

Next door, Rosie had grabbed the rifle she kept propped against her bedside table. She rattled off two accurate shots, killing the driver of the lead van and a woman in body armour getting out of the second. But the team coming downhill heard the shots from the balcony and countered with a shoulder-launched mortar shell through the window of her upper rear bedroom.

As the last of Charlie's grenades hit bodies fleeing the burning vans, the mortar explosion ripped a huge hole in Rosie and Vern's roof and destroyed the internal walls on the upper floor. Vern was hobbling to his gun cabinet when the ceiling crashed on to him, while the force of the blast knocked Rosie half out of the window as chunks of drywall flew and wooden splinters speared her back.

Harry tried breaking loose, but explosions, dust and the blow to the head had disorientated him. There was smoke and flame outside as he got dragged up the porch steps and into the kitchen. Charlie had her arms raised and two rifles in her face, while Ed's fear of going down the shelter meant neither he nor Patrick had reached safety.

Masked and body-armoured figures swarmed out front and in the hallway, while outside several moaned from grenade injuries.

'Both vans are shot up,' someone reported to Man Bun. 'Two dead, at least six injured.'

'Another dead in here,' a voice added sourly. 'Nobody told us we were heading into grenades and snipers.'

'Quit your whining,' Man Bun roared. 'If our vans are wrecked, take the Porsche and the Jeep.' Then he pointed at three guys. 'The lab is down the hatch in the living room. Get the machinery out, then start spreading the explosives around. The boss wants this house levelled.'

'Cops will have their drones out with all these explosions,' a giant superhero noted.

'Let my people worry about cops,' Man Bun said as he approached Charlie. 'Go search upstairs. If they're running a lab, they've probably got cash lying around.'

A powerfully modded guy knocked Charlie to her knees and wrenched her arm tight behind her back as Man Bun closed in.

'Long time no see, Charlie girl,' Man Bun teased. 'You'll have to forgive your security team. But, you know, these rent-a-cops have families to look out for. Except the dumb redhead, who took a bullet for her trouble.'

Charlie scowled up at her tormentor. He'd had some work done, looking years younger and without the stooped posture.

'Prick,' was all Charlie could think to say.

Across the hall, someone shouted that they'd found the lab. Harry was dazed and blood streamed from his broken nose, but nobody was looking his way, and he still wore a belt full of tools.

'Let's have Charlie girl tied tight so she can't misbehave,' Man Bun ordered. Then he turned towards Harry. 'Haven't you got big and strong since I squeezed your little boy balls?'

'Are we taking the two kids?' someone asked.

'Sure,' Man Bun said. 'If they're not wanted, they're easily disposed of.'

Charlie whimpered as the superhero tightened rope round her ankles.

'Stop fussing!' Man Bun teased, and he spun and booted Charlie in the ribs.

'Leave her alone,' Harry roared.

'Or what?' Man Bun shouted back, laughing as he opened his arms wide, to a space filled with men in full body armour.

Harry figured Charlie would suffer less if he gave Man Bun a reason to turn on him. He thrust upwards with a screwdriver, jamming it deep into Man Bun's thigh.

'Christ,' Man Bun screamed, staggering backwards into the dining table. 'Why wasn't he searched?'

Charlie screamed as a superhero yanked Harry effortlessly off the floor and banged him down on the kitchen table.

'I've got bad news for you, kid,' Man Bun announced, flipping Harry on to his back. 'A modding lab and a girl who knows how to use it are worth a lot of money. But you're not worth shit.'

'Leave him alone,' Charlie squealed, writhing as two men bound her wrists to her ankles to make a hog-tie.

Man Bun eyed a sack of home-grown onions and grabbed a muddy one, still attached to its green stalk.

'Nice veg, Harry,' Man Bun said, pulling the screwdriver out of his bloody leg as he turned to the superhero. 'Crack a few ribs for me, Hector.'

'Nooo,' Charlie screamed, as Hector's huge fist shook the

table and made Harry bawl. 'Leave him alone. He's got lung problems.'

'He certainly has now,' Man Bun said, booming with laughter as he forced the onion into Harry's mouth.

It was bigger than Harry's mouth and there was an agonising snap as his jaw dislocated.

'*Don't!*' Charlie was screaming. 'Leave Harry alone. You're killing him. I can tell you where I've got money. Ten million at least.'

'Think I need this loser to make you tell me where your money is?' Man Bun laughed.

The muddy onion forced Harry's tongue to the back of his throat. His nose was clogged with blood, the smashed ribs were excruciating and the jaw was the most pain he'd ever felt. Charlie's screams were like a drill in his brain.

'Please, please. I love you, Harry. I love you so much.'

I love you more, Charlie. I wish I could tell you that.

But where did all the pain go?

Where did the light go?

I'm above it all. I can see the superhero and Man Bun's bloody leg and Ed getting knocked down as he tries to wrestle his way into the room to save me.

And now it's all white and I'm tiny. And Mum is here. How cool is that? With her Ray-Bans and a camera swinging round her neck. Lifting me out of my crib and holding me up to blow a raspberry on my belly.

Is that my oldest memory?

So this is death, I guess.

67 FAMILY REUNION

Charlie was tied and gagged in the trunk of Vern's Jeep as the wooden house exploded.

Harry, why the hell did you stab Man Bun? What were you going to achieve with half a dozen armed thugs in the room? . . . And now I'm alone for the rest of my life. Which might not be long . . .

Rosie and Vern's place got blasted too, as the Jeep hit the highway. Tools and junk rattled, and Charlie was face down, wrists bound so tight her fingers were numb. Feeling every bump as they sped along the highway.

It took twenty-five minutes to reach Las Vegas's outer suburbs. Charlie's shoulder joint crunched when a superhero yanked her arm, scraping skin off her legs as he dragged her over a bare concrete floor and slammed her in the back of a battered delivery truck. Ed was pulled out of Harry's Porsche, tied and gagged. Patrick came last, barely conscious, with blood oozing from a split lip.

Man Bun and another guy got in the front, while a huge female superhero sat on a bench in the rear compartment and put the sole of her boot in Charlie's face. She'd walked through

Vern's cow shed and seemed amused as the stench made Charlie retch.

The sun was coming up as the second leg of Charlie's ride ended. Man Bun opened the rear doors, with an emergency wound kit strapped tight round his bloody leg. He slashed the cords on Charlie's wrists and ankles, and dragged her out. She recognised the tall pearl-coloured towers and rusted monorail track overhead as part of UrbanScape.

The trendy four-thousand-room hotel and casino had had the misfortune to open right before the first SNor outbreak and had gone bust in less than two years.

Man Bun limped to an anonymous grey door and tapped an entry card. Patrick was starting to come round, and Charlie reached across to cuddle him.

'We'll be OK,' she mouthed softly.

Ed stayed silent. His expression was difficult to read, but was possibly guilty for not obeying the order to get down into the shelter. Charlie was worried he might have a fit, which was the last thing she wanted with a psycho like Man Bun on the scene.

'I want my mom back,' Patrick whimpered as Charlie followed Man Bun up bare concrete stairs.

At the top, Man Bun tapped his pass again and they entered UrbanScape's deserted main floor. Charlie's bare feet were cold on the marble in a grand check-in area, full of giant chrome sculptures and lifeless video screens.

The air-conditioning hadn't run in years, leaving hot, dead air. Man Bun knew his way, expertly navigating the vast casino. Passing roulette wheels and endless banks of slot machines, lit only with emergency lighting and chinks of daylight.

Charlie was trembling and on the edge of tears, holding Patrick tight as she marched barefoot through a strip of restaurants. Most of UrbanScape's eateries had never opened and the big photo of Harry's aunt and hoardings for *Kirsten Channing at UrbanScape coming soon!* pushed Charlie into open sobs.

Patrick patted her arm, while the superhero dug her in the back.

'Quit your snivelling and move, or I'll give you something worth crying about.'

They reached a grand elevator lobby, unlit, its huge curved-glass aquarium filled with a couple of inches of dark green sludge. All but one elevator had a not-in-service sign and Man Bun made an elaborate sweep with his arm.

'Ladies first,' he crooned.

Charlie had never felt such pure hatred for anyone as the marbled elevator accelerated towards the fiftieth floor. Her shoulder hurt where she'd been yanked out of the Jeep and Patrick whined as she put him down.

'You got cow shit on them big boots?' Man Bun asked, eying the superhero filling half the elevator. 'You'd better not trail that on Fawn Janssen's carpet ...'

Charlie shuddered. She knew Man Bun worked for the Janssens and that Fawn was now the boss. But, somehow, her brain hadn't processed this truth until she heard her sister's name.

The superhero stayed behind, unlacing her size-fourteen boots, and Man Bun led Charlie, Patrick and Ed down a brightly lit hallway, with carpet so thick it almost gobbled their feet. Two guards with slate-grey suits and Tec-9 compact machine guns stood either side of triple-height black doors.

Man Bun got told to wait outside as one suit opened the door and let Charlie, Ed and Patrick in.

Ed gawped when he entered a lair worthy of a James Bond villain.

The office was on UrbanScape's top floor, with glass curving around three sides and a view along the switched-off signs and unwashed windows of The Strip's shuttered mega-resorts. Inside were several black leather sofas, a large art-deco-style bar and ten feet of mahogany desk. The only items on the desk were a telephone, one of JJ's football helmets and a large model of the Janssen corporate jet.

'The boys must sit on the sofa,' a short but well-muscled butler told the suited guard. 'The girl is to kneel in front of the desk facing forwards with her hands on her head. If she makes the slightest movement, give her a zap with your tasers. Miss Janssen is eating breakfast in her suite and will be here shortly.'

• • •

Fawn made them wait an hour.

'Long time no see,' Charlie's big sister said as she strode into the office, wearing yoga pants and Nikes, twirling a three-foot cattle prod like a cheerleader's baton.

Fawn was tall and dark, while Charlie was average height and blonde. But there were striking similarities in the sisters' large blue eyes and broad shoulders.

'Don't look at me, Charlie,' Fawn said sharply. 'Unless you want to get zapped.'

Fawn paused by the sofa and glowered at Ed.

'Baby bro's quite handsome for a mongo,' she said, as she stepped close behind Charlie, tapping the high-voltage prod in her palm.

'What did I ever do to you, Fawn?' Charlie asked, trying not to satisfy her big sister with a sob.

Fawn spoke in baby talk. 'Is ickle Charlie sore because her

silly boyfriend got turned to crackling?'

Man Bun entered the room quietly, dressed in clean pants. He lined up with the two guards at the back of the room as Fawn touched the cattle-prod tip against the back of Charlie's neck.

'Is this switched on?' Fawn asked, pressing the trigger. Charlie yelped, shot forward and banged her head on the desk. 'Well, I guess it is.'

Man Bun laughed appreciatively in the background.

Charlie rolled on to her back and glowered defiantly.

Patrick squealed, 'Stop hurting her,' as Fawn swung the prod over Charlie's face.

'How 'bout a zap on the nose, sis?' Fawn asked, then took a deep breath and smiled. 'You did ask an interesting question back there. Why *must* I torment poor little Charlie? Before you were born, I used to trap spiders and mice. I'd pull off their wings, or legs, or put pins in them. But when you came along it seemed *way* more fun torturing you.'

'You're a psychopath,' Charlie hissed.

'Say it once, say it loud, I'm a psycho and I'm proud,' Fawn sang cheerily. 'And look where it's got me! I was born trailer trash and now I'm the richest woman in Vegas.'

Fawn let this linger as she continued menacing Charlie with the cattle prod.

'The question is, what to do with my lovely sibling?' Fawn continued airily. 'Good lab workers are tough to find and there's always plenty of work. So I think I'll set you up here at UrbanScape. I've got four thousand empty hotel rooms to choose from. You can work fourteen hours a day. I'll give you every third Sunday afternoon off, if you behave. You seem fond of your little godson, so we'll keep him close and make sure he suffers if you don't.'

Fawn adored the torment on Charlie's face and gave her a zap on the thigh for good measure.

'Then there's young Ed,' Fawn said as Charlie balled up, convulsing from the electric shock. 'I generally think it's better if cripples and morons are disposed of. But my lab techs often need a test subject for trying new mods. Someone has to be the guinea pig and it might as well be him.'

'I'll never work in your labs,' Charlie growled. 'I don't care how you try to force me.'

'That's what your old friend Mango said,' Fawn noted. 'But we part-drowned one of her kiddies, gave her a few behavioural mods and now she's practically employee of the month.'

As Fawn said this, a white disc rolled across the floor towards the guards.

'I dropped my Icebreaker,' Ed said, jumping off the sofa to chase the mint.

'And who gave you permission to eat?' Fawn demanded as one of the suited guards stepped forward and shoved Ed towards the couch.

'Back,' he ordered firmly.

But Ed stubbornly insisted on picking up the mint and got into a little tussle with the guard.

Charlie was fearful. 'Ed, sit back on the couch, or they'll hurt you.'

'Christ he's *so* dumb,' Fawn said as Ed got pushed on to the sofa. 'Since you're so fond of Ed, I might have a taxidermist stuff him and put him on display in your lab. Though he could be a bit of a mutant after we've twiddled with his DNA . . .'

Fawn tipped up her head, laughing helplessly at her own joke.

Then the back half of her office exploded.

68 UNSEEN POTENTIAL

Harry's dead. Charlie's on the floor. Fawn is talking about doing nasty things to me. I'm seventeen. Everyone says I'm a big boy now. If I don't do something, they'll take me to a place a hundred times worse than Care4Kids.

Ed feared things crawling up his leg, so he'd woken up in a long-sleeved undershirt and jogging bottoms tucked into long soccer socks. His pockets bulged, but Man Bun's team hadn't bothered to search him.

This meant the guards didn't find the Icebreakers, one of which Ed had flicked across the floor as a distraction, or the pair of Charlie's homemade grenades he'd stuffed down his right-hand pocket as the bad guys stormed in the back at the house.

When the suited guard tried to stop Ed picking up the mint, Ed had slipped one of the little grenades in the guard's jacket pocket. The guard had just re-joined Man Bun and his colleague at the rear of the office when he noticed the lump in his pocket.

But by then it was too late . . .

'What the—' Fawn yelled, shielding her face as the blast threw her across her own desk.

Charlie had been knocked flat so the blast didn't hit her so hard, and she jumped up and ripped the cattle prod out of Fawn's grasp as an alarm sounded and sprinklers fired. The two slate-suited guards had been ripped apart by the grenade blast. Man Bun had been flung backwards, smashing through the glass panes of a bookcase, and splattered with chunks of his former colleagues.

Ed knew the blast was coming and dived on top of Patrick to shield him. The sprinklers filled the air with fine droplets, snuffing an alcohol fire that had erupted around the bar. Everyone's ears were ringing, but Fawn reached over her water-sprinkled desktop and grabbed a pistol out of the top drawer.

Charlie ducked as Fawn took two wild shots, then scrambled round the side of the desk and speared Fawn with the cattle prod.

'See how you like it,' Charlie gasped, blasting the cattle prod as Fawn collapsed.

At the back of the room, Man Bun was finding his feet and going for a pistol tucked in the front of his trousers.

'Charlie, behind you,' Ed shouted.

As Fawn felt around for a weapon, Charlie landed hard on her sister's chest and pushed the tubular cattle prod sideways against her sister's throat. Man Bun was limping and dazed. He had a gun, but Fawn and Charlie were obscured by the desk.

Ed threw Patrick behind the sofa, then picked up a dainty marble-topped end table and ran through the smoke towards Man Bun. Man Bun swung to shoot as Ed came into his peripheral vision, but the wounded leg made him clumsy and the circle of marble smashed him in the face.

Charlie got a spit shower as Fawn gave up trying to reach the gun and used both hands to fight the bar crushing her throat.

On the other side of the desk, Ed and Man Bun hit the floor and Man Bun shot wildly into a side wall.

Fawn finally choked out, freeing Charlie to grab her sister's pistol and bob above the desk. Ed sat on Man Bun's bloodied leg, but Man Bun was winning the battle to turn his pistol towards Ed.

'This is for Harry,' Charlie snarled, rounding the desk and shooting Man Bun through the eye from point blank range.

Ed staggered back, splattered in gore. Charlie's giant T-shirt was soaked through, ripped at the neck and hanging off one shoulder. Her arms and face were bloody, but there was no hesitation as she went back behind the desk and fired two shots. One in Fawn's heart and one through the temple.

Charlie leaned on the desk, coughing from dust and gun smoke. A thousand emotions and no time to deal with them. She'd been running over the debris barefoot, but now she felt the cuts in her bloodied soles.

'Go call the elevator,' Charlie told Ed, as she snatched a little Tec-9 machine gun. 'Be careful, the butler and the superhero might be around somewhere.'

She looked at Fawn's Nikes. They were too big, but there was a ton of broken glass around the doorway, so she yanked them off and pulled them painfully over her bloodied feet.

'Elevator's here,' Ed shouted through the huge doors. 'I'm holding it.'

The carpet squelched as Charlie scooped a rigid Patrick off the floor behind the leather couch.

'Little guy,' she said softly. 'I'm sorry.'

'Someone's coming, hurry up!' Ed shouted.

Fawn's Nikes were way too big and Charlie almost turned her ankle as she walked over shattered barware and blackened books. Ed stood in the elevator door and Charlie's wet sole skidded as she sprinted in, starting to do the splits.

There were footsteps getting close. Ed frantically pressed the door-close button and someone shouted, 'Hey!' as they started down. The fifty-floor ride took a thousand hours as Charlie imagined the power getting cut.

'My ears won't stop ringing,' Ed shouted, the floors blipping past.

37, 36, 34, 32, 28 . . .

'It'll get better,' Charlie said as Patrick gripped her tight. 'Try to stay calm, Ed. You were the hero. You saved all our lives.'

Charlie kept the Tec-9 poised as the elevator reached casino level. When the doors opened, there was no phalanx of guards ready to shoot them down, just acres of dead casino and green emergency lighting.

'How do we get out of here?' Charlie asked, mostly to herself.

A few steps out of the elevator lobby were arrows pointing towards The Strip. Charlie was struggling with her bloodied feet, so Ed gave Patrick a piggyback, and they jogged past rows of unplugged slot machines.

After a couple of hundred yards, Charlie led the way over a fallen banner advertising UrbanScape's *Grand Finale, All Retail 50% off*. An alarm sounded as she pushed the bar on an emergency door, stepping out into a bright Vegas morning.

The wind was still strong and it caught Charlie's sodden T-shirt, making her shiver. UrbanScape's cobbled frontage had once been a mix of water spouts, cafés and trendy bars. But everything was shuttered now and there were several dozen homeless people in tents and shelters. GENUINE HOMELESS HERE. NO ZOMBIES, was spray-painted on UrbanScape's pearl-coloured glass.

The locals weren't sure what the girl dripping bloody water and holding a machine gun was doing, but they were understandably wary and someone shouted, 'Get out of here, freaks.'

'Come on, keep calm,' Charlie told Ed, spotting a glazed expression that sometimes signalled an imminent fit.

'We're just passing through,' Charlie told the onlookers loudly, stretching her T-shirt down over her ass as the wind rattled litter and made cardboard shelters wobble.

I've got no virus mask, no money, no phone and you can see my nipples through this shirt, Charlie thought. *No taxi will take us anywhere in this state and my feet are agony.*

I should have grabbed Man Bun's wallet, but I'm not going back for it. The only place I can go is my office at the coffee shop. I don't have my key, but Gwen should be unlocking about now. But it's four miles away and we need to get off the street because Fawn owns the cops.

Owned the cops . . .

Charlie and Ed had reached The Strip. They'd hobbled about thirty yards when she noticed a concrete ramp. It still had a sign saying it was the valet entrance to a boutique hotel, but concrete slabs had been put down to block traffic.

There was a bunch of creepy-looking guys standing around, and teenaged zombie girls sat on concrete behind, wearing very little. It didn't take a genius to figure that the zombie girls were being pimped for sex.

Charlie was still pumped from killing Fawn and thought how satisfying it would be to open up the machine gun and wipe the pimps out. But her disgust was replaced by a sniff of opportunity as a silver Toyota turned off the strip.

'That's our ride,' Charlie told a confused Ed. 'Stay close.'

Charlie thought the pimps might have guns, but doubted they'd risk using them to protect a client. As the Toyota's window came down and one of the pimps slid off the wall to talk business, Charlie barged between them and stuck her Tec-9 in the face of the middle-aged driver wearing a fancy purple virus mask.

'Already killed two people this morning,' Charlie roared. 'Gimme your car or I'll make it three.'

Charlie's machine gun and blood-spattered appearance gave the man no cause for doubt.

'Faster, pervert,' Charlie ordered as the guy popped his seatbelt and opened the door. 'Keys, keys.'

A couple of the pimps were getting too close for comfort, so Charlie sprayed a burst of shots into the air.

'Stay back.'

One bullet shattered a sheet of golden glass several storeys up. Passers-by screamed as shards pelted the sidewalk and the driver was in such a panic that he fell out of the car, clutching his chest. The car was keyless, so he reached up to hand Charlie a plastic fob. As Ed threw Patrick in the back, Charlie jumped in the driver's seat and put the transmission in reverse. A motorbike swerved and honked as she backed on to the strip.

'You guys OK back there?' Charlie asked, glancing at Ed's rigid face as she put the car in drive. Her foot was agony as she pushed the pedal and accelerated down The Strip.

Ed looked half thrilled, half mortified, while Patrick complained expressively.

'My lip hurts now and my butt hurts *all* the time.'

The Strip was one red light after another, so Charlie took an easy right on to Flamingo. As she made the turn, she had a brainwave.

'I know what Patrick's been complaining about,' she announced. 'The pain in his butt.'

After three blocks, she pulled into an empty lot in front of a dental clinic that wouldn't open for another hour.

'Ed, have you got anything small and sharp in those bulging pockets?'

'I've got one grenade left and a pack of Kleenex.'

Frustrated, Charlie flipped the Toyota's glove compartment. It was crammed with junk, including change for parking meters, packs of boiled sweets and a baseball cap. But she got lucky with a floral-patterned zip-up bag, containing make-up and a small pair of nail scissors.

'Patrick, sweetie, I'm gonna need you here on my lap. Let me look at that butt.'

'What are you doing?' Ed asked as he helped Patrick step between the two front seats. 'Shouldn't we be getting away as fast as possible?'

Charlie laid Patrick face down in her lap and pulled down his night shorts to expose his buttocks

'Touch the bit where it hurts,' Charlie said.

Patrick reached behind and tapped his upper right buttock. Charlie and Rosie had both looked before and just noticed a small red mark, like a zit, but this time Charlie pinched the flesh beneath and felt a hard lump, the size of a rice grain.

I was right . . .

'Owww,' Patrick moaned.

'I know, sweetie,' Charlie said, taking the nail scissors off the passenger seat. 'This will sting, but be brave and try to stay still.'

Patrick bucked and wailed as Charlie dug the sharp little scissors into his buttock.

'I'm sorry, I'm sorry,' Charlie said, feeling awful. 'The more you stay still the quicker it will be.'

'Stop hurting me.'

'What are you doing?' Ed blurted, thinking his sister had gone mad. 'He's bleeding. Leave him alone!'

Patrick's heel kicked Charlie in the head as she pushed two fingers behind the little grain inside his buttocks.

When it neared the surface, Charlie grabbed tweezers from the make-up bag, pulled out a tiny silver cylinder and dropped it on the passenger seat.

'What is that?' Ed blurted.

'I'm so sorry, Patrick,' Charlie said, grabbing a wad of tissues out of a box in the door compartment and pressing it against the wound. 'I've taken the itchy thing out now. You need to press the tissues down hard to stop the bleeding.'

'I don't understand,' Ed said.

'Shh, shh,' Charlie soothed, rubbing Patrick's back as he continued to scream. Then she glanced back at Ed.

'It's a mini transmitter,' Charlie explained. 'The guy who killed Juno and Mikey injected it into Patrick's buttock. Fawn must have known he was my godson and that I'd probably take him home when I found Juno dead at the motel. That's how they found our house. It's all my fault. Harry died because I let them track me home.'

Ed disagreed. 'Harry was stupid to stab that guy.'

'Take Patrick. I need to keep driving,' Charlie said, sobbing and shaking as she passed Patrick between the seats to Ed. 'Try and calm him down. Keep the tissues pressed on the wound until it clots.'

Charlie wiped her face, then flicked the blood-smeared transmitter out of the car window.

'Fawn's dead now,' Ed pointed out as Patrick switched from wailing to sniffling.

'But Janssen people might not like that we killed their boss,' Charlie said, restarting the motor. 'So we need to get out of here fast.'

PART FIVE
FOUR MONTHS LATER

69 STONE DEAD

Vegas Local

MONDAY'S TOP STORIES

VEGAS NEWS – **Fawn Janssen confirmed dead as turf war leads to tragedy.**

Las Vegas Metro Police report that three California men gunned down while leaving a downtown bar late Saturday were likely victims of mistaken identity.

The shooting is the latest violent outbreak in a four-month turf war that has seen various factions seek control over illegal modding and other criminal activities.

The turf war was triggered by a power vacuum following the disappearance of Fawn Janssen, who took control of the Janssen family's alleged criminal interests, following the death of her father-in-law.

Fawn hadn't been seen alive since August. Yesterday, a forensics team confirmed that Janssen's DNA and that of three known associates was identified among human remains found in a garbage incinerator at the shuttered UrbanScape casino complex.

The search followed a successful operation that unearthed several modding labs operating in the resort's disused hotel towers.

FULL STORY AND PHOTOS (WARNING: GRAPHIC IMAGES)

WEATHER – WHITE CHRISTMAS ON THE CARDS FOR VEGAS?

A cold front that has brought unusually low temperatures to Texas and Arizona is set to reach Nevada this weekend. Clark County Transit has warned drivers to be prepared for icy conditions.

Snowfall at higher elevations may spread to the city over the coming days.

WEATHER LATEST

DISEASE UPDATE – Alert Status Amber

ASMB – No signs of recent mutation, but ensure all sexual partners have been vaccinated within last 30 days.

Killer-T – Strains 3B and 5A are active in south-west United States. Update vaccine weekly.

Melbourne Virus – Current vaccine NOT effective against strain 4C-2. Follow 8min sterilisation procedure before eating raw produce.

SNor – No current threat, but exercise cold-weather precautions in kitchens and communal environments.

Superflu – No current outbreak.

Other threats – Stone Dead jumping spider outbreak continues

> in the Henderson area. Keep insecticide spray on hand and do not allow children under 50lb to play outside as bite may be fatal. MUST be tackled by professional exterminators.

Charlie was balled up under a mound of covers wishing she'd never existed. Patrick lay on the motel suite's grubby carpet, watching cartoons on a tablet, while Ed had an ancient episode of *Big Bang Theory* going on the main TV.

'Charlie, you've got a call,' Ed said, scratching his sack as he took her vibrating phone off charge and flung it towards the bed.

Ed put his show back on and audience laughter erupted as Charlie dragged her phone under the covers, hating the light from the screen.

'Yeah, hi.'

Gwen's voice was painfully cheerful. 'Charlie, how's it going?'

'Good,' she lied.

'It's past noon. I thought you were coming into the office today,' Gwen said. 'The accounts are piling up. And we were going to discuss a staff Christmas bonus. I know money is tight, but I think they deserve it.'

Charlie couldn't cope with getting out of bed, let alone doing accounts for five coffee shops. But she felt horribly guilty. Gwen had been a loyal soldier, from the morning four months earlier when she'd turned up in a hijacked Toyota covered in blood, to the previous afternoon when Gwen picked up Patrick for a play date with her six-year-old daughter, Wendy.

'I've got a headache and pre-school is out for Christmas,' Charlie said. 'I'll come in early tomorrow, so I can have a proper go at them.'

'Shall I pick you up on my way in?' Gwen suggested. It was out of Gwen's way, but she knew Charlie might not show if she didn't. 'I can cover most things, but I don't understand the wages and accounts.'

'No . . .' Charlie mumbled. 'Actually, yes. I don't feel so great. But I know you've got your own problems.'

'I drove over to check the shop by the university,' Gwen said. 'It was doing OK, though the students are on break. There's not been a major virus outbreak this whole year. It's Christmas and people are getting their confidence back.'

'Not me,' Charlie said sourly. 'I'm a potato.'

'You went through a horrific experience,' Gwen soothed. 'Don't beat yourself up, Charlie. Getting over this will take time.'

'I guess,' Charlie said. She kicked some of the covers off and stared up at the motel suite's cracked ceiling.

'Did you see Vegas Local? They identified your sister's DNA.'

Charlie felt like her heart was being sucked out when Gwen said Vegas Local. It would always be something she associated with Harry.

'It's lucky someone cleaned up the mess,' Gwen said. 'Your DNA would have been all over the gun and the office.'

'I've been worried about that,' Charlie admitted. 'I acted in self-defence, but Ed's my only witness and, with my luck, the cops probably would have tried to do me for murder.'

'Who cleaned up, though?' Gwen wondered.

'Anyone who'd gain some advantage by knowing Fawn was dead before anyone else,' Charlie suggested. 'Any other news?'

'Just some strip-mall lady. She called saying she likes your business. She's got three dead coffee shops that she's willing to lease cheap.'

'I can't face that now . . .' Charlie groaned.

'At least one of them is a good location,' Gwen said. 'Opening another shop might give you something to focus on. And everyone says the economy is growing again. I even got stuck in traffic crossing The Strip last weekend.'

'Until the next quarantine sends it all down the pan,' Charlie said, then more encouragingly. 'We'll talk tomorrow. I don't pay you enough for what you do, Gwen.'

Gwen laughed. 'That's easily fixed, boss.'

As Gwen hung up, Charlie peered over her mound of covers. Patrick now stood at the foot of her bed, scowling.

'Are we doing *anything* today?' the five-year-old groaned. 'I'm so bored.'

Patrick was a great-looking kid, and Charlie couldn't help smiling because he'd got his T-shirt on back to front.

'Come here – put your arms up,' Charlie said, swinging her legs out of bed and catching her own funk. 'How about a game?'

Patrick grinned as Charlie put his shirt right. 'What game?'

'It's a game called pick all the dirty clothes and crap up off the floor.'

'Aww!' Patrick moaned. 'What about a proper game?'

'This room is a pit,' Charlie said, mildly motivated as she grabbed the mound of bedding and flicked it to straighten up.

Patrick and Ed laughed as one of Charlie's bras and a half-eaten pack of fries flew into the air.

'Yeah, *we're* the messy ones,' Ed said. 'Can I go across to the gym, now you're up?'

Charlie felt weighed down as she rested on one knee and picked ketchup-daubed fries off the carpet. She loved Patrick and Ed, but she was only twenty and looking after them was a twenty-four/seven job.

'Hold off on the gym,' Charlie said, wiping salty ketchup

fingers on her T-shirt. 'We're living in a sty. Did you shower when you came back from the gym yesterday?'

'I told him he stinks!' Patrick blurted cheerfully.

'Shut up, squirt, or I'll fart on you,' Ed said.

'You'll have to catch me first, lumbering ape!' Patrick grinned.

Patrick shrieked as Ed stood up with his hands in a grabbing position. It was good-natured, but the suite was two beds, a sofa and a tiny kitchenette. Charlie couldn't stand the idea of Patrick leaping between the beds and squealing.

'Quit it!' Charlie yelled, clapping twice and stepping between the boys. 'Ed, turn that damned show off, then wipe down the kitchen. Patrick, get the laundry bag out of the bathroom. Help me grab the wet towels and clothes off the floor. I'm gonna go down and do a load of laundry.'

'So can I go to the gym?' Ed asked as he sprayed Clorox over the kitchen cabinets.

'You'll have to stay here with Patrick.'

'I've been keeping an eye on him all day,' Ed protested. 'Can't you take him to the laundry?'

The motel's stuffy laundry room was Patrick's idea of hell.

'Nooooo,' Patrick whined. 'Can I go to the gym?'

'He can come if he wants,' Ed said.

'Yessssss,' Patrick said, pumping a fist as he leapt on to Charlie's bed.

The gym was across the street from the motel. It was a guys-lifting-weights-type place, rather than StairMasters and girls in Lycra. Ed had started lifting weights with Harry and asked if he could try the gym when they'd first moved in. Charlie worried he'd get teased by a bunch of jocks, but the gym's sixty-something-year-old owner, Bryan, gave Ed training programmes and kept an eye on him.

'Patrick, you're too young for the gym,' Charlie said.

'But it's school holidays so Marty's there,' Patrick pleaded. 'I can play with him.'

'Who's Marty?' Charlie asked.

'Bryan's grandson,' Ed said, as if Charlie was stupid. 'He was hanging around the motel pool half the summer.'

Charlie felt frustrated with herself. Besides feeling sad all the time and the daily fight to get out of bed, she forgot simple stuff, like people's names and picking Patrick up from pre-school.

She was wary of sending Patrick to the gym without checking, but she liked the idea of getting the boys out of her hair for a few hours. Bryan's number was in her phone and he said his bored grandson would be delighted with some company.

'All right,' Charlie said, faking cheer. 'Patrick, put on your virus mask and keep it on like you have to at pre-school. Ed, when you get back here after your workout, put those stinking clothes in a bucket with hot water and some disinfectant. Then take a shower, and wash your hair *properly* with shampoo.'

Charlie smiled as her two energetic boys put on shoes, and grabbed their virus masks and gloves.

'How many times, Ed? Turn that TV off,' Charlie barked, throwing a hoodie at Patrick. 'Put that on – it's cold out. And, Ed, take your key in case I'm still downstairs. And hold Patrick's hand when you cross. The road is quiet, but the cars come round that corner *so* fast.'

'All right, *mommykins*,' Ed said, balancing Patrick on his stocky shoulders and ducking so he didn't thump the five-year-old's head on the door frame.

70 NO MODS ALLOWED

Charlie realised how cold it was when she stood barefoot on the first-floor balcony. She was pleased to see Patrick holding Ed's hand as they crossed the street, and turned back after they'd vanished through a door with a weightlifter logo and a white-on-black banner that read *100% Natural. NO MODS ALLOWED.*

Charlie shivered as she shut the door with her heel, then felt conned when she realised the boys had escaped without helping to clean up. A huge part of her wanted to burrow under the covers and go back to hiding from the world, but she knew she'd spend the rest of the day there if she did and she hoped a shower would give her a jolt.

The erratic hot water at the house in the desert meant Charlie had often showered with Harry. The Kuchler Motel's never-ending supply was one of its best features, but if Charlie lingered too long an imaginary Harry would join her and the feels would leave her slumped in the shower tray, sobbing hopelessly.

That time Harry put one of my waxing strips on his chest and yelped so much he fell off the bed . . .

Charlie almost jumped out of the shower, knowing fond thoughts of Harry led nowhere but pain.

Keep busy.

After drying on the least grungy towel and dressing in her least grungy leggings and last clean T-shirt, Charlie grabbed the laundry basket and started gathering towels and dirty clothes scattered across the bathroom.

The basket was stuffed before she got to the clothes spread around the beds, but Charlie was on a laundry mission, so she grabbed a trash-can liner from the cupboard under the sink and began filling up with Patrick's Spider-Man underpants and Ed's aromatic socks.

After waddling down two flights with laundry in each hand, Charlie crossed the parking lot to the motel's other building and stepped through a basic UV quarantine gate into a laundry room.

One of the three dryers was rumbling and a chunky guy sat in the only plastic bucket chair that wasn't cracked at the back. He was average height, thirties, with a stocky build and a dark-brown shirt with *R&M Haulage* embroidered on the pocket.

'Hey, Charlie,' he said, peering over a comic book.

His beard had grown and he was dressed for winter, so Charlie took a second to mark him as a guy who'd hit on her when she'd taken Patrick for a pre-bedtime splash in the motel pool, back when it was still hot.

'Alex?' Charlie ventured.

'Rex,' he corrected as Charlie raised the metal lid on a washer and started dropping stuff in.

The easy smile reminded her that Rex had a one-one-seven, the socially acceptable zombie mod that kept you functioning while life floated happily by.

People with one-one-sevens tended to make good employees in mundane, non-creative jobs, though their optimistic bias gave them a poor sense of danger and their relentless smiles and trite observations made them a goldmine for stand-up comedians.

'I heard it might snow for Christmas.'

'Uh-huh,' Charlie said as she sprinkled powder on top of her first load, then opened another machine to take her whites.

'Here for Christmas, or off to visit family?' Rex asked.

'No place to go,' Charlie sighed, not wanting this banal conversation, but not ready to face her own company back in the suite. 'You?'

'Working,' Rex said. 'I was supposed to take a load home to Georgia this morning, but a tire burst on my rig and spares are tough to find.'

'I heard that,' Charlie said, nodding as she sat herself on top of the folding bench, swinging her legs.

'They've been salvaging tires off dead people's cars and trucks, but they've run out,' Rex explained. 'Getting some Mexican brand tire delivered tomorrow. But the late start means I'll be driving through Christmas Day.'

'You have anyone in Georgia?'

'Pa's in a retirement home down that way. Killer-T got my wife and my two boys, eight and eleven.'

'I'm sorry,' Charlie said instinctively, though Rex could have been reading from a weather report.

'Memories wouldn't stop hurtin' so I put a pin in the map. Drove to Las Vegas with the last of my money and started driving a truck. But a fresh location didn't change anything.'

'So, you got your one-one-seven here in Vegas?' Charlie asked.

Rex scratched his beard and nodded. 'Things came close to unbearable before I got modded.'

'Unbearable,' Charlie repeated, churning the word in her head and deciding that it summed up how she felt most of the time. 'I've heard some people have their one-one-seven reversed because it makes everything feel flat.'

'Heard that too,' Rex said, same smile as always. 'You still got your little swimmer with you?'

'He's over at Bryan's gym with a playmate.'

'I've got these big radio-controlled cars up in my room. My boys loved them. Reckon your two could blast 'em around outside. It's a big space and there's no traffic in the way.'

'Motel is ninety per cent empty,' Charlie agreed.

'You want those cars?'

'Patrick would certainly like one,' Charlie said, but she wondered if it was another angle for Rex to hit on her.

'Well, they're just taking up space in my suite.'

'Was your one-one-seven expensive?' Charlie asked.

'Dollar numbers mean nothing with inflation gone crazy. I'd say it was around one month's salary. You thinking about getting it done?'

'No,' Charlie said firmly. Then, 'I don't know. My boyfriend died and it's a lot of stress being in one big room with the boys.'

'There's a ton of empty houses for rent,' Rex noted.

'It's the effort,' Charlie sighed. 'Calling agents, viewing places.'

And wanting to stay off the radar in case any of Fawn's associates come looking . . .

'Must have met a hundred truck drivers who've had a one-one-seven,' Rex said. 'Can't think of one that has regretted it. You gotta be careful who you deal with, obviously. Especially a pretty girl like you. Some guys will try to slip you a one-five-one. That will zombie you to your eyeballs and they'll wind up owning you.'

'Where'd you get yours?' Charlie asked, then caught herself. 'Actually, I don't wanna know.'

Rex answered anyway, as his dryer made a beep. 'I used Karl's Watches. He's got a good rep. Runs out of a little jewellery booth at the outdoor mall, in front of Janssen Riverboat on the strip.'

'I won't mod,' Charlie said firmly, more for her own benefit than Rex's.

'I'm heading up for a nap now this is done,' Rex said as he scooped his dryer-hot clothes into a plastic basket. 'Gotta head out when my replacement tire arrives.'

'Drive safe,' Charlie said.

'I lost a wife and two amazing kids,' Rex said thoughtfully, as he stopped in front of the glowing UV gate. 'I've been where you're at, Charlie. But now my family is a beautiful memory, instead of something that hurts too bad to think about.'

71 THE ACCOUNTS

Christmas carols wafted up from the coffee shop as Charlie sat in her tiny office dealing with mounds of invoices, paying bills online and doing the fortnightly payroll run.

She didn't like leaving Patrick alone with Ed for too long, so she took the little boy with her. The five-year-old did OK, playing games on his tablet, building and knocking down towers made from cardboard take-out cups and occasionally getting fussed over by a member of staff.

Ellie called to say Happy Christmas. Killer-T had taken his wife. Two of Ellie's kids died of superflu and the collapsing economy meant Elliegold Media never floated on the stock exchange and made him rich. Charlie was glad to hear his voice, even though it was a reminder of Harry.

It was Christmas Eve, so the shop was closing at four. Charlie had paid the last bills and switched off her computer. Chairs were on tables and floors were being mopped. Gwen wore a novelty Santa-beard virus mask as she offered the final customers free mulled wine. Charlie decided she deserved a glass herself.

'Guys, it's snowing!' a Goth barista called Naomi yelled as she carried out trash bags.

Patrick had never seen snow. He ignored Charlie's demand to put on his hoodie, squeezing past rubbish bags and out the shop's back doors. It was a pathetic snow storm, but Charlie smiled and videoed as Patrick charged between benches in the deserted outdoor seating area, trying to catch snowflakes.

'Makes a change to see a grin on your face,' Gwen said, stepping out behind her boss as Naomi dropped trash into a Dumpster a few yards away. 'I've got my sister and ma over tomorrow. You're more than welcome to bring the boys for lunch.'

'That's kind,' Charlie said. 'But you had us for Thanksgiving. Ed still gets overexcited about presents, so I'm gonna have a quiet day with the boys and their gifts. You can't cook anything decent in that motel oven, so I've booked a table for Christmas lunch at the Brazilian barbecue place. It costs a fortune, but Ed loves it. Then we're gonna drive over and visit my former foster parents.'

'Sounds nice,' Gwen said. 'How were the accounts looking?'

'I ain't getting rich, but we're not sinking either,' Charlie said as Patrick climbed on one of the benches.

'Get down – don't be stupid,' Charlie rebuked. 'That plastic is slippery.'

'Another property guy called by the store,' Gwen said, pulling a business card out of her apron. 'Looked like another one trying to let an empty store, so he gave me this card and said you should call him.'

'He's a lawyer not a realtor,' Charlie noted as she read the card Gwen handed her. '*Shane O'Donnell, Senior Law Partner.*'

'Should I have sent him up?' Gwen asked.

'No . . . God, no,' Charlie said. 'You did good. Those property people are a nightmare. And you've been slaving since seven-thirty, so if you want to head off now I'll lock up.'

Gwen looked over her shoulder towards a Farm Fresh grocery mart. 'I wouldn't mind. I couldn't get potatoes anywhere yesterday, but Naomi said they had stacks when she was on her lunch break.'

'All right, mister, inside,' Charlie told Patrick firmly. 'It's freezing.'

There was a sinister zombie-type guy walking between some parked cars and Charlie shut the back doors sharply once they were inside. The floor in the shop was just-mopped, the drive-thru window had closed and the last customer was using the toilet before leaving.

Charlie picked a sandwich wrapper and someone's abandoned news magazine off a table. It was a New Year preview issue. The front-page headline was *When's the Next One?* and the sub-heading *Have the trillions spent given us long-term protection from synthetic diseases, or is the next pandemic around the corner?*

'I sent Gwen off early,' Charlie told Naomi, and the other remaining staff member, a modded high-schooler called Devon. 'I'm gonna start locking up.'

Naomi's fiancé was waiting to pick her up, and Charlie envied the couple as they pulled down their virus masks for a kiss. A few people had mentioned the wandering zombie, so Devon was a gentleman, helping Charlie pull down the shutters and walking her across the street with Patrick to the taxi pick-up outside Farm Fresh.

'That mulled wine goes to your head,' Charlie smiled. 'I'm swaying.'

Devon cracked a deep laugh. 'It does for sure.'

Charlie met his glance. She was grieving too much to want

a boyfriend, but Devon was hot in the way that modded guys generally were. He was only seventeen and she wondered if sex would jolt her brain out of missing Harry and hating her life. Even if it was only for half an hour.

Charlie might have made a move, but Patrick was swinging off her arm. There was no taxi on the rank, but an elderly man was hopping out of one and Charlie moved faster than a woman with six Farm Fresh bags.

Charlie felt lonely, and remembered how she liked the warm, detached feeling of being drunk. She wanted another drink, but she had no booze back at the motel and she couldn't buy any in Farm Fresh because she was under twenty-one.

'Janssen Riverboat,' Charlie told her driver.

Patrick looked curious as she helped fasten his seatbelt. 'Aren't we going home?'

'I thought we'd take a stroll. You can get an ice cream if you like.'

Every Vegas high-schooler and college undergrad knew Janssen casinos were lax about checking IDs, but there was a small Janssen-owned casino a few blocks from the motel if alcohol had been all Charlie was interested in.

I'll check out Karl's Watches. It might not even be there any more. Have a couple of drinks and get Patrick an ice cream. Maybe buy a bottle of rum if the casino has a liquor store. It's Christmas after all ... Though Ed's been on his own all day, so I can't hang around for too long.

Janssen Riverboat was a 1970s-built casino at the south end of The Strip. While the sixty-storey mega-resorts around it had crashed when the tourists stopped coming, the Riverboat's cheap rooms and nicotine-stained walls kept pulling in underage drinkers and hardcore gamblers.

Dean Martin Christmas tunes played in the Riverboat's lobby as Patrick squeezed Charlie's hand.

'This place smells funny,' he complained. 'My daddy lost all our money in a casino.'

'I don't gamble,' Charlie reassured him.

There was no ID check as Charlie bought an overpriced bottle of rum in the hotel shop, and found a near-deserted pancake place. Patrick merrily scoffed a chocolate-and-banana float, while Charlie went for a deal offering a beer and a double shot of whisky.

'Can we go home now?' Patrick asked tiredly. 'I want to be up early for my presents.'

Charlie laughed. 'I think you'll manage to wake up tomorrow.'

'Mikey hit me and locked me in his car last Christmas,' Patrick said.

'That's horrible,' Charlie said, tears welling as she left two and a half thousand on the table and grabbed the rum. 'One more stop, then home.'

The outdoor market in front of Janssen Riverboat was all enclosed stalls, selling fast food, fake designer clothing and tacky Christmas gear. The crowd ranged from messed-up-looking zombies, a lot of drunk kids, and tourists, many of whom snapped pictures of the dusting of snow on the shuttered Cascada resort across The Strip.

Charlie approached Kurt's Watches with a slight wobble as Patrick moaned that he couldn't walk any further. The covered stall's glass counter contained a few dozen cheap plastic watches, and solar-powered bobble heads of President Timberlake and a bunch of celebrities.

There was nobody serving and Charlie had almost given up waiting when an obese guy with an Indian accent stepped out of a little room behind. He wore a Christmas hat and the shirt under his hoodie read, *Killer-T wiped out my family and all I got was this lousy T-shirt.*

'You want a bobble head for your boy?' he asked. 'You can have three for a hundred dollars.'

'Friend of mine bought a one-one-seven here,' Charlie said, glancing around awkwardly.

'I don't think so,' the guy said stiffly.

Charlie snorted, drunkenly. 'Be hard to make a living selling this crap.'

'My mother told me never talk to strangers,' the guy smiled. 'You have a good Christmas.'

Charlie was frustrated. Maybe you had to get an introduction or something. But she'd picked up some cash at the coffee shop and she opened the flap on her bag to show a wad of thousand- and five-thousand-dollar bills. The Indian raised one eyebrow, looked left and right, then tutted.

'A one-one-seven costs three hundred thousand. You'll need needles and stuff to inject, which is another five, but since it's Christmas they're on the house.'

'What about auto-immune drugs?'

The guy shook his head. 'You might get sick for a few days, but it's not a big deal.'

'What are you buying?' Patrick asked loudly, and Charlie shushed him.

This is scary, but I can't go on feeling like crap all the time.

'I'm in,' Charlie said.

As Charlie counted money, the guy opened a drawer under the counter. He came up with a watch box, which he opened to show three glass vials inside. From another drawer came a clear bag containing two dozen sterile injection packs.

Charlie always paid extra for quality syringes when she ran her modding business, because she'd heard horror stories about needles breaking under the skin.

'Do you have anything better than those?' she asked.

'These are excellent,' the guy said. 'No problems, ever.'

Charlie felt sure this was a lie and her suspicion turned to the vials themselves. *I can buy a test kit online that will tell me if the mod is genuine and probably find some better needles and auto-immune pills. But this is a lot of cash. Do I really want to make this decision when I'm drunk?*

'Can we *please* go home,' Patrick begged, yanking Charlie's arm.

At the same moment, the guy behind the counter snapped. 'I can't leave this stuff on show. Do you want it or not?'

I can't stand the thought of another day waking up missing Harry and feeling like the whole world is crushing me. But . . .

Patrick tugged her arm. 'Cooooome on . . .'

'OK,' Charlie said sharply, pulling a wodge of dollars out of her bag.

But shouldn't I do more research? Those syringes are the worst. And the vials haven't even been kept in a fridge. But Rex used this place and said it was good . . .

The big Indian snatched the money, and Charlie shoved the vials and syringes inside her bag.

'I can take you in the back and show you how to inject,' he said.

'I can handle that,' Charlie said, eyes welling as she scooped Patrick into her arms. 'Happy Christmas.'

72 SISTER MIRACULOUS

Last year we had Christmas dinner at Vern and Rosie's. Their youngest was home on shore leave. Ed got tipsy on Vern's homemade wine and dozed off, so I went to bed with Harry and we had sex and fell asleep in each other's arms. One year later, Harry's gone. I can't see through tears and everyone in this shitty casino is staring at me.

'Excuse me,' an elderly woman said, struggling to keep up as Charlie dragged Patrick past the Janssen Riverboat's poker room.

Trusting your life to crappy syringes sold by a guy in a Santa hat. You should ditch the vials in the nearest trash can so you don't get tempted to use them next time your mood tanks.

But I just paid three hundred grand for them . . .

Patrick looked back as the woman got closer. Orthopaedic shoes, herringbone skirt and wispy grey hair.

'I'm begging you not to use the one-one-seven,' the woman yelled. 'I'm Sister Miraculous. May I please talk to you?'

Charlie stopped, turned and roared so loud it made Patrick jump. 'Why are you following me? Leave me alone.'

'I saw you at the watch stall,' Sister Miraculous explained as she rattled a bundle of small leaflets entitled *God, Not Mods*. 'I know what they sell there. I've told the police many times, but they don't act.'

'Believe me, sister,' Charlie said, shaking her head and starting to walk again. 'There's no god. My life is proof of that.'

'You're hurting my arm, Charlie,' Patrick whined, having to run to keep pace.

There were three steps where the casino met the hotel lobby. Charlie took the first two in one stride, then clumsily kicked her own heel and wound up flat on her face.

'Why are you crazy?' Patrick demanded, ripping his hand free and scowling.

Charlie tried to get up, but her legs weren't following orders. A burly casino security officer closed on the scene as Sister Miraculous urged Charlie to stay still and calm down.

'Take a few deep breaths,' Miraculous urged, kneeling on the carpet beside Charlie and pulling a man-sized Kleenex out of her sleeve.

'Sister, you've been told you can't hand out leaflets on casino property,' the security guard boomed, closing in.

'Do I look like I'm handing out leaflets?' Miraculous asked. 'This girl is distressed.'

Two more burly guards arrived on the scene. None seemed interested in Charlie and they formed a tight triangle around Sister Miraculous.

'You're banned from Janssen Corporation property,' a gravel-voiced guard said. 'Are you going to leave, or do we have to drag you out?'

The shock of falling had sobered Charlie a little.

'What has she done?' Charlie asked indignantly. 'Show some respect.'

Two more guards jogged in, plus a woman in a suit who appeared to be in charge.

'The sister's banned; the girl's intoxicated,' the boss woman growled. 'Ship 'em out and keep 'em out.'

'Hands off,' Charlie yelled as men with big necks lifted her off the carpet.

The woman snatched Patrick, and the guards marched Charlie and Sister Miraculous outside via the hotel reception. They passed a busy cab lane, went down a curved driveway and stopped on an isolated stretch of sidewalk alongside the Riverboat's parking structure.

'The Riverboat is private property,' the boss woman warned as she planted a stiff, tearful Patrick on the floor. 'If either of you return, we'll call the cops.'

Charlie's vision blurred as she looked around. Sister Miraculous remained a mystery, but their encounter with casino security gave them a common foe, and Charlie was reluctant to wander off because it was the kind of place where zombies lurked.

'Are you OK?' Charlie asked.

'Monstrous thugs!' the sister spat, pulling a prehistoric flip phone out of her cardigan. 'But it's my duty to protect. I beseech you to pray before using the one-one-seven.'

'I don't know if I'll use it,' Charlie said weakly. 'Christmas stirs a ton of emotions.'

The sister spoke into her phone. 'Teddy, they booted me out of the Riverboat again. Could you be a doll and pick me up in the van?'

Patrick was tearful and Charlie gave him a hug. 'I'm sorry I took you here. When you get home, you can have a bubble bath and we'll read a story together in bed.'

'Casinos are dumb,' Patrick fumed as he glowered towards the Riverboat's flashy light job.

'Well said, young fellow!' Sister Miraculous said. 'The van isn't far away. I'd be happy to take you home, or back to The Strip.'

'I'm not comfortable around here,' Charlie admitted. 'So what sort of nun gets called Sister Miraculous?'

'I was part of a variety act,' the sister admitted. 'The Miraculous Five. Magic tricks, singing, comedy. The kind of Vegas show that went out of fashion before you were even born.'

'Can you do magic tricks?' Patrick asked.

'I'm rusty,' the sister admitted. 'I didn't catch your names?'

'I'm Charlie, this is Patrick.'

The sister nodded. 'If you don't feel like going home, or you'd like to talk to someone, I volunteer at a drop-in centre close by. There's always someone there who can talk. And I'm a nun, but don't let that put you off. Terry, who's coming with the van, is a stone-cold atheist.'

'Why would I go there?' Charlie asked.

'The viruses have taken so many people,' the sister explained. 'Everyone has lost someone close. The drop-in centres help everyone, from showering zombies, to talking things through with people like you who are having a bad day.'

Charlie pointed to the leaflets. 'What about *God, Not Mods*?'

'That's my personal crusade,' Sister Miraculous said proudly as a tatty van came down the other side of the street and did a U-turn.

It was an old airport shuttle van, with a neon-pink paint job and *Las Vegas Drop-in Centers* stencilled down the side. When it pulled up, Charlie saw dents in the door and deep bands of rust around the wheel arches.

'All aboard the Wes Express,' the driver shouted as Sister Miraculous grappled with a sliding side door.

Wes was a large man with a wild ginger beard.

'Our new pal Charlie is having a bad night,' Sister Miraculous explained.

Charlie and Patrick slid on to the van's tattered seats.

'I'm good,' Charlie said. 'I can get a cab if you drop me on The Strip.'

'You've drunk a lot,' the sister said firmly. 'I'd rather see you home safe.'

Wes adopted a ludicrous robot voice. 'Please enter destination . . .'

'Kuchler Motel,' Charlie said, her vision blurring as the sister pulled the door closed from inside. 'If you're sure you don't mind.'

73 SLEIGHT OF HAND

'Snow's building,' Sister Miraculous said as the van crossed The Strip. 'Report said it'll be warmer tomorrow.'

Traffic was quiet and it took less than fifteen minutes to the Kuchler. As they rolled into the motel, Patrick saw a pair of radio-controlled cars racing across the near-empty lot. Ed and Rex sat on a kerb, wrapped up warm, each holding a control unit.

'Charlie's drunk as a skunk!' Patrick announced to Ed, jumping out of the van and hurtling towards him. 'Can I try? Please, please, please.'

'Sure you can,' Ed teased as he pulled his little car up in front of Patrick. 'You can make an appointment for two weeks' time?'

'Don't be mean,' Patrick whined, then grinned as Rex handed him the controller for the other car.

'Use the accelerator gently,' Rex advised. 'It's sensitive.'

Charlie approached as Patrick's car zipped away. She looked at Rex. 'What happened to Georgia?'

Rex shook his head, and grinned like he always did. 'By the time my tire showed, my load had been contracted out to another driver.'

'This is sweet of you,' Charlie said as Patrick banged his car into a kerb. 'I can pay you for the cars.'

'Don't bust it, dumbass,' Ed snapped at Patrick.

'Happy to see my boys' cars out of the box,' Rex said. 'Ed helped me oil them up and fix the steering on the black one.'

Charlie's bladder was feeling the beers, shots and mulled wine. 'I'll come talk properly in a second, but I gotta pee.'

As Charlie turned around to head up the stairs to her suite, Sister Miraculous gripped her wrist.

'I need to get back to the Riverboat,' the sister said. 'But, please, will you *promise* me you'll come to the drop-in centre and talk to one of our therapists before you mod yourself?'

'Oh my God, I flipped the car and it righted itself,' Ed shouted. 'Charlie, did you see that?'

But the cold was getting to Charlie and she'd have promised Sister Miraculous her right boob if it meant reaching the toilet faster.

'I totally will,' Charlie said, and she ripped her hand free and set a world record for the hundred-metre dash to the toilet.

She frantically jangled her key in the door of the suite, throwing her bag on the tiled floor, easing down her jeans and erupting a relieved gasp.

'Sooooo good!'

As Charlie peed, she saw that her bag had spilled. The weird thing was she'd put the watch box with the three vials of fluid at the bottom of her bag. But the box had spilled first, as if it had been on top. And a piece of paper poked from the seam where the halves of the box joined.

Charlie kept peeing as she leaned forward and picked up the box. Inside, the three vials had vanished, and the thing sticking out was a tri-folded *God, Not Mods* leaflet with a message on the back.

You can pick them up at the drop-in centre if you <u>really</u> want to use them.

Come and see me after you've sobered up.

Sister M.

After the message was a cell number, and the address of the drop-in centre.

'Sneaky old so-and-so . . .' Charlie gasped, remembering that the sister had been part of a magic act.

Charlie wasn't sure about using the mod, but she'd shelled out three hundred grand. She charged out of the bathroom with her jeans unbuttoned, leaned over the balcony and shook a fist at the neon van that was pulling off the motel lot.

'Get back here, crazy woman!'

Ed and Rex looked baffled as they stared up at her. 'What happened?'

'I got robbed by a nun,' Charlie said, seeing the funny side as her slurred words hit the rooms across the parking lot.

'Is this what you're looking for?' Rex asked, holding up her bottle of rum.

Charlie knew she'd behaved stupidly, but seeing her boys having fun with the cars made her feel hopeful as she stumbled down to join them.

'You can come to the Brazilian barbecue with us tomorrow, if you don't want to spend Christmas alone in your room,' she told Rex.

'I don't mind being alone,' Rex said as Charlie stood next to Ed, buttoning her pants. 'But I'll come if you'd like me to.'

Rex doesn't mind that his family died and is about to spend Christmas alone in a shabby motel room. I hate the way it hurts when I think about Harry, but I'd rather feel that than be dead inside.

'Let's try one of these cars, then,' Charlie said, rubbing cold hands.

'It's sluggish cos the battery only has a couple of minutes left,' Ed said as he handed his sister the controller. 'And some guy called Shane O'Donnell came by while you were out. He said he needs to see both of us. It's something to do with Fawn.'

Charlie felt wary when she recognised the name from the business card Gwen had passed on earlier.

'What else did he say?' Charlie asked.

'He wants to speak to you urgently. He said call any time, day or night.'

'Weird,' Charlie said, passing the controller back to Ed before she'd used it.

'Charlie!' Patrick moaned. 'I wanted to race you.'

'In a minute,' Charlie said as she pulled the business card Gwen had given her from the front pocket of her jeans.

She typed the name on the card into Google Search.

'You should have seen his car,' Ed said. 'Mercedes S-class, long wheelbase. The new model.'

'Someone's got friends in high places,' Rex said, his constant smile needling Charlie as she scanned the search results.

The internet said Shane O'Donnell was the senior probate partner at one of Vegas's biggest law firms. He was a handsome red-headed man, on the board of several local charities and tipped as a future mayor of Las Vegas.

• • •

Charlie realised her phone battery was on seventeen per cent, so she plugged it into the charger before clearing a bunch of Ed's junk off the sofa, sitting down and dialling the number on the card.

She got a snotty secretary, but O'Donnell took the call, even though it was after seven on Christmas Eve.

'The Nevada probate court has appointed me to administer the estate of Fawn Janssen,' O'Donnell explained. 'I'm assuming you've heard that your sister's DNA was identified in remains found at UrbanScape.'

'Sure.'

'I'm sorry for your loss, Miss Croker.'

'We weren't close,' Charlie told him.

'Now that a death certificate has been issued, her estate can be distributed.'

'Did she have much of her own?' Charlie asked. 'I know there was jewellery, but I've got no idea what the financial crash did to my brother's trust fund.'

O'Donnell laughed. 'When Jay Janssen died, his assets passed to his two sons. His older son was unmarried and died first, so everything he owned passed to JJ. And when JJ died it passed to his wife.'

'I thought there were lots of Janssens,' Charlie said. 'Aunties and uncles and all sorts.'

'Some shares are owned by other members of the Janssen family. But most of Janssen Corp belonged to Fawn at the time of her death. Fawn made no will. Her parents are both dead and she had no children, so under Nevada law her assets pass to her siblings.'

'Hold it,' Charlie said slowly. 'You're talking about Janssen Corp? Casinos, strip malls, private jets?'

'Once I've compiled the register of assets I'll be more than happy to send it across,' O'Donnell said. 'There will be a lot of issues to discuss with any estate of this magnitude. I'm spending tomorrow with my family, but the office will reopen the day after and I'd like to meet with yourself and Edward.'

Charlie laughed nervously. 'I'm *so* wasted right now! When I wake up tomorrow, I won't believe this call happened.'

Charlie let the lawyer get back to his family, then cracked a smile as she appreciated the irony that everything Fawn had fought, schemed and murdered for had wound up in the hands of the two people she'd hated most.

PART SIX
FIVE YEARS LATER

Vegas Local

HOTTEST 5 STORIES

1 Markets fall sharply with fears that Pakistani Paralysing Bacteria (PPB) could reach the USA within days.
2 First study shows driverless taxi fleet is popular with riders.
3 Downtown traffic gridlock as 3,000 demonstrate Nevada State ban on genetically modified workers.
4 Algarve Casino reopens north hotel, but other mega resorts face demolition after years of neglect.
5 **TOP VIDEO** – Police hunt three high-schoolers with superhero mods after mall rampage leaves girl in critical condition.

Charlie had been parked outside the quarantine station at McCarran airport for over an hour when Kirsten Channing stepped through a barred gate. She looked much younger than she used to, her slender figure clad in tight jeans and black cotton pumps and her sterilised belongings sealed in clear plastic bags.

'Thank you so much for coming,' Charlie said, cracking a broad smile. 'I can't believe I only got to meet you once before.'

'The night you brought the Killer-T vaccine to my ex's apartment,' Kirsten nodded. 'Which probably saved our lives, so I guess I owe you.'

'How was quarantine?'

'Food wasn't great, but the room was perfectly pleasant,' Kirsten said. 'To think we used to complain when we had to queue for an hour at customs. Now it's seven days' quarantine, and another five when I land back in the UK.'

A stocky man in a dark suit opened the BMW's rear doors before placing Kirsten's luggage in the trunk.

'This is my good friend and driver, Rex,' Charlie explained, walking to the far side of the car as Kirsten slid into the plush leather interior and peered into a crib. 'And the little guy in the middle is your great nephew, Harry.'

'He's *so* tiny,' Kirsten cooed, taking a big sniff of baby smell. 'How old is he now?'

'Four months,' Charlie said. 'But he came out a few weeks early, so he's extra small.'

'Is he a clone of Harry?' Kirsten asked.

Charlie shook her head. 'Clones still have horrible health issues. The embryo was seventy per cent Harry's DNA, thirty mine, plus seventeen mods. I only wanted him to have mods that would enhance his immune system, but the clinic persuaded me that you have to give a boy athletic and intelligence mods these days, or they'll have a miserable time at school with kids that do.'

'Did you carry him?'

Charlie shook her head. 'I've been super busy, with college, coffee shops and the drop-in centres. I had to use a surrogate.'

'And how old are the other two now?' Kirsten asked.

'Patrick's ten next month,' Charlie said as the BMW drove itself on to an airport access road. 'He picked up a muscle-wasting disease from a tick bite last year. He's fine now, but he missed eight months of school. I've had to get him a tutor to catch up, which isn't the most popular decision I've ever made...

'Ed's twenty-two and doing great. He's on a new medication for brain-injury patients. It has helped with his anxiety, and he hasn't fitted in more than a year. He met a girl online and he still lives with me, but he has a self-contained apartment, and he drives to and from college and cooks most of his own meals.'

'I look forward to meeting them both,' Kirsten said.

'How's life across the pond?' Charlie asked.

'London was where Killer-T started, so it's grim,' Kirsten said. 'The rest of the UK isn't so bad. My father, Harry's grand-father, passed last year. I've got a little restaurant in Devon. Only twenty-two seats. Lots of fish and locally grown produce. I enjoy the challenge of not being able to phone a supplier and get an ingredient flown from anywhere in the world.'

'Didn't Channing's reopen at the Algarve?' Charlie asked.

Kirsten nodded. 'Clark Corporation has a licence to use my name for another twenty years. But Kent Clark's wife has run the casinos since he died. She doesn't want me involved, but I still get paid licensing fees, and I'm *so* done with TV appearances and recipe books.'

'The fancy opening of the new drop-in centre is tomorrow, with the press and my foster parents, and the mayor and all of our big donors,' Charlie said. 'But we'll be passing by shortly if you'd like a tour. Or not, if you want to go back to my house and relax.'

'Tour please,' Kirsten cried, laughing. 'I've been stuck in a quarantine room for a week. I could sprint up Red Rock mountain with the energy I need to burn.'

Kirsten felt strange as she stared out of the car at barren strip malls, an unfinished football stadium and the weathered hulks of dead gambling resorts along The Strip.

'Ed and I used to own that one,' Charlie noted, pointing at the grubby towers of Janssen Riverboat.

'You sold your shares in Janssen Corp?' Kirsten asked.

Charlie nodded. 'I invested money in my coffee-shop business. Ed has enough to pay for his medical expenses and any future needs. But we transferred most of the Janssen money into a charitable trust that runs mental-health drop-in centres.'

'I loathed Vegas when I first came here with Harry,' Kirsten admitted. 'But I made some good friends and it's sad seeing it so run down.'

As Kirsten said this, baby Harry sneezed.

'Hey, buddy,' Charlie said, and she grabbed a bottle of milk out of her bag. Then to Kirsten, 'He'll want feeding in a bit, but this formula is cold.'

Charlie picked Harry out of his car seat as the BMW rolled into a parking lot, its freshly painted markings spoiled by muddy tracks from construction traffic.

The land had once housed Janssen's Cowboy Club, a small casino favoured by bikers that was grotty even by Janssen standards. The Club's replacement was a clinically white three-storey building with a sign over the door that read *Harry Smirnov Center – 24-hour Drop-in.*

Charlie gently rocked baby Harry as she led Kirsten through its automatic doors.

'This is our eighth centre in Vegas,' Charlie said, pulling a hood over Harry's eyes as she stepped into a quarantine box. 'This centre is our biggest yet. There will be therapists and doctors on hand all day. So many people's lives have been destroyed these past few years. A lot of the time, clients just want someone to talk to. Then we have counselling sessions for reversed zombies. There will also be addiction and eating-disorder clinics, and stress-relief activities, like meditation and yoga.

'Upstairs we have thirty-six rooms where people in crisis can stay for a few nights. On the top floor there's an education unit for trainee therapists and a safe-play area for kids. All the first-floor rooms have outside access and an independent air supply, so we can function as a bereavement centre if there's a major epidemic.'

'Impressive,' Kirsten said as she stepped round a chubby construction worker gluing bright blue floor tiles, then admired the sunlight pouring through an atrium above.

'I need to warm this bottle before Harry gets grumpy,' Charlie said. She pulled an electronic pass and blipped a door.

Kirsten followed Charlie into a kitchen area, so new it had plastic dust sheets over the worktops and unfinished light fixtures. As the microwave took the chill off Harry's lunch, Sister Miraculous arrived with a squeak of orthopaedic shoes.

'This must be Kirsten,' the sister beamed, blowing a kiss for the sake of hygiene and rattling words like machine-gun bullets. 'Isn't this place beautiful? Charlie claims to be an atheist, but I prayed to our Lord. This wonderful girl was delivered to me and the dark Janssen money has been turned to holy light.'

'That's one way of putting it,' Charlie laughed.

'And isn't this tiny man adorable?' the sister continued. 'Even if he is a mutated bastard born out of wedlock!'

Kirsten gulped, half expecting Charlie to sock Sister Miraculous for insulting her kid. But Charlie laughed as she grabbed Harry's bottle out of the microwave and gave it a shake.

'There's a lot of construction dust upstairs,' Charlie said. 'Sister, would you like to feed my evil mutant while I show Kirsten around?'

'Oh, you like me, don't you, Harry!' Sister Miraculous said eagerly as she sat at a table and took hold of the baby.

'Sister Miraculous seems a *little* eccentric,' Kirsten noted as they set off.

'Some people have a screw loose – Sister Miraculous hasn't got a single screw tightened,' Charlie grinned. 'She's not officially a nun any more. She caused so many fights with the rest of her order the bishop gave her the boot.'

Kirsten laughed noisily as they passed a bunch of WET PAINT signs and rode an elevator that had new-car smell.

'Charlie, this centre is amazing, but I feel *so* guilty.'

Charlie looked puzzled. 'How so?'

'I used to tell Harry that he spent too much time with you. That you were in prison for a reason. That you were a bad influence, who'd wind up breaking his heart.'

'I did break his heart back then,' Charlie pointed out. 'Though he broke mine when he died, so I guess we're even now.'

The elevator doors opened and Charlie tapped her pass, unlocking the doors of a huge play space.

'Wow,' Kirsten said as she studied a climbing wall, basketball hoops and trampolines built into the floor.

'Kids can't play outdoors with all the synthetic organisms,'

Charlie explained. 'A lot of private play spaces have opened up, but poor families can't afford them. And kids can run wild in here, while adults get treatment.'

'Harry had Vegas Local and a burning ambition to follow in his mum's footsteps,' Kirsten observed as she strolled deeper into the space. 'You have this charity and sixty coffee shops. You two were perfect for each other.'

Kirsten saw that Charlie was tearing up.

'Oh, I'm such an idiot,' Kirsten said, stepping back. 'I'm sorry.'

'No, I appreciate your honesty,' Charlie said, peeling down her virus mask to dab one eye. 'I've seen a few men since he died, but Harry's still my guy.'

'Healing takes time,' Kirsten said. 'And I'm twice your age and still seeking my Mr Perfect.'

'Sometimes it feels like a waste of time,' Charlie said, staring at the floor. 'We strive and learn, and raise kids and build stuff. But somewhere on the other side of the world there's some nineteen-year-old sociopath. He built a DNA printer in his mom's basement and he's working on the perfect germ that's gonna wipe all of us out.'

Kirsten tried thinking of an intelligent reply, but nothing came so she slipped off her pumps and stepped barefoot on to one of the trampolines.

'Harry had a trampoline for his eighth birthday,' Kirsten said as she began a gentle bounce. 'Almost filled my little garden in Kentish Town.'

Charlie smiled as she tugged off her All Stars and hopped on to the next pad. 'You did say you needed to burn energy.'

Kirsten was cautious, but Charlie bounced high, doing a back flip, then leaping back and forth between two pads.

460

'Show off,' Kirsten laughed, then attempted a flip and face planted.

Charlie got the giggles, and Kirsten clapped as she pulled off a barrel roll. The two women wound up flat on their backs, smirking and out of breath.

'I think the world's gonna be fine,' Kirsten said, lifting her virus mask to help catch her breath. 'I'm gonna get more anti-ageing mods. I'll have my first kid at a hundred and thirty and I'll die at two hundred.'

'Harry got his sense of humour from you,' Charlie told Kirsten fondly. 'I'm so glad you came over for the centre's opening.'

'I needed that stretch after quarantine,' Kirsten said, rubbing one knee as she stumbled towards her shoes.

'It's nice to act like a kid sometimes,' Charlie said, still smiling as she started putting her sneakers back on. 'But I'd better go rescue my baby from the crazy nun.'

'Harry would be so proud of what you've done,' Kirsten said as Charlie flicked her hand at the no-touch elevator button.

'I'd give anything to have one more day with him,' Charlie admitted, climbing into the elevator. 'But the fight goes on, right?'

Discover more books and sign up to the Robert Muchamore mailing list at muchamore.com

 muchamore

 muchamorerobert

 @robertmuchamore

Don't miss Robert's next novel, Arctic Zoo.

Read on for a sneak peek . . .

Walter J Freeman Adolescent Mental Health Unit – East Grinstead, UK

Georgia Pack tilted on the back legs of a plastic stacking chair, curling socked toes into the therapy room's grungy turquoise carpet. Her eyes scanned the ceiling tiles, as she tuned out, letting Henry's voice merge with rattling air-con.

Georgia was fifteen and she'd been on the unit long enough to know things. Like the knack for opening the jammed dryer in the laundry room and that Monday night's Quorn Bolognese was best avoided. On weekdays, patients who weren't psychotic or sedated had group therapy. Georgia shared the circle of chairs with four fellow teens, and a slight Indian therapist named Tanvi.

Henry dominated the therapy session. Seventeen and pretty. Floppy hair, stout legs. Canterbury training pants tucked into striped rugby socks. His posh accent and machine-gun laugh were everywhere on the unit, carrying up stairwells and booming in the dining room. Georgia even heard blasts of Henry from the smokers' patio if she opened the window in her room to shift the unit's hot, dead air.

At thirteen, Ross was the youngest patient in the unit. He sat fidgeting with a stick of lip balm and nodding approval at every word out of Henry's mouth. Laura was a shy new arrival, with elastic bandage up the arm she'd gouged when she tried to kill herself three nights earlier. The last patient in the group was Georgia's friend Alex. Broad-shouldered, with the number nine peeling off the back of an old Newcastle United shirt.

Georgia knew something was up with Alex. She liked to spar with Henry in group, but today her friend had let him grind on, ignoring obvious chances to swat his ego.

'Our au-pair drove all the bloody way from Hertfordshire with my Xbox,' Henry ranted, growing more irate with every sentence. 'I set up a death match with my buddies in the rec room. Then Keith the nurse strides in. Sees my HDMI lead going from the Xbox to the telly on the wall and tells us it's too long.

'I know we're not allowed to have long cables so we can't neck ourselves. But he wanted to take it right there, with the three of us mid-tournament. I said I'd hand the cable in at the nurses' station when we'd finished playing and get the au-pair to bring a shorter cable . . .'

Tanvi the therapist made a stop-talking gesture. Then spoke with a lisp that made *sss* come out like *thh*.

'This is where you lost your temper and there was an incident?'

'I hardly lothht my temper,' Henry mocked, sitting up defensively and tucking his feet under the chair. 'Keith tried to yank the cable. I pushed him away and he tripped on the stack of board games. Keith charged back to the nurses' station and made a tiny incident into this huge thing. The night manager came out, saying she was locking the rec room, and made us all go back to our rooms . . .'

'Let's pause there,' Tanvi interrupted. 'Henry has issues with impulse control and this is a good opportunity to discuss techniques that could have stopped a situation from escalating.'

Georgia cringed at Tanvi calling Henry's problem impulse control. Nasty thug felt more truthful.

Henry's story was known around the unit. He'd been dumped by his boarding-school girlfriend. A couple of months later, he'd seen her kissing a music student at a house party. Henry sucker-punched the student, shoved him down a flight of stairs and stomped his head into a four-day coma.

Any ordinary brat would have bounced to jail, but Henry's daddy found a fancy lawyer, who paid an even fancier psychiatrist to write a report claiming that Henry had cognitive issues and had been suffering from depression, which led to his outburst of 'uncharacteristic behaviour'.

So, Henry got to spend nine months at the Freeman Unit, bleating about his Xbox getting confiscated, instead of three years in young offenders with lads whose parents didn't own three houses and a sixteen-metre racing yacht.

'What behavioural technique could Henry have used to help control his anger?' Tanvi asked the five patients.

Ross broke a moment's silence. 'That thought, feeling, behaviour, triangle thingy?' he guessed, keen to please.

Tanvi shook her head. 'The cognitive triangle is used to understand how our feelings affect our behaviour. I'm talking about a specific technique that I mentioned earlier in this session...'

Ross blurted when he got it. 'Transposition. Like, when before reacting, you try to put yourself in the other person's shoes.'

'Brilliant, Ross,' Tanvi said brightly. 'Henry, instead of jumping straight to anger, try to imagine Keith's position. When a nurse in a mental-health facility walks into a room and sees a length of cable that a patient might use to harm themselves, what might they be thinking?'

'Keith is only a student nurse,' Ross said, lapping up the therapist's approval. 'He's probably scared about losing his job or getting in trouble with management.'

Georgia nodded supportively. 'The nurses work twelve-hour shifts. Keith was probably wiped by the time he came in and saw Henry playing video games . . .'

Georgia had eight million Instagram followers and a face that had been on magazine covers. Henry couldn't look down on her, so focused his resentment on Ross.

'Why are you against me?' Henry growled menacingly.

'Henry,' Tanvi said sternly. Therapists were supposed to stay neutral, but she couldn't completely hide her irritation. 'I'm trying to help you deal with anger issues. Please tell me something Keith might have been thinking during the confrontation?'

Henry didn't want to play. He folded his arms and his voice went high.

'God!' he blurted, knee bouncing and knuckles turning white. 'I feel like everyone in this room is attacking me!'

Tanvi was about to speak, but Alex finally broke silence.

'You're a total drama queen, Henry,' Alex blurted. 'Your stupid voice has been drilling into my head for most of the last hour. Nothing is ever your fault. Your au-pair brought the wrong clothes, some of the night staff don't let you have pizza delivered, your Xbox, blah, blah, blah . . . And the second someone disagrees or challenges, you claim we're attacking you.'

Tanvi made a simmer-down gesture to Alex. 'It's good to finally hear you contribute, Alex, but you know the group rules. Remain fully in your seat and make sure comments are constructive, not abusive.'

Alex moaned with exasperation. 'Henry almost stamped a guy to death. In the six weeks since I got here, I've heard him verbally bully younger patients, like Ross. He's yelled at nurses and lobbed scrambled eggs at kitchen staff. The point of group therapy is to talk through your problems. But how can that work with a person who can't handle the slightest suggestion that something might be his own fault?'

Henry looked at Tanvi, clutching his chest like he'd been shot. 'Are you going to let her attack me like that?'

Tanvi paused for a deep breath, stressed but projecting calm. 'Alex's tone could be less aggressive, but she's raised an interesting point about how we need to examine ourselves honestly to benefit from group therapy.'

'I'm stuck in this place, aren't I?' Henry spat. 'I got expelled from one of the best schools in the country. Am I not being punished?'

Alex tutted and grabbed her hair. 'I've been in young offenders. This place is a Holiday Inn by comparison.'

'Why should I justify myself to a girl who smoked crack when she was twelve?' Henry blurted.

Georgia shot up and yelled, 'That's out of order, Henry.'

Tanvi made two sharp claps, asserting herself before her group got out of control.

'Cool heads,' she said firmly. 'Abuse is never acceptable during group work. Settle in your chairs . . . We only have a few minutes of the session left. Let's take out the sting with some breathing exercises.'

'I can't be in a room with that knobhead,' Alex spat, hooking her fingertips inside the wrecked pair of New Balance under her chair and making for the door. 'Sorry . . .'

'We all agreed to abide by the group rules,' Tanvi pleaded. 'That includes staying in the room for the full hour.'

Georgia glowered at Henry, now wearing a triumphant smirk. When she heard Alex smash her palm against the vending machine in the lounge outside she didn't want to stay in the therapy room either. But unlike Henry, the expensive psychiatrist had yet to write her report on Georgia. She had to toe the line if she wanted to stay out of prison.

'This session is almost over,' Tanvi said, gesturing Georgia towards the door. 'Alex probably needs you more than we do.'

The deserted lounge area had a dozen sofas. Patients did group or addiction therapy in rooms that branched off either side. The coffee and snack machines were against the wall by the main doors and Alex pounded the machine again as Georgia closed in.

'Henry sucks!' Alex said, eyes glazing as Georgia gave her a hug.

Georgia knew that something more than Henry was bugging her friend.

'You were so quiet in there,' Georgia said.

Alex shrugged as she jabbed the button for hot chocolate. 'You didn't have to run out after me. You've got your sentencing coming up.'

'At least we beat the queue for drinks,' Georgia said.

When the clock hit four, the unit's teenage patients would stream out of therapy rooms, checking phones and forming a queue for hot drinks, chocolate bars and McCoy's crinkle-cut crisps. The Henry types would sprawl over the lounge, flirting and yapping until the kitchen opened for dinner, while the shy and desperate hid in their rooms.

'My stepdad spoke to his insurance company,' Alex confessed reluctantly, as her drink spattered into a cardboard cup. 'They won't extend my stay here beyond forty-five days. He can't afford to pay himself. With my drugs and psychiatrist bills, it's a thousand quid a day.'

'Sucks here anyway,' Georgia said, trying to smile, but hating that so many kids left the unit when insurance money ran out, instead of when they'd got better. 'What happened to that NHS programme you applied to?'

Alex sighed. 'Dad drove me up for an assessment, but there's eighty people on the waiting list and I'm low priority, since I've never tried suicide and I don't present a danger to the public . . .'

'They'd let you in if you stabbed Henry,' Georgia joked darkly, as she pushed the button for a caramel latte.

Before Alex could react, the double doors by the snack machine flew open. One door crashed the wall loudly as a wailing, half-dressed, figure burst through.

'I am not to be touched!' the runner shouted desperately.

The runner had been dragged out of school, wearing the bottom half of his PE kit, and a deckchair-striped school blazer over a bare chest. As he reached a dead end at the far side of the lounge, a burly Spanish nurse named Carlos and the two green-uniformed paramedics charged through the doors in pursuit.

'Julius, calm down, mate,' one of the paramedics begged in cockney. 'They're all right here.'

'Remember our chat in the ambulance?' the other one added. 'There's nothing to fear.'

'I am not mental,' Julius shouted.

Arrivals on the unit were often dramatic. Georgia had seen bodies flopped into their rooms under sedation, sobbers grasping parents, kids withdrawing from heroin wheeled to the addiction ward with puke buckets between their knees. Most common were teens who'd attempted suicide, fresh from the casualty department with neck braces, or bloody bandages.

But overpowering the admissions staff and doing a runner was something new. Julius's shocked white eyes contrasted with his sweat-beaded black face as he frantically sought an escape route. His physique was more Buddha than bodybuilder, but he was huge so it was still scary.

'Move aside,' Julius roared, as Carlos stepped closer. 'I cannot be here.'

Julius decided his best chance was back the way he came, hurdling sofas and running along cushions.

Hot chocolate splashed Alex's jeans as she backed up to the wall. Julius's head almost touched the ceiling as he vaulted between sofas, but Carlos had a plan. The burly nurse didn't fancy tackling a giant, so he grabbed the base of a sofa, tilting it enough for Julius to lose balance.

The enormous teenager became a falling tree, and a coffee table splintered under his weight.

While the paramedics moved cautiously between the furniture, Carlos was fearless, straddling the toppled sofa, then sticking a needle through the arse of Julius's PE shorts.

Julius still had some fight, despite the sedative in his blood and a gory spear of the coffee table pushed through his cheek.

'Big ones can take another,' the cockney paramedic suggested, as he threw Carlos another syringe.

Julius managed a rabbit kick, as Carlos pulled down his shorts, but the second needle sent him straight to fairyland.

'I'm not paid enough for this . . .' Carlos moaned, holding his back as he straightened up.

Now they felt safe, Alex and Georgia stepped around the sofas for a better look. Julius was a beached whale, splayed over the collapsed table, with the syringes in his arse still swaying from side to side.

Want to read
NEW BOOKS
before anyone else?

Like getting
FREE BOOKS?

Enjoy sharing your
OPINIONS?

Discover

READERS FIRST

Read. Love. Share.

Get your first free book just by signing up at
readersfirst.co.uk

Thank you for choosing a Hot Key book.

If you want to know more about our authors and what we publish, you can find us online.

You can start at our website

www.hotkeybooks.com

And you can also find us on:

We hope to see you soon!